PHOEBE WALKER

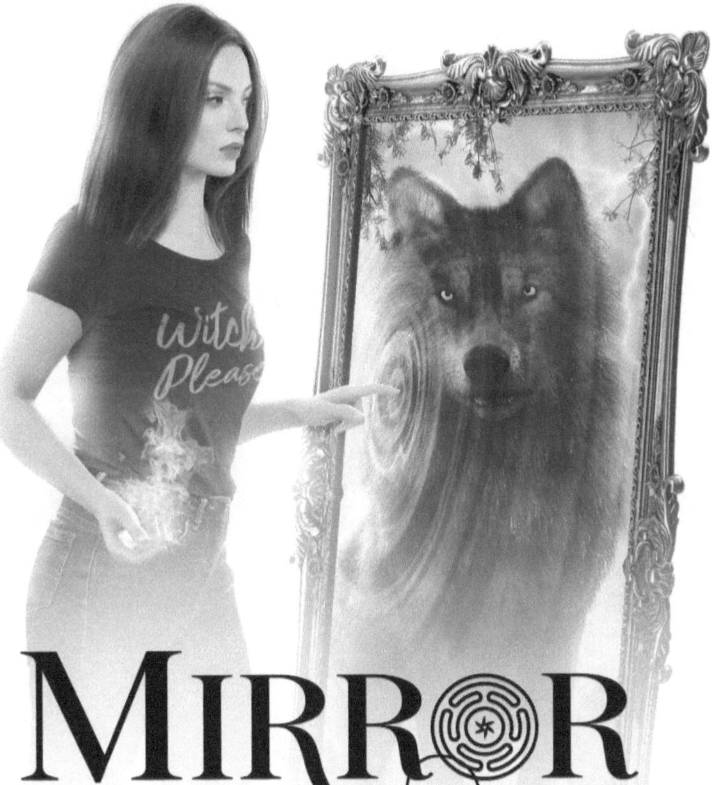

MIRROR WITCH

DAUGHTERS OF HECATE

BOOK 1

MIRROR WITCH

PHOEBE WALKER

CITY OWL
PRESS

MIRROR WITCH
Daughters of Hecate, Book 1

CITY OWL PRESS
www.cityowlpress.com

Cover Design by MiblArt. All stock photos licensed appropriately.

Edited by Lisa Green.

For information on subsidiary rights, please contact the publisher at info@cityowlpress.com.

Print Edition ISBN: 978-1-64898-313-9

Digital Edition ISBN: 978-1-64898-314-6

Printed in the United States of America

Praise for Phoebe Walker

"I'm not normally a paranormal romance reader, but *Mirror Witch* sucked me in and hooked me from the first pages. Great characters do that for me every time—future Phoebe Walker stories will be automatic additions to my TBR list!" – *Laura Moher, author of Curves for Days*

"Thrilling, suspenseful, and steamy, *Mirror Witch* is a fast-paced PNR gem featuring a resilient witch trying to understand her powers, an alpha wolf (who's a world-class hugger) trying to protect his pack, and a mystery they can only solve together. This slow-burn, fated-mates romance is unique, emotional, and unputdownable!" – *Jess K Hardy, author of the Ignisar series*

"Walker's ability to write a determined protagonist with a loving supportive cast injects life into the genre. *Mirror Witch* is a fun and exciting story that will leave you breathless for more reasons than one." – *Shameez Patel Papathanasiou, author of The Last Feather and The Eternal Shadow*

"I was completely mesmerized while reading *Mirror Witch*, and I cannot wait until the second book in the series is released as it is already guaranteed a special place on my bookshelf. I highly recommend *Mirror Witch* to fans ... of paranormal romance, suspense, action, and horror." – *Readers' Favorite 5-star review*

"*Mirror Witch* is a thrilling yet tender paranormal romance with just enough teeth to keep the pages turning. It's the perfect book for the witches and wolves among us." – *Erin Rose, author of Christmas Passion and Hot Cocoa Cookies*

"I absolutely loved Jo, and her relationship build-up with Booker was fantastic. I loved their tension but also their sweetness and understanding of each other. ... The sex scenes especially were to die for!" – *Sarah T. Dubb, author and freelance editor*

Author's Note

Because we know that some subject matter can be triggering for readers, we have content warnings for all of our books available on our website in order for all readers to determine their comfort level with our books.

In order to read content warnings for *Mirror Witch* or any of our other titles, please click here: https://www.phoebewalkerwrites.com/content-warnings

Thank you for reading!

About St. Louis Geography and the "Central East End"

For those who are familiar with the Gateway to the West and its myriad neighborhoods, it's important to note that Jo's Sanctum and Kate's Hecate's Home shelter stand in a St. Louis neighborhood that doesn't exist, as far as we yet know. (We've looked.) The Central East End of their world might be somewhere around the Gate District, just a side step or two into a different reality.

CHAPTER 1

A WEREWOLF WALKS INTO AN OCCULT SHOP

BOOKER

Sometimes finding humans was too easy.

The werewolf looked across the street into the window of the shop where his quarry was working, squinting past the bright neon signs. *Tarot. Psychic. Spells.* Its owner had chosen to call it "Other Worlds Emporium," which made him snort. It was as subtle as a frat bro doused in Axe body spray.

This woman had taken the Council eight years to find? It had taken Booker and his team only a month—but he'd worked his ass off in that span of time. Sure, she was now reading tarot in a New Age shop, like she had been before she disappeared, but she'd managed to stay elusive. She lived off the grid, working for cash, staying a short while in each place, never more than six months—but Booker had figured out her pattern, just in time to catch her here in Ste. Genevieve, Illinois. Another river town, just like all the others.

Most humans were just mobilized patterns, as far as he could see. This one was no exception.

Josephine Ellen Murphy. Born in St. Louis, raised by her grandparents after her mother's death, put into the foster system at age 16, finished high school while living in an undisclosed location. Held a few unassuming jobs, then became a practicing Wiccan reading tarot in shops and over the phone. No criminal record, no legal problems.

She would never have ended up on his radar—or the Council's—if she hadn't gotten mixed up with the Fenris.

Booker entered Other Worlds Emporium with a feigned nonchalance, but the clerk behind the counter still froze in place when she saw him. It was a hard sell, he knew—werewolves may look human sometimes, but they weren't, even when they tried to act like it. He couldn't help but sense the clerk's unease, as he did any time he affected a human's emotional state. The scent changed, or at least that's how he interpreted it.

The clerk took a step backward when he moved toward her, but when he smiled at her, flashing what he knew was a matching set of dimples, she smiled back, the tension easing from her muscles and her scent.

"Hi there!" she chirped. "Is there anything I can help you with?"

"Yes," he said, keeping his voice even and friendly. "I came in for a tarot reading. Josephine Murphy is here today, isn't she?"

"She is! She's with a client, but she'll be available in fifteen minutes if you don't mind waiting," she said, seeming delighted with this idea.

Humans.

Still, this one was harmless. He engaged in some mild flirting with the clerk, whose name was Sonja. Before the fifteen minutes were up, she had invited him out for a drink.

"I'd love to," he said, making sure his voice expressed the right level of disappointment, "but I'm only here for a few hours to visit friends. I heard some great things about your tarot reader and figured I'd stop in before leaving town."

Before Sonja could answer, a middle-aged blonde human came out from a back room, sniffling and dabbing her eyes with a tissue. She turned around to hug a petite woman with short, black hair in a pixie-style haircut, and every one of his senses zeroed in.

This was *her.* She'd changed, yes. A little. The hair was shorter and no longer the blood-red color from her pictures. Her face had more lines, but it was prettier in person, arresting in a way that wouldn't make her stand out in a crowd unless you gave her a closer look. She wore jeans, black Chuck Taylors, and a T-shirt with a grinning cartoon witch giving a thumbs-up.

He tamped down the urge to laugh. She might be the least witchiest witch he'd ever seen, but she was the one he was sent to find.

She smelled like warm lavender and sympathy.

He inhaled her scent as deeply as he could without drawing attention to himself, then cleared his throat on a soft sound that only his team, listening from outside as they covered the building, would recognize. *Eyes on the prize.*

Booker watched as Josephine Murphy patted the blonde woman on the back and gave her a gentle smile. "Don't worry—everything will work out," she said, her voice a soothing contralto. He was discovering all kinds of things about his quarry in these endless moments, and both he and his wolf were growing impatient to engage. "I promise."

The blonde nodded, still sniffling, and shuffled past him on her way out of the store. When the door closed behind the blonde woman, Josephine Murphy looked up at him for the first time. Her clear blue eyes held a look of friendly curiosity that darkened within the second. He had to hand it to her—she didn't let it show on her face, but it was the smell, every time. Her sympathy, her focus on helping her client, had turned to fear.

She knew what he was.

So, his quarry was as smart as she was pretty. Booker didn't linger over those thoughts too much, or worry too much over her fear of him. It didn't matter. The exits were covered, and the Council had given them each a small red-flannel mojo bag that was supposed to prevent anyone in a certain radius from transporting themselves. Some of the supernatural creatures he had dealt with could blip away on a mere thought, so there was every chance that a witch could do the same. It made them a bitch to catch, unless you were prepared.

His team was prepared. She wasn't going anywhere.

Josephine Murphy smiled at the clerk but stayed rooted to her spot on the floor. Booker kept his eyes on her.

"Sonja, do I have another client?"

Sonja nodded, turning to him. "This is Jo. She'll be reading for you in the back room."

Jo. He liked that. It suited her. She smiled at Sonja. "Sweetie, why don't you go on home? I'll lock up after we're done here."

The witch wanted to get her coworker out of the shop, away from him. He could respect that, but he wasn't here for the clerk.

Sonja lit up with surprised pleasure. "Thanks, Jo!" She gathered up her purse and sent him a regretful wave. "Nice to meet you. If you're in town again, come back and see us."

He gave her a brief, tight-lipped smile and a nod, unable to spare her much attention. Not when his quarry was finally right before him.

Once Sonja walked out of the store, Jo Murphy turned back to him with an expression of weary resignation that she tried to mask with a forced smile. Her fear-smell grew with every second, spoiling the scent of lavender, and her heart had begun to race in her chest—he could almost feel it beating. She gave no outward sign of the inner turmoil. She simply said, "Follow me," and went into the back room.

The store wasn't a large one, so in three strides, he reached the door to the reading room. The small, incense-flavored room held a card table covered with a cheerful blue cloth, two chairs, a large floor-length mirror, and nothing else.

She was gone. He couldn't even smell her anymore.

He muttered a filthy curse and clicked a button on his radio, asking if Nick or Max had eyes on the witch.

They didn't.

Okay, so maybe this was why the Council had taken so long to find her. He gritted his teeth, casting one last searing gaze around the reading room.

It seemed that Jo Murphy was trickier than they'd thought.

CHAPTER 2

RESTING WITCH FACE

JO

THE DREAM HELD ME IN ITS GRIP. ROPES PINNING MY ARMS behind my back, strong hands hitting me, vicious teeth biting me. The pain as real as it had been nine years ago. Still, the worst was yet to come. Once the physical violence wore me down until I was too brutalized, too drained to fight, the real horror always began.

Tonight, I was lucky: I jolted back to reality before the dream went any further. The screaming stopped when I realized where I was. *Home. Safe.*

I blinked, closed my mouth. A thin sheen of sweat had dampened my pajamas and my pillow, and every part of me trembled. From where he lay curled on the other pillow, my cat, Cole, regarded me with irritation, green eyes slitted but vivid in his midnight face. Cole didn't like the screaming, but he'd gotten more or less used to it by now. Gulping for breath, I reached out to give him his favorite type of ear-scratch, hoping to make up for the indignity of being woken up at 3 a.m. by a screeching human.

As I rubbed his ears, I looked at the tattoo on my arm, tracing the curves of Hecate's wheel with my eyes, letting the feel of the cat's fur and the familiar pattern bring me back to the present. To the Sanctum, my building. My new home. Where I was safe.

Once he was purring, I got out of bed, already feeling better. More steady. One of the perks of having cats, at least for me—petting them soothed everything.

The first order of business now was to turn on every light in my house. A lifetime of horror movies instilled that one in me, and while it wasn't true protection, it helped banish the shadows. I went through my morning ritual of yoga, hot tea, and shower. I spent more than an hour on yoga, letting the exercise focus my mind on the present moment. I had the time, thanks to the extra two hours the nightmare had given me.

Falling into a familiar routine did the rest of the work to settle my nerves and drive the dream away. Even after tea, a long shower, and breakfast, I still had plenty of time before the shop opened. Since it was just six floors down, and I was the boss, I went downstairs and got to work about an hour early to prepare inventory for the shelves and shipments for online orders. I'd planned to pawn this off on my employee Emma when she came in later this morning, but I had to keep my mind busy. Boxing up a bulk order of homegrown sage-and-lavender smoke sticks wasn't exactly engrossing work, but it seemed my best option for the time being.

As I set to work, I was reminded anew of the beauty of owning my own place —one of the advantages of this permanent move to St. Louis. I'd seen enough of the occult shop business in the last decade, the good and the sleazy, to get a feel for how to do it right. However, hanging my witch shingle on a shop and putting up a neon sign that said "Psychic" wasn't all I wanted. I'd been on my own long enough. I craved being part of a *community*. My hope for my building—which I had purchased and spent five months renovating before I opened the shop three months ago—was that the whole place would become a sanctuary for those who needed it. I'd named it "the Sanctum" in an idealistic moment of inspiration.

I'd planned the Sanctum as a place with useful products and supplies, a place where people could come and browse—not just randos, but other practitioners of the craft. I could interact with newbie witches, help them get started. They could ask questions. I could give advice. They could count on me to be here.

I could count on being here.

I mean, what was the point of being a witch if you couldn't help people?

Once I finished printing shipping labels and started putting inventory out onto the shelves, my brain returned to that problem, probing it like a sore tooth. The last time I'd had the nightmare was in Ste. Genevieve, the night before the wolf had come for me. I shivered when I thought back to him—the wolf in human skin.

If I hadn't known that he was a wolf, I would have found him attractive. More than attractive. Even though I'm short and on the curvy side, I love a tall man, and the wolf was tall in his human form, with broad shoulders and a muscular build—the kind that felt like he used his body for a living, and that living was dangerous. The body was appealing, but it was the eyes that caught me, contrasting as they did with his dark brown hair. Those eyes were focused, intense. The color of amber.

The eyes of a predator.

Yeah, I could have gotten lost in those fascinating eyes and that intimidating body. I might have if, a split second later, I hadn't registered his aura, the powerful miasma of energy surrounding him, and how it screamed *WOLF*. I'd been so preoccupied with my client, emotionally and psychically, that I hadn't realized when a werewolf had literally been in the same room with me until I looked at him.

Werewolves equaled very bad. In so many ways. So I got out of there.

I put some miles between myself and Ste. Genevieve, driving south as fast as I dared. When I felt that I was far enough away that I could rest, I found a spot out in the middle of nowhere, parked my beat-up Jeep Cherokee, and slept for a few hours. The dream started like the rest, but suddenly it changed, and I found myself somewhere else. I was no longer a captive, wishing for death. I was no longer running for my life from the wolf who'd found my most recent hiding place.

Instead, I stood on a rooftop in the city where I grew up, watching the river flow. Healthy. Safe. Powerful. Not in a Galadriel-holding-the-One-Ring way, but in a happy, secure, witchy way.

When I came back to consciousness for real, slumped back in the driver's seat, I woke with a purpose. One of the things about being a witch I'd learned the hard way in the past eight years was that sometimes I *knew* what I was supposed to do, and sometimes I could *see* what I was supposed to do. When I was very lucky, I got both.

It was time to take a stand and build my power. It was the only thing that would make me safe. I had to go home to St. Louis and find that building. So I turned the car around and headed north.

Running water and bridges were always powerful sources of energy and magic for me. I felt more powerful, more centered, the instant I entered the city, and I spent the whole first day downtown near the Arch, watching the river flow, flanked by huge bridges on either side. I'd never been able to stay too far away from the Mississippi during the years I drifted from town to town, unable to leave it, but unable to stay in one spot for long.

I'd spent that first day in St. Louis marinating in the buzz of happiness I got from being so near the river and those bridges. This was one of the Mississippi's power points—now that I knew what I was looking for, I could feel it everywhere around me. So I started making plans. For better or for worse, the city was my place, and somehow coming full circle didn't feel like a retreat. It felt like a reclaiming.

After a thorough search, I found my sanctuary. It was an older brick building in the Central East End that was borderline falling apart, but the area felt right. The roads in the Central East End were a little crazier than the rest of St. Louis, which allowed me the golden opportunity of finding a place built at a triple crossroads, which cemented the building's magical center. Hecate—goddess of witches and crossroads—couldn't have been more pleased with it if She'd built it Herself. The intersection was more of a T-junction, with the building sitting above the T like a hat, and it led into another T-junction a few blocks away where my old friend and fellow witch Kate Strega had renovated another building to create her homeless shelter, Hecate's Home. According to Kate, she had been drawn to the area for the same reasons.

Most importantly, the roof of my seven-story building overlooked the river. I was uphill from it, and between me and the mighty Mississippi, it was all parking lots and a couple of warehouses only one or two stories tall. The view from my roof was spectacular, as far as I was concerned, and it was the one from the dream—or the vision, whatever it was. I had the money, and I had the opportunity.

Who knew? Maybe Hecate had somehow set all this up and guided me to it. That wasn't for me to question, not when she had saved my life. If this was Hecate's plan, then I was going with it. It helped that I had Kate already living and working there. Witches tend not to buddy up—too much food for jealousy and power struggles there—but Kate welcomed me into the neighborhood with open arms. Being around her felt right. We had history, we both worked with Hecate, we liked each other...again, sometimes I just *know*.

The sun was fully up by the time I finished restocking and rearranging the shelves that held the shop's selection of crystals. I'd literally completed every task I'd hoped to accomplish for this week and the next, but I still wasn't any closer to working through my nerves about having had the nightmare again for the first time in eight months. Did it mean that someone was coming? That I'd been found, again?

Making a stand, putting down roots—that meant being visible to some degree. I'd put the Sanctum online with a web page and social media. I didn't use my full name anywhere, but it wouldn't take much digging to find it. All things told, it was something of a miracle that I hadn't been found sooner.

I also tried to remind myself that I was ready for this—for being found. During those months of renovations, I made the Sanctum as powerful as possible, feeding my own energy into it and taking advantage of every opportunity to magic up all aspects of the building. I put specialized charm bags in the corners, etched and painted runes in various places, placed crystals in the walls in patterns that felt harmonious—all to make sure that the building would feel happy and welcoming to those who needed knowledge or sanctuary. I added all the protections I could think to add, for myself and anyone who might enter.

The Sanctum was gathering strength all the time. It had simply become a part of my day to feed power into it and take power from it without conscious thought in a natural flow, almost like breathing.

Anyone who wants to get to you is going to have a hard time getting in here, I reminded myself as I flipped the sign in the front windows to "Open." This time of peace had been precious, and I'd used it wisely. I'd built something real here, and I went to sleep every night in my own place, with my own cat, with my own power surrounding me. The Sanctum was my home, and regardless of that damned nightmare, I felt safer here than I had anywhere, anytime, in my life.

It was good to have a home. I wasn't going to give it up without a fight.

About a half hour after I opened, the bell on my door jangled. I jumped—the first "ring" of the day tended to do that, even when my nerves weren't already frayed. I looked up from my many-times-read paperback of *Vigilant* to see Heather, one of my newer customers, and heaved a mental sigh.

Heather was desperate to overcome a phobia that she said was impeding her ability to get promoted at work. She informed me that she was ready to try anything that gave her an edge, so she'd found me. All she would tell me was that she worked in mergers and acquisitions, but she had the vibe of a power player—she wore killer suits and radiated oodles of focused energy.

Unfortunately for both of us, Heather was also a born skeptic. She refused to take the strengthening spell kit I assembled for her, turning up her nose at the small collection of ingredients and directions. "I don't want a project," she said, impatience clipping off every syllable. "I want a solution. Can you give that to me or not?"

The problem with vowing to help people is ending up in the position of having to do that even when I dislike them—the service industry in a nutshell. So I outsourced. If Heather wanted magic without the work, well, that meant she'd need a potion, and potion work was never my strong suit. I could cook well enough, but I never had the feel for magical concoctions. However, Kate was the best potion witch I'd ever met, and she could always use the extra cash.

Between the two of us, we planned and prepared Heather a potion and infused it with the energy needed to help her overcome her phobia. Since Heather had refused to share the nature of her fears, we had to make the potion more of a generalized "Phobias, Be Gone" instead of one specific to her needs.

"There's a good chance it's not going to work right," Kate had cautioned me when she delivered the finished product in a small vial. "Do these people not realize that details matter? I'm not fucking Miracle Max over here."

I shrugged. "Her money's good, and if it helps her even a little bit, it's more than she deserves."

Heather was one of those customers you get when you work in the occult: a normie whose attitude projected a mixture of apprehension and fascination that somehow combined to border on belligerence. It was a marvel that she even found my shop, let alone came into it herself. The website was *right there*.

Ah, well, I thought as I watched Heather march toward me. I may have been in the "service industry," but I was also my own boss. I could and did overcharge for certain people as I saw fit—or to deter them from buying things they shouldn't—and I was making Heather pay through the nose for this potion. If her money helped me and Kate pay our bills, it was worth it.

Heather, to her credit, didn't bat an eye at the outrageous price when I rang it up and handed her the vial, but right after signing her credit card receipt, she eyed me and said, "How do I know you aren't giving me poison?"

Sheer astonishment kept me silent for a full three seconds. I stared at her, knowing my jaw was hanging open but still not able to formulate a response.

Now I kind of wanted to poison her for even suggesting such a thing.

Heather tilted her head. "I'm serious. You drink some first."

Really? The next time she came in, I was charging her four times as much for whatever she bought. Call it a bitch tax.

I plucked the vial from her fingers. *Less fear for us all, I guess?* I took a sip, smacking my lips for effect, then corked it and handed it back. "Good enough?" I asked, reminding myself not to snarl.

Approval washed over her face. "Yes. Thank you," Heather said, her tone transformed. She sounded...satisfied. "Have a good day." She flounced out of the shop.

Merciful Hecate, may I never have to deal with that woman again.

As Heather headed for the parking lot, Emma, my first hire and my right-hand woman, walked in. Emma was a few inches taller than me, with long, black hair—although I suspected it was blonde without the dye—and flawless makeup. I had no patience with such things, but I couldn't help but admire her skills with eyeliner.

Emma had immersed herself in the goth scene in St. Louis, which was fantastic for me business-wise. Her sartorial style—all-black clothing, often form-fitting with generous amounts of vinyl—tended to make people feel they were in a "real" occult store when they came in, something that my jeans and T-shirts couldn't deliver. Even my beloved "Resting Witch Face" shirt, which I was wearing today. *Goddess bless Etsy.*

Emma was not only an employee but a newbie witch and a walking advertisement. She loved bragging about her job in "the Sanctum Occult Shop" and posting about the Sanctum on social media—something I had neither the time nor the temperament to do beyond the occasional "we're open" or "big sale" post. More than that, Emma was a born saleswoman, especially with the younger clientele. Teenage girls would flock to her, and she would guide them to the best things to buy for their needs. Emma managed to handle them with joy and care, while I did better with the adult-shaped customers. Despite my desire to help the public, I often found myself rolling my eyes at some of those girls. I mean, they'd come in and say they wanted "revenge curses" or "love spells." It made me want to chase them out of the store.

On one memorable occasion, Emma had to step in to soothe a trust fund baby who'd told me she wanted to "be irresistible to men," which would have backfired on her in horrible ways if she'd managed to pull it off.

Emma smoothed it all over, but the girl had left in a huff without buying anything, swearing a wrathful vow never to return. Apparently, asking a teenage girl, "Are you seriously that stupid?" tended to make her mad.

Who knew?

No, I had run out of patience with much of the younger generation— the kids at Hecate's Home were an important exception—but Emma would guide those customers to books that would help explain their issues or to love spells that brought love or fulfillment into their life without focusing the energy on a specific person.

On top of it all, Emma was a good friend who made me laugh on a regular basis. She was one of my all-time favorite people in the world, and I'd only known her for a few months.

When she bounced up to the counter, I gave her a welcoming smile, and she grinned back, her kohl-lined eyes alight with glee.

"Jo! I ran into one of the hottest men I've ever seen today. I'm talking *lickable.* He came up to me in the parking lot, and I have to tell you, my heart was in my throat—I was so nervous. I mean, he was hot, but he also looked kind of dangerous, and like, beautiful eyes." Emma continued on in raptures, but I could barely focus past my churning stomach. I'd only met one "man" in my life who fit that description. I'd hoped he might have given up, but it wasn't much of a surprise—once they'd gotten the scent, wolves didn't let things go.

At least the nightmare had prepared me for it.

"...he knew my name," Emma was saying when I refocused. Her lipstick-darkened mouth quirked. "I mean, *wow*." She fanned herself with the piece of folded notebook paper in her hand. "It was a major letdown when all he wanted was to give me a note for you. No fair, boss lady." Emma rolled her eyes, winking, and put the paper in my hands.

I nodded at her, trying to smile, and after a bit of awkward chitchat, I made an excuse to go back to my office. I'd split the large room behind the counter into two, creating a small hallway between an office for me and a reading room. I headed into my office, closing the door before I finally sat down and read the note from the wolf.

The words were written in precise blue ink, neat and tidy: "Sorry I spooked you in Ste. Gene. That was my fault. I need to speak with you about the Fen., but I guarantee your safety. You choose the time and place. Call this number and ask for Booker."

The word "guarantee" was underlined. Beneath the words was a phone number. There was no signature, which was smart. If he'd signed it, I could have turned the note's promise of "no harm" into a geas, and he would have to honor his word or be cursed. Not many people, even witches, had that type of natural ability, and I didn't broadcast mine, even to Emma. I wondered if Booker the Wolf knew I had that kind of power. Then again, signatures weren't necessary on something like this.

This note was an interesting development. I'd warded the Sanctum against werewolves in a big way, of course, but I'd had no way of knowing how effective the protection had been. It seemed they were working well enough. I smiled, imagining the wolf's consternation when he'd tried to saunter his big, bad self up to the Sanctum and hadn't been able to come in. He'd had to get creative.

My smile faded, though, when I looked back down at the note. Had it been from a human, I might have found it kind of charming in a passing-notes-in-class kind of way. The wolf could have called the shop's landline or sent an email through the Sanctum website, but he chose to send me a handwritten note via Emma. It could be a "trust me" move that had both a medieval and a middle school feel to it. Like, "I didn't hurt your friend, so I won't hurt you." Or it could be a subtle threat: "We could hurt her if you don't do what we want." The note didn't have that vibe, but that didn't necessarily mean much.

Oh, for the love of fucking Pete. I could've literally stood there for hours going back and forth. Gnawing at my bottom lip, I considered my options. If it could be at my time and my choosing, maybe I should at least hear what the wolf had to say.

I reached down to the tarot deck closest at hand—they were pretty much everywhere in my office and in the reading rooms—picturing the wolf's face in my mind. I picked a card at random.

2 of Cups. Positive vibes, new relationships.

Well, shit. Maybe the wolf was on the level. I thought about that slash underneath the word "guarantee," and I looked at the card again. I was historically terrible at doing full spreads for myself, but the old "draw a card" technique usually steered me in the right direction.

If I was going to be living out in the open as a witch, I would have to deal with the past at some point. With the werewolves and whatever else was out there. It was past time to face those old fears and show a willingness to make peace. I could start by owning up to what I'd done to those Fenris bastards.

CHAPTER 3

A WITCH WALKS INTO A FUNHOUSE

JO

I CONSIDERED BEING SUBTLE ABOUT ANSWERING THE NOTE—maybe even waiting until the next day. But tonight was the dark of the moon, which meant Booker the Wolf and any of his buddies would be at least a little bit powered-down. It would be smart to move now, in a tactical sense, and there would be less waiting around.

As soon as I made my decision, I picked up my office phone and called the number, willing my heartbeat to stay normal, and when a deep male voice said, "Hello?" I asked for Booker.

"Speaking." *And without a trace of recognition,* I thought, telling myself I was not disappointed. *Ah, well.* My pulse was accelerating enough as it was.

I took a breath and said, trying to sound calm, "Hecate's Home is having a carnival to raise funds for their homeless shelter. The carnival has a fun house with a hall of mirrors. Be there at 8 p.m. tonight."

Not waiting for his reply, I ended the call, my heart now galloping. I felt a little queasy from nerves, but at least I had a plan.

I still had to get through the rest of the day, though.

The store was busy enough that I didn't manage to fret myself to death. Things were running better than I could have hoped after only a few months. Much of that was due to Emma, I knew, watching as she guided another of those wide-eyed, nervous teenage girls to a helpful rather than harmful solution.

As efficient an employee as Emma was, I liked to work in the shop myself. I was generally there every day from opening to closing, which was 6 p.m. for now. My hope was to have enough trained employees in the next year so we could stay open later, but right now I just had Emma and John, my other part-time employee. People could order via the Sanctum website at any time—my way of trying to help insomnia shoppers—and the online store sold plenty, sometimes more than the physical store.

Every bit helped.

I felt like 8 p.m. had been the best choice for the meeting. After flipping the "Open" sign to "Closed" at 6, I would have an hour to deal with the million tasks involved in closing the store, and then it would be time to go. My plan was to get to the carnival at 7:30 so that I would be already waiting in the hall of mirrors by the time the wolf showed up.

Emma helped me tidy up the shop after closing, so the chores that often took me an hour were done in about thirty minutes. I wish I had five more employees like Emma—the shop would run itself and might even take over the world.

"Want to come out with me tonight?" she asked as we prepared to close everything up. "I'm going to Purgatory later."

For a moment I went blank, thinking along Dante lines. Then I remembered—Purgatory was the name of the goth club a few streets over that she loved so much.

"Hel's Belles are playing tonight," Emma continued, closing her eyes and raising her arms, miming what I assumed was her go-to dance move in the club. "Their music is the shit."

"Oh," I said, trying to hide my distaste. Emma had shown me online pictures of that band the first time she'd tried to get me to come to a show with her. The members of Hel's Belles were a brand of goth girl that always gave me the wiggins: white skin, lacy outfits, red lips. It was a look I thought of as "Victorian Dead"—it was one of the reasons I couldn't watch most vampire movies.

No, I loved Emma's look; all black suited her, and her natural paleness meant she didn't have to whiten her face. I couldn't say the same about

Hel's Belles and its band members. They had all saddled themselves with fake names—of which I could only remember "Belladonna" and "Heloise" —and their aesthetic creeped me the hell out even just looking at their pictures. Being in the same building as them? Big no.

Not to mention that the idea of listening to "trance" dance music— which was a real thing, for I'd lost precious minutes of my life Googling it— was about as appealing as drinking actual poison.

Which I had *not* sold to Heather.

"Yeah," I began, apology already in my tone, "you know that's not my kind of scene."

"Nothing is your kind of scene." Emma made a face, then cocked her head. "Hey, come on—it will be fun! We could trick you out, goth you up. Get you laid." She grinned. "I'm meeting this guy there. I could see if he has a friend." The singsong lilt of the last bit was pure Emma, and I couldn't help but smile.

"Thanks," I said, rolling my eyes. "But I've got other plans."

Her eyes flared with interest. "With big, tall, and dangerous?"

I shook my head, closing the account book with relief. The worst part of owning a business was the fucking accounting. "The Hecate's Home carnival's tonight. I'm going to go show some support."

Emma's face fell. "Oh, shit. I should go to that, shouldn't I?"

"No," I said, with a little too much force. Then I made myself smile. "I'll spend extra cash for you. No need to change your plans. Kate's going to be so busy she won't even notice."

"If you're sure it's okay," Emma said. "Wait." She rummaged in her purse and pulled out a $10 bill. "Give this to Kate and tell her I'm sorry."

"No problem," I said, smiling with real relief. I wouldn't have had the wolf meet me at the carnival if I thought he was going to be dangerous to anyone but me—I needed the home field advantage—but the thought of Emma getting mixed up in this was too much. I wouldn't risk her.

In a treacle-sweet Glinda voice, Emma declared, "You are a good witch." She paused. "We all done?"

"Yup," I said, sighing. "Thank you."

Smiling, Emma shrugged into her leather jacket. "Then I'm out, boss witch."

"Have fun," I called as she walked to the door. "I expect details tomorrow!"

"You won't be able to handle them, cotton panties."

"Ha-ha," I said. "Make sure he wears a condom at least."

Emma paused in the open door to turn and stick her tongue out at me. When I laughed, she trilled, "See you tomorrow!" as the bell chimed and the door slid shut behind her. I watched her run across the street. When she was safely inside her car and pulling onto the street, I released a breath I didn't realize I'd been holding and finally locked the door.

It only took me a few minutes of being alone with time to kill to start getting antsy, so I went upstairs and considered changing my clothes to something nicer. Then I rejected that idea and just added a hoodie since the air was turning crisp. If shit went sideways with the wolf despite my escape hatch, I needed clothes suitable for running. Plus, I told myself, I was not dressing to impress anyone.

I thought I might fiddle with my hair, since I was going out in public— and only for that reason. I tried a messy ponytail, but it turned out too messy. Then a bun. *The horror.* I sighed. There was no point in trying to make my straight, black locks look any different than usual. I tucked my hair behind my ears and let it be.

Then, since Cole was ignoring me and I knew I wouldn't be able to focus on a book or a TV show, I sent Kate a text that I wanted to talk to her when I got there and left for the carnival early.

Hecate's Home was only about three blocks away from the Sanctum, but the entire landscape of the area changed between the two properties. My building stood in the gentrifying section, where nicer building complexes, housing, and storefronts were in the process of emerging from rundown near-ruins. Hecate's Home sat atop its T-intersection in much the same way mine did, but it occupied part of the more rundown section. What used to be a warehouse was being converted into a homeless shelter for queer kids of all ages. It was still in progress, and might always be from the looks of it— but somehow Kate had been making it work.

Kate and I had known each other for years, ever since high school. She wasn't the only queer kid at our school, but she may have been the only bisexual person I knew. Later, I would come to understand that she was more of a pansexual, but at the time she only had access to male and female humans. Like me, Kate hadn't had a stable home life—her father hadn't approved of her lifestyle choices or her oddness. From what little I knew, Kate's father had been a truly horrible person, and she'd escaped that hell by staying with various relatives around the city until she graduated high school. When my grandparents died and I was put into the foster system, Kate had been there for me. Later, in those days after I left the foster system and began living out of my car, Kate was one of the few people at school who knew the truth, and she found me a couch to sleep on whenever she could.

After high school, Kate became a nomad like me, but on a much wider scale—she spent a few years in Europe, visiting relatives in Italy to learn more about her background in the craft. Even so, once she came back to the States, our paths crossed on the regular for years. She was one of those people I ran into everywhere. We would always marvel at how weird it was to see each other out of the blue in Backwater, Nowhere, and then we'd have a drink, trade stories, laugh, and move on.

I found out later that during those years, Kate had been living in her ratty van and traveling around to sell potions and items like a modern-day Bohemian because she was saving up to buy a place where she could provide a home for kids like she had been—kids whose parents refused them because of their orientation or their identity.

By the time I was settling in at the Sanctum, we'd gone from old acquaintances to real friends. I even volunteered at Hecate's Home when I had free time, and it was one of my favorite parts of my new life, aside from the shop and my mentorship with Emma. The shelter kids tended to be younger than the high-school and college students who wandered through my store like they owned it, but they were already far more mature. A few of them had some natural abilities, sparks of magic inside them that it was impossible to miss. Kate and I had agreed that at least two of them would make great students—if they wished—when they got older.

Another thing to be thankful for in this new life. Another thing to fight for.

The carnival was in full swing when I arrived, alive with light, sound, and the blended aromas of fair food—any wolf coming here was going to be constantly adjusting their senses to the surroundings. Plus, the more people around, the better—even the Fenris were hyper-vigilant about keeping their existence hidden from humans. They weren't going to rampage through the place, I reminded myself again and again.

Last year's carnival had been fun, and enough of a hit that Kate had planned the whole thing all over again. I knew the layout and had a good sense of my resources, and Kate had done what she could to ensure everyone's safety—it was on her turf, after all.

Plus, there was no harm in getting Kate and the kids a little extra funding. Wolves always had money, so I didn't feel even a little bit bad about making this Booker donate to a good cause for the chance to speak to me. No one would be in danger—except possibly me—and since he had to pay to get into the festival and into the fun house, at least Hecate's Home would benefit from this madness.

If Kate didn't kill me for inviting a werewolf into her place. In my defense, the carnival was in the empty lot beside the building, not Hecate's Home itself. I'd sent her a text a half hour ago that she hadn't even read yet.

Even so...

Shit. I sent her another text and set out to find her. It was a little after 7, so I had some time before I needed to get to the hall of mirrors.

I wandered around the carnival for a while, looking for Kate. I waved to a few of the kids and other volunteers I knew, and one of my favorite Hecate's Home kiddos, Miguel de Santos, jogged up to me. "Jo! Buy a 50/50 raffle ticket?" He held up a roll of tickets, shaking it in front of me like a tambourine. "You know you want one. The pot's growing!"

"Fun," I said, slanting him an amused glance. "The only raffle where if you win it, you're a butthead if you don't donate the whole pot back to the cause."

Miguel gave me a mock-offended look. "You don't *have* to."

"Ugh, fine," I sighed, making it as dramatic as possible. "Give me as many tickets as I can get for $10. Oh, and $10 for Emma too." I imagined

Emma's reaction if she won and I donated it all back without consulting her first. That *would* be fun.

As Miguel counted out the tickets and I scrawled our names on them, I said, "Is Kate around?"

"Yeah, but I don't know where," he said. "She was arguing with the bouncy house chick a minute ago."

"That poor bouncy house chick."

Miguel grinned. He turned and scanned the crowd. "She's...yeah, Jo, I don't see her."

"Of course," I muttered. "Well, if you do, tell her I'm looking for her."

However, Miguel was already heading away from me, having spotted some new arrivals. He called back, "No prob!"

I sighed and pulled out my phone. *Son of a bitch.* Was her phone even on? I wandered a bit more and still didn't find Kate, but I did find a gyro, cinnamon-and-sugar almonds, and some cotton candy. As I munched my way around the games and exhibits, enjoying the energy of the carnival, I watched the people around me. There were plenty of families with younger kids, a few couples out for a date night, and a few looky-loos like me wandering on their own.

I didn't see anyone who looked or felt like a wolf, but that didn't mean they weren't there. I did keep catching a hint of something unexpected in the air—a sense of something rotting or decaying. It was too hard to trace, though, with so many people and so much *stuff* around me. The carnival was a psychic kaleidoscope, not to mention an olfactory one.

I let it go, for the moment, in favor of finding an isolated table and finishing my food. Even so, I kept my eyes open, scanning the perimeter until I was done eating. I loved fair food, but it was hard to enjoy everything while I was so on edge.

I wiped my fingers and threw away my trash before I allowed myself to check my phone. *Damn, how is it only 7:20? What the hell, Kate?*

Whatever. I could kill forty minutes in the hall of mirrors. I was anxious to get this whole thing over with, and being the first one to arrive was part of my plan. I knew next to nothing about Booker the Wolf, and watching him approach might give me some more insight. Thanks to my work with Hecate, I sometimes got flashes of information about people while they were walking or when they made eye contact with me—not much, usually, but sometimes snippets of history or thoughts. It happened more frequently with those who had some magic in them, so I was hoping for some of that from the werewolf.

I wanted every advantage. I deserved that. If Booker the Wolf really just wanted information from me, then fine, I could work with him. But as a general rule, I didn't trust wolves, and I had good reason. Even if they weren't evil or crazed berserkers, they were isolationist by their very nature. That pack mentality is great if you're in the pack—but if you're not, well, sucks to be you.

If this were some sort of ambush on his part, I wanted to know sooner rather than later. I couldn't control my weird flashes of insight, but I could position myself to my best advantage to get information from them. We'd see how *he* liked being ambushed.

I bought enough tickets to get into the fun house, which consisted mostly of a hall of mirrors and some spooky rooms, with recorded screams playing with the music in the background to give that auditory bump to the brain's fear receptors. When I walked in, those screams began to work far too well on my stretched-tight nerves. I had forgotten about that kind of thing when I chose the spot, but there were other tactical advantages that made up for it. I checked my phone. 7:25. Time to find a corner and settle in.

I walked through the first spooky room and around the corner to the hall of mirrors, only to find the wolf already there, waiting for me. And here I'd worn a blue hoodie instead of a red one.

Well, shit.

CHAPTER 4

THE EARLY WOLF CATCHES THE WITCH

JO

BOOKER THE WOLF SMILED AT ME, FLASHING MATCHING DIMPLES on either side of his mouth, and I nearly laughed, despite the momentary shock and heightened apprehension electrifying my body. He was leaning against a mirror in jeans and a long coat, one booted ankle resting on top of the other, with his arms crossed over his chest. It seemed like he took the pose to look more casual and less intimidating, and it worked. Somewhat.

"I guess the early wolf catches the witch?" I said, looking away and placing one fingertip along the silvery surface of the mirror to my left.

"Something like that," he allowed, his voice as smooth as good Scotch. "And hello to you, too, Jo Murphy." Then he cocked his head, eyes sharpening, and added, almost as an afterthought, "Your hair is longer."

This time I couldn't hold back a chuckle, especially at the momentary chagrin that crossed his features. I don't think he'd meant to say it, and that momentary fumble, more than anything else, helped me relax a little. "Funny thing about hair," I deadpanned. "It just grows on you."

His grin was real this time, not calculated, and it did amazing things for his face. Goddess, what a face. It was much like I remembered it from Ste.

Genevieve: amber eyes, straight nose, high cheekbones, superhero chin. The dimples were new to me—he hadn't done much smiling back at Other Worlds Emporium—but he knew he was attractive, and he'd clearly been trying to use it to his advantage. There was power, authority, emanating from him—his aura so strong, it could casually dominate anyone who allowed it. When Booker the Wolf told someone to do something, it got done. When he wanted something, he was used to getting it.

When I walked closer to him, that aura enveloped me, although mine pushed back. *None of that here, bucko.*

I stopped when I was a few feet away, not willing to get within reach. He was leaning to the right side of the corridor, so I stayed close to the left. Damn it, he was far too appealing to me already. Booker the Wolf's body was all broad-shouldered menace, as tall as I remembered—easily more than six feet—and filling the corridor, but his smile in that gorgeous face was pure charm, and those ridiculous dimples made him seem like a harmless, insanely attractive man.

A wolf in sheep's dimples.

His eyes were locked on me now. I could've sworn they'd begun to glow a bit—*Molten honey*, I couldn't help thinking—and I found my gaze held there. *Wow.* But since I was definitely the sheep in this instance, I should maybe stop drooling over his cutie-pie dimples and those beautiful, hypnotic eyes and *focus.*

I dropped my eyes and took a deep breath, looking again at the mirror next to me. It was easier to look at his reflection. "What is it I can do for you, Mr. Booker?"

His smile more or less stayed in place, but the dimples disappeared. All business now. "Just Booker." His eyes were gaining intensity with every second that they didn't blink, and his voice took on a slight edge of frustration. "Why can't I come into your shop? I couldn't even cross the damn street."

"Because I don't want wolves in the Sanctum." He tensed, his eyes shifting away for a second. *Damn it, I offended him.* Then, directly on that thought's heels, *Why the hell do I care about his feelings? Focus, Murphy.* "Okay, Booker. What is it I can do for you?" If I had to repeat the question a third time, I was leaving.

He blinked. It was a small miracle. "The Council sent me to ask you what happened to the Fenris werewolves," he said, his deep voice rippling through me.

This was more or less what I'd been expecting. I'd figured the wolves would want to try to get vengeance on me for the Fenris for a long time now. However, the "Council" thing was new.

"A council?" I asked, unable to keep the skepticism from my tone. "Of what? Werewolves?"

He'd been giving the impression of lounging so far, but this brought him to attention pretty quickly. He straightened and took a step toward me, one predatory move, and I couldn't help but take a step backward in response. His nostrils flared, and his eyes flashed with irritation. Not rage, but alarming enough.

Don't back down.

Booker took another step forward before he checked himself. "How can a witch be powerful enough to apparently eliminate the Fenris from the known world but not know about the Council?" he asked with ill-concealed frustration.

I snorted and used my spiking alarm and indignation to fuel some bravado, although I was still shifting my body away from his. "Like this." I waved my hands in the air in a meaningless pattern that I hoped looked powerful and witchy enough for him. "Stop posturing and answer my question. Who or what is the Council?"

Booker's giant chest rose and fell, his aura shifting, and he found himself another spot good for leaning. He didn't quite get back to the nonchalance he had exhibited earlier, but it was close enough that I stopped edging away.

When his eyes met mine again, they were serious. "There's a council of supernatural beings from different races who govern the rest of us. Well, 'govern' isn't the right word." He seemed to take a moment to gather his thoughts, and I wondered if it were to create a lie or to find the best way to explain the truth. "They do what they can to keep the supernatural world as much of a secret as possible. Make it so we can police our own, that kind of thing."

Suspicious as I still was, his aura didn't feel like he was lying, and the concept made a certain amount of sense. Having a supreme authority over the supernatural community seemed like a reasonably good idea, if there were that many different types of creatures out there.

Or, given the amount of corruption that tended to seep into such groups, maybe it was the worst idea ever.

I thought back to the money. After I'd escaped from the hell the Fenris had kept me in for days, I'd come back to myself somewhere else, cleaned up, wearing clothes that weren't my own—and I had a large bag of cash. Like, a ridiculous heist movie amount. It had to have come from the Fenris den. It smelled like them, felt like them. As much as I hated knowing I had something they had touched, I'd kept it, cleansed it as best I could. A secret nest egg, courtesy of my would-be killers.

I wouldn't have been able to buy the Sanctum, renovate the first two floors and my apartment, and start the occult shop without it. It was nearly gone at this point, and I'd been banking on the shop to make my way from now on, renovating the middle floors as I went.

Booker seemed to be waiting for me to acknowledge what he'd said so far, so I did with a short nod, hoping that burst of nerves hadn't been too apparent. Then I said, "So, you're like a wolf cop?" The moment the words came out, I cursed myself, heat rising in my cheeks. *Smooth.*

He laughed, and once again it transformed his face. The delight there seemed real. "I've seen that movie too, and no. I have too many other responsibilities to my own clan and my own pack. I'm more like a contract bounty hunter. For now."

While I digested that, he frowned and added, with a harder edge to his voice, "The Fenris posed a major problem to the Council, but right when the Council was on the brink of an all-out war with them, they disappeared. The only clue left behind was a video." He paused and had the grace to look away when he said gruffly, "Of you."

It was like a punch to the gut. There was video? If there was video of me taking care of the Fenris, then that meant there was video showing why I'd done it. Of what they'd done to me.

I pressed my fingers above my chest and tried to get some air in. *That is past. This is present. Focus on this moment in time.* I focused on regulating my breathing, keeping myself calm, and all the while the wolf watched me, his eyes unblinking but giving nothing away.

When I could finally speak, I said, "So the Council knew? Your *ruling body* knew that the Fenris were abducting humans? Hunting some of them, killing them, and holding the rest as 'entertainment'—and they did nothing?" It should have come out as a scream of rage, but instead it was a raw, furious whisper.

Regardless, my words made Booker flinch and lower his eyes, fists clenching. He wasn't leaning anymore. "None of us realized the Fenris had gotten so out of hand. We didn't know what they were doing. They took people no one noticed. The homeless. The poor." He growled a little. I wondered if he knew he was doing it. Then he shook his head and met my eyes again. "The Fenris allied themselves with a bloodthirsty god and went crazy in the process. Their wolves were corrupted. By the time the Council caught on, their numbers had grown beyond what we could handle. Too many for the other packs to defeat."

Then his dark expression lightened a fraction. "Or so we thought." The wolf's eyes were on mine again, the amber a little warmer—or maybe it was my imagination. "Then they all seemed to disappear before we could make a move. The only clue we found from any of their dens was the one where you were held." He looked away again, but only for a moment. "The place was burned and wrecked, but there was an iPhone we salvaged. It had a video of you, making them all disappear." He paused. "Including, apparently, the owner of that iPhone."

I had a flash of memory—one of the Fenris in the background, a female in human form, cackling with delight while a group of them tortured me. Violated me. A pinpoint of light beaming from one hand.

Booker grunted as if he was...disturbed? Wolves couldn't read minds, though. Surely he didn't know what I was thinking. He shook his head, gestured, but didn't move toward me. "Jo, the Council doesn't deny that killing them was your right, but they do want to know how, exactly, you managed it." It was both a statement and a request, and it took my breath away.

This kind of conciliatory message was the opposite of everything I had prepared for. I finally sucked in a breath, unable to keep myself from chewing on my bottom lip as I tried to respond.

All those instincts I'd been so proud of developing? Yeah, they were telling me that Booker was sincere. That this was on the level, and he really did just want to find out what had happened.

But he was a wolf, and my head refused to let me forget it.

I sorted through my tangled thoughts, while Booker waited, averting his uncanny gaze as if he knew I needed the illusion of space. If I went with those instincts, how much should I tell him about what happened—or about how much I actually remembered?

I was on the brink of figuring it out when the energy around us changed. We'd been surrounded by people the whole time we'd been talking, but Booker's aura of power had seemed to be issuing a "stay out" warning to the laughing, talking wanderers, keeping them from invading our little corridor of mirrors.

However, a cluster was approaching us behind me, making my Very Bad Feeling-o-Meter register off the charts. I caught a whiff of that same feeling of decay and death I'd felt outside, and the hair on the back of my neck stood up.

I whipped around to see the corridor filled with what had to be zombies.

They weren't decomposing husks mumbling "braaaains," to be sure. They looked normal enough at first glance—but then the unnatural slowness, the eyes devoid of life, registered. Human-shaped, but not human anymore. I'd never encountered one in person, but they were possible to make if someone dug into some really fucking dark magic. Like necromancy.

Great. It appeared Booker couldn't be trusted after all.

Before I could move, the one nearest me lunged. It was a man in a polo shirt, his collar popped and his eyes vacant. When I stepped aside, he lurched past me, losing his balance. Four zombies filled the corridor now, but they were having trouble getting through—whoever was controlling them was unable to get them to go one by one, which would have been funny if I hadn't been feeling so betrayed and more than a little bit pissed. The wolf was growling and looking from the zombies to me, his eyes glowing as he started forward.

He was a wolf. What had I been expecting?

I tossed a furious glance at Booker the Wolf, ignoring the power of his aura and its growing intensity.

"I was going to tell you what you wanted to know. There was no need for this," I said, focusing my energy and stepping sideways, avoiding another grasping zombie. "Now I'll die before I tell you jack shit."

The expression of shock on the wolf's face as I melted into the mirror was priceless.

When I stepped out of the mirror I kept bolted to the roof of my building, I left my index finger touching its smooth surface, keeping the connection alive. The mirror magic had been another of those simple parts of my craft. On some level, I knew that I could do it—had known I could do it—since I escaped from the Fenris. Somehow, mirrors had been involved in what had happened to them. What I'd done to them. I couldn't remember it, quite, and the dreams didn't show me, but I *knew*. It was that intuition thing again.

Ever since, all I had to do was look into a mirror and think of a place I wanted to go. If there was a mirror there, I could see it. If I could fit through, I could go there. It was a skill that had saved my life several times, but even better, it felt good. Tingly.

The mirror on my rooftop was cool and a little damp beneath my finger in the night air. Part of me wanted to pull away, but I needed to see what the wolf did next.

My heart and my brain were racing. This was all so fucked. If there was someone practicing necromancy in St. Louis, and if that necromancer was working with the wolves... I swallowed at the thought. Then I considered my wards on the Sanctum.

If the necromancer showed up, I'd have to make sure my shields kept it and its shambling playthings out. Talk about a twist—I never thought I'd need to add "necromancer" to my List of Things to Fear.

As I watched through the mirror, the wolf went from confusion to rage. All that charm and ease of manner he had tried so hard to convey while I was there? Totally gone. He stood tall and looked as ruthless and fierce as he actually was. It was a breathtaking sight, one I was grateful to witness from a safe distance.

The zombies turned as if to attack him, and I wondered if this might be a show for my benefit—but no, Booker had been in complete shock when

I'd stepped into the mirror. He hadn't been feigning that. He hadn't known that I could use mirror magic, so he'd have no way to know that I could use mirrors for surveillance.

Which meant that he was now in danger. I told myself not to feel too badly for him—this mess had to be his doing anyway—but I kept watching. Just in case.

None of the four zombies would have been a match for the wolf individually, but the way they were converging on the corridor, he was going to have to act soon. As I thought this, Booker's form blurred in a surge of magical energy I could feel even through the mirror. In the next instant, a huge gray wolf crouched, growling, in the corridor—a wolf whose shoulders looked to be as tall as mine.

I took an involuntary step back from the mirror.

With the connection broken, the mirror showed me only a reflection of my short self in my silly T-shirt, a terrified woman completely out of her depth. I looked into my own blue eyes, too wide and too wild, and took a deep breath to center myself before I put my finger back on the glass.

What I saw was a flurry of violence as the wolf rampaged through the zombies like something out of one of Emma's video games. It was both sickening and fascinating—and somewhat satisfying to watch, if I was being honest. I generally abhorred violence, but I could tell that these zombies were too far gone to save. They'd been dead for long enough that they didn't bleed as much as I'd expected, but then, the wolf wasn't exactly ripping them apart in a berserker rage like I'd expected to see either.

The destruction the gray wolf meted out was far more methodical. Once they were all down, he went through each of them, ripping the heads from the bodies. With the first, no doubt because of his rage, he did it like a crazed animal. However, the remaining ones were done in less of a frenzy. He held down each body with his forelegs, and then his powerful jaws closed over each zombie's neck and snapped shut, scissoring the head off. It was cleaner than I'd expected, although still messy with the black goo that was left in their veins.

I'd read that the only way to kill a zombie was to find and kill the necromancer responsible for creating them. Guess there were more options open to a creature who could remove heads using only its jaws.

Holy Hecate, wolves were fucking scary, even when they weren't crazy.

Once all the zombies were beheaded, the wolf stood surveying the damage, flanks heaving, and shook his massive head as if in disgust. Magic surged again, in a more sustained wave than the earlier one, and within a second or two, Booker's human form was standing where the wolf had been, clothed as before and breathing hard.

I'd seen the transformation from wolf to human before, but this one was less complicated, less of an effort. From what I'd seen, werewolves loved being wolves. It took more concentration to be human.

He stood there, trembling slightly, his giant chest moving with his breaths, and muttered a savage "Fuckers," kicking a severed head away from his booted feet. After a final look around him, Booker pulled a phone out of his coat pocket and made a call to someone named Nick.

"The meet went FUBAR." His voice was hoarse and thick with frustration. "We were attacked by zombies, so now she thinks we set her up for an ambush."

A beat of silence. "No, she disappeared through the goddamn mirror, and there are a bunch of headless zombies at my feet."

He pinched the bridge of his nose between his thumb and first two fingers as he listened to the other person, then he barked a laugh. "Yeah, apparently that mirror in Ste. Gen wasn't just for ambiance." He shook his head and reached out to touch the mirror. A shock coursed through me at the connection, but I knew it was one-sided. "She's got skills."

I swallowed. *He can't see you. He can't feel you.*

He was quiet for a few seconds—more listening. Then, "Thanks. I'll keep people out until the clean-up crew gets here. Text Max too, get him digging up more info. I don't know that the Council is operating with all of the facts—or if they're not telling us everything." He took his hand off the mirror. "Just in case that's on purpose, let's keep it out of their hands for now."

His mouth was grim, amber eyes glowing with intensity once more. He shook his head again and muttered, "There's something else going on here."

He looked around the corridor one last time, phone still at his ear, then left, presumably to head people off at the entrance.

With a shuddering sigh, I took my fingertip off the mirror and turned to Stanley the gargoyle. "Well, you're not going to believe what happened to me today."

Stanley perched on one corner of my decidedly non-Gothic building. He was crouched forward, legs bunched beneath him, his massive arms planted in front of him—muscular and scary-looking, as all proper gargoyles should be. His taloned hands curled over the edge of the building, and his huge wings arced out to each side as if he was preparing to take off. He was big, but not so much bigger than me that it made me feel dwarfed. If he'd stood up, he'd probably have been about seven feet tall.

On my first tour of the building, I had paused my inspection to admire him and then to sit down and look out over the city with him, finding a perfect spot on the bulky ledges that ran along the roof's edge. I could only see his face in profile, sadly, as he faced out toward the river. From the side, I could see that he had the typical gargoyle frown-and-snarl—only the curl of his lip seemed to imply a sense of humor. He looked like he might enjoy hearing jokes, so I'd started telling him the worst ones I knew that first day. If he didn't like them, he never told me to stop.

I'm not ashamed to admit that I fell in love with him then and there. He looked like a Stanley, so I'd thought of him that way ever since. It was only fancy that made me think of Stanley as the protector of my building and, by extension, me. I'd never heard of a real gargoyle in my admittedly sparse knowledge of the supernatural world. Hell, there weren't even any other gargoyles in this neighborhood, and yet here was Stanley, looking like he'd be more at home on a cathedral. I took time to sit up on the roof with Stanley nearly every day, sometimes for hours, usually nestling in under one of his outstretched wings and leaning against his side. I would meditate, look at the city, watch the river, feed energy into the Sanctum—and of course, I spent plenty of time talking to him.

It was the best when it rained. If I sat close enough, Stanley's wings worked like an umbrella, and I could stay dry while I watched the water wash the city clean.

However, regardless of how he got there, I equated Stanley with home and safety, so I made sure my huge, heavy rooftop mirror faced his direction. The access door was in the center of the roof, so I'd made it into a covered porch area to keep the mirror in relative safety during any kind of weather. It had been a right bitch to set up on my own, but it was worth it—all I had to do was think about Stanley and being home, being safe, and I would step through to this location.

This wasn't my only option, of course. I had full-length mirrors in all the important parts of the building, and at least one on every unfinished floor. I could imagine my bedroom, the work office, or the back room in the shop, but this mirror was the one that I used the most. I lived inside, but the roof was an important part of what made the Sanctum...well, my sanctum.

I stepped away from the rooftop mirror and went over to look at the river with Stanley, grateful to have him there with me after everything I'd seen that night. As a protector for the building, I couldn't have improved on him if I tried. As a friend, he was unparalleled. After all, if Stanley weren't here, I would just be the crazy lady on the roof, talking to herself and sometimes her cat.

You're home. Safe. I breathed deep and tried to relax. The night blanketed the city in murky dark, nearly black in some places, brightly lit in others. The air held the promise of a chill. Fall was around the corner—usually my favorite time of year. Still a little out of breath, I sat down next to Stanley and let my feet dangle over the edge of the building, my arm resting on his leg, my head resting on his stony side. I watched the river and told Stanley about my adventures today and how they had ended.

Stanley was a great listener—and unlike Emma or Kate, he never freaked out about me sitting on the edge of the roof. Once I finished my story, I sighed and fell silent. After a moment, I added, "All that said, I think if the necromancer were working with the werewolves or whoever this Council is, the wolf wouldn't have destroyed all the zombies. He seemed pretty pissed off about it." I thought about how he'd sounded when he talked to his buddy Nick. *Now she thinks we set her up for an ambush.*

Regardless, that wasn't definitive evidence against him being involved. Aloud, I mused, "Maybe the zombies weren't supposed to attack until after the meeting was over? Maybe they attacked too soon, and he lost his shit because the necromancer pulled the trigger before he got what he wanted." I paused. "But it didn't feel that way. He didn't feel like he was going berserker. It felt like he went after the zombies because they were a threat." My brain went back to the tarot card I'd pulled. "I drew the 2 of Cups before I went."

Goddess, I was talking myself in circles. I thunked my head against Stanley in frustration, then winced. "Ouch." I sighed, resting my head against him again, and quipped a half-hearted "It's another fine mess I've gotten us into, Stanley."

We sat and watched the inky darkness of the Mississippi for quite a bit longer. Then I bid Stanley a good night and went downstairs to create the most powerful zombie wards I could before I went to bed.

CHAPTER 5

WHY DID THE WITCH CROSS THE STREET?

JO

THE NEXT DAY, I WENT DOWN TO THE SHOP EARLY. AGAIN.

I'd spent my few hours of sleep that night plagued by nightmares new and old. These had included zombies lurching at me and a gray wolf, huge jaws open wide.

After a maniacal cleaning spree, the likes of which the shop hadn't seen since I opened, I texted Emma around 7 a.m.—as early as I dared—to tell her not to come in today and to wait to hear from me about tomorrow. I promised to call later. I wanted to see her, but more than that I wanted to keep her as far from the Sanctum as possible for now. Werewolves, necromancers, zombies? Not the kind of thing I wanted her around.

A half hour passed, and no response. *Damn.* I hoped like hell she hadn't lost another phone at Purgatory the night before. From all her stories, that club seemed like even more of a black hole than most.

I texted John, my other part-time worker, as well, even though he wasn't on the schedule until the next day. I hated taking a shift away from him, but being alive trumped being solvent every time.

Then I texted Kate and asked her how the carnival went and if there were any problems. I figured that if the wolf hadn't gotten everything cleaned up well enough, she'd know. There was nothing on the news websites, at least, but she might have hidden it.

Of course, she didn't text back, either. "Am I the only damn person awake right now?" I muttered.

Once that was done, I thought I might be able to relax. That was foolish. I was amped up on too much magical work the night before and too many questions—and there had been neither enough restful sleep nor enough answers to offset it all.

Completely out of busywork by this time, I parked myself behind the counter, laptop open, and began Googling what I could about "council" and "werewolves," and then "necromancer" and "zombie," and then any other combinations of applicable words I could think of, bookmarking the possibly worthwhile pages and sites as I went. Unfortunately, there weren't nearly as many of those sites as I had hoped.

It reminded me of when I'd begun researching "witchcraft" online after high school, when the odd things that kept happening to me seemed to point me toward the craft. Along with a few interesting but vague books, the bulk of my knowledge had come from chat rooms and the community of mostly well-meaning New Age pagans I connected with there in those first few lonely years.

I studied and I practiced, I gathered better books and materials, and I learned—slowly but surely. Goddess, how I'd yearned for practical guidance from another human being. While intense study created a great foundation for later practice, nothing beat someone with experience giving pointers. However, I didn't know anyone like that among my flaky New Age acquaintances, none of whom seemed to have power like mine. Life had already taught me by then that people weren't permanent, so there seemed little point in seeking out a mentor.

Between accumulated knowledge, trial-and-error practice, and wary connections with a few other witches during my years of travel, I'd learned a lot on my own, but I didn't want others to have to go through that. I'd thought the Sanctum could be the way I was meant to help others like me. I'd already found my first fledgling witch in Emma, and I'd made a few other contacts so far. For the first time in recent memory, I was making friends. Putting down roots.

Then, werewolves and zombies came crashing in. On the same day.

That was the real frustration of it all now: how little I really know about the supernatural world, highlighted by Booker the Wolf's disdain over my ignorance. Granted, I didn't know much. Yet. The Sanctum was on the fringes, both literally and figuratively, and the fringes were a great source of information. People who were interested in the occult tended to live there, and fringe people noticed things other people did not. If one knew what one was doing, one could learn a lot about what might be coming from those fringe people and what they had seen—if they were willing to share.

I closed my laptop and stretched my arms over my head, sighing with the movement. It was a moot point right now, anyway. With the shop under lockdown, I was on my own with what I had available. Time to go analog.

I gathered up the books I had available to look up information, both in my personal collection and in the shop's inventory. The problem was that my collection wasn't that impressive when it came to the supernatural world, as it mostly focused on witchcraft. I yearned for a set of dusty tomes with the information I needed.

However, I wasn't totally at a loss. Over the years, I'd seen or heard of some books that might be useful, so I searched for them on Amazon and sprung for next-day delivery on the ones available.

Once all that was done, I stared off into space and thought back to the night before.

In the hours since I'd left him in that mirrored hallway, I had leaned back toward the idea that the wolf hadn't set me up. He wouldn't have killed all of the zombies if he'd been in league with them, and the conversation I had heard from his end wasn't the "curses, foiled again" type. Booker had been frustrated and angry, and I still wasn't sure he'd told me his entire agenda—in fact, I was certain there were things he was holding back.

However, at least one thing did feel certain: there was a larger supernatural community operating in the shadows on a major level. Now that I knew this was the case, I wanted to learn everything I could about the Council and that community so I could stay out of trouble with them. Unless, of course, they caused trouble with me. I certainly hadn't gone gunning for the Fenris, and they seemed to know that, if I could trust what Booker had said.

The crazy thing was that I did feel I could trust Booker, at least on the surface level. I wasn't sure if I should take everything he said at face value—

what Booker had said about the Council not having realized how bad the Fenris had become seemed fishy—but I did believe that *Booker* hadn't known about it. His disgust at the Fenris and what he knew of what had happened to me had been real.

Or maybe I'd drunk just enough of Heather's "Phobias, Be Gone" potion that I'd lost the roughest edges of my very healthy fear of wolves and their kind. That...wasn't necessarily a good thing. Still, there was that card pull. *2 of Cups. A new partnership.*

I drummed my fingers on the countertop, wishing I didn't feel like I was treading water above a bottomless ocean trench.

I looked out the window, noting the wisps of clouds and the empty parking lot across the way. I'd had windows installed with reinforced glass so that I could see outside in two directions if I chose—and with extra charms to keep them from being easily broken. It made me feel better to be able to see around me even when I was behind the counter. The only time I could handle being in a windowless room was when I was reading tarot.

My phone vibrated. A text from Kate: "YES SO GOOD. Lots of $$$. A fucking mess tho."

Eyebrows raised, I texted back: "Mess?" *Goddess, please don't let it be zombie parts.*

After a second, "People are filthy creatures," with a picture of the lot beside her building, still cluttered with tents and rides in various stages of being broken down, littered with all the debris you might expect from a busy fair atmosphere. I could see in the photo that the fun house had already been mostly disassembled.

Almost lightheaded with relief, I texted back: "Looks like the kids are going to have fun cleaning that up."

She responded with three cry-laughing emojis.

Despite everything, I chuckled. I'd have to tell Kate what was going on, but it could wait. There were too many people milling about Hecate's Home right now for there to be too much risk to her.

I hoped.

Even with all this—and "this" was fucking plenty—the bad penny in my cluttered thoughts was the idea of talking out loud about the Fenris again.

Aside from Stanley and Cole, I'd never really told anyone the whole story of my abduction and torture by the Fenris, even Kate. At first, that had been mostly out of self-preservation. I spent some time working with various counselors and rehab workers after the attack, and they were all trauma specialists. It had helped, for the most part. However, I couldn't tell someone who lived in the ordinary world, where gods were myths and supernatural creatures were fairy tales, the truth of what had happened. How much worse what had been done to me was by virtue of them being werewolves.

That would have landed me in a straightjacket and a padded room, and I had no intention of being imprisoned. Not ever again.

Kate would have understood, but—and I knew how tragic and absurd this was—I was ashamed to tell her anything more than the bare facts. Kate, being Kate, didn't push me. She had her own past traumas that rode with her everywhere.

Now I was supposed to just rip myself open and explain the whole terrifying, traumatizing thing—or at least all the parts I could remember—to a werewolf?

To Booker and those unblinking amber eyes?

My heart flip-flopped in my chest once, then twice, a sure sign of an incoming panic attack. I clenched my fist, focusing on my hand, and started some yoga breaths. *In through the nose, out through the nose. Inflate the belly, deflate the belly.* I wasn't clearheaded enough to meditate, but this was better than nothing.

After a few minutes, my heart calmer and my shoulders looser, I opened my eyes. When I looked out the window again, Emma's car was parked in the lot across the street. At an odd angle.

Emma herself stood on the sidewalk across the road, looking over at the shop. In the same clothes she was wearing yesterday. She looked...lost? Injured? Sick?

I was moving before I even made the conscious decision to do so. Heart pounding anew, I called Emma's cell phone one more time, leaving the phone on speaker on the counter as I retrieved my .38 from the lockbox beneath the cash register.

Make sure it's loaded. Make sure the safety is off. Don't accidentally shoot Emma. Or yourself.

The ringing from the speakerphone blared loudly in the quiet of the shop. I looked out at Emma, but she didn't even look down to indicate that she heard the phone. *Something is very wrong.* I didn't wait, couldn't wait, grabbing my phone and shoving it into the back pocket of my jeans as I headed out the door of the shop.

I didn't bother to hide the gun, keeping its reassuring weight tight in my right hand. The street was deserted—this area didn't wake up until 10 a.m. on Saturdays. I checked to make sure no one was lurking on the other side of the door before I went out. Nothing was out here except for Emma's car, and Emma herself. Was she drunk or high? Had she been attacked?

"Emma," I called from my sidewalk. She didn't seem to have heard me. Her expression was unreadable from here. Were those bruises on her face, on her neck? I reached my mind, my power, out to her and felt nothing. *Please, Goddess, no.*

I hesitated only for a second before I ran across the street to her.

"Emma? Talk to me, sweetie, okay? What happened?"

I was beside her, reaching for her with my free hand, gun still low, my entire soul in anguish, before I registered the smell and understood why Emma wasn't responding.

She wasn't Emma anymore.

Before I could move, the Emma thing had her hands around my neck and had half-kicked, half-stomped the gun from my hand. Not that it would probably have done much good.

Then it was all squeezing, terrible pressure while I stared into the glazed, dead eyes of my friend—*dead, she's dead*—and scrabbled my hands in desperation at hers. *Stupid, stupid, stupid, stupid witch!*

A joke for Stanley popped into my oxygen-depleted brain. *Why did the witch cross the road?*

To get strangled to death by a zombie right outside her impregnable magical fortress.

Gathering my strength, I tried to plant my feet and push into her, get her off-balance. She didn't budge—not a surprise. I'm no fighter. I've learned some basic self-defense over the years, but I always figured my best chance in a fight was my magic.

Real fucking smart, Murphy, I thought as I struggled to breathe and center my power. I hadn't done real magic outside of the Sanctum in so long that I couldn't grasp the power, could barely even reach for it.

All the while, the Emma zombie's grip kept tightening.

Stop panicking echoed in my mind, and I heard shouting somewhere around me, as I began to black out. The words helped me clear my head. I cast my mind out and asked my Sanctum, my home, *Help me. What do I need to do to live?*

I was fighting to stay conscious, and as soon as my mind focused on the question, the answer exploded through my mind. *WHAT DOESN'T BELONG?*

The answer was the necklace around the Emma zombie's neck, which was now dangling outside of the cleavage of her black, vinyl tank top, nearly in front of my nose. A rune of some kind. An amulet.

I tried to grab it and couldn't get my arms to move. Black spots floated in front of my eyes, and my ears popped. *No, no...*

...no...

FOCUS.

The power rushed through me like prickly heat, shaking tears loose from my wide eyes—and I focused on the amulet.

When it burst into flames, the Emma zombie's hands loosened enough that I gasped in painful gratitude.

When the Emma zombie was tackled and hauled away from me by a giant form that burst into my periphery, I stumbled away and fell to the ground. Weeping, crawling, grabbing my gun.

I rolled to my back, trying desperately to clear my head and ignore everything that hurt, willing my numb arms to lift the weight of the .38, which seemed to have increased its density in impossible ways.

When I did finally raise the gun enough, I had it leveled—well, trembling, but aimed squarely enough—at a furious, snarling Booker, whose eyes were glowing amber suns of rage and whose hands were locked around the Emma zombie's neck.

CHAPTER 6

RUN, WOLF, RUN

BOOKER

SOMETHING WAS UP WITH EMMA CONNORS, BUT DAMNED IF Booker could tell what it was. He'd had his binoculars trained on her ever since she'd pulled up to the parking lot across the street from Jo's Sanctum.

Frankly, he was surprised. Jo hadn't changed the shop sign to "Open," so he was willing to bet she was battening down the hatches for the moment and had told her people not to come to the shop.

It was what he would do if he were her.

Sleeping in his car had been uncomfortable, but he'd managed it. He'd kept both eyes on the building for as long as he could keep them open, and then he'd called Nick to tell him to get Max on watch duty. But he couldn't go back to his offices until he had a chance to talk to Jo again.

Someone was trying to kill the witch he'd been sent to find, but he'd been so preoccupied when they'd been talking in the fun house that he hadn't realized it until it was almost too late.

Booker had known Jo Murphy was in the hall of mirrors before he saw her. The smell had changed—the stale air with hints of the olfactory cacophony outside was eclipsed by the scent he'd been searching out for months. Warm lavender, not quite like anything he'd ever smelled before. Except once.

The carnival had been an intriguing choice for their meeting. At first, he'd wondered why she'd bring werewolves onto Katerina Strega's ground, but he already knew Jo's Sanctum and Hecate's Home were like twin pillars of power, built on a set of triple crossroads unlike any he'd ever seen before. The whole Central East End reeked of magical energy, and the last time Booker had been there, Kate Strega had given him a demonstration of power that he'd yet to forget.

He'd gone to Strega during the first months of his search, weeks before he'd gotten the tipoff about Jo's presence in Ste. Genevieve. The records showed that Strega and Jo Murphy had gone to high school together, so them both turning out to be powerful witches couldn't have been a coincidence. Where he'd screwed up was in underestimating Strega's regard for Jo. In his defense, he had no evidence that they'd been close friends, and witches didn't tend to play well with other witches. From what he knew, "covens" were for wannabes and movies.

So he'd gone to the shelter and found Strega working outside with a group of tweens and teens. Booker introduced himself and explained why he was there, amping up the charm the whole time.

Strega had been polite and had stepped away from the side of her brick building, where half a dozen kids from pre-teens to college-age were doing landscaping, to speak with him. She'd listened as he said his piece, then, instead of addressing his questions about Jo, she'd smiled, her gray eyes nearly as pale as her long, wavy hair. "Have you spent much time in St. Louis, Mr. Booker?"

"I have, actually," he'd said, somewhat taken aback by the question. He'd been in and out of St. Louis before she was even born, not to mention his new status as alpha to the St. Louis pack of Diana's Wolves—but he left that part out. Something told him she wouldn't like that at all.

"Good." The witch nodded. "I'm sure you know all about the channel catfish that swim the Mississippi. Some of them get to be as big as six feet. Can you imagine that? A channel cat, well, it eats just about anything that comes its way." She cocked her head, her smile gone now, her gaze holding his in a way that very few humans—magical or otherwise—usually could.

"It's nice, living so close to the Mississippi. I make sure to give the river an offering whenever I can."

A sly grin then spread across her face, and in that instant, he couldn't breathe. The air had been taken from his lungs, its absence creating a horrible vacuum in every molecule of his body.

It had been only for a few seconds—a surreal, terrifying few seconds, surrounded by laughing kids working in flower beds while he suffocated outside on a clear spring day—but it had been enough.

When he could breathe again, he'd tried not to gasp out his relief. Her smile had widened, pure innocence. "Goodbye, now," she'd trilled, turning away from him in a swirl of skirts and hair.

He'd left without another word. He was tenacious, not stupid. That experience had been vivid in his memories as he'd walked through the carnival to the fun house, and both he and his wolf had been relieved not to run into Kate Strega along the way. He shuddered at the thought again, rubbing at the scruff on his jaw and frowning through the binoculars.

He just needed to make sure she didn't run away again. In general, he didn't want to scare her. Her fear-smell bothered his wolf, made them both restless.

They'd talked during those few minutes in the fun house, and she'd made him smile and laugh more times than he had in some time. He had noted with interest that his smile—not the one he pasted on to deal with humans, but the real one she brought out of him—seemed to have an effect on her. It was subtle, but difficult to hide. He wondered if she found him attractive, but reminded himself not to get distracted.

Then, of course, he'd let himself get fucking distracted.

First it had been her total ignorance of the Council. It hadn't smelled like she was lying, and her eyes had been clear, if still alive with mistrust. This woman had been wandering around the Midwest packing the magical equivalent of Class 4 weapons, and she was completely ignorant of important aspects of the supernatural world she inhabited. Booker had had to work hard to keep his temper from spiking, thinking about how many ways Jo could be in danger. Then he'd blown it—buoyed by irritation, he had taken a step toward her, not thinking of it as a predatory move, until that fear-smell assaulted him and she took a step backward.

That had just pissed him off even more.

He'd prayed to Diana for patience and had backed off. Then he'd had to figure out the best way to explain the Council to her. He'd kept it simple, trying not to go overboard with information she didn't need—and that would probably freak her out. She had listened, and everything in him had noted the change with relief when her scent went back to normal. Then he'd had to tell her how the Council had known that she was involved in the disappearance of the Fenris.

Her reaction had churned Booker up again—he'd registered her fear, pain, anger, sorrow. It was everything he didn't want her to feel, and he kept getting spikes of it, flashes that made it all worse. This wasn't like his usual insights into his quarry. He knew terrible things had happened to her at the hands of those werewolves, and it bothered him, infuriated him. Intensely.

Distracted.

Then those gods-damned zombies had shown up, and she'd blamed him for it, delivering a killer parting shot before walking right through the mirror like fucking David Bowie in a deleted scene from *Labyrinth*.

Yes, Jo Murphy was most definitely trickier than anyone had even dreamed.

Booker hadn't heard of any magic-user being able to move through mirrors. Scrying with them was common enough, but Jo had melted into the surface, walking through it like a door. When he paired this ability with the still unknown fate of the Fenris, he was beginning to worry that his report to the Council was going to result in some very unwelcome attention for Jo and her Sanctum.

Yet another problem that would need solving. First, he had to keep Jo alive long enough to get the information he needed and make the damned report. Now that she thought he'd betrayed her trust, that was just going to be more difficult.

Once he'd taken care of the zombies and left Hecate's Home, he'd gotten in his car and headed straight to the Sanctum, settling into one of the parking lots that offered a good view of the front and side of the building.

The lights on the top floor had soothed him a little. She was home and safe, at least, and he'd hoped like hell she was busy warding her magical fortress against zombies.

Like it or not, Jo Murphy was his responsibility now. That was how the Council would see it.

It was how he saw it.

When he'd seen Emma's car pull unsteadily into the parking lot, Booker had immediately sat up. He'd gotten out of his own car, taking the binoculars with him, and he'd texted Nick and Max: "Connors here. Be ready."

They'd acknowledged with thumbs-up reactions, and then he'd watched as the girl parked clumsily and got out of the car. It had appeared for all the world like she was seriously impaired—her movements were slow and precise, halting, but then she'd gotten to the sidewalk, still across from the Sanctum, and she'd stopped moving.

Something was definitely wrong.

Now a text from Nick buzzed on his phone, startling him: "Witch is on the move."

He stared at it for a second, then swung the binoculars away from Emma to see Jo crossing the street, a gun in one hand and an expression of terrified concern on her expressive face. Her mouth moving, calling to her friend.

His wolf snapped to attention. *No, Jo. Stop.*

She made it across to Emma, and he was up and running. Emma's hands closed around her neck before he got his stride.

Too far away. Too far.

This was a fear he'd not felt in a long time. His throat burning, his heart about to burst from his chest. It was the kind of thing that would have triggered a change if his body hadn't seemed to understand that shifting to his wolf mid-run would be a huge tactical mistake. Going from two legs to four at full speed, sorting out the extra legs and muscles and the change in size in a fraction of a second? He would have gone down hard.

So Booker stayed in his human form and ran, and at some point he began to shout words, threatening words, angry words, as he watched Jo's arms drop to her sides and her head start to droop.

Too far. Too late.

When he was only a few yards away, Jo straightened, her eyes flared red. A bright flash of flame on Emma's chest—then Emma froze, and Jo fell free of her grip.

He was on Emma, who wasn't Emma at all. His hands were on the zombie's throat, about to rip the head from its shoulders with a cold, vicious pleasure, when Jo pointed the gun at him. It had barely registered, but then she had stopped him with one ragged, whispered word: "Amulet."

When he pulled the charred, stinking amulet from around the dead, wretched thing's neck, the zombie collapsed. Whatever magic had animated it was gone, leaving him fighting for breath, for control of himself.

He stared at Jo, knowing that his eyes must look terrifying to her but unable to calm himself. "Haven't you figured out by now that someone's trying to kill you?" he managed to growl, his voice deep with fury.

She sat up, leaving the gun beside her on the sidewalk. She tried to speak, and then swallowed and tried again.

"Don't." It came out sharper than he'd intended. Her fear and pain hammered away in his skull, coming in from too many of his senses. *Focus.* "You'll hurt yourself. It was a stupid question anyway."

He knelt beside her, reaching out but stopping short of touching her. "Is anything broken?"

She shook her head almost imperceptibly.

"Are you hurt anywhere other than your throat?"

Another tiny shake.

Thank the gods for that much. He sighed, feeling some of his rage draining. She was hurt, traumatized, but she would recover. He looked at the body of her friend beside them. He dragged in a deep breath. Even the air was tainted with the taste of her pain. "I'm sorry."

Jo's eyes, the whites pink with burst blood vessels, filled with tears, which she dashed away impatiently. Another shake. "My fault," she croaked.

"No," he said. "Someone did this to her. To get to you."

Another shake. More tears.

"Jo." He tried to make his voice gentle. "Let me take you to a hospital."

Another shake. She pointed to the Sanctum.

He ground his teeth, but before he could argue, a text from Nick came through: "Clean-up on the way. Get her off the street."

"Jo, we're going to take care of Emma."

She looked up at him, tears tracking down her face despite her palpable anger. "She's someone. She matters. You can't just make her disappear," she rasped, forcing the words out despite the damage to her throat.

Fucking hell. "We're not the Fenris," he growled. "We don't kidnap humans for sport or kill them for fun. Our ways are nothing like theirs. I'm not going to explain the details to you while we're out in the open and anyone could get at you. Or drive by and see this."

Booker stood and offered her a hand. Jo didn't take it, instead rolling to her hands and knees and pushing herself up to a standing position, bending down again to pick up her gun and putting the safety on before she raised her eyes again. She was trembling, but she held her chin up. He could admire her for all that, if it didn't give him an excellent view of the red marks on her throat that were already turning to bruises. His wolf growled, but Booker swallowed the sound.

Lock it down. You're going to scare her again.

"Let me get you inside," he said. "Let's figure this out together. Can you take down some of the warding so I can help you?"

She looked at him, more sorrow than rage now. "No," she croaked.

His chest was going to cave in under the pressure if he had to handle much more pain. From her. From his own reaction. "Damn it, Jo—"

"I need time." The words were stronger, more forceful. Her blue eyes were wide, her pupils still dilated with shock, but everything in her stance and bearing told him no matter what he did or said right now, she was going to *take* time. However much she needed. Because she wasn't going to beg, and she wasn't going to relent. Not until she was good and ready.

Booker took a deep breath, mostly to calm himself again, and that warm lavender scent stole into his senses. It was still tinged by emotions his wolf didn't like smelling from her, but it was still Jo. He liked it. He liked *her*—it was impossible not to.

More than anything, he just wanted her to not only be safe, but *feel* safe. To feel safe with him. It was an unpleasant realization, especially considering it might never happen. Not after everything she had been through.

He gave her a short nod. "You know how to reach me."

She nodded in return, and then she turned and walked away from him, back into her building where he and his kind weren't welcome.

It was hard to blame her.

CHAPTER 7

WITCH, HEAL THYSELF

JO

I DON'T REMEMBER MUCH ABOUT STUMBLING INTO THE SHOP. I know I locked the door. I know I put the gun carefully on the counter.

I know that I walked straight into the back and through the mirror to the roof.

Huddling against Stanley, sitting against the side of him that hid me from the front of the shop—away from where Booker's mysterious clean-up crew would be taking what was left of Emma away—I wept. The sobs tore out of me and my damaged throat, and they hurt, but it was nothing compared to the loss of Emma.

My fault.

At some point later, I ran out of tears. My T-shirt was wet with slobber and snot, but I managed not to get fluids on Stanley. Or on Cole, who I realized was curled up against my other side. I wiped my face with a dry section of my shirt and rested my hand on Cole's warm fur.

Then, because I had to do something constructive before I lost my mind, I focused my energy on healing my throat.

Healing via magic was tricky. I hadn't done much of it on myself, although I'd tried—and mostly failed to help much. Kate had shown me a few techniques for creating a power flow into the damaged areas, but I had trouble controlling the stream and letting it continue on a steady, slow progression.

When I'd blasted a bruise with enough energy to make it worse rather than better, Kate had thrown up her hands.

"Jo. You cannot just wave your hand and make the boo-boos disappear. This isn't a TV show."

Impatience, thy name is Josephine.

I opened a small channel, let the Sanctum's power trickle into me, envisioned it repairing my larynx, trachea, throat. While I did that, I thought about my options.

Which boiled mostly down to finding that necromancer and making the fucker pay.

Vengeance, thy name is also Josephine.

At some point, I got up and went back into my apartment to brew a pot of chamomile tea. While I was waiting for it to steep, I did a saltwater gargle, wincing with every movement of my throat muscles.

When my tea was ready, I dosed it liberally with honey and went back up to the roof, trying something different with each sip—envisioning the healing energy flowing down with the tea. After a few minutes of this, I was feeling a little better, at least in the physical sense.

I stood behind Stanley, taking comfort in his presence, and looked at the river. The clouds had dispersed and the sun was out, warm on my face, taking some of the crisp chill out of the air. It was a lovely day.

And Emma was dead.

I took another swallow of tea, a bigger one this time. It didn't hurt quite as badly.

I didn't know much about Emma's family. Her mom wasn't in the picture, and her dad lived somewhere around Chicago. Emma had been taking a few required classes at one of the St. Louis Community College campuses, but I couldn't remember which. She hadn't chosen a major because, as she so often said, she didn't know what she wanted to be when she grew up.

Emma had glowed with compassion and life and humor.

It was surreal that everything she had been was now past tense.

My fingers tightened around the handle of my mug. The anger and grief built up again, back toward another crying jag. I just let it happen, too tired to fight it off.

Eventually, I went back into my apartment. I went to the computer and printed off a sign that said we were closed for the time being due to remodeling. Then I put the same message on the Sanctum website in big, bold, red letters with the date. I also posted the same thing to the shop's social media accounts. I didn't have a huge following, as I'd only been open for a few months, but I had a responsibility to my customers. I ignored the notifications from Emma's account, staying away from the Sanctum Occult Shop's profile. Tamping down that pain yet again.

I summoned the last of my energy to go downstairs and tape the sign on the locked shop door. I tried not to look across the street, but when I inevitably did, the sidewalk and parking lot were empty. You could say one thing for wolves. They worked fast.

That last necessary task done, I went back upstairs and flung myself into bed, burrowing into the covers. It was a relief when Cole followed me, settling against my back, a warm, purring presence.

My throat still ached. My cheeks itched with dried tears. My insides were empty, a hollowed-out husk. Even so, I despaired of finding rest. *There's no way I'm going to be able to sleep.*

That was the last conscious thought I had for some time.

When I woke, the sunlight streamed in from the other side of the room, its muted glow signaling that the sun was on its way down. For once, I hadn't dreamed of anything.

Which was good, because the reality that hit me from the waking world was bad enough. When I went to my bathroom and looked in the mirror, I saw that my eyes were puffy but nearly back to normal, and my throat bruising was not nearly as bad as it had been earlier. When I drank some water, the soreness was there, but far less pronounced. "Thank you, Goddess," I muttered, the words a little hoarse but otherwise clear.

I still felt like hell, but at least I would be able to function.

My first move was to call Kate. It was time to bring her in on this, to whatever point she was able to get involved. Her priority had to be her kids, of course, but she had to know what was going on. What had happened to Emma.

If someone was declaring war on me, then there was every chance Kate might also be in danger—even if just by association.

I kept the rundown brief. Thankfully, Kate endorsed the meeting at the fundraiser by not commenting on it. As I finished the story, her horror at everything morphed quickly into rage. "So what are we going to do about this?"

"I'm considering my options," I said. "I'm thinking it's going to have to involve the wolves."

Kate nearly hissed. "You can't trust them."

"Oh, believe me, that's been my biggest problem." I shook my head at nothing, forgetting she couldn't see me. "But I think this one, Booker, is on the up and up. Plus, they have resources we don't. I pulled the 2 of Cups before the meeting, remember."

"That's not a guarantee. If you need firepower—"

"Not that," I said. Kate's fearlessness always amazed me, but in this case, it might be more of a liability. "Power isn't the problem. Besides, they have information. They know about so much that we don't—well, I don't."

Kate was quiet for a moment. "This is true. I don't know that much more than you when it comes to the 'supernatural community.'" I could hear the air quotes around the words when she said them.

"Like it or not, they're our way through this mess—on what I hope is the right side. They have resources, money, contacts. Plus," I said, thinking of Booker's gray wolf snapping the head off a zombie in one bite, "they're fighters. Everything's been physical with these zombies." I swallowed, feeling the roughness in my still-healing throat.

"Can you bind them?"

"I don't know. I don't know how their alpha would take to that. Booker feels like a straight-enough arrow, but when it comes to his pack, I really have no clue."

"Fucking wolf. He wasn't supposed to come back here."

"Come back?" I croaked.

"Before you moved here, back when he was hunting for you." While I was recovering from this news flash, she added, "I told him I'd feed him to the channel cats."

I nearly laughed, but then my eyes filled again. Kate sensed it. "Hey, hey, hey." Her voice was low, crooning. "Hey, hey, Murphy. I'm here."

"I know," I said, hating how pathetic I sounded, trying to collect all my grief again and put it away. "I know."

"I'm coming over."

"No," I said, the strength in my voice snapping back like a rubber band. "You are staying away from the Sanctum for now. Stay with your kids."

"Then you come here."

I started to protest, but the offer was too tempting—especially since of the two of us, I was the one who could travel without leaving our respective buildings. "Yes," I said and ended the call. Then I took a deep breath and stepped through the mirror in my room to the mirror on the back of her bathroom door.

I breathed in the familiar smells of incense, took in the mess of Kate's room, which wasn't too far removed from the usual state of my own. Yet oddly, both Kate and I were sticklers for cleanliness and order in our work areas. *Maybe every witch needs a little chaos somewhere,* I thought, bemused, and sat down on the edge of her rumpled bed.

After a few seconds, Kate ran in. "I was down in my office," she said, breathless, coming straight over to sit next to me, gathering me up in her arms. "Goddess, you're so cold."

I buried my face in her hair and let more tears come, and she rocked me, crooning something—one of her Italian lullabies—on repeat in her dulcet tones. I could carry a tune, but Kate could *sing*. She used it in her magic sometimes, as her grandmother had.

I let it wrap around me.

After I'd stopped shaking and shuddering and my breathing had returned to normal, Kate pulled back, keeping her hands on my shoulders. She inspected me, her pale gray eyes sharp and assessing. "Let me see that throat," she commanded, and when I raised my chin, she touched one warm finger to the bruising there. "I'm going to give you a potion, and it's going to taste like shit, but you're going to have to drink it all."

I gave her a tiny smile. "Yes, *Mom*."

"I'm actually pretty impressed," she said, smiling for the first time when she let go of my chin. "You did some good work on yourself here. I can feel the remnants of the worst of the injury, but it's healing up well."

I shrugged. Kate gave me a pat and headed out of the room, coming back a few minutes later with a glass vial and a drinking glass.

"Here." She handed me the vial and the glass. "First the potion, then the other."

I took down the potion well enough—it tasted like an earthen floor and a forest had had a liquid baby, but I was prepared for that. If Kate said a potion was going to taste like shit, she meant it. My senses still overwhelmed by the potion, I took a slug from the drinking glass, expecting water.

It was vodka. I hadn't been able to smell it because of the damned potion.

I sputtered out an "Uggghhh" and slanted her an accusing look. "What the hell?"

"Drink the rest," Kate commanded.

With a glare that even I knew was childish, I did.

"You needed that," she said, taking both the empty vial and empty cup from me.

While I hated to admit it, my head was feeling clearer than it had in a while—since before the nightmare had returned, maybe. I shook my head and flopped back on her bed. "Why is this happening?"

I didn't see Kate move, but then she was lying beside me. "I'll take Questions Neither of Us Can Answer for $500, Alex." She sighed. "I'm not getting anything from Hecate either."

I hadn't even tried. Of the two of us, I was the least likely to contact our goddess, I suppose from some passive idea that I'd be bothering Her. Of course, Kate, who was mostly aggression, was unburdened by such fears.

I looked at her. "So we're on our own."

Kate turned her head, studying me. "It sounds like you're not going to be alone for much longer if you let wolves into the Sanctum."

"True," I said, looking back up at the ceiling. "If they're my best chance at making it out of this alive—and if they can help us understand more about what's really going on out there—it doesn't seem like I have much choice."

"There's always a choice," Kate said, her voice hardening. "After what happened to you, you're within all your rights to deny them anything they ask."

I swallowed. Good Goddess, it almost felt normal. Kate really was a damned amazing witch. "2 of Cups, remember. These wolves aren't the Fenris," I said, parroting Booker's refrain. I think I was reminding both of us.

"Remember. They're wolves. Still potentially dangerous," she said, eyebrows clenched tight. "Whatever you do, be careful."

When I returned home, I headed to the rooftop rather than my apartment. The dark sky stretched out above me, stars shining there, and I simply took them in for a moment as I shivered in the cold. The temp had dropped sharply when the sun went down, another sign of autumn. It was usually my favorite time of year.

I took out my cell phone, and I put in the numbers I'd memorized from Booker's note. Had that only been yesterday? It felt like years ago.

When he answered, it was with a terse "Booker."

"Hi," I said, knowing my voice was still a little hoarse.

His voice changed, becoming that soothing baritone I remembered from when he was trying to charm me. "Jo." Even so, the intensity of his interest, his focus, was palpable. I shivered again. "How are you feeling?"

"Like shit, but I'll survive." I took a breath. *Pull it together, Murphy.* "I'd like to meet with you. Tomorrow."

His breath caught audibly before he rumbled, "Yes. I want to help."

"I think I believe that," I said, looking up again at the starry sky. I wished the thought of his help soothed me more than it bothered me.

"Will I be allowed to come into the shop? I promise you," and his voice deepened, roughened, "no harm will come to you from me or mine."

Such a generous offer. I shook away the snide thought. "I'll allow it, with the condition that it's just you. For now." I took a deep breath. "Can you be here at 8?"

"I'll be there."

"Don't come early this time," I said, feeling a ghost of a smile flit across my face. "I won't be lifting the last of the wards until 8 on the dot."

"You're the boss." He paused. "Thank you, Jo. For being willing to trust us. To trust me."

When we hung up, I went back over to Stanley and settled into my spot.

"Well, Stanley, it appears that tomorrow is going to be the day we let a werewolf into the Sanctum." I leaned my head against him.

Stanley didn't answer, of course, but I pretended that he had. "Tell me about it. If you've got any better ideas, I'm all ears."

I let the silence sit for a few seconds, then I sighed. "Yeah, that's what I thought."

CHAPTER 8

WHERE WOLF? HERE. HERE WOLF.

JO

KATE HAD GIVEN ME ANOTHER POTION BEFORE I LEFT, A LESS hideous brew that tasted mostly of peppermint with hints of valerian and passionflower, plus something else I couldn't identify. I drank it all before I went to bed, lying down for another bout of dreamless sleep.

After I woke up, a little sore but much improved, and did my morning routine, I began the laborious project of taking down my wolf warding. Which was far easier in theory than in practice.

The first step was to remove the wolfsbane charms I had placed at the four corners of the building and replace them with henbane, an herb sometimes called "stinking nightshade." Wolfsbane is more commonly known as "monkshood" in the St. Louis area, and it's just another name for aconite.

They're both incredibly poisonous.

You'd have to actually eat henbane to get sick from it, but wolfsbane could be dangerous even to touch. Plus, no known antidote. I always wore thick rubber gloves when handling both herbs. Best to treat the poisonous plants with the reverence they deserved. If I wanted to harness their protective power—and aconite, sacred to Hecate, was incredibly powerful stuff, as witnessed by how effective it had made my wolf wards—I had to respect them. If I didn't, I might not live to regret it.

Like any witch, I had more herbs than probably necessary, both in the shop and in my private stash in my apartment. I'd put up two shelves in the kitchen on either side of the oven—one for the cooking herbs and one for the magical ones. It was an interesting contrast, since I bottled and labeled my own, to see OREGANO and THYME on one shelf and MUGWORT and BLACKBERRY LEAF on the other in otherwise identical bottles.

Of course, some things, like BAY LEAF and GINGER ROOT, were on both. It was a touch more work to maintain duplicates, but it was better than risking an accidental mix-up.

I mentally prepared myself for henbane's uniquely awful before opening the jar. One sniff ensured that my supply was still fresh, so I took it via the mirror up to the roof where I'd already gathered the four charm bags, wrapped in clean red cloth.

Stanley and Cole were used to this process, as I switched out the herbs once a month. It would have been time for me to do this soon anyway.

The process of putting the charm bags together was pretty much the same. By switching out the wolfsbane for henbane, I just had to substitute the name of the creature I wanted to keep out.

So I did, deciding to use this to double down on the nature of the zombie warding. I pulled on my rubber gloves and carefully changed out the herbs just as I changed the wording of the spell, substituting "undead" for "wolf." Just in case there was some other kind of reanimated creature that a necromancer could send against me.

First, I put the charm bags back in the four corners of the roof. Then, I centered myself and mentally redrew the large, permanent circle of protection I had placed around the building. I fed the circle my fear, my anger, my pain, and whatever other jittering feelings I had left over from the previous day and night, which were plenty.

The circle encompassed the building, the trees along the walkway, and the street. I fed it the energy from these heightened emotions, imagining it encompassing the whole area in a powerful shield of protection.

Kate referred to her protections for Hecate's Home as a "bubble," but that word never sounded strong enough to me, and visualization is one of the keys to working successful magic. Bubbles eventually burst, and it was hard to keep that idea from my head every time I heard the word. The more complicated and important the spell, the more important it is to have the right sensation—hence, why my throat-healing worked better when I tied it to the tactile process of drinking tea. But for this, it was all visual.

When I first created my shield after moving into the Sanctum, I pictured my circle not as a bubble, but as an egg. However, the opaque, thin-shelled nature of an egg still didn't feel strong enough. Then, I drew on something else for inspiration. Practically every TV show set in space—of which I had watched many—featured shields. Once I started thinking of my circle as a protective force field, instead of a bubble or an egg, it became much more solid and real to me. The shields around the Sanctum felt to me like the shields around the USS *Enterprise*—and I was both Captain Kirk and Scotty, so to speak, as the captain and chief engineer.

Half the time, witchcraft is just figuring out what works best for you.

I'd found that even when the energy contained negative emotions, it was still extremely successful and strong. Unlike many other things in witchcraft, the intent and negativity didn't foul up the magic of the force field. It held more happiness and love than anything else—those had been closely tied to my feelings about the building and my new life—but all strong emotions create energy. If I had to be upset, I might as well use it for something that benefitted me. The force field went far, far down into the earth, so the shield's energy was constantly cleansed and grounded.

I thought of the whole thing simply as "the shield." I'd gotten so used to feeding energy into the shield that I did it without thinking much of the time, almost like ignoring one of my many aloe plants. I fed it when I woke up, and often as I was going to sleep, and I fed through it whenever I needed —just like taking a clipping from one of my aloes for healing or spells. I'd also learned how to create shields around myself, too, when I wasn't in the Sanctum, but that required more preparation and concentration, both of which I'd been lacking when the Emma zombie attacked me.

This was just another reason I was so proud of what I'd done with the Sanctum. How powerful it had become and how much it was progressing—not only outside, but inside. I'd planned to try taking on tenants later in the month for the finished apartments on the second floor—my employee John was going to be my first full-time resident.

Yet another thing that had been blown up by the madness of the last few days. I didn't know how I was going to explain it to John. How I was ever going to not fear for the well-being of those who would be coming and going through the doors of the Sanctum. They would be safe here, of course, but their lives outside my shield would be in danger just by virtue of being associated with me.

I let the bitterness of that thought feed into the shields and then repeated words that would reinforce the new directives. *Wolves are welcome here.* I did my best to mean it.

Once I had expended what energy I could into reprogramming the shields, I went back to the mirror and stepped through into the shop. The last step would be the one that should break the last of the wards, but it was going to wait.

I'd told Booker 8 a.m., and I'd asked him not to come early, mostly because watching him waiting outside the shield would only make me nervous. It was a weird test, to be sure—I wanted to see if he would honor my request. I wasn't naïve enough to think that he didn't still have the Sanctum under surveillance, but if he could show me that he would play by my rules...well, it might help us start building some trust.

If I looked outside and saw him standing on the other side of the street right now at—I looked at my phone—7:52, waiting and doing everything but tapping his foot, it was going to be difficult to keep from being irritated. *Show me you can follow simple directives, Booker. Show me that you're taking me and my needs seriously.*

At 8 a.m. on the dot, a black SUV pulled up into the parking lot. Booker got out, and once again, I had the opportunity to get a really good look at him. In the purely physical sense, Booker was what the Hecate's Home kids would call "foine." Emma had referred to him as "lickable." When my throat threatened to close up over the memory of Emma, I banished that thought.

The last time I'd seen him, Booker had been disheveled, in clothes that looked like he'd slept in them and stubble thick on his jaw—his hair falling over his wild, glowing eyes. This Booker was more like the one who'd found me in Ste. Genevieve, that strong, angular jaw clean-shaven, brown hair combed back off his forehead. His eyes were hidden under black aviator sunglasses, but I knew them all too well.

His long legs were encased in worn jeans, hands in the pockets of another of those long jackets—this one a charcoal gray that reminded me of his wolf. *It's just ridiculous how attractive he is,* I thought in a weirdly acute sense of despair, looking down at my own jeans and plain, high-necked black sweater, the better to hide the lingering bruises. For a second, like a high school girl about to meet a movie star, I wished I'd spent a little more time on my appearance.

Stop that. Focus.

It was time to lift the last barrier.

I put my hands down by my sides in a makeshift mountain pose—not necessary for the spell, but it helped me feel grounded, even when I was wearing shoes. I conjured in my head a vision of the shield, the street, and the front door of the shop. Then I put a wolf—Booker's gray wolf, so big that his head would be at the same level as mine—in the vision. I imagined the Booker wolf walking across the street and into the open door of the shop, letting the power flow out of my fingertips and into the grounded shield. *Wolves are welcome here. This wolf is welcome here.*

I couldn't see Booker's expression from this distance, but I could see that his entire body had gone on high alert, his head high and focused on the shop. I didn't know if he could see me through the window, but I knew he could feel the magical energy flowing through the shield in front of him.

After a second, the shield just...allowed him to pass. He recognized the change when it happened, his head cocking to the side, looking for all the world like a curious dog caught in the thrall of some new, unexpected command.

After taking one tentative step down from the sidewalk onto the street, Booker made his way across the asphalt without incident, in a loose stride that betrayed nothing physically. I watched him closely, focusing my power, and thank the Goddess, I could feel him for a second, read him like an open book. What I got was a surprise, to say the least—Booker was nervous too. Hoping this would go well. He was...excited to be here. To see me.

Huh.

He stopped at the door of the shop, hesitated for a second, and then knocked. It was such an unexpected, kind of ridiculous gesture of respect that I nearly laughed—he knew I was right there, but he would wait for me to let him in.

It was very difficult not to like this particular werewolf.

Damn it.

When I opened the door of the shop, Booker caught the doorknob and opened it the rest of the way. It opened out, which I'd planned so as to make it easier for departing customers carrying their purchases from the store. However, it did make opening the door for someone from the inside a little awkward, so I appreciated the move.

"Please come in," I said, glad that my voice wasn't so hoarse. Still not fully healed, but that would take more time.

At least it didn't hurt to talk, because Booker and I had a lot to talk about.

I backed away, giving him space to enter the shop. He did, pulling off his sunglasses and shoving them into one of the pockets of his jacket, unveiling those uncanny amber eyes. They swept around the shop with his usual intense, thorough regard, and then he turned and closed the door behind him, locking it once again.

I swallowed a little surge of fear. *He's locking the bad guys out. This is not a trap.*

When he turned back to me, his nostrils were flaring. "Just as a precaution," he said, as if he knew what I was thinking. "People don't read signs if they don't think they have to, so anyone might walk in."

I nodded, ordering myself to relax. Booker watched me carefully, and then he took a slow, easy step nearer to me. I felt his aura of power, just as I had before, but this time it was familiar—more comforting than threatening. When I didn't move away, he sighed, just a little. "How are you?"

"Super," I drawled, unable to stop myself. "How are you?" He winced, and it shamed me. It was childish to take refuge in sarcasm when he was being so earnest and trying to be so honorable. I bowed my head and bit my lip. "I'm dealing," I finally said. "It's hard."

When I looked back up, his eyes were still locked on me, dropping to the knit fabric that didn't quite cover my throat. "No witch T-shirt today?"

He'd noticed that? "Not really feeling it."

His mouth firmed, then relaxed. "You're healing though," he said, reaching out one hand toward the faintly bruised skin above the sweater's collar. He was almost close enough to touch it, but he didn't. "Your voice sounds better."

"Witchcraft," I said, shrugging and summoning up a tiny smile.

Booker nodded. "Good."

Booker smelled good—like cedar and soap. It mingled well with the various smells of the shop, although I hoped they weren't too much for him. Werewolf noses were sensitive, which was a point I'd exploited by making him come to the carnival.

Then, he'd been a potential threat. Now, we were on the verge of becoming allies.

I turned then, motioning for him to follow, and headed to the back room where we could sit. Once we were settled into the tarot room, and I had a table between him and me, I felt a little better. More in control.

"Did you have any problems with...the body?" I asked. It took effort to ask, but I had to know.

Booker shook his head, eyes unblinking on mine. "No. It's taken care of."

"What did you do with her?"

Booker sighed, a muscle working in his jaw. "Do you really want to know?" His gaze was direct, matter-of-fact.

I didn't. "No," I said. Then, again, a little stronger, "*No.*"

"She'll be found," Booker said, his deep voice soothing. "Her family will be able to bury her. They won't know what happened, but they won't be left in agony, hoping that she'll come home someday."

I swallowed, feeling tears prick at my eyes again. "She's not close with them."

He nodded. "Jo." He waited until I looked him in the eyes again. "It would be best if you reported her missing later today. You don't have to, but it'll make things easier—for the authorities. For you, in the long run."

At the look on my face, he leaned forward. "Just tell them the truth," he said, his voice a gentle rumble. "The last time you saw her was Friday night when she left the shop. Because what you saw yesterday—it wasn't Emma."

I closed my eyes. He was right, but that didn't mean I had to like it. "I will," I said shortly. Then, after a second, I added an ungracious, "Thank you."

Booker leaned back again. "You're welcome," he said, allowing a hint of irony to creep into his voice.

"So." I curled my hands around the arms of my chair. "We need to talk."

"We do," he allowed. "Where do you want to start?"

"Do you know who the necromancer is? Did they follow you here to St. Louis?"

Booker blinked—a rare occurrence. "My note guaranteed your safety," he said, sounding affronted. When I just cocked my head, his lips pressed together in obvious irritation. "If I knew a necromancer was trailing me, do you think I would have given you that kind of assurance?"

I raised my hands. "How was I supposed to know that? You were just some scary wolf who tracked me down. Twice."

His eyes narrowed. "There was something about preferring death to telling me what I wanted to know."

"That was a mistake on my part," I said, knowing that I was losing the upper hand here. "Miscommunication based on an incorrect speculation."

"You thought I betrayed you, went back on my word." He was getting angry, but there was no violence in it. Just injured feelings.

"Again," I said, hanging on to my patience with my fingernails at this point, "I didn't know who you were. How was I to know that you were any different from the Fenris?"

That muscle ticked in his jaw. "I am one of Diana's Wolves. When I give my word, I mean it."

I couldn't hold in a short, scoffing laugh. "*Diana's Wolves.* You say that like it's supposed to mean something to me."

He considered me for a moment, then cocked his head. "This is going to be a long conversation," he said. "It'll be more productive for both of us if you can at least give me the benefit of the doubt here." He leveled his gaze at me. "You allowed me into your sanctuary, and I'm grateful for your trust. You told me once to stop posturing—remember that?" When I nodded, he did the same. "Okay. Now I'm asking you to please give me a chance. I can't do that if you're deliberately going to keep closing yourself off."

I could feel the truth and sincerity in every word. It fairly emanated from his pores. He believed what he was saying. I took a deep breath, and before I could talk myself out of it, I asked, "You okay with heights?"

Those dark eyebrows raised. "Yes."

"Come on," I said, standing up. "Let's go up to the roof."

Booker hesitated only for a second. "Sure," he stood, brushing something imaginary from his jeans as he did so. When I didn't start toward the door, he looked around and saw the mirror.

"Through there?" The stunned disbelief in his tone made me smile—a real smile—for the first time in days.

"You afraid?"

He tilted his head one way, then the other, his mouth scrunching, before he looked at me again. "Little bit?"

That did it. I laughed, and I was rewarded for this by the reappearance of those dimples. Once again, he made my heart lose balance for a moment.

"Fine, then, scaredy-wolf," I said. "We'll take the stairs. The elevator is out of commission." I paused. "Permanently." Not only was the elevator old and rickety, but it would just make it easier for someone to get to me on the top floor.

"Sounds good. I'd like a tour of your Sanctum." He paused, searching my face for a moment. "If you're comfortable with that."

"Um, sure," I said, mystified but game.

He stood aside and extended a hand toward the door, doing everything but sweeping an imaginary hat from his head and bowing. "After you, Jo Murphy."

CHAPTER 9

THE WEREWOLF, THE WITCH, AND (PIECES OF) HER WARDROBE

BOOKER

BOOKER FOLLOWED JO BACK THROUGH HER SHOP, LISTENING intently as she described the features of the building, memorizing the layout and the information as they went. She knew them intimately, which meant that she had been involved in the renovations as much as possible even if she hadn't swung a hammer.

He'd requested the full tour, and thankfully, she'd taken him seriously.

He made note of a few key things: the building had three entrances—one that went through the shop, one on the side that led directly up to the apartment floors, and a double door around back that had access to both. There was a stairwell door in the back room that led upstairs to two tarot-reading rooms, an apartment, and storage for the extra inventory she kept for online orders.

She led him through the back room up the stairs, which felt sturdy and well-made. The finished areas on the second floor were nice—appealing to customers, he imagined. Nice hallways, subdued lighting. Cozily decorated rooms. She did tarot and palm readings as well as Reiki sessions in those rooms, she told him, but she kept the room downstairs, the one where they had talked, for when she was working the shop alone and someone came in for a reading.

He asked questions, keeping them quiet and respectful. Although she gave him strange looks at first, it didn't take much for her to open up about her plans for the building—and he enjoyed her excitement, even though she was speaking in hushed tones as if she were leading him on a tour of a museum. He got the feeling that she hadn't had many opportunities to talk about the minutiae of her renovations and her plans for the future. Her warm lavender scent was a happy one, so he basked in it along the way.

Her first plan was to make more rooms on the second floor. "I'd love to be able to have a psychic fair someday, and we'd need at least six readers to make it a success," she explained, adding that meant at least six individual reading rooms. Currently, she had three total, with the one downstairs and the two finished ones here on the second floor. "I could probably negotiate the space in this apartment," she indicated another doorway down the hall from them, "for three reading rooms. Or I could have as many as nine."

She paused there and added, "Although I might go for six reading rooms and just rent out the apartment. We'll just have to see. It's going to take time and money."

As they headed up the stairs to the third floor, Jo explained the shape the building had been in originally. For an old apartment building, it still had good bones, but much of it had been run-down and in need of repair. She'd had to have the whole thing rewired and plenty of pipes replaced for the plumbing, and it pleased Booker when she was able to answer his questions about what had been done and the types of materials used with specifics.

As a property owner himself, he respected anyone who invested their time and energy into renovations as personally as she had done. Yet another thing to like about Jo Murphy.

The third floor intrigued him, as it was full of apartments that had been cleaned out, rewired, and plumbed, but as yet unrenovated. Wheels turned ferociously in his mind, but he had to wait for the right opening.

The three floors above that were basically gutted open spaces. When he'd asked what she was going to do here, she shrugged and said, "For right now, I'm not sure. Maybe larger apartments? Full-floor? I'm kind of waiting for inspiration here before moving forward."

He nodded, making mental notes as he inspected the areas.

Finally, they reached the seventh floor, which was Jo's personal living space. "I didn't expect to be bringing company up here," she warned him. "You're going to see it warts and all."

Booker just smiled and shook his head. She had no idea how much it gratified him that she was showing him her Sanctum, that she would share with him so much information. He'd enjoyed watching her talk, watching her hands move, watching the lights play over her black hair as they'd walked up and through the building. He'd enjoyed her warmth, her smell, her contentment. She'd probably considered her tour to be boring, but he'd appreciated it thoroughly.

The first thing he noticed when he saw her home was the lack of walls. Jo Murphy seemed to crave space. She'd kept the layout simple, leaving the floor plan open with only her bedroom and a large bathroom with a walk-in closet sectioned off. He approved of this.

The second thing was that there were floor-length mirrors everywhere.

There was at least one mirror on every floor, he'd noted as they'd made their way through the building. But here, it was as if she wanted to have as many doors open to her as possible. The windows, too, had been widened and lengthened when she'd had this floor done. It was as open as any living space in an old city building could possibly be.

It made sense. Any creature who had been held captive would want to live in a place with few walls.

However, his business side of him, the one that had worked in professional security most of his life, was dying a little inside. *At least let the fucking glass be thick.* He kept his voice neutral, leaving out the F-bomb when he asked this as a question, and he was relieved when Jo said it was half-inch glass and was tinted to ensure that someone outside wouldn't be able to see in.

Booker could vouch for that part. Not that he was going to tell her he'd been watching her place.

"I'm not, like, a crazy exhibitionist, but sometimes I forget where my bra is," Jo said and then winced when he grinned at her. "In my own home, I should be able to walk around naked if I want."

Booker laughed. *Do not think about her walking around naked.* Today was for business, and business only. "I agree," he said. "Anyone has the right to live in chaos if they want. You keep your office and work areas clean."

"If I don't, I get totally lost," she admitted, but then she narrowed her blue eyes. "It's not exactly *chaos* up here. It's not that bad."

Booker said nothing, just walked over to a chair and picked up from the cushion a white cotton bra that had seen better days. He slung it onto the couch and sat down, then gave her an innocent look.

Jo rolled her eyes, a blush rising in her cheeks. "Fine, it's chaos, but it's my chaos. I know where everything is when I need it."

"No argument here," Booker said, watching as she puttered around, picking up some clothes and tossing them in a wicker basket, then adding books from the couch—plus the bra—and marching them into her bedroom. He had a feeling she'd get pissy if she knew how adorable he thought she was right now. Then he wondered how much she could read of his emotions and his aura. Some witches had almost telepathic abilities, but Jo didn't seem to have that kind of direct power.

When she came back, her cheeks were less pink. "Plus, I wasn't planning to have people over," she added. She settled herself cross-legged on the couch and scanned the room one more time—he assumed for more wayward underthings.

"Oh, I'm people now?" It was only half a joke, but he grinned.

"Generally speaking," she said, trying to suppress a smile and failing, her scent blooming. Yes, she was responding to him again. Warmth spread in his stomach.

Keep it conversational. "You have a cat," he said. "Name?"

"Cole," she said, casting a glance around. "I have no idea where he is." Then she cocked her head. "How did you know?"

Booker tapped his nose. Her apartment contained a variety of smells, most of them appealing—except that one. The litter box scent was muted, but it was still easily detectable.

She gave him an exasperated look. "I put all kinds of herbs around the litter to keep the smell down, and I scoop constantly."

Booker shrugged, hiding a smile.

"New subject," she said, rolling her eyes. "No more twitting the witch about her housekeeping." She paused, gesturing toward him. "So. Diana's Wolves? I'm assuming we're talking about the huntress Diana. Are all werewolves pledged to a god?"

"It's not quite that simple," he hedged, wondering where to start. She was watching him expectantly. "Yes, Diana's Wolves belong to the goddess Diana," he said. He rolled up his sleeve to show her the tattoo on the inside of his forearm, a bow with a nocked arrow. "Diana's Wolves are protectors and providers. We don't harm women or children—it's a matter of honor to keep innocents safe."

"So, the Fenris belong—well, belonged—to Loki?" Jo asked. "Fenris wasn't a god, if I remember correctly."

Booker nodded. If she was able to follow the mythology, they were halfway there. "Loki enjoyed exploiting the connection between the werewolf and his wolf-child," Booker said, working to keep a snarl from his voice. "The Fenris were...an abomination. They allowed themselves to be corrupted. By our nature, werewolves are supposed to be the protectors. We have an instinct to hunt and kill, but that is purely to ensure survival. Provide and protect."

Booker paused, willing his hackles back down. His wolf didn't like this part of the convo at all. However, Jo was nodding, and that was good—because he was about to tell her something she didn't want to hear. "Like I said, Diana's Wolves follow that code: provide and protect. We don't kill for the pleasure of it, but we do when it's necessary." He cocked his head. "I won't lie to you, Jo. It is often necessary."

Jo nodded again, and her smell didn't change, so he continued. "When it comes to mingling with the human world, many of us do. More so than some werewolf packs." He considered going into his family's leadership role when it came to North American wolves, but that would be a whole other conversation. "Most of us work in some sort of field that gives us the opportunity to extend that kind of service to others—doing security, taking gigs as bodyguards. You'd be surprised how many people in law enforcement are Diana's Wolves." His mouth turned down. "Although these days, I know that's not always a ringing endorsement."

Jo looked away, but then she met his eyes again. "Okay, so that's your clan. Pack."

He raised his eyebrows. "We have clans, but that's my pack."

"Hey, I live to learn. If you guys have some kind of manual for werewolf culture, I'd love to read it." He grinned, but her pale blue eyes were mostly serious. "For real. A manual would be..." She glanced heavenward, as if something might fall from the ceiling. "...really helpful."

Booker chuckled. He hadn't laughed this much around someone who wasn't pack in a long time. "I'll see what I can do."

"Thank you," Jo said. "Now. What happened to the Fenris? Loki corrupted them?"

He sighed. Ignored the twist in his chest. "They were unpledged wolves. There used to be a time when werewolves could just have packs, and that was the end of it. Then Loki decided that he needed the wolves. For Ragnarok or just for kicks." Who the hell knew what motivated a chaotic god. "It's anyone's guess. The unpledged wolves would hear him whispering to them, calling to them, telling them we were special. Told them that we shouldn't be in hiding—we should be hunting humans. Become the true top of the food chain. It's a lie, but a dangerous one."

Jo's wide eyes seemed more curious than afraid. He contemplated how to explain it, then decided just to be direct. "The whispers of supremacy. The temptation to give in to the wolf. Even family bonds aren't always enough to keep you from listening. Without the pull of a pledge to a clan and pack to anchor you, it's hard to resist." Booker sighed, hoping Jo would understand this part. "Turning into the wolf, it's...easy. Being a wolf is fun. Natural. It's easier to stay in that form—for most of us, it feels...better. In certain ways." He paused. "It's simpler."

Jo hadn't moved, hadn't changed that absorbed expression, so he continued. "It's harder to change into a human from the wolf form. Man into wolf isn't a huge jump, but wolf to man is. I think it's because humanity is a choice for us."

His wolf whined uneasily inside him, and he tamped down the urge to give himself a soothing shake. Instead, he settled for a human variation and rubbed his face with both hands, briskly. Then he dropped his hands and continued.

"The Fenris wanted to be wolves all of the time, but they were unnaturally vicious. Blood-mad. Wolves hunt for food, and they like the hunt, but killing for pleasure doesn't make any sense. It's a waste." He shook his head. "These werewolves embraced Loki and loved being his Fenris because they wanted to be more like their wolves, but they ended up corrupted. Not wolf, not human. Worse in every way. That's why we call them an abomination."

Jo was as silent as before, but now her lovely eyes were stricken. Her scent bittered with sadness. Booker leaned toward her, elbows on his knees, hands clasped in front of him. He was pleased when she didn't lean back. "Jo. What happened to you was an abomination. No true werewolf would have countenanced it." She lifted her chin a touch, but she kept eye contact with him. "What I said to you downstairs, about keeping an open mind? I'm asking you not to paint us all with the same brush—the brush *they* gave you."

For a moment, they just stared at each other. Booker was impressed— most humans couldn't or wouldn't keep his gaze for so long. But Jo was measuring him. He could feel it like a tingle in his blood. More than almost anything, he wanted to measure up, be deemed worthy of...well, whatever it was she wanted from him. He'd told her that Diana's Wolves were protectors and he'd meant it, but he had a feeling she didn't quite grasp the extent of that.

If Jo asked for his help, he'd be bound to her and she would be bound to him. That was how it worked, how his pack honored Diana and why she was their sworn goddess. As alpha, Booker would be personally responsible for Jo's well-being. For maybe the first time in his life, he truly wanted that responsibility for someone else. He wanted to be bound to her. They were on the cusp of something that had the potential to change both of their lives. Her fascinating abilities, this powerful building. His fixation on her smell. Him finding her just as the necromancer decided to strike. His inconveniently growing need to be around her.

It was hard not to feel like Fate was working on them both.

Booker didn't have a problem with Fate, so long as it went along with his nose—and his nose was telling him that Jo Murphy, and her Sanctum, were important. Not just because of what happened with the Fenris, but because of what was happening here, right now, in this area of the city.

Not so very long ago, he'd made the decision to come back to St. Louis after confiding in his father that he'd been feeling he was needed in the city. Arthur Booker had been only too happy to offer his only son the St. Louis branch of the family business. He wanted nothing more than for Booker to quit working for the Council and truly commit himself to his duties as alpha. Booker had accepted the position and moved his growing pack here, was starting to get them settled while he finished this last job for the Council.

It was entirely possible that Josephine Ellen Murphy was the reason those instincts had kicked in.

He waited for her to speak, sending a quick prayer to Diana that his feelings about the situation weren't wrong. The more quickly they began working together to find this necromancer, the better. For both of them.

Chapter 10

Who's Afraid? The Big Bad Wolf?

JO

What I'd told Booker was true: I did live to learn. For me, it was part of being a witch and would be a lifelong endeavor.

But holy shit, I was learning a lot more than I could possibly have bargained for just then. I so badly wanted to pull out a notebook and take notes while Booker was talking, but he was staring at me so much during the whole thing that I would have been worried about offending him.

Still, a manual would be really handy—I hadn't been kidding. A manual on supernatural creatures in general, werewolves in particular. Maybe there was a whole supernatural library out there—one with multiple levels and rolling ladders where I could whirl around like a character in a musical. The image made me smile. If there wasn't any kind of informational literature on werewolves, maybe I could write one. Would Booker let me pick his brain?

Speaking of, it was odd how at home Booker looked in my apartment. His size was manageable here, unlike in the reading room downstairs or the narrow corridors of the hall of mirrors. Sitting in one of my overstuffed chairs, leaning toward me in a deceptively casual way, I could almost forget that he was a wolf when he wasn't a human tree. An attractive one.

Then he would fix me with that unblinking amber gaze, and...oh, yeah. He'd just given me a whole lot to think about with his spiel about the Fenris.

About himself.

He'd just asked me to keep an open mind. Not to paint him with the same brush as the Fenris. I was just about to fall into those beautiful eyes, succumb to that aura of power. The smell of cedar, sandalwood, and male in my personal space. It all fit.

With effort, I broke eye contact with him and laughed. It was shaky, despite my best efforts. "Fair enough," I said. "I can't promise you anything, but I will try to keep an open mind."

"I think the fact that you called me shows that," he said.

I gestured to our luxurious surroundings. "And the fact that I brought you up here," I said.

"Truth. I like your Sanctum, Jo Murphy, and I like your apartment." His smile was warm. His tone caressing.

Answer him without stuttering, please. "Thank you," I said, before something else popped back into my head. Something that I'd wondered about earlier when he was giving me his werewolf-culture lesson. "Wait. Diana doesn't seem like the type of goddess to have a bunch of werewolves pledged to Her. Especially males. I mean, don't your penises offend Her?"

Booker's surprised bark of laughter delighted me. I was going to have to keep making this man laugh on a regular basis. Those dimples were killing me.

It took him a few seconds of fighting chuckles before he could answer, and even then, his voice was threaded with amusement when he said, "We don't do things with our dicks She'd disapprove of—which is remarkably easy, I might add, when you're not a piece of shit. Unlike that guy in Alton." Booker arched a brow at me. "I'm sure you're not surprised to hear that you made an enemy there. He's the reason I knew you were in Ste. Genevieve."

Ugh. Tony Preston, asshole abuser extraordinaire and owner of a strip mall in Alton where I'd read tarot just before moving on to Other Worlds Emporium. "He made an enemy when he refused to stop hurting my friend. Goddess knows how many other women." I paused. "So, you made a deal with Tony?"

Booker had the grace to look uncomfortable. As well he should, doing business with scum like Tony fucking Preston. "He tipped me off."

"He tell you about the geas?"

"He didn't know what it was—he thought it was just a run-of-the-mill curse—but I figured it out." Now Booker was staring at me again, with approval. "Well done there. You did the women of the world a favor with that one."

"Yeah." I'd slapped Tony with a geas, courtesy of his signature on my paycheck, that made him powerless to harm women—in any sense of the word, which for that scumbag meant sexual encounters too. "The best part is that there's an escape clause in it. He just has to stop trying to inflict pain on women, touch them without anger for a certain number of times, and it'll go away." I sighed, remembering. "He'll never break it, of course, but he's punishing himself in the end." Delicious, delicious irony.

"Diana would definitely approve. To answer your question, She likes werewolves." He raised his hands in an expressive shrug. "She's goddess of the hunt, so She's one of the fiercer protectors out there. We're good for that. She once told me that I was resilient cannon fodder." This last held a hint of what was, to my mind, some very misplaced pride.

"Resilient cannon fodder?" I laughed in disbelief. "That's Her liking you?"

He shrugged. "She may have been kidding, but Her humor can be pretty dry," he said. At my look, he asked, "Don't you commune with your goddess?"

I thought about my communications with Hecate and grimaced. Rather than delve into the millions of questions I had about Diana's dry humor and what She was like as a goddess, I figured it was time to get down to the matter at hand.

I took a deep breath, then let it out slowly. "So, someone's sending zombies after me, and I have no idea why."

Now he was alert, sitting up and keeping his eyes bright on me. "How many attacks have there been, total?"

"Just these two."

"So the first was when you bailed through the mirror and let the zombies have at me?"

"I thought you'd brought them at the time, so I didn't think I was leaving you in danger," I snapped. "Besides, you killed them all pretty fucking quick. You *weren't* in any danger." He smiled, looking like the wolf who'd caught the canary, and I realized that I must have confirmed that I had been watching him through the mirror.

Damn it, this wolf was going to be able to figure me out in seconds if I couldn't stop being a blabbermouth around him. The dimples were out again, seducing me into smiling with him again. *Goddess, why does he have to be so attractive?* Booker's head was tilted toward me, his smile fading a bit, his eyes beginning to glow. Or maybe that was just my imagination. *Hecate, help me here.* Thinking about my goddess helped a bit.

Keep it together, Murphy. This is business. "You need to know what happened to the Fenris, and I need to be alive to be able to tell you about it." Booker's unblinking gaze returned to its normal, steady state, and for once, I found that comforting. "If you help me stay alive, help me find the necromancer, I'll tell you everything I know." Honesty compelled me to add, "There are some things that I'm not sure about. I think I can figure it out, remember it. I just...haven't tried."

"I think I have a pretty good idea of what happened to them," Booker said, raising his eyebrows. I couldn't tell what was going on behind those eyes.

The Fenris were the only bargaining chip I had. If Booker said no, my options were limited. I didn't want to think of needing the help of werewolves, of all creatures, but Booker had dealt with a bunch of zombies in something like a minute, while I'd been nearly strangled to death by just one. I could stay in the Sanctum and stay safe, but how long would it take the necromancer to start striking out at my friends? I didn't have that many to begin with—and thanks to the necromancer, that count was down by one.

Booker had a team. He had resources, and as I'd told Kate, he had information—information I needed if I was going to function in this world. If the Sanctum was going to function the way I'd hoped it would.

If I tried to find the necromancer on my own, I'd probably get killed. If I brought Kate into this, she would probably get killed—and where would that leave the Hecate's Home kids? That course of action put everyone in danger. The wolves could protect me, keep me from having to bring anyone else into this. Together, we could stop the necromancer and get that darkness out of the city. I could get vengeance for Emma.

Resilient cannon fodder. I'd thought Diana was being callous in Her assessment, but wasn't I kind of thinking of the wolves that way, too? That wasn't fair.

However, the Fenris had been gaining power and kidnapping people like me for years before Booker's Council had figured out what was going on. That wasn't fair, either.

Plus, Booker had said that his pack were protectors. I couldn't imagine that they weren't used to risking their lives. Unless, of course, he decided that this wasn't his fight and denied my request for help. My offer to trade.

If Booker said, "Sorry, but that's too much trouble," would I figure out a way to fight the necromancer? Or would I go back on the run again and call my time in St. Louis a failed experiment? Running had worked in the past, even if some vital parts of me balked at the idea now. It felt wrong.

I put my hand to my throat, which had started to ache again, and tried to flow healing energy—gently—from my hand to the injury. If I concentrated on that, I could keep from worrying for a few seconds.

Booker was still silent. Waiting. Watching. How much of my inner turmoil could he sense? "Well, it's your call," I said, keeping my voice neutral, my face blank. Trying not to betray every tangled emotion that threatened to spill free. "If you don't want to get involved in this, I understand."

He shook his head, leaned forward again, his voice deep and determined. "You misunderstood me. I want to help you. I'm going to help you." The rush of relief filled my limbs, made them weak for a moment. He paused, blinked, then continued on. "Like you said, I need to know any details you can give me about the Fenris, and I'm perfectly willing to keep you alive and help you figure out what's happening. Plus, a necromancer weaponizing zombies in an urban area? *My* urban area?" He smiled briefly, but it was fierce. No dimples this time. "I would have involved myself in that problem without being asked."

As he kept talking, the relief and gratitude built up, making me almost lightheaded. "You sure?" *Shut up, Murphy. Don't look the gift wolf in the mouth.*

Booker's brooding amber gaze lightened, warming, when he looked at me. "I'm sure."

Thank the Goddess. Yours and/or mine. "Thank you." I smiled at him, and for a moment, an energy, an awareness, crackled between us. I could almost see our auras touching, connecting. *Wow.* I pulled my gaze back and stood, needing to move. Work out some of my suddenly awake nerves. "Want to come up and see the roof?"

The roof access was at the very top of the main building stairwell—to everyone but me. I kept the doorway to my floor locked, of course, as well as the doorway to the rooftop staircase. At the top of the staircase? Yup, more locks.

In this, at least, I could feel Booker's unspoken approval as he watched me unlock each set. I knew he was skeptical of my window-riddled apartment—despite it being on the seventh floor, with extra-thick glass—but I had made sure to have excellent locks installed throughout my building, even if the doors themselves weren't the best. I planned to open the Sanctum to residents eventually, but I also meant to keep my own spaces private. Safe.

It helped that I usually didn't have to bother with the locks during my many trips to the roof. It was a lot of damn locking and unlocking to get Booker up there, since he'd expressed another polite but firm refusal of my offer to take him through the mirror. This time, however, he again cited wanting the "full tour"—which meant gauging the roof access accurately.

Once we finally got up there, however, I could tell that he liked it. Booker walked out of the door into the sunshine, tilting his face up to the warmth. Then, with a slow grin, he turned in a deliberate circle, walking as he did so. It was an education, just watching him survey the area around the building. Those sharp eyes missed nothing.

I waited until he was done, then gestured toward the river, saying, "The building would be worth it for this view alone."

He walked over to stand beside me. "You love rivers." It was a statement, not a question.

I shrugged, not moving my gaze from the churning, gleaming darkness of the waves. "Especially this one."

"It was how I found you initially, you know." His voice went deep, a little rougher. "Your pattern. Whether you went north or south, it was always Mississippi river towns."

I could feel my jaw sag. Goddess, how could I have been so predictable? I hadn't even realized I was doing it. I finally tilted my head up to look at him, studying the set of his jaw in profile. Given how things were working out, I couldn't be entirely sorry.

Booker bent his head toward me a bit, then said, as if confiding a secret, "I'm very good at my job."

"I'm very bad at being untraceable," I muttered, then watched his dimples flash again as he turned toward me.

Suddenly, I was too aware of everything. The heat of his body, the size of him, his proximity—it was all too much. To cover my sudden flash of anxiety, I cast my eyes over and saw Stanley.

I sidestepped away and around Booker, trying not to be awkward, and then said, as cheerfully as I could manage, "Come over here. I'll show you my favorite spot." I went up to lay a hand on one of Stanley's arcing wings and motioned to the gargoyle. "Booker the werewolf, this is Stanley the gargoyle. Stanley, this is Booker. He's agreed to help me in exchange for information."

I figured Booker would be amused at this, or at least skeptical of me trying to introduce him to a stone statue, but instead, Booker came over to stand at Stanley's side and bowed, slowly, deliberately, while looking at Stanley's profile.

"It's an honor to meet you, Stanley," Booker said, with complete sincerity, as he straightened. I got the distinct feeling that my new partner in necromancer hunting was showing respect, but not deference, to my officially unofficial guardian gargoyle.

Yeah, "May your life be interesting" was definitely both a blessing and a curse—in my case, the jury was still out.

Shaking my head in bemusement, I smiled at Booker and hopped up next to Stanley like I had a million times before. However, before my butt landed on its usual perch, strong hands grabbed me by the shoulders and pulled me backward, jerking my body off-balance for a heart-stopping moment before my feet hit the surface of the roof again, the hands still holding me in place.

"What are you doing?" Booker growled from behind me, and my skin prickled, hair raising, at his tone and the anger in his aura. The full-on shakes started when my mind flashed back to another time when hands with that kind of strength had taken hold of me. Restrained me. Hurt me.

I burst free of Booker's hands without a sound, stumbling hard into the shelter of Stanley's wings, and I took a deep breath and put a force field around myself. *Focus. This moment, this time. Present time, present time, present time.* I put one hand on Stanley, felt the smooth stone beneath my palm. *Here. Home. Safe. Here. Home. Safe.*

The emotions wanted to be in charge—they wanted to freak the fuck out—but I was better at controlling them now. It had taken a lot of time, plus a lot of meditation and yoga, but years later, the flashbacks to my time in captivity had mostly subsided, despite the occasional dream rerun. I thought I was doing pretty well, all things considered. Even now.

By the time I had my breathing regulated and could be reasonably certain that I could talk again without trembling, I opened my eyes to see Booker pacing around the rooftop. Well, "pacing" if you were on speed. I'd never seen anything like it. His long, jeans-clad legs weren't running, but they were also not walking. I caught flashes of a tense jaw and clenched fists. Felt his aura like a whirling miasma of self-castigation and regret. Rage, but not at me. Concern for me. Bitterness for himself. I wasn't just getting flashes from watching him this time—I had to keep myself from getting pulled directly into the storm.

I let my force field go, flowing it back into the building, and debated how to approach him. In the end, I decided to stay where I was—I didn't want to risk getting run over. Instead, I just said, pitching my voice a little louder than normal, "Um. I sit there." When Booker flashed me a tense, glowing glance, I pointed to the spot next to Stanley where I'd sit and watch the river. "It has the best view," I finished lamely.

Booker looked away and paced the length of the roof and back a few times. Something that would take me a few minutes, but took him a handful of seconds.

Then he stopped, but he didn't look me in the eyes. From this wolf, that kind of deference was on the edge of disturbing. "I'm sorry," he said, his voice sounding tightly controlled. "It looked like you were about to jump off the roof." He gestured, then dropped his hands. Fists again. Clench, unclench, clench. It was mesmerizing. "From the angle where I was standing, it didn't look like there was a platform there. It just looked like you'd decided gravity no longer applied to you. I didn't—" He bit off what he was going to say next, turned, and continued speed-pacing.

Incredibly, it seemed that I had scared the big bad wolf.

Or at least, the thought of my impending death had.

The implications of this went in two directions for me, one of which—his concern for my well-being stemming from some personal interest—was a little too far-fetched for me to dwell on for too long. The other was more likely.

If I died, Booker wouldn't get what he had been sent to fetch. This Council must be pretty damned intimidating if not getting the story on the Fenris was such a big deal.

As for me, well, I'd turned away from him without a second thought. *Stupid.* Turning your back on a werewolf was never a good idea—and, as a result, I'd gotten grabbed. Of course, I believed Booker when he said that he'd thought I was jumping and, therefore, thought he was helping. I could feel those emotions rioting through him. He was upset. Logically, I knew Booker didn't mean me any harm.

However, the remnants of fear still rode the adrenaline through my system, and they got a little jolt while I thought back to how terrifying it had been for him to touch me like that. Once again, I had to work to steady my breath.

Damn it.

While I reined in my fear, Booker continued his pacing. Part of me wanted to tell him to stop before he wore a hole in the roof, and then I imagined what it must look like if anyone was watching us.

The snort was a mild one, but then I couldn't contain it anymore. It was definitely nerves, but also just the craziness of this whole situation. The lousiness of the last few days. The insanity of the world in general and mine in particular. Either way, I burst out laughing for real, and it brought Booker to a sudden halt a few feet from me.

I imagined him digging in his heels to stop his forward momentum like Wile E. Coyote, leaving a skid mark behind him, and then the giggles got real.

"What the hell is so funny?" His voice wasn't entirely steady, but it was also mystified.

I bobbed my head, still shaking with laughter. When I could, I managed to say, "The world is weird, that's all," hoping he would let it drop.

He didn't, of course. He just stared at me, waiting for me to explain. Fucking werewolves—they never let anything go.

"It's nothing," I said, wiping a bit of moisture from beneath my eyes and stepping out a foot or two to show him I wasn't afraid of him anymore. Because I wasn't. I was far more afraid of my past. "It's only funny if you're me."

Booker shifted his stance so that he was now facing me, and some of the tension leached out of those giant shoulders, his head tilting a little.

I sighed, spread my hands wide, and finally was able to sober myself up. "I just got you all worked up and myself in a nearly full-on PTSD flashback...all because I wanted to show a werewolf my favorite place to sit during his tour of my building." Just saying it out loud had me smiling again. "It's absurd."

Booker's expression grew even more serious, which shouldn't have been possible.

"See? I told you it's only funny if you're me," I said, trying to break his frown by smiling at him. A real smile.

I was standing with my back to Stanley's, his massive wings on either side of me. Booker took a tentative step or two toward me, but it didn't make my fear spike again, thank Hecate. Although I was glad that he didn't come too close. I was a little too raw yet.

Still, I didn't want to lose him. His help.

I took another breath. I couldn't apologize for the misunderstanding because it wasn't my fault, but I could extend an olive branch. I said, "I hope you're still okay with working together—"

While at the exact same time, he asked, "What do you charge for rent?"

Chapter 11

Through the Looking Glass (And What the Wolf Found There)

JO

Could this day get any weirder?

"I haven't decided about rent yet," I said, trying to mentally switch gears. "I have a potential tenant lined up for one of the apartments, but he's not ready to move in yet." The last time I spoke to John—*Was it just three days ago? It feels like three years*—he had told me, with some sorrow, that he would probably need to move soon. He was a live-in caretaker for an elderly woman who had just been put on hospice, so it was only a matter of time.

I had planned to finish the apartment on the second floor for him—a matter of painting and replacing a few fixtures—this weekend.

Now there were four tragic words that Fate always conspired against: "I had planned to."

Booker's eyes sharpened with curiosity. "Is this a friend?"

"An employee," I said. "And a friend."

When Booker nodded, expression neutral, I took another step toward him. "So you want to know about rent for one of my apartments?" *The bulk of which aren't finished yet?*

Booker took one breath, then two. His aura had calmed again. "I'd like to know about the apartments, sure. But I'm more interested in how much you would charge per floor."

If he didn't stop, my jaw was going to unhinge and fall right off my face. What was going on in that overly handsome head? I took another step closer to him. "Per floor?"

He crossed his arms over his chest. "This place has a lot of great space," he said. "You have three floors that have yet to be designed. I have access to contractors. Those floors would be extremely valuable property to me and my pack, if I could design them to my specifications."

I nodded, trying to comprehend this.

He leveled his amber gaze at me. "I'd like to talk to you about a five-year lease, minimum."

Holy Hecate.

"I'll plan out and pay for the renovations, with your approval, and pay you rent," he continued. "Once the lease is up, we can renegotiate." I hadn't moved since the five-year lease comment. He tilted his head at me, not breaking eye contact. "It goes without saying that I'll update and maintain your security systems as part of our agreement."

Of course. "Give me a minute to think," I said, a little weakly.

Booker inclined his head and took a few steps away, and I turned back to Stanley and the river. This was the definition of "too good to be true." I couldn't have asked for a better deal—I had been low-key dreading having to advertise, interview potential tenants, create multiple contracts. The renovations had already eaten up most of my nest egg, and the shop wasn't running in the black yet. It likely wouldn't be for at least another year, and that was if I was lucky.

But to invite wolves into my building? The thought of being surrounded by wolves again made my entire body tense up. I crossed my arms in front of myself, rubbing my elbows.

Five years of guaranteed cash flow, plus free renovations and security? My entire building completely finished and rented, without having to beg people to move in? The thought of it made my aspiring landlady's heart go pitter-pat. That would mean stability on a level I'd never dreamed.

Of course, the downside would be...a whole pack of werewolves. In my life. In my space.

A whole pack sworn to Diana, I reminded myself.

As wolves went—and I stole a quick glance over to where Booker had turned away, ostensibly studying the skyline—this one wasn't so bad. I had already decided to work with him, and by extension, his team. They would be protecting me and the Sanctum, not trying to take it over. It would be like having a team of guard dogs who wouldn't piddle on the rug or chew up my shoes. In theory.

I sighed, then turned to Booker. "If I say no to the lease, what happens to our agreement about the necromancer?"

Booker turned to me, his expression serious. "We'll still work together to find and stop that bastard, regardless of what you decided about the lease. We won't stop until you're safe." Then one corner of his mouth curled up. "I hope you'll give us a chance."

I nodded, then shifted my attention back to Stanley. I wished I could talk this over with him, but I'd already made up my mind, hadn't I, when I let myself consider all the benefits of this agreement. When I decided to trust Booker with my life despite my longstanding fear of wolves.

I hoped Heather's potion was working half as well for her as that one sip seemed to be working for me.

Well, if I was going to agree to this lease, I was still going to need to set parameters. I was sure Booker would install some airtight security measures, although he was going to get a fight from me if he tried to do anything to my apartment windows. However, I had to admit, when it came to real protection, nothing would beat having fighters living on-site. Which no doubt was at least part of Booker's game plan. He appeared to be taking his promise to help me very seriously.

If he would agree to sign a contract that could also work as a geas...and if every wolf who came into the Sanctum would sign a similar contract...yes, that could work. For all of us. Booker seemed to truly like the Sanctum, and that was something I hadn't anticipated, that the magical energy here might feel good to nonhuman supes, however many types there might be.

Yes, that could work.

I also wasn't above reinstating my anti-wolf charms if things went south. I had enough wolfsbane in stock to clean house ten times over, and it would be easy enough to include a nuclear-option clause into the contract.

I pulled out my phone and did some quick math on the calculator, taking what I had been thinking of charging John, then doubling it—John was getting the friend rate. Then I took that number and multiplied it by four to get a tentative amount per month per floor.

Once I had the number and rounded it up to the nearest hundred, I winced. To me, it seemed like a fortune. Surely he wouldn't want to pay that times three.

If he refuses, we can negotiate. I'll be open to that. Within reason.

I took a deep breath and put my phone back in my pocket, and then I walked over to Booker. *Hecate, be with me on this.* Booker turned to me, giving me his full attention—thankfully, I was starting to get used to his all-consuming stare.

"Okay. If we're going to do this, here's what I'll need." When I explained the contract and quoted him the price, Booker blinked. Then, he took two slow, easy steps toward me, and when I didn't move away, he traced his fingers down my cheek with the lightest of touches. Everything inside me went still, hyperaware of him, the warmth of those fingers, the slight roughness of the tips. This time I was the one curling my hands into fists at my sides. Something in me was trembling. But not, I realized, from fear.

Heat unspooled in my stomach when his fingertips dropped to trace the faint bruising on my neck. "You price yourself too low," he murmured, his gaze dropping to where he touched me, then looking back up, those amber eyes glowing into mine for a long, breathless moment.

Then Booker sighed and took a step back from me and shook himself, almost like a dog would after a bath. He began to pace again, but this was regular human pacing, not the frenetic agitation of earlier. "Anywhere else in this area, I would be paying double what you just quoted me," he said. "And that would be for places that aren't anywhere near this heavily protected." He stopped in front of me. "I'm going to give you the opportunity to change your price. To something more reasonable for you." Then he quoted a monthly rent that made my original one curl up with its tail between its legs.

I had a wild urge to shake myself in much the same way he had to force my brain to start working again. "That's too much."

Booker frowned, his jaw set. "Can you trust me on this one? I've got some experience with real estate in this city."

"Booker—" I began, and then stopped. "Booker. Like, Booker Brothers Security?"

He cocked his head at me, and I could swear that some of his tension began to ebb. "I wondered when you'd make that connection."

Still trying to wrap my brain around it, I regarded him thoughtfully. "I hadn't thought too much about it until now, but given that werewolves tend to have money—and it's not that common a name..." I blinked at him, trying to keep myself from looking gobsmacked. "So that's your family?"

Finally, the dimples made another appearance—and, ironically, they were a little sheepish. "Yes," he admitted. "I'm in charge of the St. Louis branch of Booker Brothers Security. For Booker Enterprises."

I shook my head. "Holy shit." When his grin deepened, I adopted what passed for a British accent and drawled, "The auld firm."

It wasn't an exaggeration. Booker Brothers had been founded even before the Pinkerton agency sometime in the early 1800s. I'd gone through a Wild West period in my youth after watching *Tombstone* and *Young Guns* too many times to count, and my grandpa had encouraged it. The Bookers were initially just guns for hire, bodyguards for the rich and famous, that kind of thing, but after the Civil War they became experts in security, investigations, and a whole host of other interests. They were all over the country, or at least, in most major cities.

Here was one of them, standing in front of me.

I could imagine Booker as a gunslinger all too easily. His big, lean body alert as he strode down a dusty street, gleaming eyes squinting and shaded beneath a wide-brimmed hat, broad chest covered by an embroidered waistcoat, two Colt revolvers on his hips...

Fucking hell, I'm 13 again.

Do not ask him to say he's my huckleberry.

Then I envisioned Booker saying it, but instead of Val Kilmer's smooth Southern tones, it was gruff and a little confused at why he wasn't just killing his opponent already. I couldn't help chuckling a little.

He opened his mouth like he was about to say something, then took a breath and closed it. There was the head tilt again, which seemed to be his I'm-trying-and-failing-to-figure-you-out stance. At least he was still smiling. "Do I even want to know?"

He was going to have to get used to this kind of thing if he was going to be living in my building. "I'm picturing you as a gunslinger," I said, making finger guns and pulling them out of imaginary holsters. "I read about Booker Brothers and their hired guns when I was into Wild West stuff."

He laughed hard at that one, some pink mantling his cheekbones. "Remind me to tell you some family stories," he said when he could draw enough breath, still grinning. "I'd be happy to show you the offices sometime. The St. Louis one isn't our oldest, but it dates back to the Civil War."

That did sound amazing, but we had more pressing matters. "Maybe after we find and stop this necromancer," I said, hating the way it drained all the energy out of me to remember it. We'd been having fun for a second there.

Booker's smile faded. "Right." He nodded. "So, back to business. I own a few buildings here and there, beyond the family holdings. I want to pay you a fair price—and considering the amount of power and magical protection this place provides, you deserve it."

He made a good point—and it didn't hurt to know that he was loaded, even above and beyond what I considered normal for werewolves. "Okay, then. I'll accept your revised quote," I said, albeit still reluctantly. "You don't have to do a five-year lease. If you want, we could just do a one-year agreement and then see how it goes."

"Thank you," he said, his voice grave. "But I'm not going to give you the chance to get rid of us that easily."

My face scrunched up at that. I wasn't trying to shoo him or his money away just yet. However. "We'll see how you feel about living with a witch in the building and another down the street," I said, unable to keep a hint of challenge from the words. "We may not be your cup of tea."

Booker shrugged. "We're used to witches," he said, and I know my eyes betrayed my surprise. "Diana's Wolves have several on the payroll. None of them like to work together, so things can get tricky. There's one who's a healer—she's probably the best we have." He gave me an innocent look. "Although she's nowhere near your caliber."

"Thank you so much," I said, dry as dust. I really did have a lot to learn about the supernatural world. "Do you do magical security then, in addition to all the other stuff?"

Booker cast his eyes briefly upward. "*All the other stuff* just happens to be the best physical security in North America," he said with pointed emphasis. "But yes. We just don't advertise the magical element."

I thought about this. "I want to be kept in the loop on all the magical security, just to make sure it's compatible with mine." *Also, I want to see if you and your payroll witches know some tricks that I don't.*

"Absolutely." There was no hesitation, which was reassuring. "I won't add anything to the building—physical or magical—without your knowledge and consent."

I was falling back into those eyes again, that steady, warm amber gaze. "It's appreciated," I managed to say.

"Excellent. Just for clarity, I want to rent the four apartments and the three empty floors," he said.

"I'll need at least one of those apartments for John," I interjected, and at Booker's disgruntled expression, I gave him a quelling look. "I can give him the one on the second floor. That would probably work best for him." That reminded me of something else. "By the way, I know that not having an elevator isn't overly attractive to renters, but I don't want to have one installed unless I have to." I didn't want my building to be inaccessible to people with disabilities, but I couldn't bring myself to make it easier for other people to get to me—or at least, I hadn't before.

"No problem," Booker said easily. "I've yet to meet a wolf who doesn't love stairs." He raised an eyebrow. "Again, just for clarity, will you be good with making sure the Sanctum is open to the wolves who work for me?"

I'd been thinking about that. "Are all the wolves who work for you Diana's Wolves?" At his nod, I said a silent prayer of thanks. Trusting Booker also meant trusting his pack—which would be easier if they were all sworn to a goddess I respected, even if She wasn't mine. "Then yes. I can do that." I paused, then added, "I know you couldn't feel it before I lifted the wards, but I've really tried to make this neutral ground, more than anything."

Booker seemed to relax a bit—I didn't realize he'd still been holding on to that much tension. Did the guy ever totally relax? "So we have a deal?" That gaze was direct and searching again.

I took a deep breath and nodded. "We do," I said. "Welcome to the neighborhood. Pending successful contract negotiations." I extended a hand.

Booker looked down at my hand, and then he gently closed his own around it. His was warm and strong, a little rough, and there was a tingle at the point of contact that I could feel in my knees. *Wow.* Best to just try to ignore that though.

I gave his hand a firm and brief shake. "A gentleman's agreement," I said, then couldn't resist adding, "between a witch and a werewolf."

Booker released my hand, grinning. "There have been stranger bedfellows."

Do not think about beds.

I went over to Stanley. "We're probably going to have some new tenants," I said. "Don't worry. They're friends." Then I turned to Booker. "We'll need to talk about the lease, the contract paperwork, some other details. Remember, if anything feels hinky, I reserve the right to cancel all this."

"Of course," he said, spreading his hands. "When can we get started?"

"No time like the present." I headed toward the door. "Let's go down to my office."

Before I could get past him to the roof-access door, Booker held out a hand to me. "I think I'm ready to take the shortcut back down," he said.

I gave him an approving smile. "Look at us, trusting each other." I stepped over to the mirror, and when Booker joined me, I took his hand in mine. Again, that delicious frisson of contact, and again, I was close enough to him to feel the warmth of his body. I breathed in the cedar and sandalwood smell of him. "Just walk in right behind me, and don't let go," I instructed, and then I brought him into the mirror, envisioning the shop as I walked through.

When we emerged, I immediately turned to examine his reaction, make sure he was okay. Mirror-walking had become so second nature to me now that it was like walking through any open doorway, and Kate had come through with me before, although it wasn't her favorite thing—it gave her vertigo. I'd brought Cole through with me plenty of times with no discernible effect, but I had no idea how a wolf would react.

As it turned out, I needn't have worried. When I made eye contact with him, Booker's expression melted from momentary shock into such a blazingly happy smile that was so genuine and unfettered, I wondered what exactly I'd gotten myself into. He looked like a kid who'd just gotten to ride on the biggest roller coaster at the park for the first time.

Those amber eyes wide and a little giddy, he shook his head with a low, delighted laugh. "Josephine Murphy," he drawled, "you definitely price yourself too low."

CHAPTER 12

LET'S MAKE A MAGICAL DEAL

JO

BOOKER AND I CAME UP WITH SOME GENERAL NOTES ABOUT everything immediately after his mirror trip, but he got a call and had to leave. Which was for the best. I needed to be alone in the Sanctum and collect myself—and think about this deal.

Was this what I should be doing?

Since I was worth fuck-all at reading tarot for my own future, I went to Kate—rather grateful that I was going to her place, not bringing her to mine, so she wouldn't freak out over the differences in my warding.

As it turned out, the mere story of Booker the Wolf's plans for my Sanctum was enough to do that. Her exact words were, "This is batshit crazy."

When I laughed, she gave me a penetrating look—and when Kate decides to do that, you feel it in your spine. "Funny? You think it's funny that someone who was on the run from werewolves for years is suddenly opening her magical fortress and letting them in?" She took me by the arms, the rings on her fingers cool on my skin, and gave me a little shake, then peered into my eyes. "Did he do something to you?" Her wintry eyes went unfocused, and she hummed a little—part of her scrying process. She was

apparently using my eyes as a reflecting surface, which was impressive. I'd
never heard of anyone doing that before.

I let it happen. Hell, given my relative lack of fear when it came to
Booker, it was probably a good idea to have Kate poke around my
metaphysical person and make sure everything was aboveboard.

After a stretch of quiet as the soft prickles of Kate's magic filled the air
around us, her unfocused eyes flashed white for a split second before they
returned to pale gray. They weren't narrow anymore.

"Well?" I spread my arms wide. "What's the rumpus, grumpus?"

Kate's mouth was firm but not flat. "Nothing. And..." She paused,
clicked her tongue. "Nothing. Sit." She gestured toward the bed. "I'm going
to read for you, see if that helps me understand."

"And me," I pointed out. "More than one witch here."

She waved her hand, impatient now, and grabbed the nearest tarot deck.
Her entire house was littered with them, different types scattered on various
surfaces. When I first met Kate, she had one tarot deck. Since she started
reading professionally, like me, she'd had hundreds. Most people can have a
deck for life because they use it once a day or once a week, or for those really
not into doing readings, maybe once a year. However, when you were
constantly shuffling and handling them, only the very best decks could last
for years on end. Human hands were hell on tarot decks. Since many
companies had switched to crappy card stock for a lot of decks, many didn't
even last that long. I'd had customer complaints already with certain decks,
so I refused to stock them anymore.

The deck Kate grabbed was one of the ones I'd stopped stocking, the
Sun and Moon deck. The cards were gorgeous, and the artwork would make
even those lacking psychic skills have an evocative reaction. The first few
decks had a nice protective coating, like any deck of cards should, but
subsequent reprints hadn't bothered with this. I'd used the first decks until
they were faded and falling apart, but when I replaced the deck, I found it
could barely be shuffled without the cards splitting. The Sun and Moon
tarot artwork was probably my favorite of all time, but there was no way to
use the cards practically. I'd missed it.

The deck Kate pulled out was one of the older versions with the more
durable cards. She barely shuffled the deck and all but threw the cards out. If
there was a pattern or a method to her card placement, I couldn't follow it.

With tarot, the card placement is important, so without knowing what spread she was using, I could only look at the story unfolding before me.

Ace of Wands, 3 of Wands, 5 of Wands, 6 of Wands, 4 of Wands, the High Priestess, Justice.

"Holy shit, that's a lot of fire," I said.

"You're the torchbearer, fire-bringer," Kate said, her eyes and voice unfocused and far away. *"You bring justice and victory. What you build isn't for you, Jo, the single entity, but you, Jo, the plural. Diana the virgin brings the unborn into the world. You started it, but we will finish it. Booker is essential. Kate is not. Yet."*

The last sentence had a deeper voice and an echoing quality that sounded more like a comment than a prophecy, and for a moment, Kate's eyes were unearthly. I couldn't tear my gaze away even after the echo faded, and then, in one second, she was Kate again—and her expression was comically stunned.

I couldn't stop myself—I laughed. I'd never seen someone look so exasperated, annoyed, and relieved all at the same time.

We both sat on the bed, looking at the rumpled cards on the rumpled quilt. "Yeah," Kate said, sounding resigned. "I'm getting the distinct impression that Our Lady of the Crossroads wants me to butt out. So to speak."

I choked back an incredulous laugh. "You're kidding." Only a goddess could tell Kate with impunity to mind her own business. Kate Strega believed the world needed saving and that she was the one to save it. "You mean, you aren't essential somehow? *Yet?*" That wasn't super fucking ominous or anything.

Kate sighed. "Nope." She looked down at the cards again. "I thought I felt something when I scried, and this just confirms it. For whatever reason, She's...okay, I guess?...with this insanity."

I thought about it. About the new danger, about the wolves seeming to arrive just in the nick of time. "It makes a certain amount of sense," I offered.

"Oh, fuck off. It doesn't." Kate stood, crossing her tattooed arms over her chest and tapping one toe.

"Look at the cards, Kate. Look." I tapped the first and then second cards. "Clearly, I built the Sanctum—the ace and the three. While I'm not sure of your positioning here, the High Priestess could even be part of that. I stand between the worlds more often than most. Also, I was led here in a way, just as you were. I mean, come on. No way it was coincidence, me finding the Sanctum less than a block away from you on a fucking *triple crossroads,* for Goddess's sake. Hecate's Home is also on one too, you know —" Kate gave me a narrow-eyed look. "—and *yes,* you do know. Just go with me here."

I took a breath, then pointed to another card. "5 of Wands is clearly the attacks on me. Here's the 4 of Wands, and I feel like that's Booker working with me to make the Sanctum better. Hell, he's going to be literally making it better by taking the rest of the remodeling off of my hands and paying me to boot."

Kate looked down at the cards, her mouth a moue of irritation. "Well, if Hecate spoke through me—" She paused and shouted at the ceiling. "—*without even asking, which is rude,* to tell me to butt out, I should butt out. That said, the cards make it seem as if Booker is important to this endeavor and that you'll enjoy working with him too. It's like being told the moon no longer exists." She blew out an irritable breath. "You should try to communicate with Her."

Yeah. The last time I communicated with Hecate, the Fenris disappeared and I woke up covered in scars with a bag of cash and a whole boatload of PTSD. "Nope." I gathered up the cards. "I don't do the burning bush stuff." At Kate's exasperated look, I shrugged. "If She needs to tell me something, She will. One way or another."

Since nothing Kate could say would refute that fact, she let it go. Instead, she gave me a hard hug and another awful-tasting potion as a parting gift.

I busied myself for the next two days writing up the contract, agonizing over the wording, and consulting with a lawyer Kate recommended—an older Black woman with a squat body, an iron-gray helmet of hair, and a perpetual grimace. I liked her immediately.

I also spent those days texting Booker about progress. I hadn't planned on it, but it was either that or answer the phone when he called. We hashed out plans for the geas as a contract that worked both on a legal and a magical level when it was signed.

Once the contract geas was in shape, I texted Booker to come to the shop the next morning.

Kate had insisted that she meet Booker before we signed the paperwork, and that was the kind of main event that I might have been able to sell tickets for in the right circles. *Place your bets—who's going to look away first, the suspicious Stevie Nicks-gone-steampunk witch or the charming urban cowboy Big Bad Wolf?*

As it turns out, I needn't have wondered. Once Booker and Kate stood face to face, it was clear that Kate wasn't intimidated. "Hello," Kate trilled, her entire being alive with malicious energy. "It's you again."

Booker held her gaze just for a moment, as if to make clear that he knew what all this was, and then held out a hand, lowering his gaze to his own palm. "We weren't properly introduced last time."

I waited, wondering if she was going to give him the cut direct—unable to blame her if she did—but she flicked her eyes to me, then him, and finally took his hand, giving it a brief, brisk shake. "Kate Strega," she said, her mouth relaxing a little.

"Booker." He raised his eyes to meet hers with a faint smile.

"If *anything* happens to Jo or John, or my kids, or anyone else in this whole neighborhood once you and your pack are living here, you're going to wish I'd gone ahead and introduced you to the catfish." Kate's pale eyes gleamed.

Booker swallowed and nodded once. "Understood."

"You're lucky Jo is allowing you to be here."

Now he looked at me, the intensity of his gaze taking my breath. "I know that."

Kate huffed out a long breath, then turned to me, long skirt swirling around her legs. "Okay. I'm going now. Just...be smart."

It was an echo of what we'd always said to each other when we were on our different roads for all those years: *Be smart. Be safe. See you around the next bend.*

After she left, I cocked my head at Booker. "Gotta love those channel cats."

He grimaced. "Apparently, they're big enough to eat anything."

The first thing we had to talk about was the price for the rental, which stayed fairly close to the one we'd come to on the roof. Then he outlined his renovations for the building, and I was both pleased and a little amused to see that he'd had detailed plans drawn up for each floor. Apparently, being a Booker meant quick access to pretty much any service a person might need.

I made some adjustments to his plans, absorbed his minor consternation, then pointed out that there was one large room with no windows. It seemed like an oversight, but I should have known better. "A gathering room," he explained. "Well-ventilated, with comfy, easily movable furniture." He paused, then smiled at me. "A projector and screen for movies."

It was nearly impossible not to smile back at that. So wolves liked to watch movies—who knew?

Once we ironed out the renovations—and he gently but firmly denied my offer of paying a percentage for the cost—it was my turn to tell him about my plans for the geas. "There are two basic kinds of geas," I said, pulling out both versions of the contract I'd drawn up and laying them on the desk between us. "One is kind of a binding agreement where you simply cannot break it. Should you want to, you couldn't. The other is more vengeance-based—that's something like the one I did on Scumbag Tony. The kind that if you break it, some curse will befall you. That curse can be specific or vague."

I paused, then added, "I'm open to talking about either version. However, if you're looking for a long-term commitment on something, the second always seemed more like shutting the barn door after the horse was running free. I prefer the first." I tapped that version of the contract.

Booker's stillness was complete—not even a muscle twitched as he studied me, long enough that I had to look at anything else. His voice was deep and dispassionate when he finally spoke. "Could you amend the contract geas after it was signed? Change some element in order to curse the signer after the fact?"

I gritted my teeth, trying not to glare when I met his eyes again. "Not for the first type of geas, which is what we're talking about. I wouldn't do that to you."

"But you could?"

I was supposed to be the one with trust issues. "Theoretically, maybe—if the language of the contract geas didn't prohibit changes by either party without the presence of both." I folded my arms. "Of course, that's where reading the fine print comes into play."

"So we'll work out the fine print." Booker finally moved, leaning back in his chair and folding his arms. I tried not to gape at his muscled forearms, exposed by the rolled-up sleeves of his plaid shirt. He'd dressed for work today. "Would you be amenable to copies being made of our original agreement and being held by Booker Enterprises under another witch's magic?"

"Yes," I said flatly, daring him to come up with some new objection.

His gaze was level and calm, steady on mine. "I should think that you of all people would understand taking precautions."

"I do understand." It came out a little petulant, and I swallowed the unexpected, very inconvenient lump in my throat. I'd thought I was the one with the trust issues here. "I'm just...I don't know. I guess I just assumed that you'd trust me."

"I'm a businessman. I have to be able to explain this to the pack knowing all the angles, anticipating their questions." He unfolded his arms and leaned across the desk toward me, not breaking eye contact. "*My* trust —*my* instincts—alone aren't going to cut it for some of them, and that's reasonable."

I could smell him now, feel his warmth again, and I began to relax, unfolding my arms, leaning toward him in return. Booker's power aura was intense—and soothing, now that we were allies. I wondered what it felt like to people he didn't like. "So, your instincts say I'm trustworthy."

"I wouldn't be here if they didn't."

When was the last time he blinked? I dropped my eyes to the paper in front of me, where I had been making notes.

"Fine, so we'll make sure the contract can't be amended without some kind of proof of both parties present—thumbprint maybe? I'll check into it." I took a deep breath and let it out. "Now, for the focus of the geas. I was thinking an across the board 'peace' agreement. Being in the building means being peaceful—and that should help forestall any violence or wolf-outs on the premises." I paused and finally looked up at him again. "Unless that's going to cause problems for your wolves."

"In general, no. When the moon is full, we will change, but I have a plan for that." He nodded and cocked his head at me. "We'll talk about it when the time comes."

"That means," I thought for a second, "a little over two weeks?"

"Two weeks, three days, and seven hours—give or take a few minutes." He grinned, letting the dimples out to play. "We always know."

The next hiccup was over the warding. Booker wanted to ward against practically everything that wasn't werewolf or living human. But now that I knew there was a whole galaxy of creatures out there, and that so many of them seemed to be just living their lives like anyone else, I was reluctant to shut them all out.

"I'm running a business here, and I am—or was—building a community," I argued. "I want this to be a place where people, whatever that means, can come together, talk, and hang out. I don't want this to be the Werewolf Place."

"It's the Sanctum. It's your place."

"But your pack is going to affect the feel of it, in major ways." I raked my hand through my hair and tugged on it for something like the twentieth time. "I have to make sure that once this whole necromancer thing is over, I can get back to building a community. I want witches and peaceful supes to be able to come here and find what they need, as well as humans." It felt weird saying "supes"—it was hard not to picture the row of Campbell's products at the grocery store—but Booker had used that term casually with me before, and it was less of a mouthful than "supernatural creatures."

Booker grunted.

I pictured Emma's smiling face in my mind, helping a curly-haired high school senior find the right crystals to balance anxiety and success. "That's the way I always meant it to be."

Booker's amber eyes were on my desk for a moment, then they raised to mine. "Remember when you said you wanted a manual?"

The thrill that went through my body at those words was laughable.

Hey, some women love diamonds, some flowers. I love knowledge. I truly do live to learn. "Yes," I said, trying not to sound too pathetically eager.

"I can get you a list of known supes in the area."

"A list? Or a manual?"

He shook his head, raising his eyebrows for emphasis. "There isn't a manual." My disappointment was visible. I know, because Booker laughed. "But there is information. I can see what I can do to get something compiled for you. Or find some books. That'll help you research the wards you need, add some magical ammo."

I bit my lower lip and sighed in mock-ecstasy. "You know what girls like."

He grinned, his eyes darkening just a little as they flicked down to my mouth. "Yeah, right." Then his expression turned serious, eyebrows lowering. "Once you get those wards lined out and we can get started in here, we're going to find that bastard necromancer and get that abomination out of our city."

Our city. Hecate help me, but I liked the sound of that.

CHAPTER 13

WOLFAGEDDON

JO

OVER THE NEXT WEEK, WOLVES SEEMED TO BE EVERYWHERE IN the Sanctum. Especially Booker. He was always coming to me with measurements, confirming new building plans, setting up the signing of contracts. He was also bringing me fancy hot chocolate. Chatting about the weather or a new movie he'd seen. Offering to help me with this or that. Getting me to talk about my favorite books. Talking over his goals for the day. Asking me questions about my preferences in the apartments. Bringing me paint color samples for perusal.

"I don't really care," I told him apologetically one day as he brandished five shades of blue at me. "That top one is pretty, but they're all pretty."

He gazed down at them again. With his brows lowered and lips pursed in consternation, he looked like a more dangerous Property Brother. "It's your building. You told me how much you liked working on the shop and your apartment."

I rolled my eyes. "Well, it was fun when it was my stuff." At his disgruntled look, I couldn't help but chuckle. "The whole point of this is that I don't have to look at paint colors and pick out flooring and all that.

It's your problem now." In my head, for better or for worse, I had begun thinking of them as his apartments. "I'm sure I'll like what you pick."

"Fine," he groused, slipping the paint samples into his back pocket. Then he put both palms on the counter and leaned in just a bit. "But I'm still going to show you my final pick for each one. I don't want any surprises when I walk you through the rooms."

It was impossible not to smile at the earnestness in his amber eyes. Or the lock of brown hair that had fallen over his forehead. Or the tanned, corded forearms that were directly below my line of vision, exposed by the rolled-up sleeves of his red plaid work shirt. I waved him away, making a show of turning to my work computer. "Fine," I said.

It only took a few days for me to begin expecting to see Booker around. Not exactly looking forward to it. But not *not* looking forward to it.

Maybe looking forward to it a little bit.

The parts of that week that stayed crystal clear were the unpleasant parts —the first and worst being talking to the cops about Emma. As Booker had suggested, I explained that I'd closed the shop because of renovations, that I hadn't seen her since she left work that night. On a burst of grim inspiration, I suggested that they speak to someone at Purgatory.

That made me wonder if Purgatory had something to do with what happened to her, so I began monitoring their website. They had no official social media. Odd.

I also spent time searching for the rune on the necklace Zombie Emma had been wearing. The one I had burned. I had dozens of books on runes, but this one wasn't in any of them—and believe me, I checked. Preliminary checks online turned up squat. Kate had reached out to some contacts in Italy for help, but so far, nothing.

On that, I was stuck.

I managed to make the most of the week otherwise and stayed as productive as possible. In addition to cleaning and doing the million little things I'd been meaning to do around the shop and my apartment, I did phone tarot readings for a few of my regular clients, updated my online shop, and filled online orders. When the noise from upstairs became too loud or too much, I put on noise-cancelling headphones.

In order to capitalize on the free time and get ahead, I set up some social media updates about the renovations and scheduling more for the next month—just a few a week. This inevitably meant I would make another trip to Emma's profiles, looking at the messages there. She was gone, and people knew it. I couldn't bring myself to post anything on her profiles—it was one thing to tell the cops a half-truth and another to post a blatant lie of "where are you" online.

Any time I thought about Emma, I also thought about the necromancer who had killed her. Who had done worse than kill her.

So, I also spent some time researching zombies, mind control, and necromancy. Because necromancy was a form of witchcraft, Kate and I pooled the knowledge we already had and began compiling more. I had a notebook that was getting filled up. Booker approved of the research and added what little he knew, but he wanted me to wait before we made any direct moves forward on the investigation.

I got it. Once the apartments were livable, he'd have his pack with him. Hell, *he'd* be living here—he'd shown me the apartment he was working on for himself and a few of his right-hand wolves, and I couldn't help but notice that it was the closest to being complete. Once that was done, we could start the hunt in earnest.

Speaking of the "supernatural community," while I was adjusting to the wolves in my henhouse, I'd also been trying to figure out the way these zombies worked.

Knowing that tearing off the rune necklace stopped them was an important detail, but I didn't really want to get that close to them again. I wasn't a weakling, but I was still human—and the power surge that had helped me burn the rune was something I'd yet to fully explore. Fighting something as supernaturally strong as these creatures was best done at a distance.

Preferably, not at all. In many ways, I was content to more or less stay put in the Sanctum. Even though that meant growing accustomed to sharing space with werewolves.

Sharing space was kind of an understatement. I was never really alone. Even at night, at least one or two of the wolves were sleeping on cots somewhere in the building—I could feel them. I think it was meant to be comforting. I did notice that the wolves were extremely careful to stay within my line of sight. No one came up behind me even once. On the first day of Wolfageddon, I had been coming out of the back room when I realized I'd forgotten to put on the music. I spun around to go back in and change it, and this one wolf—Darius, I think—practically fell over himself making sure he wasn't at my back. I pretended not to notice, but made sure that I was a bit slower in my movements after that.

What kind of orders did Booker give them? Don't spook the witch?

Booker must have staggered arrival times too, because there were never more than two at a time coming in or going out of any of the common areas.

When I'd met each wolf to get their signatures on our officially approved geas, they'd all been respectful, polite. Curious. Weirdly, they all seemed to get a little high off of signing the geas—all of them had grinned like goofballs once the spell took hold but one, Ethan, who seemed a natural stoic, and even he had cracked a half-smile. There had been no complaints, that was for sure. In my experience, wolves were happiest when they were indulging their inner beast, as it were. A happy werewolf carrying lumber upstairs felt like a very weird thing, but most of the wolves around me seemed pretty happy.

Maybe if wolves were happy, they didn't need to kill people for fun?

I made a mental note to ask Booker about that if he ever stopped moving for five minutes at a stretch.

Before too long, I was on a first-name basis with Nick, Max, and Ethan, Booker's main security team who were also helping with renovations. I also got to know four other wolves who were there specifically for renovation work, Darius, Shannon, Anthony, and Opal. All four of them were so eager to be useful that despite them being men and women mostly in their twenties, I couldn't help but think of them as Booker's puppies. All four of them were part of a construction crew I'd seen plastered on billboards during my infrequent trips to other parts of the city.

Yes, it was beginning to dawn on me just how ingrained the supernatural community was in what I had previously considered the "real" world.

Meanwhile, Booker brought in two other wolves to work on the security system. I'd told Booker to hold off on the magical protections until I knew what all of them were and could compare it to what I had already done.

As he'd done with the apartment renovations, Booker made sure I knew everything I wanted about the system—and it did feel very straightforward. It was up within a few days, and we'd be working on the magical element the following week, when one of the pack's witches could do her part.

I guess I was also becoming a pack witch. For better or for worse.

The day before I reopened the shop, I called John, my part-time worker and now my only other real friend aside from Kate. He was relieved to hear from me, and again I felt like shit—I'd been keeping him at bay with texts about the progress and telling him I'd have him back in when I could. Kate and I had protected him and his building with temporary shields, but I was uneasy about having him back if that meant putting him in danger.

Kate reasoned that if he was still planning to move into the Sanctum, it would be the safest place for him. Booker had agreed that John could live there, and since the geas meant no turning into wolves—or violence—John wouldn't be any the wiser about his neighbors and my new tenants. Theoretically.

After filling him in on the renovations and the new leases, I asked him if he could come in to work for our grand reopening the next day. There was every chance we'd have an onslaught of customers, and I had to face him at some point.

"Sure," John said. "Have you heard anything about Emma?"

"No," I said, hating myself. "Still no news."

John came in the next morning at 7:30 a.m., and we got lost in the morning minutiae. I'd forgotten how calming John could be. Just working with another human was nice. As much as I'd grown to accept the wolves and get used to their odd quirks of habit and manner, it was nice being around someone who blinked at regular intervals.

John was almost Emma's opposite: quietly good-looking, with blond hair and blue eyes. Like me, he favored jeans and T-shirts, although his were far more fitted and tidier, and since he was on the lean side and neither short nor tall, he tended to blend in to any crowd unless you were looking for him.

However, John also had a sense of humor and was keenly intelligent. He seemed to be interested in everything around him, and I often thought he was the type of person who could go to school forever and be completely happy. He was in the process of getting his second degree, although his work as a live-in caretaker and his job at my shop meant he generally took only a few classes at a time. "I'm not in a hurry," he always said, smiling. "I've got time."

I'd been right about the customers, so the steady flow of people in and out kept us busy until nearly 10:30. Usually, the busiest part of our day seemed to be right before school let out, so I figured we'd get another influx around 1:30 or 2.

"We're out of the red candles again," John said, coming up to the counter where I was logging purchases.

"There's more in the back," I said. "Grab some of the lavender and sage incense." I'd also forgotten how odd the shop smelled after so many people came and went.

He did as I asked, and after we lit the incense, John raised his eyebrows at me. "So, how are you? What's going on with the new tenant?"

"You want whole truth or half-truth?" I asked him. This was a game he and I played one day when getting to know one another. The half-truth was the nice way to sum up a situation, and the whole truth was often long and involved. After a while, the phrase came to be shorthand for any sort of bad situation, bad customer, bad day, bad whatever—even though I knew this time I was going to have to play a little fast and loose when it came to the "truth" element.

He frowned a little, but then said, "Half," to my great relief.

"I'm not great, but I'm dealing." I shrugged, then shook my head and added, "It just sucks, that's all." My eyes got a little damp, but I blinked it all back. If I started crying in front of John, I might never stop.

"I know. I'm sorry, Jo." John's mouth twisted. "I keep hoping she'll just waltz in here one day with some story about how she met some guy and took off to San Francisco to see a metal band or something, you know?"

I laughed, but it was raspy. "Yeah." Then I cleared my throat. "So, the renovations. Those are happening because I have a new tenant who's very motivated to get everything up and running."

I filled him in a bit on Booker and his plan for the three floors he'd rented, and John recognized the name immediately, although his expression morphed into one of frustration. "Damn," he said, and when I blinked, he shook his head. "Don't get me wrong—I mean, that's awesome for you, but I was really hoping you'd have a spot for me here."

"John, don't worry—I kept you in mind." I gave him a reassuring smile.

"You'll have one of the second-story apartments. Booker's going to make sure it's ready for you once he's got things under control."

John's expression eased a bit, but not entirely. "Would it be possible to move that date up?" I opened my mouth to ask why, but John kept going, sadness creasing his brow. "Margie passed at 2 a.m., and her son told me I shouldn't come back, so all my stuff in is my car right now. I was hoping I could rent one of your places."

I knew that Margie meant a lot to John, and I hated that I didn't have a finished apartment for him. On top of that, I knew what it was like to have nowhere to go except your car. I thought fast. "Wait. You know the reading rooms upstairs? You could stay in one of those for now." He perked up, but I held up a hand. "They're not really ready yet, so you'd be roughing it a little for now. The plumbing works and the wiring works, at least. If you don't mind living in a construction zone, we could fix it up during your school hours. Lord knows it's going to be noisy here anyway."

"That would be amazing." It was good to see the tension ease and the stress lift from his body. "I don't have a ton of money right now but—"

I waved him into silence. "I can do a work for rent thing for now, if you like. I don't know how many of your hours were taking care of Margie versus how many are at school, but now that Emma…" I paused, not wanting to finish that sentence. "Well, right now, it would be great to have you here more during the week. I'm going to have to be out of the shop a certain amount pretty soon, I think."

Considering I was going to have to begin hunting for a necromancer pretty soon, having an already-trained worker to pick up a chunk of my usual hours would be a benefit.

"Sure," John said, surprise lighting his face. "I'm only taking a couple of night classes this semester anyway, so that will work out pretty well."

Oh, thank you, Hecate. One potential problem solved, at least. Well, two if you count John's. "Thank you," I said, giving his shoulder a bump with my fist. "It'll be really good to have you here."

John grinned, but then his face turned serious. "Thank *you*, Jo. I've always loved being here. This place—it's special."

You don't know the half of it, my dude.

CHAPTER 14

THE COMPANY OF WOLVES

BOOKER

BY A WEEK AFTER THE ZOMBIE ATTACK ON JO, EVERYTHING AT the Sanctum was going so well that Booker was beginning to wonder when the other shoe was going to drop.

He hoped like hell that it didn't drop when he brought Grace to stay there.

The geas signing had worked exactly as he and Jo planned. She'd drawn up the contract with a close eye to detail—according to the pack's lawyer up in Montana, it was damn near perfect, although she had frowned over the "will not assume wolf form in the building" clause.

"That's an infringement of rights," she insisted over the phone. "As a natural-born shifter, you have the right to insist on that being part of the contract."

"No." Booker had shaken his head, although the lawyer couldn't see it. "We won't need to shift in the building—that's part of the point."

The lawyer had relented, but she was still skeptical. Booker wondered exactly how much time she'd spent in cities, working around humans, in her life. Being a werewolf in remote areas, and even in smaller cities like Billings, wasn't quite the same kettle of fish as living in the Midwest. Up north, the clans had access to plenty of land to run and hunt during the full moons and various annual gatherings, and one of Booker's first tasks as alpha of the St. Louis pack was to secure more wooded acreage within easy driving distance of the city to accommodate runs for the increase in the werewolf population.

Being a werewolf in the modern human world meant being on edge most of the time. Some had to actively fight the urge to change under any duress—especially wolves who had sensitivity or behavioral issues, not to mention PTSD. The more anger and frustration built up, the more the wolf demanded to take over and deal with those human emotions by making them a non-issue—not just during pack runs and hunts, but all the time.

It was one thing to love being a wolf. Booker absolutely did, and he cherished his monthly opportunities to let the wolf take over and be free. However, he knew he could do far more good for his pack in his human form, and since he dealt so much with other supernatural beings and humans, he'd become adjusted to spending eighty percent of his life in human form.

Just because he looked human, though, didn't mean that his wolf just went to sleep during that time. The wolf was always there, mentally perched on his shoulders, sharing his thoughts. The longer he went without a change, the harder it could be to keep the wolf from emerging without warning or taking over his reactions. That kind of burden wasn't exactly a relaxing way to spend your waking hours.

However, being in the Sanctum was the most calming experience of his adult life. He'd felt it when he'd gone there that first day and spent time with Jo, and it hadn't taken him long to realize that her place was special. The whole neighborhood held power, of course, but once she'd taken down the werewolf wards, he could feel that calming energy as soon as he'd walked into the shop door.

Once he'd signed the contract geas, that sense of peace was elevated to another level. It was like the wolf climbed off his shoulders and sat beside him—still part of him, but not on top of him, not bracing itself to spring to the fore at any moment. Instead, its tongue was lolling out and its eyes were half-closed. *Happy wolf, happy Booker.* He couldn't remember the two parts of him being so in sync or so relaxed since he was a kid.

He remembered the look on Jo's face, curious and amused. "Are you okay?"

He'd shaken his head. Stopped himself from laughing out loud, and instead gave her the grin he knew she liked. "Yeah," he said. "I'm good."

He'd acclimated to the feeling within a day or two, but it still spread over him like a welcoming shower every time he stepped into the Sanctum. From the reactions of Nick, Max, and the pack members on his renovations crew, it wasn't just him. The buzz was beginning to spread through the pack, despite his best efforts to get them to keep it at least somewhat on the down low.

The building itself was everything he'd hoped it would be. Just looking at the space, going over it with his architect, he'd known exactly how to partition it out and how to utilize it to fit about a dozen of his immediate needs for the pack. Some of them could live there permanently, while others could stay on an as-needed basis—and he'd already bought another building nearby with plans to create another Sanctum-like apartment building. He hoped. If everything went well with Jo.

Booker hadn't been able to keep himself from pouncing on the chance to rent out most of the building, once he'd seen and felt its power, once Jo had asked him for help and he'd felt that bond with her. He supposed he should feel somewhat guilty about taking advantage of the situation, offering Jo such an extravagant lease to make it so she couldn't say no.

However, she needed his help, in more ways than one. Her building, with all its potential, was crying out for attention.

Just in the half-remodeled apartments alone there were dozens of swatches of paint colors everywhere. It was clear she had no idea what to do with the rest of the place, as there were chaotic piles of tools, home-improvement books, and other reference materials all over the place. A few rooms had paint streaked on the walls but not much else, as if she had tried to decide on color and then gave up altogether. He'd chuckled when he saw that, and he hadn't been able to resist teasing her by showing her paint samples on the pretense of getting her to help him choose.

He was having fun here, even as he scrambled to get the building ready for his pack. Even as he knew that the larger problem—the necromancer who was still out there, likely regrouping and planning another attempt on Jo's life—still loomed beyond these walls.

Concentrating his energies on the building was a good distraction. Because any time he let himself think too much about the necromancer who'd tried to kill Jo, it made the wolf and the man snarl, even inside the peace of the Sanctum. The problem was that they had very few leads outside of Purgatory, the club a few blocks away. He had two wolves watching the place at all times, following anyone who felt like a threat, but until Jo found something more to go on, he wasn't ready to make a move. She was safe, for now, and doing research on the rune from the necklace. He was busy, for now, because getting the pack settled and ensuring Grace's health and the well-being of her and her unborn babies had to be his first priority.

Then, he'd promised his wolf, they would find and kill that fucker.

Because they were both rapidly beginning to think of Jo as theirs.

Booker knew how important it was to keep Jo alive. To help her. Diana's magic worked in strange ways, and once one of Her wolves agreed to help someone, providing that help became a compulsion. Thankfully, it was such a part of them that he'd never yet heard of any pack members being forced against their will. It had to be a true need, and it had to have importance. The more important the call, the more strongly they reacted to it.

When Jo asked him for help, the tattoo Diana had branded into his skin Herself had flared hot. He'd heard the goddess in his head: *Help her, or she will die.* He knew then that somehow Jo was important.

He just hadn't known how important she was, or how much he would feel driven, on a deeply personal level, to help her. Protect her. He wondered if his ever-increasing need to be around her was part of that compulsion to protect, or if it was just part of his rapidly escalating attraction to her, but the pragmatist in him didn't care much. It was all for Jo, regardless.

Still, he wasn't ready to tell her about that just yet, not when she was just getting used to him and his pack being around her all the time.

The building and everything it offered felt almost like a reward for giving her the help she requested. Even with him inflating the price she'd offered initially and taking on all the expenses of the renovations, the price wasn't so far from what he'd pay elsewhere, and this area was already beginning to boom. In a few years, it would be completely unrecognizable. Jo and Kate had started a magical process that was already transforming the neighborhood. He could feel it and purchased property accordingly—he understood the city the way his father understood the forests and mountains. Booker may have been born in the northern wilderness, but St. Louis was his home.

During the past week, his home had found a beating heart in Jo's Sanctum.

This was a huge step, finding a place like this, and he wanted that for his entire pack—not just the ones currently in St. Louis who were most in need of a sanctuary. He wondered if the peace could be extended to the whole neighborhood, if he could develop this whole area into a safe, stable calm-wolf zone. But first things first—he was getting himself and his pack settled in, and they were going to stop this necromancer, and then he could make those plans.

Because without Jo, there was no Sanctum. She was tied so directly to it that the whole place smelled like her. Even in the apartments he was renovating, beneath the odors of drywall and paint, there was that warm lavender scent. He found himself hunting for it sometimes during the day.

Hunting for *her*.

It was relatively easy to find excuses to be around Jo. At first, it was mostly just to get her used to him. She was skittish, so he stayed in her line of sight always, but he talked to her every time, even if it was just a "I'm heading up" or a "Do you need anything?"

She never needed anything. So he brought her things he thought she might want. A croissant from the bakery down the street. Hot chocolate from her favorite coffee shop. A book about runes from his father's collection. She'd given him the smile he liked best, the delightful crooked one that made her eyes crinkle at the edges—it was how he imagined she must've smiled when she was younger, before she'd been taken from her normal life and thrust into his in the most violent way possible.

Best not to linger on those thoughts though. He was here with Jo now, and that kind of thing was never going to happen to her again. He'd fight and kill to make sure of it. He'd die, if necessary.

After seven full days of work, he'd given Jo the go-ahead to open the shop again. Most of the noisy construction work was done, and two of the apartments were ready for their new tenants. Not a moment too soon, because Nick's anxiety over his wife's pregnancy was beginning to distract everyone on his team—including Booker. Nick was Booker's right hand, and he loved the man like a brother, but Nick's wife Grace was also one of

Booker's best friends. They'd all grown up together, and Booker was damned if he'd let them down when he was so close to giving Grace a safe place to have her babies. He needed to get her settled in the Sanctum ASAP.

He could also admit that he was looking forward to introducing Grace to Jo. He had a feeling they were going to get along just fine.

Just after the shop's closing time on the first day of reopening, he drove to one of his apartment buildings in the Central West End to pick up Grace. She met him at the entrance—Nick had already taken her bags to the Sanctum and wanted to have everything ready for her before she set foot in the apartment. Her loose maternity dress looked cheerful enough, but she'd worn her hair in a wrap, a sure sign that she didn't have any energy.

She waved one hand, her other curved under her protruding belly, as he walked up to her, then he put his arm around her shoulders. "Ready to go?"

Grace Taylor sighed and leaned heavily on his arm. "Are you sure about this?" she asked, lines of stress and fatigue etched on her lovely face. It made his heart clench a little. "Moving to a new place when I'm so close?"

They walked slowly together to his car. "Believe me, it'll be worth it." *I hope.* He opened the passenger door for her.

"I keep hearing that from Nick." She eased herself down into the seat, grunting with the effort. "But it's hard to believe." When she finally settled in, she let out a sigh and leaned her head against the headrest, looking exhausted. "Just seems too good to be true."

"Gotta trust me, Gracie Lou," he said, helping her buckle herself in. "You'll feel a lot better very soon."

Grace Louise Taylor's dark eyes narrowed. "Okay, just for that, you're going to have to buy me a very large cheeseburger on the way," she said.

Booker laughed. "Fine. The pregnant tyrant will be appeased."

The drive-thru burger helped her a little, put some color in her cheeks, Booker was glad to note. She could eat only half before she gave up, the lines of stress tightening around her mouth again. Werewolf pregnancies are always tricky, but Grace's had been problematic all the way through, although their doctor had said there was nothing wrong with the fetuses.

When they parked around back of the Sanctum, Grace peered out her window in silence, taking it all in. It was on the tip of Booker's tongue to ask her if she felt anything different, but he tamped it all down. There was always a chance it wouldn't work on her.

Diana, please let this work. Please let this help her.

Booker led Grace slowly through the halls in the back of the building to the shop, where Jo was restocking shelves. She turned to them and smiled, wiping her hands absently on the hem of her T-shirt.

Today it was a shirt with a cartoon of three hags clustered around a cauldron with huge grins on their faces, using their long-nailed fingers to pop colorful bubbles as they floated up from the pot. All three of them were saying, "Cauldron bubble!"

Booker was pleased to see that Jo seemed fairly relaxed, even with a new wolf in the building. Although Grace was tall and strongly built, it would be difficult even for someone with a major werewolf phobia to be afraid of the hugely pregnant belly and the haggard face he was presenting to Jo now.

"Grace, this is Jo. Jo, this is Grace. She's Nick's mate. Wife."

"It's nice to meet you." Jo reached out a hand to Grace, who took it carefully. After Jo shook her hand, her gaze sharpened, and she looked at Booker. "How about we go to my office and sit down?"

They were all relieved when the short walk to the back room was over and Grace was able to lower herself into a chair.

"Grace and Nick are going to move into the first of the finished apartments—we got it ready for them today." He watched, pleased, as Jo smiled at Grace. "She'll need to sign her own contract, but it needs to be more binding than the regular ones."

"Okay." Jo reached over to a minifridge and pulled out a bottle of water, leaning forward to hand it to Grace, who gave her a grateful look. Then she leveled her eyes at Booker again. "How much more binding are we talking?"

He kept his voice firm. "In addition to the signature, she'll add three drops of blood and a blood fingerprint."

Jo's expression turned grim, and her smell turned dark in his nose. Anger tinged with fear. His wolf wanted to sneeze. "A threefold binding is pretty damn close to mind control. Does she know that?"

"Yes." He looked at Grace. "She needs this."

Jo frowned, then turned concerned eyes to Grace. "We're not going to do anything you're not comfortable with." The steely gaze she flicked at Booker added a silent *or anything I'm not comfortable with.*

Grace held up a hand. "I appreciate all this." She turned to Booker, worry etching deeper lines around her mouth. "I can feel a little of what you were all talking about just sitting in here but..." Both of her hands curled around her belly.

Booker put a hand on her shoulder. "It gets better the instant you sign the geas," he said. "I promise."

Grace sighed. "I trust you, Booker."

Jo watched this, frowning. "Okay. I think we need to get a few things straight. Unless everyone who comes in signs this with threefold binding, then Grace will be helpless to defend herself if any of the standard contracts are broken. She can't be bound like that if there's even a remote chance that someone could harm her." Jo was shaking her head. "This place is as safe as I can make it, but there's always a chance."

"It's okay," Grace said. "I don't mind trusting my safety to the pack."

"It's *not* okay, and *I* mind," Jo growled, "which is especially important since I am the one making this geas."

Both wolves stared at the human across from them. Then Grace grinned, suddenly looking something like her old, fierce, take-no-shit self. "You were right, Booker. I do like her."

"Jo," Booker began.

Jo held up both hands. "Look. It goes against everything I've been and experienced and...fuck." She paused, appeared to collect herself, then placed her palms flat on the table. "I'm getting that there's something going on here that has nothing to do with me and everything to do with the fact that she's pregnant and you're both worried. But I'm not going to do this kind of binding without an explanation."

Booker took a deep breath, tamping down his impatience. "Fair." He looked at Grace. "The short explanation is that pregnancy is hard on werewolves. It's not a wolf pregnancy, and it's not a human pregnancy—it's something in-between. You already know that we can't always control the change when we're angry or afraid." He clenched his jaw. "Pain does it too. Stress. Worry."

Jo nodded, some of that dark anger fading from her smell. "Like pregnancy complications? Giving birth?"

This time, Grace answered, "Changing while pregnant can have odd effects on the babies. I'm carrying three." She smiled, but it was fleeting, and she rubbed her belly with both hands. "With the stress on my body and all the hormones, that urge to change is constant. The magic that makes us what we are gets unpredictable. So it's best if I can stay human during the pregnancy as much as possible." She sighed, shifting in her seat. "Especially staying human during the birthing process."

"For more than one reason," Booker said, unable to keep his voice from going rough.

"Then the peace contract—the no-change contract. That'll help you?" Jo's voice was fully sympathetic now.

Grace tried to smile again. "I hope." She paused, then added, "We...lost our last pregnancy. Two that time." She swallowed and wiped tears from her eyes. "I couldn't...well, my body just couldn't do it."

Jo's expression was one of sorrow and resolution. Booker could see her answer before she gave it. "Well," she said, with a decisive nod. "Let's get you a contract."

Booker stayed quiet while Jo produced a copy of the geas and showed Grace all the important elements, bringing it over to Grace's side and kneeling down beside her to make sure she could clearly see everything she was agreeing to. He listened to the murmur of their voices and kept up a steady stream of prayers to Diana.

If this worked...if it really worked...it would be a game-changer for his people. They'd given Jo the thumbnail sketch, but the truth was that werewolf pregnancies were just difficult, even under the best of circumstances. They weren't as fertile as either wolves or humans, and their pregnancies were as long as humans' but twice as hard on the mother's body as a human pregnancy. They needed to eat more, sleep more, rest more—and even with modern healthcare, the miscarriage rate was still abnormally high. Pregnant werewolves were only too aware of this, and it only added to their burdens and stresses—as did the concerns of their mates and their families.

The fact that shifting outside of the full moon could cause the babies to be born as wolves had its own dangers. Werewolves born as wolves had a harder time with nearly every part of the human aspect of their lives. Worse, it made the children more susceptible to Loki's manipulation later in life.

They didn't know why, but something about the wolf form, about the werewolf connection to mythical wolves, seemed to be part of it. Either way, werewolves born in wolf form were more likely to become Fenris. Or at least, they had been.

He supposed it wasn't such a surprise that this woman—this witch—who'd somehow rid the world of the Fenris might be the key to stamping out Loki's influence on his people for good. His only regret was that they hadn't found her sooner.

Once Jo was satisfied that Grace understood every aspect of what she was signing, Jo handed her a pen and an athame. "It's sterilized," Jo said, and she held the clipboard steady for Grace as she signed the paperwork and then pierced her index finger. Three drops of blood hit the paper beside her scrawled signature, and then Grace took a small breath and pressed her finger into the paper as well.

Booker held his breath, but he let it out in a huff of surprise when he felt the magic swell in the room, a tide of warm energy that pulsed gently as it began to ebb.

"Your promise fuels the magic," Jo murmured to Grace. "It is done."

Once the magic around them settled back to its familiar pleasant background feel, Booker turned to Grace and was relieved to see her smiling, looking as relaxed as anyone so hugely pregnant could. Her smell had even changed, subtly, the tang of stress gone. Now it was mostly just Grace and shea butter—Nick also smelled like that, since it was his job to rub it into Grace's skin every night now that she couldn't reach everywhere.

"Oh, that is nice," Grace said, looking over at Booker with a smile and a happy sigh.

Booker grinned, feeling almost as light-headed as Grace looked. "It worked?"

"Oh, it worked," she said, stretching her arms over her head. "Wow. I feel almost human."

"It's like setting something down, isn't it?" Booker said.

"Yes," Grace said, rolling her shoulders and looking up at Jo, where she stood holding the clipboard and watching the two of them. "Wow. I can't thank you enough."

Then Booker and Jo both said, "You're welcome," at the same time.

Grace snorted. "I was talking to her."

Jo raised her eyebrows and cocked her head at Booker—who shrugged—and then turned a warm smile to Grace. "You're very welcome." She shot another glance at Booker. "We're going to need to have a longer talk about this. I want to understand what worked here and why it worked. Especially if this is going to become a thing." She tapped one red sneaker on the floor. "As you know, I live to learn."

He'd expected no less. "Let me get Grace settled in with Nick, and then I'm all yours."

After Grace and Jo said their goodbyes, he led Grace out of the office and up the stairs. She used him for balance, but otherwise was walking more freely than she had in months. Booker silently thanked Diana—and for good measure, Hecate. Best to cover all the bases.

Then Grace chuckled to herself.

"What?" he said, slanting her a smile.

She side-eyed him slyly. "You're all hers, huh?"

"Ah." He knew his grin turned a little goofy. "Shut up."

"Oooh. Nick wasn't kidding." She jiggled his arm. "Booker's got a crush."

He rolled his eyes but couldn't stop the warmth rising in his cheeks. "Gossip is beneath you, Gracie Lou."

"Do that again, and I'll tell her your full name."

He mock-gasped. "Bitch." Her full-throated laughter made him smile.

CHAPTER 15

THREE DOORS DOWN, WEREWOLF-STYLE

JO

STILL BUZZING WITH THE INCREDIBLE ENERGY OF THE MAGIC, I watched them both leave, waving at Grace one last time, then paced my office a few times. *Holy Hecate, the rush.* Big magic did that, and this had been Big Magic.

Grace's reaction seemed to answer my biggest question—why all of Booker's pack members acted so odd after signing the geas. It apparently eased their inner wolves. One mystery solved.

This whole werewolf pregnancy thing opened up so many more.

Okay, have to get some fresh air.

I marched over to the mirror and without breaking stride stepped through it to the roof. It was still mostly light outside, but with fall weather coming, it wouldn't be for much longer. The crisp air felt good in my lungs, so I breathed it deep as I walked around. I should be chilly—I'd brought a sweater out with me last night—but the energy still had me too amped up.

While Grace seemed like a lovely person, and my heart truly broke for her lost pregnancy and her fears over this one, I simply didn't know how to feel about being party to bringing more werewolves into the world. Granted, Diana's Wolves—as Booker had pointed out more than once—seemed to be

as different from the Fenris as Quakers from neo-Nazis, but still. It just...
required thought.

After some Booker-worthy pacing, I finally went over and sat down next
to Stanley to watch the river. "So, did you know that werewolves have
difficult pregnancies?" I asked him. "I sure didn't."

I'd just finished telling him about the threefold binding when some sort
of commotion erupted down on the street. I looked down and around to see
four or five of Booker's wolves running around the building.

"Shit," I muttered. *What now?*

I picked up my phone to see that I had missed a call from Booker. Two
calls. Plus two texts asking where I was. "*Shiiiit,*" I hissed again, and then I
called him back.

When he picked up, he wasted no time. "Where are you?" he growled.

"On the roof. Why? What's happening?" I asked, still scanning the area
for zombies or whatever else might be agitating the wolves.

"What's *wrong* is that no one could find you. We left you in your office, I
told you I'd be back, and then you were no longer there. And two missed
calls," he said, as if I were a simpleton.

Irritation had my free hand clenching into a fist. To be fair, I normally
let Booker know when I was heading up, and the wolves were all more or less
used to my normal schedule. Still, I'd forgotten, in the relative peace of the
last few days, that the wolves were also there to guard me.

Grace and the Big Magic and the reminder that all this was very, very real
and very, very new to me had me off-balance. I forgot, while I was thinking
about werewolf pregnancies, that slipping up to the roof might freak
them out.

That said, it wasn't my fault they couldn't walk through mirrors. While
it wasn't entirely Booker's fault that he was an overprotective control freak, I
was in no mood to take any of his shit.

"Would it make everyone feel better if I went back to my office?" I asked,
feigning meekness.

He gave a bark of laughter. "You aren't sorry at all, are you." It wasn't a
question.

"No, I'm really not."

He paused, said something to someone else that I couldn't hear—*Yes,
please call off the puppies before they attract too much attention*—and then

sighed into the phone. "Well, I need to talk to you. Should I come up or do you want to come down?"

I looked up at Stanley. "All the doors that access my floor and the roof are still locked."

Booker gritted his teeth—I could almost hear it. "That didn't answer my question."

It was absolutely the magical energy zinging through my veins, but I couldn't resist. "Oooh, you come up. I want to see how long it will take you to get through all of the locks."

The phone beeped at me, Booker having apparently hung up. A little stunned at my own audacity, I counted by Mississippis and got to five before he burst through the roof-access door.

I swiveled myself so I faced Booker, my back to Stanley's side. Never issue a challenge to a werewolf. Locks are definitely a moot point if you can rip the door off its hinges.

"Did any of the doors survive?" I asked, eyeing his disheveled hair and controlled expression. He might be irritated, but he didn't really look it.

He brushed some splinters and dust from his shirt. "No, but I was going to replace them anyway." He sauntered toward me. "They were ugly. And fragile."

When I laughed, he did too. Against all the odds, Booker looked lighter and happier than I'd ever seen him. It wasn't that he was grinning or bouncy or anything. It was more a lack of a weight on his shoulders. A relaxing of tension. He loped over to where I was sitting, looking more amused than irritated.

I looked up at him, unable to keep from smiling. We really did have a weirdly similar sense of humor, and it never failed to surprise me.

"Now." He blew out a breath, then caught my gaze with his own faintly glowing one. His voice dropped to a low, almost reverent tone. "Thank you for what you did for Grace. It means the world to us. Not just me, Grace, and Nick—the whole pack." He paused, then said, "I don't think you get how important you're becoming to us. You really did panic the wolves when they couldn't find you. You gave them hope, then disappeared."

I started to speak, but he held up his hand. "I mean, I kind of figured you went from the mirror in your office to the one up here, but I called to make sure first."

I hissed through my teeth. "Then I didn't pick up."

"We all got worried." He gave me a rueful smile, then scratched the back of his neck. "I know you don't get why it's a big deal, but I mean it when I say you're important to us. You asked for our help, and we don't just *want* to help you—we *have* to. We're bound to you now. It's been days since the attack, and we're all kind of wondering when something bad's going to happen. We're on edge. It's...uncomfortable when we don't know where you are." He sighed and rolled his shoulders. "We just want to keep you safe."

Gah. How am I supposed to not melt right now? He was being so open and earnest. He hadn't gotten mad when I basically made him break down three doors to get up here.

"I'm sorry that I worried you," I said, making my eyes big. "I don't want to freak anyone out. Around this place, I don't even bother with stairs or anything. I like mirror-walking." I paused, then shrugged. "I'm willing to check in, let someone know what room I'm going to, but I am going to continue to travel about my place freely." I made it as firm as I could. "This mirror thing—it's a part of me, and I know there's even more I can do with it if I practice."

Booker nodded. "Knowledge enjoys being used," he said, looking me in the eye in that way he had. Not blinking. Not wavering.

It was getting easier to meet those bright amber eyes and not look away. To not want to look away. "Yes." He really did understand.

"Fair enough. We can adapt to that," he said. This time, he was the first one to break the held gaze, looking out over the river and smiling. "You still price yourself too low."

Well, didn't that just make a girl feel good? "Come on and sit down," I said. "I'm not going to keep craning my neck while you answer a thousand questions about werewolf pregnancies."

Again, that bark of laughter, and then he came to sit on the ledge with me. "So long as Stanley doesn't mind," he said, settling himself down.

"I don't think so," I said. "I'm guessing he'll let you know."

Booker smiled at me, and his eyes went a little soft. "How are you doing with everything?"

"Well." I leaned back against Stanley a little more. "Still a little buzzed from the magic. Still a little confused about the whole thing." *Still not sure I want to help build up the werewolf population, even if it does make you treat me like I'm a goddess.*

"Understandable," he said.

"So. Do I get to know what's going on with this?" I hated being out of the loop, especially when my own energy was still humming in the air like electricity.

He nodded. "You remember what I told you about Loki and the wolves? How he grooms us to try to make us go Fenris?"

Not likely to forget that lovely bit of nightmare fuel. "Of course."

"It's difficult to maintain a human form during pregnancy. You know that. However, if the mother is in wolf form, then the babies are born in their wolf form. When that happens..." His eyebrows pulled together, and he sighed. "They have more trouble integrating into the world beyond the pack. They have a shorter rein on their temper, so they tend to die young. To make matters worse, they have a stronger compulsion to follow Loki."

"So they become Fenris." Some of that energy drained out of me at the thought. "Or they did."

"Right. We don't yet know if that's going to change or just get worse now that they're gone." Booker rubbed his hands over his jeans, looking down at them before he met my eyes again. "Couple all those problems with how difficult it is to make it through a pregnancy in the first place, and it's caused a serious problem with our numbers."

There must be werewolf census takers. I imagined humans in suits with wolf heads wearing glasses. It amused, but not more than the idea of the Fenris swallowing up werewolf pups disturbed.

Booker wasn't done. "To make matters worse, sometimes we don't get the human woman back." He stared at the ground, then looked back at me. "After a month or two as a wolf, many of our women tend to stay wolf, especially if their pups haven't shifted yet." I could feel the sadness radiating from him.

"This happened to someone you know."

"My cousin," he said, his voice raspy, a near-growl but not at me. "Being a werewolf is the balance of the two. If you ignore either form, it's an unnatural state for us. If you live too long as the wolf, you disappear into the wolf."

"So being here would be almost like checking them into a hospital for bedrest and helping them deliver safely," I said.

His mouth lost its grim slant. "That's how I've been hoping it could work. Then they go back to their normal lives and raise their young as usual."

"Wow." I'd never thought of myself as a midwife, but this sounded almost appealing. Talk about helping those in need.

Except, of course, for the fact that they were werewolves.

"Of course," he murmured, "that's contingent on one very important thing."

Still lost in thought, I said, "What's that?"

"You," he said, reaching out to tap one long finger on my hand. The contact was brief, but it jolted me back to reality. "This won't work if you're not comfortable with it."

I didn't know what to say, so I stayed quiet.

After a moment, he said quietly, "I would understand if you didn't want to help bring more werewolves into the world."

I closed my eyes. "It's not quite that simple." Then my eyes popped open again. "That's why you didn't tell me about this before, right? Why you wanted me to meet Grace first."

Booker shrugged, but his lips quirked. "I did think that if you met the kind of pregnant werewolf you'd be dealing with here, it might help you understand the magnitude of what this means for us."

"I suppose I get that, but I have some conditions for doing this."

Booker's posture stiffened, but he kept his expression neutral. "What kind of conditions? We're talking about the pack's children and the possible future of my species."

When he said it like that, it sounded awful. "Conditions for me and the use of my power," I corrected, as gently as I could.

"What kind of conditions?"

"Let me think." His aura had flared with fear and anger and worry, and it was doing its best to scramble my brain. I didn't want to scare him, but this was my magic, my energy, and I had the right to ask questions and put some limits on things, regardless of how he felt about it. I took in a deep breath and blew it out.

When I felt I could ask the right questions, I began. "First, the babies... pups?...that are going to be born here. Will they all be Diana's Wolves?"

"No," Booker said. "When you become an adult, you can choose to follow one of the clans or not."

"Okay. Tell me more."

At my encouraging nod, he rolled his shoulders, and his aura began to calm. "Some adults aren't pledged to anyone, but since the rise of the Fenris, those are rare."

"Has anyone ever pledged a baby to Diana?"

"That has to be a choice. When you follow one of the clans, the rules of that clan become the way you live your life. That cannot be imposed on anyone. They must be free to choose their own way."

Like the Amish, I thought. That was going to make things more difficult, but I supposed there was some honor and common sense to that approach. Before I could stop myself, I asked, "Do teenage wolves get to do a *rumspringa*?"

Booker laughed, his aura clearing out the rest of the way. *Yay.* "No." He cocked his head at me. "Amish references aside, I think I know where you're going with this."

"That I may be helping to give birth to potential members of Future Fenris of America?" I raised my eyebrows. "Big-time yeah."

"Yeah." He sighed. "I can't guarantee that you won't. The Fenris are gone, but Loki isn't—we know that for certain."

"You said that some hear Loki's call when they're young. If the children were already dedicated to Diana or some other acceptable god or goddess, maybe they wouldn't be able to hear the lies and the promises and be tempted. By the time they're adults, it's too late."

Booker frowned and scrubbed one hand through his hair. "I know that but it's law." His aura was roiling a little again. "Forcing someone to pledge to a god or goddess when they're too young to make that big a decision is taking away a precious right."

It was a hell of a thing, to be sure. "The thought of doing this, and having one of the children born here potentially go Fenris..." I shook my head.

"You don't want them coming after you."

"No." Just like that, I was as angry as he had been. "I don't want to come after *them*. I don't want to help them be born only to remove them from existence down the road. That's just...twisted."

Booker's amber eyes were resigned. "You'd feel responsible, and you'd have to act."

I nodded, rubbing my hand over my heart. "The wolves born here aren't going to live here," I said slowly. "They'll go back home, and they'll grow up. The only way I'd know if they were going Fenris was if I could read their auras, but making a bunch of young wolves parade through here on an aura check is a logistical nightmare."

"But not impossible."

No. Hecate, give me strength. "I think we can do better," I said, finally getting to my point. "I don't suppose any of these wolves are Catholic? Do you christen your children? Ask for protection of any specific deity?"

"No, we don't have a lot of Catholics, although plenty of our children here go to Catholic schools—this is St. Louis, after all." He gestured out at the city, then gave me a considering look. "I think I follow your line of thought. Bless the pups with the protection of a goddess until they can come of age and choose themselves. Do you think that would keep Loki's voice from their ears?"

He was leaning toward me now, his expression intrigued. I started to mirror him, leaning in toward his warmth and cedar and sandalwood scent, but stopped myself and looked out at the river. "Honestly, I'm kind of making this up as I go along." I shrugged. "If pledging yourself to a goddess means you also have their protection from going Fenris, it couldn't hurt to ask if that same protection be extended to your children, until they reach the age of choice." I paused there, thinking hard, then I slapped one hand down on the ledge. "Yes. I even have a few books in the shop that can give us some tips and guidelines. It's called a wiccaning."

"So, basically, you're just wanting to protect our children from Loki until they become adults? *That* is one of the conditions?" He seemed incredulous.

I nodded again, wishing I could read his mind instead of just his emotions.

He stared out at the river. "Things like that have been attempted before, but they weren't as much protection as we hoped." *Well, damn it.* I sagged a little, but he laughed gently and met my gaze again. "However. We've never had Jo Murphy on the case." The glow in his eyes made something sweet twist in my belly. "I have no doubt that you'll be able to make it work."

I smiled, feeling unaccountably bashful. "Okay."

He smiled back, the tenderness in his glowing eyes almost too much to look at directly. "So that's one condition," he said. "Any others?"

"Yes." I took a deep breath. This one was important. "I don't hold babies."

He cocked his head, for all the world looking like a curious dog. "What?"

"I don't hold babies," I repeated firmly. "I don't babysit. My apartment is not kid-friendly. My shop is not terribly kid-friendly. If you are going to be here for five years, that's potentially a lot of children being born. I know people will be grateful that I helped give them sanctuary, and that means they will want to show me the kids, and I am asking that they, um...don't? At least not in person." At his questioning look, I sighed. "I don't hate kids, okay? I just don't feel very comfortable around babies and toddlers."

He laughed a little and nodded, but then he was back to studying me. I got the feeling he was curious, had some sort of mental list of things he wanted to ask me, but he didn't say anything. Instead, he gave me an amused half-smile. "Done."

"The last thing I have to ask is somewhat mercenary. If you're going to want me to continue doing the thrice-binding geas, I'm going to have to charge more." I sighed. "The energy and magic involved are intense. I was kind of buzzing from it earlier, but I'm starting to feel some serious exhaustion."

Booker's expression immediately folded into concern, and I waved a hand in his direction. "No, no. I'll be okay, but it takes a lot out of me. Now, the good news is once you've signed it, you never have to again. Grace could come back here in thirty years, and she'd be able to walk right in the door and get that peace back. Her geas would still hold." Booker appeared thunderstruck, and I shrugged. "That kind of quality is important. I put a lot into it. So, it deserves its own payment."

I quoted him a price that was expensive in my mind, but not outrageous —people have paid more for a high-end tarot reading—but it wasn't cheap.

Besides, it wasn't really about the money at this point. Placing a value on what I was doing made this whole situation feel more like a business transaction. They were getting something of value, and I could hopefully keep myself somewhat removed from them.

Hopefully. I was getting used to the wolves and even beginning to like most of them—and I had to admit, Grace seemed like potential friend material—but I still didn't want to be an honorary werewolf.

Booker was shaking his head. "I was going to offer you more than that. You're still pricing yourself too low."

I waited a second, then narrowed my eyes. *I may price myself too low, but you sure don't mind taking advantage of the discount.* Ah, well. I was already getting a small fortune from the deal already. Plus my own werewolf army.

"Okay. Here's the last thing, which has become a more pressing issue." I reminded him about John and explained his situation, watching Booker carefully for any signs of irritation.

"Was that all you were worried about?" Booker's eyes searched mine.

"Well, no, but I didn't exactly know how you would react, and I just couldn't let John down."

"You ought to know by now that I understand what it means to have a pack. John is obviously part of yours, and I respect that."

I finally gave him a tentative smile. That went easier than expected.

We sat in silence for a moment or two, and then I closed my eyes. All that energy from before was gone, and it felt like my whole body was wilting. I already knew: I was going to do this. I was going to help these wolves. The thing was...I *wanted* to.

"Gods, why does it feel so right to do all this?" I hadn't meant to say it out loud, but there it was.

When I opened my eyes, I saw that Booker was very still. "You mean—"

I cut him off. "I'm not sure what I mean." I massaged my eyes for a moment with my fingertips. "I just fell off a cliff, magically speaking, so I'm tired as hell right now. But..." I paused and met his gaze again. "It felt really good to help Grace. So, I say we hold these terms for the five years of your lease—assuming neither of us die in the meantime—and then we renegotiate."

"Agreed." Those dimples came out, and I responded as usual. At least there were some upsides to being manipulated by Fate, werewolves, and Hecate knew what else. "That is really, truly fantastic to hear. Thank you. Again."

"Yeah, yeah." Then something struck me. "Hey, how many others are there? Pregnant right now?"

"In St. Louis? Three, but Grace is the farthest along. The other two are in their second trimesters, and I'm thinking maybe moving them in two months before the due date, if that works for you."

This was still mind-boggling. I'd only thought of the geas as making sure someone behaved themselves to my specifications. It was one of the natural magics I had at my disposal, but I'd never liked the mind control element of it—that felt wrong to the nth degree. That said, I'd never thought of using it like this, as of course my defensive, traumatized brain tended to lean negative on such things. It would never have occurred to me to use one on myself for magically enforced self-control.

"So, I'm guessing the pregnant ladies will need to basically be inside the whole time, since the geas only works in the Sanctum."

"I think Laura—she's the next in line—is still working remotely, so she might keep that up while she's here, at least for a while. She's a video editor and is something of a workaholic. Grace has taken maternity leave from her job, but she'll have Nick here with her."

"The pack members will make sure everybody has what they need?"

"Well, sure." He cocked an eyebrow. "As will Amazon, DoorDash, and so on."

I felt my cheeks heat. "Right. I wasn't thinking."

"This will be our home. Legal address and everything. We're not hiding here." To his credit, he didn't say it like he thought I was an idiot.

However, I knew my face was still red. I could just launch myself off the roof right now, although with his reflexes, Booker would probably catch me. Then growl at me. "Of course." I looked down at my hands. "I guess I haven't really considered that you live in the real world too." I thought about it and shook my head. "Hell, probably more than I do. You're out there every day, interacting with people. Humans."

I've been more or less cowering here.

Booker shrugged, but those amber eyes were bright and intense. *Molten honey.* When his hand closed warm over mine, I didn't pull away. "You've been afraid for your life for good reason. You've figured out how to make yourself safe, make the world come to you, on your terms." He leaned toward me a little, and I caught his scent again. "You're not a coward. You're smart." Then he flashed his dimples again. "You've given me a run for my money the whole time I've been on your trail."

I smiled at that. "True."

We sat there for a few moments in the fading light, looking out at the river, and the breeze picked up. His hand didn't move, and I didn't mind.

CHAPTER 16

YEAH, BUT SHE'S MY WITCH

BOOKER

BOOKER PACED HIS OFFICE IN THE BOOKER BROTHERS building downtown.

It was amazing how quickly the Sanctum had become home for him. He resented the office for being here—in this historic downtown building that he used to love—and not there, but he knew that his lack of presence in the workplace had been noticed.

The wolf growled, and Booker shook his head. No one had any reason to doubt that he was doing his job when it came to his territory. When it came to Jo. He'd sent reports, and he'd been sure to keep checking in. That was the whole reason he was in his office—he was waiting to hear back from one of the Council's Fae historians about the rune. After his report about the zombie attacks on Jo, he'd requested access to runic histories, and they'd finally honored his request. The elder historian had found and copied samples to send over to compare to the necklace, but he refused to release the books in question. The old Fae didn't like the internet, which was so fucking backward that Booker couldn't stand it.

The ancient bastard insisted on using the Booker Brothers' fax machine. He or his assistants or whoever the fuck was supposed to send it were taking their sweet time. He cast another glance at the silent fax machine and grunted. Diana help him, all he could think about was getting back to the Sanctum.

Back to the renovations. Back to strategize with Nick. Back to check on Grace.

Back to Jo.

She was adapting to his pack remarkably quickly, and he was hoping now that Grace was there and feeling better every day, she and Grace could be friends. It helped that curiosity about Jo was eating Grace alive, which Nick found hilarious. Neither one of them seemed to think it was odd or problematic that Booker was getting so tangled up in the life of a human, which was a relief. Grace openly encouraged it.

Jo wasn't an ordinary human, to be sure, but werewolves tended not to form long-term attachments with humans, unlike some of the other supernatural races. It was hard enough for werewolves to conceive and achieve a full-term pregnancy with other werewolves. There were no records of any mixed-species offspring, which he thought would probably be just fine with Jo, given her feelings about children.

Gods, he needed to stop thinking along those lines, but it was hard to. He'd never reacted to anyone—wolf, human, or otherwise—the way he'd reacted to Jo. Never felt about anyone the way he felt about her.

Now the future stretched wide open. Protecting Jo had felt right from the beginning. Now it felt necessary. His reward for finding her and helping her was that the species as a whole might start actually wanting to have children again. With the population dwindling over the last few decades, this was excellent news. He had begun to fear if he lived too long, he would see the end of his wolves.

In one fell swoop, Jo had given back hope to them all.

Most witches he dealt with in the past would never have given such a gift so freely. She really had no idea of the magnitude of the power she had collected in that building. Just the sheer force of her will held most of it together, but it felt rock solid. He could tell when she gave him the tour that she had anchored her power in various places, so the whole building would hold together without her there, but most of the magic was just her. Witches really came into their power during their third decade, and she'd just started hers. He'd had a feeling when the Fenris disappeared that things were about to get really interesting, and there was no doubt she was the center of the evolution of his world. Wolves survived by adapting, and pack leaders knew that better than most.

She'd agreed to all his terms, as he'd agreed to hers, but she was charging him for the threefold geas, and he thought he understood why. He'd kept track of her emotional state along the way, and she seemed content, more relaxed, but still wary at times. In the past, she would run away rather than get too involved in other people's lives, even people she'd truly cared about —he'd met enough of her temporary friends while he was tracking her to figure that out.

It wasn't just werewolves that scared Jo. It was the thought of forming emotional bonds with anyone else.

Yet here he was, a werewolf forming an emotional bond with her, whether she liked it or not. He ground his teeth. The Sanctum anchored her, but there was still every chance that she might try to disappear one day rather than fall deeper into the werewolf world.

Booker paced faster. Would that goddamn fax ever come?

His stomach clenched when he thought about the mystery of the Fenris. The Council needed to know, but he hardly cared anymore. The idea of pushing Jo to tell him made his wolf uneasy. No matter how he kept trying to logic it all out, he'd felt compelled to protect her since he first saw her on that video—the video of her torture by the Fenris. The Council had been concerned about her, certain that she was a power to be feared, especially when they hadn't been able to locate her for so long.

When they'd put him on the case, they'd shown him the video, and it had become the center of his world as he prepared to find her. He'd watched the horror show more than once, despite his rage at what he saw—pushing himself to be analytical, to figure out what he was missing. They knew from the info they'd gathered that the Fenris had taken Josephine Murphy two days prior to the day the video was shot. They had hunted her down for unknown reasons, and they'd beaten and raped the woman for two days, then the woman had waved her hand, and they all disappeared.

Good fucking riddance.

Some of the torture had been on the video, but it was the last part that he kept watching and rewatching. What he saw was a cornered animal trying to get away, and that's what he'd initially told the Council. The fact that Jo then disappeared for eight years backed up his theory. He'd found out everything he could about her prior to setting out, and everything he knew of Jo told him that whatever had happened, she wasn't out to destroy the world. She was just trying to keep herself alive.

It surprised and humbled him that she was adapting so well to having him—a werewolf—in her life. He knew it meant she trusted him, even if he still scared her sometimes without meaning to.

He'd scared her on the roof that day by grabbing her from behind. Her fear-smell in his nostrils had completely obliterated the normal soothing smell of lavender that was essentially her, and the reason for her fear brought the wolf to dangerous levels of anxiety. The wolf wanted to protect her so the fear-smell would go away, not realizing that in that moment, what she needed was the man—keeping it all tamped down had been a test of his control.

Of course, the wolf had already been on edge because of the attack. Replaying that episode in his head made his hackles rise again. The bruising around her throat, the stench of her fear and grief and anger clogging his nostrils, the blue eyes swollen and red. She'd been shaking with fear and pain, but she'd refused his help.

Even so, he knew he was screwed.

His emotions were already in play when it came to her. He wanted to soothe her fears, bundle her off somewhere so that no one would ever hurt her, mark her as his so that she'd have the safety and support of the pack. The wolf thought that was an excellent plan and was irritated that it wasn't being carried out. Booker the Wolf didn't understand that Jo wouldn't appreciate any of this, but Booker the Man knew she would look at it as interfering with her free will.

Freedom. Was there anything more important to someone who'd been kidnapped and violated as she had?

The wolf didn't care, but the man needed Jo to trust him—and the thought that she was beginning to do just that was precious to him. If he tried to railroad her into compliance about the Fenris thing to get an answer to the Council sooner or if he tried to push his affections onto her before she was ready...

He couldn't risk that. *Patience*, he told the wolf.

So he'd tell Grace in no uncertain terms that he didn't need or want her to be a wingman—Jo was more likely to run away from him than run to him if she knew the direction his feelings about her were heading.

Jo needed a friend.

Preferably a friend who didn't wish him at the bottom of the Mississippi. The memory of Kate Strega's cold stare made his wolf's ears flatten.

Booker thought he might drop a bug in Grace's ear to keep it chill but approach Jo casually. He knew that Jo hated doing the books for the shop, so maybe Grace could help her out. Jo might feel more comfortable asking her questions—his witch craved knowledge like other people craved chocolate.

She'd definitely run if she knew he was already thinking of her as "his."

He itched to talk to her. Find an excuse to hold her hand again. Find other ways to get his skin against her skin. However, he had obligations and responsibilities, so he couldn't be at the Sanctum 24-7, as much as he wanted that very thing. This was his territory, and he'd have to keep his head in the big-picture game if he wanted to manage it properly. At least his most trusted pack members were living there, now that they'd gotten most of the essential renovations done. It was easier to be away knowing she would always have protection.

His phone vibrated in his pocket, so he dug it out, and the name on the caller ID stilled his restless legs. He smiled when he answered. "Dad," he said.

"Son." Arthur Booker's voice was slow and graveled. "You've been busy."

"I would have called, but I figured you'd see the reports." He'd been careful about how he'd revealed what he'd learned thus far in his emails to the Council. Being vague with Art during direct communication when his father wanted details was nearly impossible.

"I did. Very interesting find, your mirror witch."

That didn't even begin to cover it. "We're on the brink of something major here."

He filled his father in on Grace, and when he was done, his father was silent for a full minute before he said slowly, "That's better than we'd ever dreamed."

"We'll have to see how it all turns out, but I have a good feeling about it."

Art chuckled. It was like two boulders tumbling over one another. "In your nose or in your heart?"

His father knew things about Booker that no one else did. When as a kid Booker had tried to explain how "a good feeling" smelled to him, his dad had laughed just like that and told him that when he could sense that good feeling with his nose *and* his heart, he should chase it down until it solidified.

"Both," Booker said. Renting Jo's building had been like that. Despite Jo Murphy's tumultuous life and the danger she was in, he'd known that she would somehow bring him peace. The fact that it extended to his entire pack—possibly his entire race—was a happy miracle in the middle of all the chaos.

"Good." Art paused. "Anything more on the necromancer?"

Booker glared at the silent fax machine. "If the Fae get their asses in gear, we might have a chance of getting closer to identifying the rune on the necklace."

"The pictures you sent weren't enough?"

Booker sighed. "The burn marks caused some trouble." His mirror witch had fire in her. He wished that made him feel better.

"Even so, it's not a good sign that no one recognizes it."

Booker grunted. Something outside the experience of the Council—especially the centuries-old members of it—was never good. It meant that the gods were probably involved.

"If you need more resources, you only have to say so. I can send you what you need—and if I don't have it, Theresa will." Art's sister Theresa was the co-leader of Diana's Wolves in North America. While Art handled everything north of the Mason-Dixon Line up to Inuit lands, Theresa led all the packs south to the Panama Canal. By tacit agreement, the siblings had ceded authority in an ever-growing section of the Midwest to Booker, although he was nominally only in charge of St. Louis and the surrounding areas.

Even though he only really wanted St. Louis and the surrounding areas.

The thought of playing interclan politics with his father and his aunt sounded exhausting, when all he really wanted to do was focus his energy on his own city and his own wolves. Let Art and Theresa deal with Odin's Wolves and the Lobos de Quetzalcoatl/Lobos de Guadalupe drama. He was working on something different but equally important—and not just to their clan, but to wolves everywhere, if things went well.

Instead of voicing any of this, Booker simply said, "Thanks, Dad."

"Given what happened with the Fenris, I'm surprised she wants to help us."

It was said idly, but Booker's hackles raised. "No one's more surprised than she is."

"The Council's getting antsy. Are you sure she really doesn't remember?"

"She's working through it. She's still scared and traumatized by what happened." Booker told his racing heart to slow. Art was his father and his alpha, and if Art began to push...well, the less Art knew, the better, until Booker had more concrete answers to give him. He didn't want the Council trying to interfere while he got his pack settled in the Sanctum, and he had a feeling that once they got a better sense of the scope of Jo's power, they would try like hell to interfere.

"Just remember, son, she's a human and a witch. They don't think like us." He paused. "Their priorities are different."

Booker remembered the earnest expression, the determination in those big blue eyes as she'd explained how she wanted to protect the pups from Loki. To give his species yet another fighting chance. She'd thought he wouldn't go for that idea somehow. It had taken his breath away for a moment.

Yeah, but Jo is my *witch,* he wanted to say. *I like the way she thinks. I understand her logic. Her priorities make sense to me.*

The fax machine buzzed to life, and Booker sent a silent prayer of thanks to Diana. "I have to go. I'll call again when I know more."

While the paper printed, Booker texted Nick to make sure all was still well at the Sanctum. Nick texted back that all was well, and Max was helping Jo rearrange shelves. That made Booker smile—Max's ridiculous height would be uniquely suited to the job. The big wolf's extroverted nature had also come in handy for once, as Max had been the first of his wolves to make a real effort to befriend Jo. The two of them already had an inside joke about the "long and short" of it.

He couldn't help but feel a warmth in his chest every time he saw signs that his wolves were bonding with Jo—and he really liked the idea of someone being with Jo when he couldn't until this was resolved. Possibly even after that. He never wanted to see her looking bruised and scared again. He never wanted to endure her fear-smell again—to his way of thinking, the best way to do that was to make sure she was protected.

The ideal way to do that was for him to stay close to her.

As long as she wanted that, of course.

In the supernatural community, werewolves were notorious for never letting things go—their prey, their alliances, their grievances. When they found something important, they stuck with it.

He hoped Jo would be ready for that sooner than later, because it would be hell on him to find a way to let her go.

CHAPTER 17

AND YOUR LITTLE DOG, TOO

JO

THE DREAM CAME TO ME AGAIN, JUST AS IT HAD THE DAY I MET Booker. This time, I didn't wake up. I had to relive the whole experience in my dream, where it seemed to happen all at once. Four days packed into a few hours of sleep, but my brain managed to do it. The fear, the blood, and the constant pain flooded into my mind. In the dream I fought back, just as I had in real life—at least, at first. Before they broke me, body and soul.

My subconscious tried to swim away from the dream, tried to get out of it, but it moved relentlessly on and on.

The beatings in the dream were always vivid but surreal. I felt the torture—the hits, the cuts—but it was more like ghost pain.

Being aware that I was dreaming it all again was almost worse than being in it. It was like my mind was doing it all to me. I fought to wake up before having to relive the rapes. I didn't even know how many times they'd raped me while I was there. The violation, the agony, had just seemed endless.

Unlike the torture, this part wasn't surreal in the dream. The pain wasn't ghostlike but vivid as blood dripping from a razor blade, and I could feel my body twisting in the bed, trying in vain to evade it. *Don't scream.*

Don't scream. They'd loved it when I couldn't hold back the anguish, their human mouths and half-wolf mouths hanging open in delight at the sounds I made.

At a certain point, the exhaustion and the pain and the fear meant I couldn't control it. I opened my mouth and got a flash of a female figure I knew was Hecate. "*Not yet,*" she said, and touched my forehead.

Just like that, I was awake and screaming, covered in sweat.

I cut off the scream with a choked gasp, pushing myself up and turning on the bedside lamp, flooding the room with gentle light. *Here. Not there. Not there. Here. Safe.*

I grabbed the nearest pillow and hugged it, letting myself rock back and forth a little bit. Cole sat on his haunches beside me, his green eyes sleepy and filled with annoyance. I'd forgotten to check if he was on the pillow I'd grabbed. Clearly, I'd stolen his property.

"Sorry, dude," I managed and reached out to run a hand down his back, which he tolerated.

I closed my eyes and adjusted my breathing into yoga breaths. *In through the nose. Out through the nose.* When my heartbeat slowed a little, I looked at the clock. 5:41. Well, at least it wasn't 3. This was close enough to my normal waking time. Since the wolves had moved in, I was up by 6, taking an hour for yoga and meditation, then getting down to business long before I opened the shop at 9. It had been a pretty productive two weeks.

Since the wolves had been here, I'd been sleeping better. Less anxiety, fewer incidents of waking up in the middle of the night. No nightmares. *Huh.*

Until now, of course.

I sighed and grabbed my phone to turn off the alarm before it sounded when the phone started vibrating in my hand. It was Booker.

"Good morning?" I said when I answered, hoping it sounded more like, *Why are you calling me so early?*

His voice was deep and brusque. "You were screaming and no one could get to you. What's going on?"

"Oh, nothing. Nothing," I said, knowing my voice wasn't fully steady enough to sell it. "Just a bad dream. It happens sometimes."

"The screaming?"

"It's a really bad dream." I sighed. "Screaming seemed the only appropriate reaction."

Booker grunted. "The wolves working on the floor below you said they couldn't get to your door. Some sort of force field prevented them from even touching it."

Interesting. Was I erecting magical barriers while I slept? That was pretty cool, if a little bit scary.

I took a breath and reached out with my mind—sure enough, there were barriers in front of all of the doors to my apartment, as well as the doors to my bedroom. They felt like miniature versions of my Sanctum shields.

"Huh," I muttered. I looked at Cole, who seemed to think none of this was terribly important. "Just a second."

I concentrated on the barriers for a second, and the flow of their magic seemed to crawl back to the various magical anchors I had placed around the building.

"There shouldn't be any barriers now," I said, relaxing back against the headboard and laying a hand on Cole again. He began to purr. "That said, I'm just fine and don't need to be checked on." I closed my eyes, soothing myself with the rumble of Cole beneath my palm—and yes, with the knowledge that Booker, as grumpy as he was right now, was on the other end of the phone. Was in the building one floor down. Was concerned. "It was just a bad dream."

The silence from Booker's end was damning even before he said, tightly, "Here's a tip. Wolves like me, ones who have more magic in them because they're in charge? They'll know when you're lying. You are not fine."

I gritted my teeth. That was inconvenient as fuck. "Fair enough. Here's the truth. I'm not physically injured or in danger right now. I had a bad dream. An awful dream. I've had it before. I am going to get up, work out, and shower. Then I will be fine."

I could almost hear him narrowing his eyes. "Fine then." He blew out a breath, then muttered, "I'll see you at the shop," and hung up.

He wants to see me. That little flutter in my belly was nearly as inconvenient as finding out that he was a lie-detecting werewolf. *Of course he's going to see me,* I reminded myself. *He's living here now, and we're meeting to talk about the rune today.*

Besides, he was waiting to find out about the Fenris.

I remembered that very last moment from the dream. Hecate had said, "Not yet."

Yeah, that wasn't creepy or foreboding at all.

I went through my morning routine to help focus myself on the day ahead of me. Yoga, shower, food, and Cole. Mornings were my favorite time with him. He had a food dish that I of course kept full all the time with dry food, but every morning I gave him a can of wet food as a special morning-time treat. While he ate his tuna and veggie mixture that morning, I sat beside him and talked to him about everything and nothing. It was my apology to him for leaving for the day.

Of course, he often found his way down to the shop and out onto the rooftop on his own. He always came back in, so it didn't worry me too much—my Sanctum was an old building, and I certainly didn't know all of its nooks and crannies. It wasn't like mice were an issue. If the little tokens of affection in the form of a paw or a head I sometimes found on the floor were any indication, Cole wasn't about to let any rodent run free in his domain.

For the first time since the wolves had been in the Sanctum, I considered dabbing on some lavender essential oil. I never wore perfume, but I loved the smell of lavender. I had lavender bubble bath and lavender soap, and I kept bottles of lavender lotion scattered throughout my apartment, office, and shop. It kept my nerves from getting too frayed.

I'd been going easy on the lavender because wolves have such keen senses of smell, using my lavender soap and lotion, but not the oil, thinking it might be as loud as a shout in the noses of the wolves. Today, as shaky as I still felt, it might help to power up the soothing element.

Wait. Was I really sitting here worrying about what the wolves thought about how I smelled? Letting them affect how I prepared myself for the day? Irritated, I grabbed a pair of jeans and a T-shirt from the closet. This one was my Wicked Witch of the West one, with an illustration of Margaret Hamilton in full costume looking like a badass and the quote "...and your little dog, too!" on it.

I dabbed on some lavender oil. *Screw the wolves. I'll smell how I want and need to smell.*

Then I groaned. *Wolves.* Holy Hecate, but they were just *everywhere.*

The odd thing wasn't that I had the nightmare last night—the odd thing was that I'd had only one incident of near-panic attack since they'd been here. I never thought I'd be able to be in the same room as one wolf without hyperventilating, let alone have twelve of them in my building, and yet it had been two weeks, and I hadn't lost my shit. Even the nightmare this morning didn't seem connected to them. Again, I saw Hecate in my mind. *Not yet.*

I even kind of liked the wolves being around. They were nearly all so nice, and they all looked at me as if I was doing them some sort of huge favor, as deferential as handmaidens. Nick and Max had started to joke with me a little, and even Ethan didn't seem unfriendly so much as not particularly interested.

Also, they'd changed the feel of the Sanctum and its magic just by being here. Wolves tended to have lots of energy, and their hefty auras took up a lot of space—but in a way that charged it up rather than draining it out. Their happiness flavored that energy with good feels, as Kate's kids might say. While the air was heavy with wolves, it wasn't in a negative way.

And Booker...well, I liked having him around. That warm feeling of knowing he was on my side, that he would help me figure out what was happening.

It didn't hurt that he seemed as fascinated by me as I was by him.

Remembering the way his hand had rested on mine, those bright, unblinking eyes gazing at me like he was checking out my soul and finding it pleasing, my stomach twisted deep down.

In a good way.

A very good way.

Good goddess, when was the last time I'd gotten laid?

Far too long.

One of the things I needed to do before I met with Booker, Nick, and Kate this afternoon was gather up my notes and make sure everything was ready. We'd all been doing as much homework as possible, and I knew that Booker had been in communication with his Council about the rune—he'd gone back to the Booker Brothers office building yesterday to get some info from a Council historian, although he was fairly vague about the details. Once he'd gotten it, he'd set up a meeting.

I'd found jack squat, as had Kate as far as I knew, but Nick had been able to track and account for all of Emma's movements that evening. Everything led to Purgatory—it was the last place anyone had seen her before she turned up zombified outside the Sanctum.

I still had the rune, wrapped up and placed in a hex box to keep its magic muted and muffled—the rune needed to be there. I made sure everything was on my desk and ready to go. It was beyond time to find Emma's killer.

Emma. Out of a new and depressing habit, I checked her Facebook and Instagram accounts. I saw something posted on Instagram the night before from one of Emma's friends, blk_I_lnr32, who'd tagged Emma: "Miss u so much, @gothicallyemma!!! Hope ur at the HB show 2morrow"

I clicked through the pictures, trying not to tear up at the sight of Emma in the goth-glam clothes her body had been wearing when it showed up to kill me.

Then I saw something that made my eyes pop wide.

John and I were going over afternoon inventory when Booker walked into the shop around 2 p.m. with a manila envelope in his hand. He was frowning at first, as if preoccupied, but when he saw me, he lit up with a happy smile that stole my breath. *Hello, dimples.* I couldn't help but smile back, despite everything—it was the first time I'd seen him since yesterday afternoon, and his gorgeousness just smacked me in the face like it was the first time, period. I mean, the guy was attractive in a rough-hewn way even when he was serious, but when he was grinning and his aura expanded with happiness? No one could resist.

I came around the counter to indicate that I was ready for our meeting, and he took two strides toward me and wrapped his arms around me in a bear hug before I could even tense up in anticipation.

Shock melted into surprised pleasure in every fiber of my body—the feel of his solid body against mine, that cedar and sandalwood smell enveloping us both. His heart beat solidly beneath his jacket, right under my ear.

"Definitely a good-feeling smell," he said, and I felt the rumble of the words in his chest. In my knees. Other places.

What the hell did that mean? "Okay?" I murmured. Maybe this was just proof that the lavender oil wasn't a problem.

The hug was warm, friendly, and over far too quickly, just as I'd started to lean into it.

When Booker stepped back, his grin had softened, but he was still so happy he was nearly bouncing. I knew I had a dazed smile on my own face, because I was trying to get myself to stop.

I glanced over at John, who was staring at us both in bemused astonishment.

"John," I said, taking a breath. "This is Booker. Booker, John."

"We've met," Booker said, letting his eyes linger on me for an extra second or two before he turned to hold out a hand to my employee. "Good to see you again. Let me know when you're planning to move in any furniture, okay? We'll help however you need."

John clasped Booker's hand, his smile curious. "Will do. Thanks." He flicked his gaze over at me, and the smile widened. "I guess it's time for your meeting, Jo?"

Ugh. He did everything but waggle his eyebrows—although, to be fair, only someone who knew John would get that he was doing some subtle teasing. I narrowed my eyes. "Yes. You need anything else first?"

John shook his head. "Nope. I can close up if you need me to."

Yeah, I might need that, but not for the reasons his amused eyes were implying. "I'll let you know."

I looked back at Booker, who was still watching me expectantly, doing everything but wagging his tail. Damn, I was going to ruin all that good-feeling smell for him soon enough, so I figured I'd wait and let him enjoy it. "Ready?" I said, trying to smile again, and I started up the stairs.

Unfortunately, he was spookily observant, and his own smile faded as we headed up the stairs side by side. "What's wrong." It wasn't a question.

"Let's get everyone together first," I said.

Less than ten minutes later, we were all in one of my second-floor tarot rooms, which had been repurposed for the time being by Booker as a meeting room for his teams. Booker had his construction wolves and his hunter wolves—I didn't know what else to call them—and this was where the hunter wolves met. Nick Taylor was Booker's second-in-command, a stocky black wolf with a rare but sweet smile who was married to Grace. Max Jorgenson was a huge tree of a blond wolf with a sly sense of humor—he and I had already bonded over bad jokes and our extreme height differential, and I'd put him and his freakish height to work in the shop more than once over the past week. Then there was Ethan Lang, a slim but powerful-feeling wolf who reminded me of Simu Liu but seemed to have literally no inclination to smile. Ethan didn't appear to have interest in anything but his own business, which was being the tough, silent type—and business seemed to be booming.

From what I had gathered, Booker and Nick had grown up together, along with Grace, and Max and Ethan had been working with them for at least a decade. Ethan had been promoted to a leadership position recently, which I assumed was because Nick would be spending more time with Grace once their babies were born.

Max and Ethan weren't at the meeting today, as they and the rest of the team were keeping guard and out on patrol, but Kate flowed in with Nick, who'd gone to escort her over, and she gave Booker some side-eye before she sat by me. "I've only got the bare minimum of info, so I hope someone else had better luck," she said.

After a brief murmured conversation between Booker and Nick, Booker said, "The Council historian sent these, and they're open to answering questions and sharing more info." He grimaced. "They'll do it over the phone."

It sounded like that was some kind of concession on their part, and a major annoyance for Booker.

I took a breath. "I couldn't really find anything until I checked Emma's social media this morning. One of her friends posted pictures of the Hel's Belles show Emma went to that night. Emma is in them, and so is the amulet. She was wearing it that night, while she was still alive."

Booker and Nick were on full alert. "So someone gave it to her at the show."

"That seems to be the case." I sighed grimly. "Hel's Belles is playing again tonight. It's their first show since the one Emma went to."

Kate was leafing through the faxed pictures. "Look at this one."

We looked. It wasn't our rune, quite, but it was close. Close enough.

It was a rune associated with a deity that none of us particularly wanted to face. "I thought she was more of a traditionalist," Kate murmured. "She sticks to the Old World. Europe. I've always heard she doesn't go in for modern pagans so much."

"Apparently, she's branching out." Booker's voice was grim.

I picked up the picture of the rune. It was marked "Symbol of Hel, Norse Goddess of Death."

"Well," I said, trying to smile. "At least we know it's not just a clever name."

CHAPTER 18

A GAME OF CONFRONTATION AND CONFUSE-THE-WITCH

JO

IN THE SILENCE THAT FOLLOWED MY VERY LAME JOKE, I WENT ahead and took the reins. "So," I said, "we'll all go to the concert."

"I'll go," Booker corrected. "You'll stay here and stay safe."

Nope. Not this time. I'm done being passive. "Emma was my friend," I said. "I'm going to check out this scary-ass band, and you're not going to stop me."

He stood, his unblinking eyes boring into me. "It's to our tactical advantage if we send a team of wolves in to scout the place." I cast a look of disbelief at Kate, who shrugged as if to say, *You're the one who brought a werewolf into your life. What did you expect?*

Meanwhile, Nick looked like a dog watching a tennis match, his dark brown eyes alert and interested as he looked from me to Booker and back. Without blinking, of course. *Damn wolves.*

I rose from my chair as well. Booker may have had the height, but he wasn't the only one who could stare. "Do we have a tactical advantage? They obviously already know who I am and where I am—I'm willing to bet they know who you are by now too." I raised my hands. "If we all go together, we're united. There's no point in splitting up now—there's more power in numbers. And..." I paused. "...and, well, *power*. I'm going."

I crossed my arms over my chest, cocked my head to one side, and gave him my best *what do you think you could possibly do to stop me?* look.

The urge to blink, to look away, grew with every second. Jesus, it was hard to stare down a wolf—and Booker was an alpha. My expression morphed into an incredulous *why are you so stupid?* look. In response, I could feel his aura getting bigger, more imposing. I hadn't realized that he could pull menace into himself, but he was doing that now. Trying to intimidate me. Like he was trying to keep me in line the way he might with one of his pack members who challenged his authority. I may not be a wolf, but my hackles raised.

Oh, yeah? Well, fuck you, buddy.

I opened up my own aura, pulling energy from above and below to make it bigger and stronger than the one trying to impose itself on me. When mine was the size of his, I pushed it forward and rammed his aura back into him.

The shock of that seemed to bring him back to himself, and his glowing amber eyes returned to more or less normal. With a touch of chagrin.

I took a deep breath and let it out. My voice always shook when I was really pissed off, and I hated that. "I was being nice that time," I warned, proud of my steady, serious tones. "Don't try to impose your will on me again, or 'nice' won't show up to play."

Definite chagrin now from Booker. "I'm sorry," he said after a second, still looking a little stunned. "I'm used to dealing with wolves and humans. Wolves don't care about imposing auras all that much. They have their own. Regular humans...don't really notice." He looked into my eyes again. "I wasn't trying to impose my will on you. I swear." He scrubbed the back of his neck with one hand. "I just really want you to stay here. Where I know you're safe."

While I appreciated his concern, he was still being pushy—guilt was just another tactic. *Well, fine.* I could push back.

"I sensed the zombies the other night before you did," I said. "That's a tactical advantage. I know wolves have super-smell powers, but I can sense other things that may help figure out what's going on." Then I leveled my own stare at him, wishing I could make my eyes glow like his. "Beyond all of that, I'm going. Period. Besides—" I gestured toward the mirror in the room. "—you have no real way of stopping me." The look on his face was priceless. *The witch wins again.* "We can work together on it or separately, but I'm going."

Still seated, Kate and Nick looked like they wished they had popcorn. I looked back at Booker expectantly.

He wasn't happy, but he wasn't going to push me again. "I'll adapt," he ground out.

From there, it was all a matter of planning things out. Kate was going to be our person in the chair, listening in via the neat earpieces that Nick provided.

I tried not to get too excited, but it felt like a sting operation in a movie.

Booker's irritation and concern finally began to ebb as I made it clear during the planning that I wasn't going to go rogue or half-cocked. I may have laid my good-soldier attitude on a little thick, but since I faced him down in front of his second-in-command, I was in a good enough mood to be willing to give a little back.

Honestly, the worst part of the whole business was looking up all the info we could find about Hel's Belles, which included watching some video of their performances.

They didn't have a website, seeming to have created their online presence out of social media hype. The lead singer was named Heloise, and she was blonde with long, straight hair parted in the middle, usually in an elaborate updo. Her "sister," Belladonna, played piano and wrote their music. She was a redhead. I'd already known most of this beforehand, just through Emma's chatter and social media posts about them. I'd just figured they'd named the band after the first syllables of their names— which had to be fake, like the hair. They didn't look enough alike to be sisters for one thing, and even if they were, I refused to believe that any parents would choose to name their two daughters Heloise and Belladonna. The two dark-haired band members were Leonora, who played guitar, and Magdalena, who played synthesizers—also fake names, I assumed.

Hel's Belles was a relative unknown until about eight months ago, when they started playing in the St. Louis area. Around the same time I bought the building and decided to make a home, they exploded in popularity. They became the featured band at Purgatory nearly three months ago, which was timing that definitely bothered me, as it was when I'd opened the shop.

No one knew their real names or where they came from, although there were some interesting Reddit threads and various other chatter online. This both added to their mystique and frustrated reporters who couldn't find a backstory on them even after six months. They didn't do interviews aside from one feature in the *Riverfront Times* when they hit that Purgatory niche and became minor goth celebrities.

However, most of the talking in the article was from their manager, a guy who called himself Nigel Hades. Kate rolled her eyes at that. "Gods. Could he be any more of a douche-canoe?"

I studied pictures of them, trying to examine the structure of their faces. The hair and makeup obscured most of their individuality, so I couldn't be completely positive, but none of them looked like anyone I knew or had known. The still photos creeped me out, but the footage of their live performances was even creepier. Everything about them made me not want to look. I couldn't keep my eyes on the video for too long before I'd have to look away. It was easier to look at the crowd, which certainly seemed to be affected by the sounds, but was it more than a normal reaction?

Kate noticed my unease. "You sure you're going to be able to be there in person?"

This of course invited the attention of the two wolves in the room. Nick's face was concerned, but Booker's was intense.

"Yes," I said, a little too forcefully, for everyone's benefit. "I will be able to handle it."

Once we'd reconned everything and made plans for charm bags to carry for protection from any magical mesmerism or control, Nick took Kate back to Hecate's Home. I promised to mirror-walk there to pick up charm bags before the show. It would be four hours before we'd need to leave.

That left Booker and me alone in the room. I regarded him with suspicion. He hadn't been angry with me, not really, but he seemed to be on edge.

"You okay?" I asked, as I gathered up my notes and the pictures from the desk. He grunted, large arms crossed in front of him as he watched me. I shrugged. "Whatever."

Before I left the office, he hugged me again. The happiness from before had changed, mingled with something darker and sharper, but his aura cleared exponentially once I leaned into the hug and slid my arms around him. I relaxed and breathed him in, all sandalwood and cedar, all warm male. I should be wondering what was up with these hugs, but damn, I couldn't resist them. It felt like it had been years since I'd been hugged by anyone, and I didn't realize how much I'd missed it. How often had anyone hugged me after my grandparents passed away? I don't think I stayed around anywhere long enough to form the kinds of attachments where hugs happened.

Maybe Booker was equally starved for affection, because he didn't break off the hug like he did earlier. Instead, he leaned down and kissed the top of my head, holding onto me for a moment longer, and then let go when I stepped back, awash in a new confusion. *Kisses on the head? From the wolf who was irritated that I wouldn't stay at home like an obedient little witch?*

With a more relaxed smile, he nodded to me. "I'm going to check on the workers, and then I'll gather the wolves upstairs for a debriefing before we leave. If you need anything, just text."

"Sure," I said, hoping I didn't sound as flustered as I was. Maybe it was a wolf thing? Confuse the prey? This just served as a reminder that I still knew relatively little about werewolves. It's difficult to learn much about something you're actively hiding from.

I went back downstairs and found John helping a customer, so I busied myself until he was done, then showed him how to open the shop. He'd been a closer during his part-time days, but now that he'd be living here and taking on more hours, he was going to need to be more well-versed in all aspects of the business. Luckily, he was all for it—and even luckier, he didn't razz me about Booker.

My only disappointment was when I asked John if he was at all proficient with bookkeeping. "I failed my stats classes twice," he said, all apology. "I think I'd do more harm than good."

Well, fuck. "No problem," I said, sighing. "Just thought I'd ask."

When closing time came, I left John to finish the process and headed upstairs. I'd neglected lunch, so my stomach rumbled major complaints. I figured I'd be able to go up to my place and eat a sandwich with Stanley and Cole and try to relax a bit, before we went to Purgatory around 10 p.m. Which sounded so fucking awful I couldn't stand it—how is 10 p.m. a reasonable time to start anything? I was too damned old for this shit.

Following my instincts, I texted Booker to let him know I was heading upstairs, but instead of going through the mirror, I walked up. I'd been a little curious about the progress of the middle floors.

However, on my way up the stairs, I paused when I heard music coming from the fifth floor. It sounded like more of that awful trance electronica, so I took a detour and found a group of wolves gathered in the large room Booker had originally earmarked as the meeting room. The lighting was low, and the walls were still unpainted—stripes and spots from mudding and taping marked the bare drywall—but the room was furnished with couches and chairs already, plus large floor pillows.

Sure enough, the wolves were gathered there, watching footage of Hel's Belles. Booker was in one of the chairs holding a remote, and when I peered in the doorway, he and several other wolves looked my way. I waved, and Booker gave me a half-smile in the darkened room when he waved back.

I found out later from Nick that there was about two hours of footage from different shows, and they watched that footage at least three times. They watched shorter videos that showed more of the club dozens of times. They watched everything so that they could verbally plan how to best get in and out without being noticed or ambushed, how to ensure an exit strategy.

I had to admit, I was transfixed by the sight of them. It was like seeing a bunch of dogs wholly engrossed in watching something, but to the nth degree. Apparently, wolves are very visual thinkers. At least, that was my assumption from context. Even during the few minutes I stood there, one would mutter a word and the others would nod as if a whole conversation had taken place. Probably for them, it had. At no point did they look away from the screen. My own eyes got blurry when I tried to figure out if they were blinking.

After this, I went straight upstairs and made myself a sandwich, and I was getting ready to step through the mirror out to the roof when I remembered to text Booker again. After I sent the message, I sighed. This was going to get old real quick. I'd have to find some memes and save them to my phone to use—that would make it more fun.

I began to step across the threshold of the mirror, and Cole meowed at me, sounding somewhat plaintive. He'd been doing fairly well with having wolves in the building, but being so busy with the wolves and research and the shop hadn't left me much time with him, so I picked him up and carried him up to the roof with me.

I never worried about Cole being on the roof. It was seven stories up, with no buildings connected to ours. Our neighboring buildings were industrial in nature, mostly warehouses. Cole never seemed too interested in leaving the Sanctum in general. I'd adopted him pretty much the day after I moved in, and he'd taken to the place immediately, with little of the fear cats usually display when moved to a new place. He'd always just kind of roamed around like it was home.

When I set him down on the rooftop, Cole trotted right over to Stanley. I sat down on one side of the gargoyle, and Cole took the other side.

While I ate, I proceeded to tell them both the news of the day, including the upcoming trip to Purgatory to see the shiver-inducing Hel's Belles and how the wolves were really into watching videos.

As always, Stanley listened attentively with no judgment. As for Cole, the sandwich was tuna salad, so I had his complete attention, and since I was a complete sucker for that rapt gaze, I rewarded it with pieces of tuna here and there.

I didn't tell them about how Booker had hugged me twice—the first time because he seemed so happy, the second because he seemed to need the contact—and I wasn't sure why.

CHAPTER 19

WITCH AND WEREWOLF SUV: SPECIAL FASHION VICTIMS UNIT

JO

THE WOLVES WERE SILENT AS WE DROVE TO PURGATORY IN A large black Yukon—the kind of vehicle I'd seen FBI agents and mob guys drive on TV. I'd always thought it was overkill to have a huge SUV, but being crammed into the thing with Booker, Nick, Max, and three other wolves whose names I was still learning made me grateful for the space. Ethan and more wolves were trailing us in an identical Yukon to keep an eye on things outside the club.

The silence wasn't threatening, but it was eerie. There was no good-natured talk or anxious chatter. I'd tried a "Ready to have fun stormin' da castle?" to Nick and another wolf I was pretty sure was named Kristen, but they just nodded briefly. Booker had flashed me a small, tight grin. No dimples.

I gave up. Clearly, they were all focused, so I just sat with them and tried to do the same. I did a five-minute meditation and clutched the charm bag Kate had made for me. The wolves all had their own charm bags, but mine was different—it had physical protection woven in.

It was funny, in a sad way. Emma had tried for months to get me to go to a goth club with her, and here I was, going to a goth club because of her death. With a bunch of werewolves.

The drive was short, absurdly so. When I ventured to ask why we didn't walk in the first place, Booker would only say, "Armored transport," and left it at that.

None of us had bothered to dress the part. The wolves were in their street clothes, but all their outfits involved black, and Booker had switched to a black jacket—I assumed this to be a nod to the Purgatory ambiance. They didn't need to do much, though, I had to concede. It wasn't that they were all incredibly attractive in their human forms, but it was more the air of confidence and focus. The auras of power that surrounded even the younger wolves in the group would make them more attractive to any regular human.

As for me, well, I had exactly zero clothes I would consider to be dress-up goth stuff, but I had plain black clothes. Luckily, my black hair, pale skin, and light blue eyes worked to my advantage, so I wore dark jeans and a black shirt with some silver jewelry and a tiger's-eye necklace for clarity. The amber in the stone reminded me of Booker's eyes.

After we parked, I became the center of a moving wall of wolves. I wished I had stilts or something, but unfortunately, my black Chuck Taylors did nothing. I couldn't see anything. After we paid the cover and went inside, they gave each of us a necklace. It was a different rune, a more common Norse one, but otherwise, it was exactly like the one I'd taken off of Emma. However, this one had "Hel's Belles" etched on the back. Some kind of weird promotional merch?

I gave Booker a look, and he asked the door guy, with a casual air, "What's with the necklace?"

The door guy, a stocky, barrel-chested dude with a long, blond beard and a Purgatory T-shirt, said, "Complimentary with your tickets. If you have to leave, show it to whoever's on the door to get back in."

"Cute," I muttered. *So how do we get the weird ancient runes that turn us into zombies? Asking for a friend.*

Booker gave me a warning glare, then nodded at the guy and put the necklace in his pocket. The wolves mirrored his actions. I followed suit, but I noticed that most people we passed as we pushed into the crowd were wearing theirs. Even with my limited visibility, due to Wall o' Wolves Inc., I could tell that none of the necklaces I was seeing were the zombie ones.

Curious.

As we got into the open bar and dance area, the wolves separated from around me, still keeping a perimeter, but I could breathe again. Well, for the most part. I could breathe in the heavy, people-scented air of a totally new place. Purgatory definitely contained power that felt just a hint wrong, and I tried to dig deeper, but the noise and the crowd were doing a number on my anxiety. I hadn't been out of the Sanctum in nearly two weeks, not that I'd been a social butterfly before that. I'd always turned down Emma's invites to shows with the "I don't like that music" excuse, but even if one of my favorite bands had been playing in the city, I probably wouldn't have gone.

Old habits died hard...as did old PTSD.

Booker's presence on my left steadied my nerves—I used his rock-solid aura as an anchor. The place was a renovated warehouse that had been gutted, so it was huge and full of people. The owners had put a lot of thought into catering to different types of crowds. Plenty of dancing space, but also good seating. There was a large stage set along the east wall—empty for the moment—and a huge dance floor packed with people, a hundred at least, dancing to some flavor of electronica controlled by a DJ in a booth off the stage. On three different floors, balconies with separate bars circled the dance floor. People sat at the tables on the large balconies, eating, drinking, and watching the dancing below them.

Booker directed me to an empty table as the other wolves spread out in the club. Whatever ESP or shorthand they had had them each hurrying off in a different direction. I wasn't sure exactly what their plan was. I was told we were coming to see Hel's Belles perform and then leave. A scouting run.

Apparently, Booker had planned things so we would arrive before the band began to play. I decided to focus my energies on finding another of the ancient runes. There had to be some rhyme or reason to who got those and why. Maybe hardcore fans, like Emma? People who were more susceptible? People who had magical abilities? I needed to get a better sense of the magic at play here, if I could just find my center.

Booker ordered two bottles of water from a passing server, then he leaned in and pitched his voice low. "Are you okay?"

I shrugged, trying to relax the tension in my shoulders. He frowned but didn't push it. Instead, he kept up his casual scanning of the room.

When we got our waters, I didn't open mine, just spun it between my hands, feeling the cold plastic on my skin. Could the damn band just get out here and play already?

As if they'd heard my wish, the lights dimmed, and the DJ faded out the current endless song. "Y'all ready to get your trance on?" he asked, his voice booming and echoing over the speakers. The crowd roared in answer, and I winced. When I glanced over, I could see Booker clenching his jaw.

"You know it! It's time for the main attraction...Purgatory is proud to present our own Hel's Belles!"

The crowd's cheers faded as the smoke machine went to work and the blue and white lights began to weave patterns on the stage. Suddenly, four figures stood there: Leonora and Magdalena on either end of the stage, with Belladonna and Heloise in the center. It was like they all simply appeared onstage, but I knew that was just a matter of clever placement and perspective. I couldn't smell any real magic at work yet.

I had to give it to the band members—their live-show aesthetic definitely paid forward the Victorian Dead flair. Their looks were similar to their pictures on the Purgatory website, with only minor variations in their dresses and hairstyles.

Heloise's blonde hair shimmered nearly white in the lighting, and her dark eyes and red lips were startlingly vivid in contrast. Her dress was white lace, unlike the black worn by the rest of the band. When she took the microphone in one slender hand, even I had to admit that she possessed an ethereal beauty like nothing I'd ever seen in real life. She stood out from the rest of the group like a white swan in the center of a group of large ravens— all beautiful, but in different ways.

When she began to sing, and the band followed her lead, the effect bordered on hypnotic. I had trouble taking my eyes from her long enough to glance over at Booker, to see that he, too, was focused on her, unblinking, as were the other wolves.

Then, almost unconsciously, I put my hand in my pocket and grasped the rune there. It gave my hand a little bit of a shock, like when too much static builds up. The jolt wasn't much, but it worked its way into the center of my chest before I realized what was happening.

I came back to myself with a start, forcing my hands to release the necklace. "Booker," I hissed, leaning toward him. "Don't touch that rune."

He jerked, and I saw him draw his hand from his pocket with an extremely pissed-off frown. He did something that signaled the other wolves.

After that, we just watched the rest of the crowd, most of whom were wearing their necklaces. They were more than involved—they were mesmerized, swaying and moving with the beat of the song, some with their hands up and loose, their eyes coming back to Heloise again and again. She was drawing them in with the song, a chant in some language I didn't understand.

The hairs on the back of my neck stood up, and I caught my first glimpse of the energy, the power, she was drawing from the crowd. They gave it to her willingly, letting her pull their will out of them so she could shape it into her own power. While I watched, I could almost see it forming around her, disappearing inside her. She wasn't ready to wield it. Not yet. But I got the sense that she was powering up, like a witch-shaped Death Star.

I tried to avoid looking directly at her, but my gaze was pulled in her direction—and when her wild, crazed eyes caught mine, she smiled a wide, blood-red grin. She moved as she sang, and I saw into her, intuition kicking in so hard it nearly hurt. Something was *very* off about her, horribly *wrong* with her, but all that was pushed aside by something more frightening.

Heloise knew we were there.

She knew about the wolves and about me. We probably had less than a minute before all that stolen power and energy would be unleashed on us. I didn't know what she planned to do, but no fucking way were we going to stick around and find out.

I jumped from my stool. "We have to go. Right now," I said. Booker was up immediately, all the wolves following suit, and we headed back to the front door. "Drop those necklaces. Now."

They all did as I bid them. Pack mentality had its uses. I took a second and tucked mine into my charm bag—the charms would dampen its powers, and I needed to study this thing alongside the other rune—and let myself be swept out of the club by a Wall o' Wolves that I was suddenly, desperately grateful to have all around me.

Goddess. Those eyes.

I couldn't tell if anyone followed us, but I figured Booker and the wolves were on top of that situation. All I knew was that I was in that giant, stifling club full of tranced-out people and malevolent magic, and in the next breath I was outside in the fresh air—well, as fresh as it got in St. Louis. The Mississippi smelled like dead fish, but it was a welcome, familiar scent after the club.

Once we were all in the Yukon and driving away, Booker leaned back from the passenger door. "Are you hurt? Did she do something?" His low voice was urgent but warm.

"No." I took a deep breath. How odd to be relieved to be in a vehicle full of wolves. "Not to me. She was drawing energy directly from the crowd." I swallowed. "I could actually see them giving her their will, their energy. The rune necklaces were the key. She's using them."

Booker's eyebrows raised. "Something you've seen before?"

"Not like that," I said. "You?"

He frowned. "I'll have to consult with the Council."

"She knew about me. She knew about the rest of you," I said. "She was... glad we were there. She wanted to show off."

"We figured that much," Booker said nonchalantly. "It was set up like a lure, but we didn't take the bait the way they expected."

"Oh, really?" I snapped. *Resilient cannon fodder, huh? Diana, you definitely picked the right wolf.*

"That's why I didn't want you to come," he said, adopting a let's-be-reasonable tone. "You were right—we learned a lot more with you there."

"I'm so very glad," I drawled, reminding myself that I was the one who'd insisted on going, so I shouldn't get too bitchy with Booker. All that irritation at him simply faded into fear—not for me or the wolves, but for the innocents back at the show. The ones that Heloise was controlling.

"You know, I'm not really into concerts or the goth subculture or any of that, but it seems like a fucking rotten thing to get your will sucked out of you and possibly die just because you're a fan of music." I didn't realize I'd said it out loud until the wolf sitting beside me grunted in agreement.

Booker also nodded back at me. "It's also not smart to bring a bunch of wolves into your stronghold just to show them that you can." He paused, his mouth grim. "I wonder if they thought we'd attack right there. If they wanted us to."

My eyes went wide, considering the kind of bloodbath that might have been. Zombies generally don't notice their heads being torn off. Live people get very upset about it. Briefly. "Holy Hecate." What the hell would that have proven? What could it have accomplished?

What did Hel's Belles really want, aside from my death?

"We wouldn't have wanted to hurt any of them, but there's no way the band could have known that," Booker said. "Still, I find it interesting they recognized us right off the bat. They seemed to want us to know they were the ones sending the zombies. That's pretty damn brazen."

Great. Brazen bad guys. My favorite.

CHAPTER 20

WHENEVER I WANT YOU, ALL I HAVE TO DO IS SCREAM

JO

BACK HOME AT THE SANCTUM, I TRIED TO SHAKE OFF THE ICK factor of the club and the unease about Heloise and the memory of those wide, insane eyes. *You're back on your own turf, Murphy. Relax. The crazy goth necromancer-witch can't get you here.* I took a few cleansing breaths and did a quick binding spell on the Hel's Belles necklace—I would study it further the next day. For now, I was ready to go to sleep.

Booker had watched me carefully during all of this, his wolves having gone up to do a quick debrief with Nick and then retire to their respective apartments. He stayed to watch the binding after having inspected the rune himself again.

Once I was done, he gave me a long stare. "You're not steady," he began gruffly.

"I'm tired," I retorted, not wanting to be soothed. I wasn't steady. I was spooked. I was worried. So I didn't argue when he walked me up to my apartment.

I did come close to arguing, though, when he came in the door with me.

"I'm just going to sleep on your couch tonight," he said. "After the nightmare this morning, and the club tonight, I just want to make sure everything is okay here."

"Everything" meaning me. Of course.

I wanted to be fierce and independent and tell him I'd be fine. Then I felt his aura, considered that strength. Remembered how I'd used it to keep me steady and anchored while we were in the club. Booker the Wolf's presence comforted me, as strange as that might be. He was a little autocratic at times, but I could work around that. What had he said when he conceded to me earlier? *I'll adapt.*

I could do that too. Within reason. And he did seem reasonable. Easy to talk to, most of the time. Considerate. Funny. Plus, he was a great hugger. A wielder of attractive dimples.

Besides, he was already living here. His apartment was on the sixth floor, and it was clearly meant to be not only his place but also a place for other wolves to stay as needed. He'd turned it into a dormlike place with four bedrooms and a large central area with copious seating in front of the television, right next to the kitchen, creating an eat-and-play area. He'd shown it to me a few days before, and his pleasure in it had been rather adorable.

However, I couldn't help but notice his bedroom was right beneath mine. I wanted to file that away as a coincidence, but nothing this wolf did seemed accidental or random to me.

He'd be sleeping near enough to me anyway. What difference did one floor make?

I shrugged and got him a pillow and a blanket for the sofa. When he thanked me, showing his dimples, I flushed a little. I could feel it. "Well, good night," I said. "If you're hungry, there's some food in the fridge. Help yourself."

When I turned to escape into the bathroom, he did one of those werewolf-fast moves, and suddenly, he was beside me. Very gently, he lifted a hand and stroked my flushed cheek with his fingers. His touch was whisper-soft. I wanted to lean into it.

When I looked up at him, his amber eyes were glowing down at me. Very slowly, he started bending down, maintaining eye contact, and I found myself drowning in sandalwood and cedar in the very best way. I leaned up against him as I stood on my tiptoes, a little twist inside my belly at the feel of him, the lovely warmth of his body, tipping up my chin and pressing my lips to his in a light kiss.

His lips were warm and soft beneath my own, and there was a hint of response that stole my breath, but the next second his lips were immobile, the rest of his body rigid with tension, his aura darkening.

Crap, crap, CRAP. Misread those signals, Murphy.

I withdrew from him, stepped back, but his eyes were closed. Maybe he was going in for a hug instead? Or maybe he wanted to whisper something to me? I mean, that was ridiculous—there was no one in this room but us, but whatever. There was some reason. No one freezes up like that for welcome advances.

Had I been blushing earlier? No. Now the blood truly rushed to my face in what must've been a furious tidal wave of blotchy red, one of the true curses of pale Irish skin. I took a step back from him and looked away. I may have stammered out something like, "Whoops. Sorry." The particulars were unclear during the raging storm of my mortification.

I pulled in a deep breath and took a second step back from Booker. *Well, that happened. No way out of the situation but through it. Someday, we'll look back on this and laugh.* His eyes were open now, so I pasted an attempt at a smile on my face and dove in.

"I'm sorry," I said. "I didn't mean to put you in an awkward position by kissing you. I thought you were leaning to do that, but clearly, I read that wrong." I said it all way too quickly, then tacked on, "Can we ignore that just happened?" *Holy Hecate, please say yes so I can hide somewhere and ride out this horrific embarrassment alone.*

Booker's eyes had taken on that molten-honey glow, and they were locked on mine. He hadn't moved, but his focus was rapt and active, like I was a puzzle he was trying to figure out.

"No. We can't ignore that." He spoke slowly, enunciating carefully. "You kissed me."

I couldn't meet the intensity of that gaze any longer, so I focused on his chin. A strong chin, defined and angular but with an appealing squareness to it. *Gods damn it.* This wouldn't be happening if he wasn't so attractive. If he wasn't so appealing. If I weren't so lonely. If he didn't feel so good and so bizarrely *right*.

Clearly my instincts had led me down the wrong road there. "You didn't kiss me back. So." I shrugged, willing my cheeks to stop flaming. "I was interested. You're not. There isn't really much else to say, is there?"

When he didn't speak at first, I frowned at him. *Now he chooses to be a sucky communicator.* "Can we just let this go now?"

Of course, a werewolf wouldn't let it go. Not this wolf, who'd chased me up and down the Mississippi for months, then pulled me into his life when he found me—for better or for worse.

When he finally spoke, his voice had dropped an octave, and it made me shiver. "I'm more than a foot taller than you," he said. He sounded almost... offended. "If I hadn't wanted you to kiss me, you would have had to get a stepstool, and even then, you couldn't have managed it."

I narrowed my eyes. "Oh, really?"

He took a step toward me. "I was showing *restraint.*"

I didn't back away. His aura had changed, and the charge there was intense. Aroused. *Oh.* I gazed up into his burning eyes, let that warmth travel through my whole body. "Well, what would it be like if you weren't showing restraint?"

He smiled a positively wolfish grin. "Would you like a demonstration?"

Um. I felt that one in my toes, my knees, and other parts. "I live to learn," I quavered before I could think better of it.

Within a moment, the space that remained between us ceased to exist. He had his hand in my hair, cradling the back of my head, and then his lips were soft and hungry on mine. Coaxing me to open for him, for his tongue. I sighed into his mouth, and he growled with approval before bending forward and lifting my body off the ground, his arms under my legs, molding me to him.

So much heat. So much energy. Our auras mingled. Both of us lit up from the inside. He turned, taking me to the nearest wall and pressing me up against it. His mouth, hot and urgent, demanded constant attention, and I arched into him, raising one leg and then the other to wrap around his hips. Every part of him was rigid again, I noted with satisfaction and not a little alarm, and I wanted him that way. His fierce need nudging into my warmth.

Goddess. I was already attracted to him, but there was nothing hotter than the way he seemed to want me. His aura was enveloping me as surely as his arms, as enticingly as his tongue, so tight that I was breathless with it. Larger auras for larger beasts? Maybe a bigger sex drive? My mind wandered off for a second, but then he moved one hand to the curve of my bottom to tilt me up into him, and I couldn't think anymore.

I'm not sure how much time passed, but eventually he slowed the rhythm, eased back on the friction of our bodies, soothing the fire, and I finally got the mental and physical strength to push against his shoulders a little, rather than pull on them.

The instant I pushed, he ended the kiss, setting me down with care. Luckily, he kept his arms around me for a minute. My knees were definitely wobbly.

I swallowed and ran my tongue over my lips, still feeling them tingle. He was watching me, but I kept my eyes level with his chest as I stepped to the side to get a little bit of space between us.

"So," I said, trying to get back my breath. "That's unrestrained?"

He watched me, not blinking. Our auras were still connected, mingling like lovers. "No," he said, a rumble from his chest. "Not even close." He tried to grin again, tried to be playful, but he was too intent. No dimples. "There were too many clothes between us." He paused, his voice rougher. "I don't want to spook you."

I raised my eyebrows and hooked my hands in the pockets of my jeans to give them something to do. "What am I, a horse?" I think I meant it as a joke —because I knew what he was going to say.

"Jo." He stepped closer, and for a moment I thought he was going to reach for my hand, but he didn't. *Don't touch the witch. Don't scare the witch.* "I know your history." He sighed, and the patience in that instantly pissed me off. "I don't want to move too fast with you and then have you regretting it, or being upset by it."

I tried really hard not to let my anger out, but today had already been too much. Now he was going to use what happened to me with the Fenris as an excuse? Because I couldn't handle that? Ever since I met Booker, he'd been trying to convince me that he was nothing like the Fenris. He'd all but succeeded. If he was afraid he was going to somehow break me or scare me during a healthy bout of sex, this—whatever the hell it was between us—was dead in the water already.

"Thanks so much for making that choice for me," I snapped. "For the record, just in case you're curious about how I really feel, if it's a choice between you not responding at all versus you going wild, I'll take wild." I pulled myself up to my full, if pitiful, height and met those unblinking eyes with my own, letting him feel the full force of my anger. "I may have issues, but I'm not fragile. I won't break. If you scare me, I'll tell you. Quit with the kid gloves and get over it, or don't even bother."

Booker didn't say anything to that, and I didn't wait for a response. I was exhausted and tired of dealing with people.

And wolves.

And crazy goth necromancer bitches who wanted to kill me.

I turned and went into my bedroom, did my bedtime cleansing and routine, put on sweats, pushed an irritated Cole off my pillow, and went to sleep.

While I slept, the Fenris dream came, and it lasted longer than it ever had before, went deeper into that awful time period than it ever had—big surprise, given that I was exhausted emotionally, physically, and spiritually. There was screaming, as there always was, but it stopped when I jolted awake, my cheeks cold with tears. I turned on the bedside table lamp, rubbing my hands over my face. Trying to breathe.

My cell phone rang. It was Booker. I didn't bother saying hello—I just answered it and put it up to my ear like a sleepwalker.

"Barrier. In front of the door to your room," Booker growled into the phone. "Take it down." After a beat of silence, he added an even growlier, "Please."

I hung up and concentrated on the bedroom door, coaxing the energy back into the stones in the walls. It took more time than normal, but then, I was shaking more than normal. Cole's ears were back, but he was still on the bed, watching me.

I'd been having the dream way more than usual. It was a favorite of my subconscious, of course, but as I'd learned to process it and heal from it over the years, the dream had dwindled to only three or four times a year.

Now I'd had it three times in less than two weeks. Twice in two fucking days.

Thanks to what I'd seen in the dream's extended-play version, I thought I finally knew why.

As the energy finally dissipated, Booker came into the bedroom on the balls of his feet, checking first me and then every corner of the room. "What happened?" It reminded me of how he'd looked that day he'd helped me stop Zombie Emma—wild, half-crazed, ready for anything. His hair stuck up on one side, the grain of a beard beginning to show. He was in his jeans, but barefoot, his shirt in disarray. "Are you okay?"

Not even close. It was an unconscious echo of what he'd said earlier. I breathed in and out. "It was a nightmare."

"Again?" He came to me, urged me to sit back down on the bed. I hadn't even realized I was standing.

"I'm sorry," I said, wiping at my cheeks again. Was I still crying? "I didn't mean to scare you."

"Jo." He sat beside me on the bed, his warmth reassuring now that his fear was fading. "Will you tell me about it?"

I sighed. "It's...just a nightmare."

"Don't lie to me," he said, but this time it was gentle, soothing. His hand was on my back, gently rubbing my neck with his fingertips. "What was it about?"

I leaned back into his fingers. "The Fenris."

He nodded, as if that were a given. "What happens in the dream?"

I almost smiled. Of course, stalling like a child had zero effect on Booker. To tell him the whole story was to relive it. I was afraid it would take more than I had left in me to tell him what I'd learned tonight.

"Just tell me about the dream, Jo. Please." Booker's hand moved up to my hair, then back down to my shoulder and neck. A caress. He was petting me like I would pet Cole. "Then I'll go away."

I swallowed, and it tasted almost metallic. "Well, the dream itself is just about being captured by the Fenris and everything that happened there." I finally turned to him, raising my eyes to meet his. "I think I know what happened now."

His body went still, but his fingers still curved around my neck. He didn't appear to be able to think of any more questions to ask me.

I tried to smile, but it was as wobbly as my knees had been after his kiss. "I guess I know that you still need me to help your pack. You signed the lease, but I have to ask." I took a shaking breath. "Will you still be here for me tomorrow if I tell you tonight about what happened?"

Now his other hand, warm and gentle, closed over mine where it lay clenched into a fist on my leg. He coaxed it open, linked his fingers with mine. "You price yourself too low, as usual." He caught my gaze with his, smoothed a lock of hair back from my forehead with his free hand. "I'm here. I'm staying. Tell me what happened."

CHAPTER 21

THROUGH THE LOOKING GLASS (AND WHAT THE WITCH FOUND THERE)

JO

I HAD BARELY TURNED 23, AND I'D BEEN LIVING OUT OF MY CAR since before my birthday. The "friend" I'd shared an apartment with, Shirley, had gotten us evicted—I didn't realize she'd been spending our rent money on drugs until the eviction notice had been served. I'd been going to school and working, so I really only slept there, but that had backfired on me big time. Why had I trusted her with our money?

Oh, 23-year-old Jo, you sweet summer child.

It wasn't as big a setback as it might have been, given my history. Since my grandparents died when I was 16, I'd been in a couple of foster homes, but after the first few, I started living on my own. My foster families had been nice people, but their houses never became my homes. I was a guest, basically just killing time there. So I'd cut out the middleman and stayed on friends' couches or in my ancient Honda for the last part of high school.

Therefore, being homeless for a few months while I got some money together wasn't a new thing for me. Inconvenient and a trifle pathetic, but not new.

What was new was the way people were disappearing—especially the people on the fringes where I had found myself. I would see certain people for weeks, parked or camped out in specific places, and then poof, they were gone. I'm sure the homeless population didn't seem to have dwindled to anyone who wasn't out there, who wasn't a part of it, but I could tell. There were fewer of us, and the vibe had become one of fear. Paranoia. I was luckier than most, because I had a car with doors that locked.

In the end, of course, locked doors didn't matter. The Fenris had seen me and decided they wanted me.

So they took me, ripping the car door off its hinges one night and pulling me out of a sound sleep and into their world.

That first night was the hunt. They took me to a place outside the city and left me in the woods, loosely bound and blindfolded. Once I wriggled my hands free and removed the blindfold, they had disappeared, and I was left wondering if I'd been the victim of some kind of awful practical joke. I didn't know then that the supernatural world existed. I thought my burgeoning magical skills were just some form of telepathy, like maybe I was a mutant. Yeah, I'd read too many comic books.

I had no idea I'd been taken by werewolves at first. I just knew I'd been taken.

I tried to find my way out of the woods, and they watched. Then they played with me. I'd stop to rest and find myself grabbed from behind, carried to another spot, and released again. I screamed for them to stop, and they laughed. That was the first time I realized how horrible the situation really was—hearing that crazed, delighted laughter ring out from all parts of the forest around me.

There were just so many of them. I could swear that each time, they hunted me as a different group, some in human form and some in wolf form, although my brain hadn't yet processed that they were all werewolves. They thought it was loads of fun to watch me tear ass blindly through the woods, only to be pulled up short again and again. After the third or fourth time they let me go, I just stopped trying to run. My attempts at escape made them happy, and anything that pleased them felt like a bad idea. I already knew I wasn't going to win, so I refused to play the game, even though it angered them.

Even back then, sometimes all I had was a fuck-you attitude. I didn't know if that made it better or worse for me among the Fenris.

When I stopped playing the hunt game, they decided they wanted to smell my fear. They brought me to their den, which was a big building somewhere, possibly a warehouse they'd been using. It was furnished in Modern Meth Lab and stank of wolf odors, human odors, and death. By then, I was already dulled by shock, but they managed to bring the fear they wanted out of me. They put me in a cage in the main room, then told me stories about other people they'd taken, hunted, killed, beaten, and raped. Some of these were people I knew, had met on the streets.

The Fenris got what they wanted, because I couldn't help being scared, but beneath the fear was rage. With every story they told me, with every bit of excruciating detail, my fear and rage built. I was angry that these creatures —I knew by then that they weren't just humans, although I hadn't yet processed "werewolf"—were doing this to people I knew. I was even angrier that they were doing it to me.

It's weird, the things your brain will do to protect you. To keep you from breaking. My anger did that for me.

That didn't mean I was safe though. Far from it. My brain tried to give me mental blocks of denial to keep me from panicking, to help stall the anticipation of the pain. Right up until they threw the first punch, I told myself they weren't going to beat me. Even after the first beating, I told myself they weren't going to rape me. After the first rape, I convinced myself they would just kill me. They wouldn't do it again.

Then, they did it all again.

And again.

And again.

Each time, I endured it all. Somehow, I lived through it, even though by then, I didn't want to.

At one point, one of them mentioned my mouth. He was in human form, wearing a pair of cut-off jean shorts and a Pantera T-shirt, and he was certain I was beaten down enough to give him a blow job—or at least, not resist. He was wrong.

His erect dick was in my mouth, and I was crying, breathing through my nose as best I could and trying not to gag at the taste. At one point, my wildly rolling eyes caught sight of his bare feet. They were filthy, with long toenails that had collected dirt beneath the ragged ends. All that anger and hate swelled up inside me again.

I didn't have a lot of strength, but I had just enough, thanks to the rage, to command my jaw to close on him. There was so much blood that it still filled my mouth even after I spat that disgusting chunk of flesh out onto the dirty floor. He screamed like a hyena and broke my jaw.

That was the end of day two.

By day four, I was broken, body and soul. Exhaustion had consumed everything I had left except the glowing ember of rage deep inside. They never really left me alone, so I never had any real time to recover from one thing before the next thing happened. My jaw was broken, my shoulder dislocated, and something was wrong with my legs. I couldn't feel them, and one was bent wrong. By then, they'd left me out of the cage to save themselves the trouble of dragging me in and out to play their games.

That last night, I tried to crawl away. I don't really even know where I thought I was going to crawl away to, as my body was too battered to do more than inch toward the door. Every inch of me burned hot or numb. None of them even noticed.

So I stopped. Since I couldn't move, I did the only thing left to me: I took all the knowledge I'd gained in my baby witch studies and I prayed.

Not for revenge, but for death. An end.

I called to Hecate. She'd been the goddess to whom I'd gravitated once I knew who She was. Hecate, the goddess of witches, crossroads, keys, dogs. The threefold goddess.

Just a few days prior to being taken, a Wiccan friend of mine who was apprenticing to become a tattoo artist offered to give me a free tattoo if she could use me for practice. I gave her a picture of Hecate's wheel, and newbie artist or no, the tattoo on my wrist had been flawless. That night, I looked at the Hecate's wheel on my wrist through eyes that were nearly swollen shut, and I prayed for Her to come and take me. I begged Her to come and end my life. I put everything I had into my call, including that one small ember of rage that still burned in my ruined body.

For years, this was all I really knew of my experience with the Fenris. It was all I remembered. It was all I ever dreamed of those endless days, and it was plenty.

However, after tonight's dream, I knew what had really happened.

Hecate answered my call that night. Personally.

She must have brought me between the worlds then for the first time, because suddenly I was no longer a broken thing in that stinking torture place but whole and healthy, sitting on a log in a fragrant moonlit meadow with my goddess.

Hecate sat with me in Her maiden form, glowing in a simple dress and golden sandals. She was smiling at me.

"Am I dead? Is it over?" I wasn't sad, just curious. Peaceful.

Hecate shook Her head. "No, Josephine," She said. "You don't get to die just yet. I have plans for you." She waved her hand in front of us, showing me a vision of the Fenris wolves in groups clustered there. There were so many of them, and all of the wolves were linked by a golden thread. "Still, I can help you."

"How?"

Hecate looked around. "You walk between the worlds, Josephine. It is one of your gifts already, though you don't know it." She nodded to the images of the Fenris. "Werewolves straddle two worlds. The Fenris have left themselves vulnerable. If you grab the golden thread, you can pull the Fenris out of the world, where they cannot harm anyone ever again."

Without hesitation, I reached forward to grab the thread, but the image collapsed.

"You cannot do it here. You must be in their world first."

Even the peace of that place wasn't enough to keep fear and anger from trickling back in at the thought of going back.

Hecate gestured with Her free hand. "I have healed your injuries from the damage they have inflicted. It will not hinder you." Her eyes glowed white. "You have the strength to do this. Grab their thread, hold them with your will. Use your rage. Use the memory of the pain. Ignore your fear."

When I nodded, She smiled again, but it was not a smile of comfort. "Once you have them, place your palm on the mirror and bring them here. To me."

Between one breath and the next, I was back on the concrete floor of the den, naked. Somehow in all of the torture and all of the agony, I hadn't realized that my clothes had been entirely ripped from me, but I could feel it now, and I trembled with cold.

Getting feeling back in my legs should have been a good thing, but for a

moment I was paralyzed. If they saw I was healed, they would hurt me again
—I was still covered in my own blood, so hopefully they wouldn't notice
that my wounds were gone. I stayed down and looked around for a mirror,
finally finding one on a wall to my left.

Get to it. I crawled again, agonizingly slow, before a female wolf realized
I'd gotten farther away than they'd realized. "Hey, sweet thing," she cooed.
"Where do you think you're going?" She grabbed my hair and yanked me
up. "This one's ready for more," she called out to the others.

The instant her grip on my hair loosened, her gaze off me, I exploded
into action, knocking her off-balance and propelling myself the last few feet
to the mirror, a cheap rectangle at head height.

I turned then. *The golden thread.* When I unfocused enough, looking
through them instead of *at* them, I could see it, running through all of the
Fenris there and extending out from the building.

I used one hand to gather the golden thread to me, wrapping it around
my palm and *pulling*. The wolves began to struggle, but they couldn't move,
so I wrapped it around my right hand, gathering them all, glorying in having
them at my mercy. Then I wrapped it around my wrists. The wolves fought
against it, howling and screaming, and their terrified confusion fueled me.

It felt *good*.

I pulled the Fenris to the mirror, turning to place both palms there,
pushing them and the golden cord through the mirror, stepping through
with them. Hecate was there, waiting for me, and She smiled, reached out to
take the golden thread from my hands. When the gathered thread was in her
hand, I saw it for what it had become: one long, golden leash on a number
of Fenris wolves now too numerous for me to count.

She gave it two tugs, and all of the Fenris turned into dogs.

My shock must have shown on my face, or perhaps She just felt it.
"Neutered dogs, spayed dogs," Hecate told me, then looked over them.
"They will be much nicer this way."

She turned to smile at me again. "Well done, Josephine. You are free."

Somehow knowing I could, I walked back through the mirror into the
filthy, stinking den, the empty space echoing around me. I cleansed myself as
best I could, still as if in a dream, and methodically packed a bag full of cash
from the Fenris' counting table. Then I stood in the doorway, surveying for
the last time the vile den where I'd been tortured. Where I'd wanted to die.

That was when I realized that Hecate had left me that ember of fury, burning hot in my chest. I knew I would use that ember, expanding it with my magic, my energy, to burn it all down before I left that place, and the person I used to be, behind.

Booker sat silent for a few seconds once I finished my story, one hand still warm on mine, the other back on my neck, rubbing gently. I was more grateful for that skin-to-skin contact than I could say.

Finally, he spoke. "Hecate took the Fenris out of this world and into her own? *Neutered* them into dogs?" Then he started to laugh, shaking his head.

Wolves are weird. I'd have glared at him if I had the energy. "You don't have to believe me, but that's what happened," I said. "Hecate gave me back the memory. I think She took it from me initially. Maybe to help me heal? Or maybe because She wanted to keep it from me until now for Her own purposes?" I sighed. Since he wasn't moving, and since his thumb was stroking over my skin—*petting me again*—I leaned my head against his shoulder.

"I believe you," he said, the rumble of his voice deep and reassuring. "I have no doubt that's what happened." He paused. "What you described—it meshes with the video, at least the physical aspects."

"It also explains some stuff that I didn't really understand," I mused. "The walking through mirrors thing. She showed me how. Now that I can, the threads that bind things are so much easier to see."

Booker nodded.

"Also...my hair turned black that day," I said. Might as well get all of the crazy stuff out in one session.

Somehow, that was the detail that surprised him. "It did? I saw pictures of you from before, when it was a deep red. I just thought you must have colored it."

I wish. I kind of missed coloring my hair. "When I came back to myself after the fire, my hair was black. Can't be bleached or colored." When he didn't respond, I added, "Speaking of things I can't change, the gold thread left scars. That's where these came from."

I lifted my head, tugging my hand free from his and showing him the

tiny white scars on my hands and arms where the gold thread had been
wrapped around them.

"You know, it didn't even cut me," I said, examining them. "All of my
injuries were healed, but even though the thread didn't hurt, never bit
through my skin, these are the only physical scars I have from the whole
thing."

Booker traced his fingers over a few of the white lines. "These were in
your files, but no one knew what they were from."

"Them and me both."

He took one of my hands in his again. "Okay, so you came to
somewhere out in the middle of nowhere with a bag of money."

"Knowing I'd been taken and tortured by Fenris werewolves, having all
those memories, but not knowing how I got out of there." I nodded.
"Goddess, it was a small fortune. I bought a new car, gathered up what little
I had left of my personal possessions, and I ran."

That money had been enough to keep me going, along with my side
jobs, for eight years—and I leveraged it to build up my nest egg. It was the
height of ironies for me that the Fenris had basically funded the Sanctum.

Booker was doing his unblinking wolf stare again. Would I ever get used
to that?

"Everyone has been so worried about you, about your power and how
you might use it," he said. "We should have known that you were just
defending yourself."

I lay my head back on his shoulder because it was wide and warm and
there. He smelled even better, somehow, than he had the night before.
When we kissed.

After a moment, I said, "I don't regret doing it. I'd do it again. Although
maybe just a lot earlier."

He grunted agreement, coasting his thumb over one of my scars.

In the time that followed, Booker asked me a lot of questions—about
my life, about my magical abilities—and I answered them freely. It felt right,
the intensely personal nature of it. It was the kind of weird early-morning
conversation that sometimes happens between two people who are awake at
an odd time. It felt like we were the only two people in the world, or that
maybe we'd shifted into a pocket universe with each other. No one else
existed.

I was just fine with that.

"I was pretty much a cut-and-dry pagan before the Fenris got me," I said during a lull in the conversation. "I built on what I learned over the years when I was on the run, but it was nothing like what's happened to me since I've been here in the Sanctum." I sighed. "The longer I'm here, the more my abilities flex their muscles and become more apparent. Maybe it was being on the run for so long. There's never enough time to get into a routine on the road."

Booker nodded. "Two things I've learned. The first is that witches often come into the meat of their power when they enter their third decade, and here you are." I shrugged and resettled my head on his shoulder to continue listening. "The second is that most witches do better with a seat of power. As much as it's a cliché, witches like castles. They like to have big places that are fortified and protected. You've done that here."

Holy Hecate. Once again, I was confronted with the depth and breadth of my ignorance about the supernatural world and my place in it. "So, again, is there like a manual or something?"

He chuckled and shook his head.

"Yeah, I guess that would be too easy," I grumbled, making him chuckle again.

Well, if witches like holding fortified positions, I was set up pretty well. The river near me, the bridges as brackets, and the triple crossroads as the foundation for it all. It occurred to me then that I must have been doing exactly what Hecate wanted me to do.

I have plans for you. She'd said that to me directly. Back in Kate's bedroom, during the vision/visitation, Hecate had spoken through Kate to tell me I was the "torchbearer, fire-bringer."

What you build isn't for you, Jo, the single entity, but you, Jo, the plural. Diana the virgin brings the unborn into the world.

The clarity and renewed, growing power I'd established here had to mean I was walking down the path I was meant to take. With one of the allies I was meant to walk it with. *Booker is essential.* We had to work together on this.

Booker murmured something, and I felt his lips in my hair. Had I said any of that out loud, or was it just because we were so connected in that moment? Did it matter? I'd shared everything with him already—he knew all the darkest, most painful parts of me—and he wasn't walking away.

I already trusted him. I already wanted him. I knew that he was on my side.

Whatever it was that had brought me to this place—zombies, wolves, goddesses, and all—I was glad he was with me.

CHAPTER 22

WON'T YOU PLEASE, PLEASE HELP ME?

JO

AT SOME POINT, REALIZING THE SKY WAS BEGINNING TO lighten, I asked Booker for some privacy so I could do a few yoga stretches and get myself ready for the day, and he complied. John was opening the shop that morning, so I didn't have to rush, and I needed that bit of normalcy. The routine.

Once I'd showered and dressed, I went out to the kitchen to grab some breakfast and open a can of Fancy Feast for Cole. He'd been mostly in hiding since Booker had been in the apartment, but I figured werewolf or no werewolf, Cole would be present for his breakfast. The cat did not fuck around when it came to his wet food.

However, when I got into the kitchen, Cole was on the countertop, already eating a bowl of raw meat—also known as the hamburger I'd been planning to use to make tacos later. Booker was standing next to Cole, also eating raw hamburger from his own bowl, albeit with a fork. Both of them paused every now and again to regard each other, then went back to their food.

The incongruity of the image stopped me in my tracks. It was...sweet? I guess? I mean, the boys were bonding. With raw meat? *Gross.*

"You're going to spoil him," I said, walking over to stroke Cole's back and be totally ignored by him. "What if he turns up his nose at Fancy Feast forevermore?" Booker gave me a somewhat guilty look and swallowed, while I tried not to think about what had been in his mouth. "Hey, you didn't save any for me?"

He laughed, as I'd intended, and I grabbed a bowl and a box of cereal. The three of us ate together, standing up in the kitchen, in a companionable silence.

When Cole finished, he sat on the counter and washed himself, ignoring Booker but making it clear that he wasn't intimidated by the wolf any longer. *Good for you, dude.* Although I knew he'd played right into Booker's hands.

Booker washed out both his and Cole's bowls and put them into the dishwasher, and then he smiled at me. "I'm heading over to talk to Nick and Max, then do more recon on Hel's Belles."

"I'll be in the shop, and I'll research while I can," I said. "Text me if you find anything."

"Ditto," he said. There was an awkward moment, but then he flashed me his dimples again, looking almost shy. "See you later."

When he was gone, locking the door behind him, I let out a long breath, then tidied up my own dishes and grabbed my phone to pop down through the mirror to my office. When I emerged with some paperwork and invoices, John was already there, and sitting next to the cash register, looking very pleased with himself, was Cole.

I greeted John and narrowed my eyes at my cat. How the hell did he get down here without me? I guess I shouldn't have been surprised. When a cat knows there are other interesting places to be, he'll find a way to get to them.

When John left the counter to help a customer, I went over to Cole and rubbed his head, scratching him behind his ears in the way he liked best.

"Dude, if you absolutely must be everywhere, I understand, but please try to stay inside the building," I said. "My protections won't extend past that, and I like you. Got it?" I knew he didn't understand me, but maybe something might sink in.

After such an auspicious beginning, my work morning became surprisingly quiet. I was tired, but a clean kind of tired—like I'd divested myself of something that needed to be purged.

John had an afternoon class, so he took off around 10:30 a.m., leaving me alone in the shop without even wolves around. I looked up more about the runes and tried to find out about the chants in the lyrics from the night before. All the while, I wondered about that ember of fire that was still inside me. I meditated, trying to find it, but I couldn't focus enough.

Before I could dwell on it too much, the sound of someone moving in the shop made me whip around, startled. It was Grace Taylor, who must have come in from the back stairwell. *Damn.* I was going to have to put a bell on the back door as well.

She smiled at me as she walked in. "Hi," she said. "Is it cool if I come down here?"

For a moment, I just stared at her in awe. Grace had looked so fragile when I'd met her, despite her height and strong build. Today she looked like a fertility goddess. A blue maxi-dress displayed her still enormous belly, but her dark skin was glowing, and her crown of natural hair gleamed, no longer appearing wilted and dull. Her eyes weren't rimmed by shadows, and her aura felt clear and strong. Not quite at Booker strength, but there was no doubt that Grace was a powerful wolf in her own right.

I smiled. "I'd love some company." The many questions I had already amassed about werewolf culture crowded into my head, but I held back for the moment. *Do not interrogate the pregnant werewolf before she's even had a chance to sit down.*

Grace grimaced good-naturedly. "Just company?" she said. "Is there anything I can do to help you out? I'm going crazy up there. Nick keeps pushing a remote in my hand and telling me to find something new on Netflix." She rolled her eyes, and I chuckled.

"If you're sure—and if I won't get either of us in trouble—I could find something. What do you do?"

It turned out that Grace's day job was working as an accountant. *Hecate, be praised.* By the time Grace had finished talking about her job, I'd put her in front of my computer and begged her to help me.

"I do all the accounting for the shop, building, and leases myself," I explained, "but I don't really know what I'm doing. I constantly worry I'm doing it wrong, and someday someone's going to show up and take me away to IRS jail."

Grace laughed. "Got it. Well, let me take a look."

Over the next hour, Grace made short work of a chore that would have taken me the better part of a day—all while we chatted casually about our lives. When she was done, she showed me her work and informed me, amused, that I would not in fact be going to "IRS jail."

Too excited to be offended, I blurted, "Could you work for me while you're here? It'd only be a few hours a week, the way you do things, but it would be wonderful to have your help."

Grace's eyes lit up. "You bet. I'd love that."

It was then I remembered, *Whoa. She's a werewolf.* Then I thought, *So? Werewolves are apparently people too. Do you really want your accountant to be a werewolf? Does it really matter? Thanks to Booker, werewolves are just a fact of life around here these days.* How the hell had my life done such a one-eighty within the span of just a few weeks?

At least some of my uncertainty and irritation must have shown on my face, because Grace said gently, "You all right?" She tilted her head in a manner much like Booker's, her brown eyes keen. "You look disconcerted."

"I *am* disconcerted," I grumbled. "And thanks to Booker, a little smothered, but I'm tolerating it because you can't ask for protection and then get irritated when it's given." I sighed, leaning on the counter beside the stool where Grace sat. "It's just...my life feels like it's completely changed." Grace nodded, her expression sympathetic, so I kept going. "I feel like I keep making these little decisions, and I turn around and there are these huge ramifications, and I don't know why or where they're coming from."

Grace sighed. "If it helps, I think I know how you feel," she said, rubbing her belly. "It's chaos when you're used to order."

"Exactly," I said. *See? The pregnant werewolf gets it.* "I swear, ever since I asked Booker to help keep me alive and safe through this zombie thing, my own life feels like it's out of my control."

Grace made a faint choking sound, and I peered at her in alarm.

But she wasn't choking. She was laughing, and once she saw my confusion, she was very nearly howling with it. It lasted long enough for me to start getting annoyed. Maybe Grace wasn't quite the friend material I thought she was. *Fucking wolves, man.*

Eventually, she began to calm down, wiping her eyes. "Oh, child," she said, pausing for another titter. "You asked *Booker* for help?" She finally looked at me, a sly, lovely smile stretched across her face. "You may as well have just proposed marriage."

"Excuse me?" I couldn't imagine what my expression must have looked like, but whatever it was set her off again into another giggle fit.

"Jo, honey," she said when she could draw enough breath. "You're *so* screwed."

I tried to be patient while she got herself back under control, because to say I had questions at this point would be the understatement of the fucking millennium. Finally, I couldn't take it anymore. "Grace?" I said, laying one hand on her shaking shoulder. "I like you a lot, and I'm in awe of your skills with numbers, but you're killing me here."

She sobered up, although it took a bit, and gave me an apologetic smile. I rolled my eyes and smiled back, then gave her a tissue. "Clean yourself up. Then explain."

She dabbed at her eyes. "All right," she said, voice still rich with amusement. "I'm so sorry. First, for the record, I also like you." She paused, as if to emphasize that, and I gave her a reluctant smile. "However," she continued, "you have to be careful when you ask Booker for help."

"Okayyy," I said. "Why?"

Grace shifted her bulky body on the stool and turned toward me. "Well, to be fair, it's not just Booker. Any of Diana's Wolves are honor-bound to give help or protection to someone in need if it's requested. Even me, and I'm not a fighter."

Wow. I could see how that was both truly noble and seriously problematic.

"Booker in particular has a broad definition of 'help.' He tends to render assistance *his* way, which is usually by taking over everything." She spread her hands in a shrug. "Most alpha wolves are like that. Plus, you asked him to 'help keep you alive and safe.'" She air-quoted my words. "Booker will too. Until you die of old age." She paused, appeared to consider it. "Or until he annoys you to death."

Horror struck me directly in the solar plexus. "*No*," I said, aghast. "No, *no*. I don't need that. I don't *want* that. I just wanted his help with the zombies. The necromancer. I didn't want to obligate him for life."

Grace shrugged again. "Well, he'd only be obligated to help with the necromancer. That's true. It's just that Booker likes to take on more responsibility than any sane person needs to." She paused there. "His dad always said that Booker has an overdeveloped sense of honor. It's what makes him an excellent pack leader." She smiled and rubbed her belly. "It's why Nick and I are here—we've all been friends since we were in diapers, but we always knew that when Booker formed his own pack, we were going to be part of it."

I digested this. "I'm not part of his pack. I just thought we were making an agreement: my life for information."

"Information?" She frowned, considering this. "Did you give him what he needed?"

I thought back to those moments sitting on my bed in the early morning, when we were in our own universe together. "Yes."

"Then it was never just about the information," she concluded. "Not for Booker. Especially not with the way he feels about you." Before I could process that terrifying, tasty tidbit, her eyes widened. "Goddess, but *wait*! He'd been searching for you for months, right? Following your trail?"

I nodded, then said mechanically, "Eight months. After I escaped from him the first time."

Her mouth made a delighted O. "He got your scent, and then you got away from him. After he finally found you again, finally got you to talk to him, you turned around and asked for his *help*?" She practically vibrated with glee. "Wow. You couldn't have made yourself more enticing wolf bait if you'd tried. Poor Jo. Poor Booker." Grace chuckled again.

Damn. I couldn't be annoyed with her—I could tell she cared about Booker a great deal, as the laughter was more commiserating, an amusement born of love and familiarity.

I was plenty annoyed at myself now though. Good to know I was wolf fetish material. I'd thought I just had really great chemistry with Booker, but everything had moved really fast. Too fast. Magic could often speed situations along, and maybe it had fueled his obligation to help and compelled him to be around me.

Maybe it wasn't just me and my magic to blame though. Maybe Diana had added a sense of physical attraction to motivate her wolves to help whoever had asked, although that would be a weirdly sexual move for a virgin goddess, and surely that couldn't extend to everyone, like children or the elderly.

I pushed the thought out of my mind and excused myself to go to the bathroom. Where I hoped to regain my composure.

Being rational here was the only course. The best thing I could do was just un-ask Booker for help. My inclination was to call him right away and just say that I didn't need his help—the obvious downside being, of course, that I really did need his help, and more than that, I wanted his help. I wanted him around. I wanted...him. I hadn't felt alone since I met him, and it was nice to have someone to talk to who could hold up his end of the conversation. I mentally apologized to Stanley and Cole for the slight.

The real problem was that I *hated* compulsion spells. Taking away someone's free will was never a good thing to do, as I'd tried to explain to the man himself when I was worried about the geas. If Booker had been mystically compelled to help me, it hadn't really been a choice. Or at least, not *his* choice, freely made. No one should be forced into anything so potentially life-altering against their will or their better judgment.

When I went back out to the shop, Grace and I talked for awhile longer —Grace having steered the conversation into more innocuous areas like TV shows and books—but a portion of my brain just sat stewing. In typical Murphy fashion, I was making problems for myself using only the power of my brain. Forget walking through mirrors or controlling fire. That was my true superpower.

When Booker showed up around lunch, I asked Grace if she could watch the shop for a few minutes so I could talk to Booker in my office. She agreed, her eyes darting between the two of us with ill-concealed interest.

Booker followed me back, and when I turned to face him, I saw that his body had tensed up, his expression wary. He'd looked at me that way a lot over the past couple of days, and it was getting old.

"Okay, so I don't really need your help with Hel's Belles or the zombies anymore," I began with as much conviction as I could muster. "I've already told you about the Fenris, so I've kept my part of the bargain. So I am officially un-asking for your help." I gave him a smile, hoping that pronouncement would undo whatever Dianic magic had compelled him.

He turned and closed the office door carefully, then he crossed his arms over his chest and leaned back against the door. His jaw looked tight, and his eyes were beginning to glow. "*Okay, so,* considering that your first sentence is a lie, I'm going to ignore the second one." I glared at his gentle mockery, but before I could speak he added, his voice a little deeper, aura a little darker, "Don't lie to me again. Please. Why don't you just tell me what's going on?"

Damn it. I'd hoped it wouldn't ping as a lie. How bloody fucking inconvenient could this get?

I sighed. "I was talking with Grace, and she explained the finer details about Diana's Wolves and the obligation to help." I crossed my own arms over my chest and the "Witch, Please" screen-printed there—two could play at the defensive body language game. "I didn't want to force you into helping me. I was just trying to make a deal. But..." I paused, then frowned and forced myself to continue. "You never really had a choice about helping me, and that's not fair."

His aura began to lighten and ease back. He unbent his arms enough to scratch his chin. "You're worried I've been forced to help you. That I'm being compelled."

I nodded, feeling wretched.

His smile was soft and startling in its sweetness. "Well, let's put those fears to rest right now. The Council wanted me to investigate who sent the zombies and why, anyway, once they found out. So even without you, I'd be doing the same thing I'm doing now," he said. "The necromancer is in *our* city, remember?"

I did remember.

"As for the rest, I took the pledge as an adult wolf," he said, leveling his gaze at me. "I knew what it entailed, what that would mean for me and my life, and I would do it again."

I nodded, alarmed when tears gathered behind my eyes, but Booker wasn't done. He took a step closer to me. "But you...I decided to help you a long time ago. What happened to you—*that* was not fair. I saw how much it had done to you that night I found you in Ste. Genevieve." He bent his head down, capturing my gaze with his. "I was glad when you finally asked me directly, but that just became my excuse. A way to justify it all."

His eyes were warm on mine. "Obligation or no, this is how things would have panned out. It's how I wanted it to go—minus the mortal danger aspect."

I smiled a little and blinked back the tears. "You sure?"

He came to me then, raising one hand to my neck. There were no clear marks left, thanks to all the healing energy and Kate's awful potion, but we both knew where the bruising had been. "You're healing," he murmured.

Just the touch of his fingertips on the bare skin of my neck had my whole body on high alert. His warmth, his scent—I closed my eyes. I wanted to lean in and bury my nose in his neck and breathe him in deep. Forget my fears. Forget the zombies. Forget everything but him.

With a low sound of need, he tilted my head up with his thumbs and brought his mouth down on mine. The kiss was soft and sweet, gentle as a whisper. *Not enough.* I pushed myself up on my toes and wrapped my arms around his neck, bringing my body flush against his, and his kisses turned hungry.

His hands mapped my body, starting at my neck and moving in a long, sweeping glide down my back, lingering on the curve of my bottom and trailing down to the backs of my thighs. I parted my legs a little on a moan, wishing he would move his hands to where I needed them most.

Booker didn't oblige, instead bringing those wonderful, talented hands back up to my neck, gentling the kisses again. I mentally groaned in frustration. Now that I'd decided I wanted Booker—werewolf or not—I was fairly burning to have him. I mean, would it be so bad if we just had sex on my desk? I didn't think so, but Booker apparently had other plans.

We have some self-respect left in here somewhere, Murphy, so let's not throw ourselves at him, hmm?

Well, not more than I already had.

Booker broke away from the kiss fully, then leaned his forehead against mine and looked into my eyes. He did that a lot. I was going to have to find a non-werewolf person in the know to ask if all wolves were able to put the whammy on regular humans with that look. Every time Booker did it to me, I was putty in his hands. It had to be some sort of supernatural thing.

"Would you like to come to lunch with me?" he said, not moving.

Coffee, tea, or me? I sighed, certain I wouldn't be on the menu. "Sure, but I'll need to check on Grace and make sure she's okay."

When we came back downstairs, Grace took one look at me and laughed. "Hmm. Didn't work, did it?" When I shook my head, she clucked her tongue at Booker. "Yeah, I can see that he dismissed it without a thought."

Booker glowered at Grace with mock-intensity, and she stuck her tongue out at him.

To me, she confided, "He's always been bossy, ever since we were little."

"I wasn't bossy," Booker explained. "It's just that my way was always the right way."

Booker and Grace's good-natured bickering reminded me of siblings—she took delight in tormenting him, and Booker gave it right back, but he also managed to glean a great deal of information about how she was doing. Booker would tease, and Grace would respond with information. That way, he could satisfy himself that she was okay without outright asking. For a walking lie detector, it was a subtle and respectful strategy—much better than aggressively demanding information.

I enjoyed watching them together, their interactions displaying ingrained habits between them. I may not have had a guide to werewolf behavior, but I was already learning a lot of things that I liked about it.

CHAPTER 23

HOW TO (NOT) BAIT-WALK YOUR WITCH

BOOKER

As it turned out, taking the woman you were trying to protect out for a bait-walk disguised as a lunch date did not make for a calm wolf. Booker began to regret the choices he had made the instant they stepped out into the fall sunshine, and his discomfort only got worse the longer they were out in the open.

Leaving the Sanctum with Jo felt a little—fine, *a lot*—like being on the move with a priceless treasure.

Booker had invited her to lunch, and although she was surprised when he said they would walk the few blocks down to the Central East End's commercial area and her favorite take-out place, she didn't ask questions. It was after 1 p.m. and John was back, so Grace had been able to go back upstairs for a nap.

Hence, Operation Priceless Treasure, otherwise known as Operation Can We Draw Out That Murderous Bitch Heloise in the Daylight?

Booker reminded himself that he'd taken every precaution. He had two small teams on them from both sides at all times, plus Max staking out Purgatory to keep an eye on movement. He'd loaded up with charm bags. If the attack came magically, he hoped, they'd know before it even hit them.

He wouldn't have had to do this if the morning had yielded anything usable. The Council was looking into Hel's Belles, and he'd also put the considerable resources of Booker Brothers behind it. He had no doubt that they would find out who the band members really were, eventually, but that wasn't helping them right now, and he was no longer sure finding out their identities would lead them to a motive.

All of his intel indicated that the reason the band members of Hel's Belles couldn't be traced to any other location or their personas linked to their real names was because they were simply living at Purgatory when they were in the city. They should have been able to take a team into Purgatory and perform a surgical strike, but Max had reported that there were wards up against wolves there now.

Because of course there fucking were. Heloise might be brazen, but she wasn't suicidal.

Purgatory was only a few minutes from the Sanctum for a running wolf. So he wanted to see what would happen if Jo was outside the Sanctum during the day.

Of course, he didn't tell Jo that. He and Jo weren't talking about plenty of things today. He kept having to push several recent distracting memories to the back of his head. That mind-bending, ill-advised make-out session that made lust roar through him every time he thought about it. Her telling him she preferred it when he was wild. The screams and tears that had made him desperate to get to her. Their endless, heart-rending talk that morning.

All of these were distractions that could get Jo killed outside of her fortress. So he ruthlessly shut them away.

Had he been able to fully relax, he would have enjoyed walking with Jo through the neighborhood. It was brimming with potential development, and the air had that muddy, river-laden tinge that he somehow found pleasing. Jo was bouncy in a way he hadn't seen her, the energy in her body fresh, her bright blue eyes animated as she talked about Grace's talents as an accountant and how she'd set the Sanctum books in order in just an hour.

That sounded like Grace. Booker remembered how happy and healthy his friend had looked and how pleased he'd been to see them both together. Two of the most important women in his life.

Not that he would tell Jo that. Yet.

"This place has the *best* hummus," Jo said as they entered the restaurant.

"I'm still perfecting my recipe, but this place has it down cold. I can't get that creamy texture though—it's a kind of miracle."

Booker smiled down at her, and although his wolf was standing beside him, ready to jump if a threat materialized, they both enjoyed her happy-smell—the lavender of her overlaid with something sunshiny and clean. His chest tightened.

Lunch was a friendly and smooth affair. Booker let Jo lead the conversation this time, remembering how he'd already inundated her with questions that morning, after she'd shared the dream with him.

It gave him chills to know what had happened. He was grateful to Hecate even as he worried about the goddess's Grand Plan for his mirror witch—although it seemed fairly clear that Hecate was very open to having him and his pack be a part of Jo's future. That was good at least. Knowing that Jo's power set apparently contained fire as well, part of him wondered how she was going to handle it, while the other part wondered if they could utilize it in the fight against the necromancer.

Nope. Not going there yet. Jo's not ready.

While they ate, they talked about ordinary stuff—favorite books, movies, television shows, and music. They had enough overlap to make things interesting, but she surprised him with some of her choices. He loved her amusement over the wolves' loving movies and TV, laughing when she told him about her experience watching them in the video room.

"That sounds right." He tried to explain the pack bond that made that possible—sharing information and thoughts without verbal expression. "It's like we're all in tune with each other, so all our senses give us info. It's sight and smell cues, plus a dollop of emotional telepathy."

She nodded and swallowed a bite of food. "Is that how you know when I'm lying?"

He froze for a second, but then his pride in her bubbled up. She surprised him all the time. "Pretty much." He gave her more details.

He left out the part where she was his mate, something that had become crystal clear to him in the past twenty-four hours, if it hadn't been before. Their bond was different, and eventually—once they both acknowledged the bond—they'd be able to read each other's minds.

Again, she wasn't ready.

So many things he had to hide from her. The guilt and impatience chasing each other through his thoughts made his wolf sneeze and give his giant head an ear-slapping shake.

Unfortunately, patience was one of those things he'd been meaning to work on, but just never got around to.

Booker guided Jo back to the movies-and-TV thing. "So, yeah, most wolves really love TV—the better the sound and the clearer the image, the better." He smiled, showing her his dimples. "Of course, loving movies and TV doesn't mean wolves have good taste. I'd be willing to bet the average wolf has a lower bar, entertainment-wise, than the average human."

Her eyes laughed at him. "Really?"

"Most wolves will watch anything once." He leaned forward. "That's actually part of why I wanted the big open space on the fifth floor. We've made a large section out of it as a home theater."

That seemed to interest Jo. "So, you guys have, like, pizza-and-movie nights?"

"Basically," he said. "Ever since I came back to St. Louis, I've been trying to do a movie night every week. This area is even more accessible for most of my pack, so I'm hoping more wolves will be able to join us. We need the camaraderie. We need to be around each other."

"A place where wolves can just be wolves together?"

"Yeah." He chuckled. It sounded so casual when she said it like that, but maybe it really was that simple. "Pretty much."

Jo chewed a bite, her eyebrows clenching together. When she saw him looking, she shrugged. "No offense, but I'm trying to imagine if movie night with a bunch of wolves would be cool or creepy."

He laughed. "I don't know, honestly. We've never had a human at a movie night," he said. "You could be our guinea pig."

She made a face. "Charming image."

After lunch, Booker asked her to show him some of the new shops in the area, under the guise of scouting out properties. His text message check-ins all said no activity, and he tried to be glad about that—but he still wanted to keep her out of the Sanctum a little longer. Enjoy the fall sunshine. So they walked and talked, and he kept up a periodic scan of the perimeter.

They went into a bookstore, and Jo browsed and spoke with the owner while he kept a watch on the entrance. Jo purchased a book on Norse runes and the latest J.D. Robb release, which he supposed said a lot about Jo right there.

When they stepped back outside, Booker was checking their perimeter, trying not to scowl, when Jo took his arm in a companionable way and said, "You know, if you want to use me as bait, we might have better luck if we actually walk by Purgatory."

He stopped in his tracks, raising his free hand to scrub it over his face. *Damn it.*

She wasn't done. "Plus, if you let me know ahead of time, I can do things like leave the anti-zombie charm bag I made this morning at home."

He cursed under his breath. "Witches," he muttered.

Jo smiled, and her eyes sparkled up at him. "You should keep me in the loop. I can foil your plans less if I know what they are."

Booker tried not to be charmed by this. He failed. "How did you know?" He took advantage of the moment and reached down to snag her hand in his before he started walking again. Her awareness of him ratcheted up a few notches, making him grin.

She shrugged. "I had a feeling something was up when you suggested we leave my stronghold without the Wall o' Wolves."

Booker burst out laughing so hard that he had to stop walking for a moment before he could recover. She laughed too, which didn't help. Finally, he recovered enough to ask, "Without the *what*?"

"My entourage!" She gestured out to where he knew two wolves were stationed, watching them. "My protection detail. 'Wolf Pack! Form! Of! Mobile body shield!'"

Booker barked out another laugh and tamped down the suddenly overwhelming urge to kiss her right there. His witch was fierce and powerful, but she was also too cute for words. No wonder she'd captivated him so thoroughly. "So, I guess if we stop back by the Sanctum and ditch the anti-zombie charm bag, you'll be good with taking a walk near Purgatory?"

"Sure," she said easily. "And you can explain to me why I'm not allowed to lie to you, but you can lie to me."

He winced. *Direct hit.* "How about we have that conversation later?"

"I'll allow it," she said, then pinned him with eyes like pale blue lasers. "But don't think I'm going to forget."

They stopped back at the Sanctum to find John behind the counter. "John, are you cool here alone for another hour or so? It's been a pretty slow day," Jo said.

"No problem," John said, holding up a trigonometry textbook. "I've got plenty to do."

"Thanks," Booker said, and they nodded at each other. Booker hadn't been able to pinpoint exactly what kind of supernatural creature John was, but he knew that John didn't smell bad—his was a pleasant but nonthreatening aroma, almost like good oatmeal—and he knew that John harbored real affection and loyalty to Jo, and Jo felt the same for him. That was good enough for now.

Eventually, they'd probably have that conversation, because he was fairly certain John knew that Booker and the other residents were werewolves. However, that could wait.

Booker and Jo went back out into the sunshine and walked over to Purgatory, both quiet for the moment. Booker caught a glint from Max's binoculars on a rooftop a few streets over and gave his friend a nod.

Meanwhile, Jo was looking closely at the area around the Purgatory building. "I know you've already noticed this, because you're you, but the third point of the triple crossroads is here." At Booker's nod, she cast her eyes up to the top of the building, then back down. "So, Hecate's Home, my Sanctum, and Purgatory."

Booker had already sent someone from Booker Brothers to City Hall to look for the original plans for the buildings and their development, only to find that, *oops*, no one knew where the documents and blueprints were located. And no one knew the name of the original architect. Of course.

"It's not a coincidence," she said.

"Definitely not."

They walked around the building, getting as close as they dared. Close enough that Booker felt the wards on the building warning him away.

Still no action.

After almost an hour—during which Jo joked that she was being as enticing as she knew how to be, bait-wise, which made him want to both laugh and groan—they gave up and went back to the Sanctum.

Nothing. Not even a minion out and about. "Even catching a zombie would be something," Booker muttered.

"What good would that do?" Jo's voice was horrified.

"We can trace back the magic. See if it goes back to the group or somewhere else. Sometimes zombies talk too."

"You can trace it? I didn't think wolves did magic."

Again, she brought up something that was too complicated to fully explain. "We don't," he began. "Our transformation isn't really physical—not like in the movies. We have different forms, and we take them magically. It's inherent to our being."

She nodded. "I saw you change at the fun house. It wasn't like I expected."

"What did you think..." Goddess, he suddenly felt as awkward as an adolescent with a crush. He swallowed. "I mean, were you scared by the change?"

Jo seemed to think about it. "I already knew you were a werewolf, so I wasn't, like, shocked. It was a little scary when you ripped into the zombies, but you weren't a rampaging beast." She smiled a little. "Your fur was gray. Beautiful. For a wolf."

Booker the Wolf wagged his tail, mouth open and tongue lolling with a grin, and Booker the Man fought back a pleased blush. "Well. Thank you." He began to walk again, pulling her with him.

Jo was still thinking though. "It seemed like the transformation back to human took more out of you."

"Accurate." He remembered how it felt, like suddenly turning against the current and trying to swim back upstream.

"Anyway. We *are* magic, but we don't wield magic. The Council has a witch who specializes in tracing magics back to their source—she's looking into it."

This time it was Jo who stopped, staring up at him like he was an idiot. "Seriously?" She waved her hand up and down in front of herself. "Witch. Right here. You could have asked me."

Booker cocked one eyebrow. "Do you know how to trace a zombie back to its creator?"

Her shoulders slumped, indignation fading. "No." Then she started walking again. "Fine."

Because he couldn't help but poke at her, he leaned down and said, "It's okay. You aren't that kind of witch." He grinned when she side-eyed him. "Everyone has their skill sets. Hers are just different, that's all."

Jo harrumphed, and he chuckled softly. She was adorable, his mirror witch.

By the time they reached the Sanctum, Booker had become philosophical about their bait-walk. "I'm sorry it didn't amount to much," he said, pausing at the shop door, but it had been fun.

Jo shrugged. "We can do another one tomorrow," she said. "I'm cool with doing this as much as we need to. I don't want to just sit and wait—and we learn more every time we interact with them. It makes sense to me."

He looked down at her, bringing one hand up to her chin. "Definitely a priceless treasure," he said, before he remembered that she wouldn't understand what he was talking about. She smiled anyway, and they were back at the Sanctum again, so he and his wolf were both happy.

"I have to head up to the wolf floors," Booker said, with more than a little regret. "It's renovations and Council stuff, both, and I'm not sure how long it will take, but I'd like to come and stay in your apartment again, if that's not going to weird you out." He paused. "Just in case you have another dream."

Yes, there was that deeper, warmer scent again, the one that he adored from her. The arousal smell. It made him want to roll around in it and make a fool of himself—which he'd come close to a few times with her.

But it wasn't the right time yet.

Patience.

It really was overrated.

Chapter 24

A Tale of Two Couches...and One Big Damn Kiss

JO

True silence is impossible when you live in a city, but that evening my apartment was the closest thing to quiet I'd had in weeks. I took the opportunity to putter—cleaning, putting together some potions and a few charm bags that might be useful, listening to Stravinsky on low. It relaxed me to the point that I actually took the time to lie down on one of my couches. The two couches and my oversized easy chair made a U shape in the living room. In theory, I'd set the area up thinking it would be the perfect place to have people over. In reality, I generally just sat on one couch and folded clean laundry on the other.

I never had people over. Not even Emma or John. Just Kate, and she couldn't stay long because of her kids.

Maybe that would change. I envisioned Grace coming up and hanging out with me. Maybe Nick too—I hadn't had a chance to get to know him, but he and Grace obviously adored one another. I thought Kate might like them too. I mean, when judged by human standards, wolves were weird, but I liked their odd straightforwardness. Or at least, Booker's odd straightforwardness.

Always Booker.

I closed my eyes, remembering the way he'd looked at me outside. The easy way we'd talked. Maybe we'd actually get to have sex tonight. The idea made my lower stomach bottom out with a twisting pressure—it really had been too long, and I wanted Booker more than anything I'd yet encountered in life. So much that it made me uneasy if I thought about my feelings for him too much, dug into them too deeply.

I didn't know how I felt about potentially falling in love with a werewolf.

I did know how I felt about having this particular one for a lover.

So I'd wait for him here, see what happened.

I felt Cole hop up onto my chest, curling himself into a ball. "Hey, cat," I murmured, petting his furry warmth. "Did you have a good day?"

Cole ignored my question, but he didn't leave me hanging. His purr began as I let my hand rest on him. The music filled the air, and my brain emptied, lulled to sleep shortly thereafter.

At some point later, I drifted awake, groggy from a dreamless night, to the odor of some truly awful breath. I opened my eyes to see Cole's nose almost touching mine.

"Dude, you have some serious tuna breath," I muttered, scratching him behind the ears. As Cole started to purr—no doubt I'd simply played into his fiendish scheme to wake me and make me pet him—I noticed that light was glowing in through the windows. *Morning already?* I shifted a little, turned my head, and saw Booker asleep on the other couch.

I didn't remember Booker coming in last night. I also didn't remember putting a blanket on myself, so that must have been him. I smiled what no doubt would look like a very goofy smile if he were awake to see it.

It felt normal for Booker to be here. It was sweet that he'd covered me up, but it was dangerous to get used to something like that. In my experience, people were never permanent. It was something I'd learned the hard way before I went on the run. Getting used to them was just setting myself up for heartbreak.

I told myself to remember that, but watching a sleeping Booker drove just about every other thought from my head other than *Wow*. His brown hair was tousled from sleep, and even without the dimples, his face was gorgeous. Strong cheekbones, the superhero chin. His face and his body were peaceful, almost boneless, all of the tension I'd seen in him at various times in the past two weeks completely gone. I remembered what it felt like to be held close to that body—all muscles and heat. I loved his arms, which were long, muscular, and solid beneath the sleeves of his T-shirt. His hands were huge, with long fingers. Those hands had memorized my body, running up and down. God help me, I even liked his bare feet, tangled together and peeking out from beneath the worn cuffs of his jeans. I wasn't big on feet, but these two? Attractive.

I took my time staring at him, memorizing the details of his body. I wanted to go over to him and smooth his hair. Many people looked younger when they slept, but Booker simply looked like a relaxed man, something I rarely saw when he was awake—he was too vital, too full of energy and his aura of power. His sense of responsibility to his pack, to me, fueling him at every second.

Far too late, I wondered if it was wrong of me to ogle him like this, even if he was unaware of it. Wolves may be fine with staring, but I wasn't quite comfortable being caught staring at someone. Especially someone I could stare at for hours.

In these stolen minutes of the early morning, still a little sleepy, I could admit to myself that I could get used to Booker being around. I was already used to him, something he had been prepping me for—I could see it now as clearly as I'd been able to catch on to yesterday's bait-walk. First, idle chitchat. Being around all the time. Then, casual touches on the hand. Escalate to a full hug. Then, a kiss on the head.

Don't spook the witch, indeed. I'd asked him if I was a horse, only to belatedly realize he'd been gentling me like one.

There we were again with the cowboy imagery—which really shouldn't have turned me on.

I still didn't know much about werewolves, but I did know something about men. Booker had begun moving in on me pretty quickly. Of course, it could be that this was part of the security job or his freelance work with the Council—if he traveled around the country dealing with different types of supernatural crises, maybe it was a girl-in-every-port situation. It was difficult to imagine him spending too many nights alone.

Whether it led to anything more or not, if I had my way, he wouldn't be spending his nights alone much longer. For however long it lasted, I was going to enjoy him.

I smiled a little, squirmed a little at the thought of being naked with Booker, so of course he opened his eyes. He went from being completely relaxed and asleep to completely awake and alert. His amber eyes stared into mine, so pretending I hadn't been staring at him would have been futile. Instead, I just stared back.

When he smiled at me, it was like the sun coming out.

"No nightmares tonight?" he asked.

"No, and I'm glad." I turned my attention back to Cole for a second. "Four hours of sleep a night isn't enough for me. Another day or two of that, and I would've cracked." When I looked back at him, I could feel myself smiling that goofy smile from before, so I forced myself to look away.

Wow, Murphy. Crush on the werewolf much?

Instead of staying there, I got up, much to Cole's dismay, and began to get myself ready for the day. When I was showered and dressed, I went into the kitchen to see Booker and Cole sharing a companionable breakfast, although my already worked-up stomach was relieved they'd given the raw-meat bonding a rest. Instead, Booker had found the Fancy Feast for Cole and a banana for himself.

"See," Booker said. "He's not spoiled." With more misplaced pride, he stroked Cole as the cat daintily licked the wet food from the plate.

"Yes, I can see." I shook my head and got a banana for myself. "I just didn't want him to get used to you giving him raw meat. 'Cause I'm certainly not going to."

"I've signed a five-year lease. Where am I going?" he said, petting Cole again.

"You know what I mean. When the whole bodyguard gig is over, you'll be back in your own place. Staying in your own apartment." Holy Hecate, I wished I hadn't said anything at all. *Let your mouth get you into trouble—it's the Murphy way!*

Booker had finished his banana and was examining me like I was a problem he needed to figure out.

"Want to hear some boring werewolf stuff?" he asked, walking over to throw away his banana peel.

I began to peel my own banana. "I live to learn," I said, trying to sound jaunty. "Hit me."

Booker washed his hands at the sink, then turned to lean one hip against the counter, folding his arms—muscled biceps bulging sleekly under the sleeves of his T-shirt, I couldn't help but notice—before meeting my eyes again. "I traveled around for Booker Brothers and the Council for years. It never occurred to me to do anything else. Also, wolves need to hunt—travel's a great way to channel that instinct, especially for younger wolves or very dominant wolves."

I nodded, and Booker continued. "A few years ago, I decided I wanted a break. I followed a very strong instinct and decided to take over the St. Louis branch of Booker Brothers, which had the side effect of making my dad really happy—but that's another story."

He took a breath, pausing a moment before he went on. "You've spoken to Grace, and I know she's mentioned me being bossy. She might have told you that I'm an alpha. Well, I hadn't intended to set up a wolf pack of my own, but one formed around me. Nick and Grace were a part of that. I remember my father telling me that's how it worked for him when he stopped traveling and settled in Wyoming."

I knew already, just from paying attention, that Diana's Wolves comprised a large number of the werewolves in North America. Some were together in packs, some alone, and sometimes just a family here and there. According to Grace, there were territories, especially to the north, that were almost entirely comprised of werewolves, and it was an open secret. St. Louis had never been one of those places. There were a few families of wolves here and there in the area, but most of them preferred to stay on the outskirts of the city. The fringes. More space to run.

"Much of being a wolf is instinct." Booker's unblinking gaze became even more intense. "My instinct led me here. Many of my wolves here came here the same way. Enough instinct in enough wolves, and it's considered a movement. So," he spread his hands, "a movement of Diana's Wolves settled in St. Louis, instinct leading them to see if forming a pack under me would be better for them."

I nodded again to show him I was listening, even if I wasn't certain why he was telling me all this. "So far, none have left and more keep coming," Booker said, and his voice took on a rougher cast. "I'm responsible for all of them. I declared this territory mine, and wolves prefer to be around each other. Part of why I leased out this building is because it's half a block from the new Booker Brothers offices I'm planning to open in the next few months. There are a few other properties in the area I'm looking at too."

Oh.

He tilted his head. "This is my territory. I'm supposed to be here. Just like you're supposed to be here." He pushed himself away from the counter in one smooth motion, going back over to Cole. "I won't be going anywhere," he said, scratching my cat behind his ears again. I could hear Cole begin to purr. "I can bring *Cole* anything he desires for breakfast every day, if he wants the company." He emphasized Cole's name in such a way that it was clear he wasn't just talking about the cat.

I wasn't sure how to respond. It felt like a clear statement of intent, but things between us were still too murky relationship-wise. I settled for, "Thank you for telling me about this."

He gave me a half-smile. "You're welcome." Then he nodded, going into the living room again to gather up his wallet and put on his socks. Meanwhile, I cleaned up from my own small breakfast and gathered the potions and charm bags I'd made the night before in a tote bag to take down with me.

Once he had his boots on by the door, I turned to say goodbye, but he spoke first. "There's Council business, and they need me there today in person. I can't postpone or put them off." He didn't seem happy about it. "I'll be out of town for most of today to meet with the Council, but I should be back this evening." He paused, casting his eyes to the ceiling briefly as if debating what to say, then took a deep breath before he looked down at me. "Jo, I'd like your promise that you'll stay in the building today. Just while I'm away. Please."

Definitely debating what to say—or at least how to say it. Luckily, I didn't take offense. It was more gentling from the urban-cowboy werewolf, but I didn't mind so much. "Yeah, no problem there," I said, moving closer and smiling up at him. "It was nice to go walking yesterday with you, but being here hasn't bothered me. Not when I have the roof and Stanley for fresh air and company."

"And Grace, I hope."

"Definitely," I said. "I like her."

"I'm glad. You'll be good for each other." He was close enough that I could smell his sandalwood and cedar scent. Did he use some kind of special soap or was it just part of his wolf thing? After a second of silence, he gathered me up in his long arms and pulled me into him. Holy Hecate, the guy could hug.

"I probably won't be able to text much. If you need something, ask Nick or Max," he murmured into my hair. "They'll help you."

"I know." I rose up on my toes, burying my face in his neck. "I'll miss you." That was the infatuated girl inside me talking, and I cursed her weakness.

Booker urged my head up and sought my lips with his. It was sweeter, more gentle, than the teasingly soft kisses, more deeply stirring than the devouring ones. There was arousal here, but not the kind of raw lust we'd stoked in each other before. The sweetness of his mouth and the warmth of his embrace had me leaning into him, and his arms tightened. I never wanted it to end, but it had to of course. He had work out of town, and I needed to open my shop. Still, I lingered a little while longer, sipping at his lips with my own, sliding my tongue slowly against his, showing him my affection in return.

Kissing was always pleasurable, but this was more. It felt like he'd poured his feelings into the kiss and then wrapped me up in them. The strength of that emotional tide caught me off guard, and for just a few seconds, I opened myself up to the rapport we shared, letting my emotions swirl around me. Our auras mingled, melting into one another, like they had before. All of my anxiety flowed to the top, but beneath that was respect, delight, and affection—and of course, a healthy amount of lust.

I'd kissed and been kissed plenty in my life, but nothing had compared to this kind of communion.

Booker slowly pulled back from the kiss, rested his forehead on mine, and laughed softly. His words were a little shaky when he said, on a sigh, "That's a lot of information to take in at once."

It was a shock, having him acknowledge it—that odd straightforwardness again. I had no idea that emotions could be shared like that. I could often feel the emotions of others, but it wasn't a two-way street. I received information; I didn't *share* it.

With effort and an odd sense of loss, I closed off my emotions, stopped letting their energy out. It was necessary, I told myself. The wolves already took over most of the floors of my building, I didn't want them—*him*—to be able to read my damn mind.

With a sigh, Booker pressed his lips to my forehead and took a step back from me. He smiled at me, all sweetness again—*had I ever seen him like this?* —and I gave him a little wave, not able to trust my voice, before stepping through the mirror and down to the emotional safety of my office.

CHAPTER 25

WOLF, EDUCATE THY WITCH

BOOKER

WHEN BOOKER HAD FIRST STARTED WORKING WITH THE Council a lifetime ago, he'd agonized over wearing exactly the right thing when summoned to an official meeting. He was still young enough at the time that he'd tried to win over their good opinion. *Dress professionally, act professionally. Show them you are no creature's dog.*

He'd rapidly discovered that the more anyone tried to curry favor with the elders on the Council, the more quickly the Council dismissed them, so he adapted. If there was no way to win approval aside from doing his job and doing it well, he may as well handle all his interactions with them his own way.

In the years since Booker made that decision, it seemed the Council felt he could do no wrong, but he no longer cared. The Council was a useful tool and a necessary ruling body—and it paid extremely well—but he turned down a good half of the jobs they'd offered. The Council members were powerful, but several of them were old and petty. Any job that smelled even a little bit like personal retribution or agenda wasn't for him.

But they'd summoned him, and this time they had good reason to. As much as he'd been loath to leave St. Louis, even for a day trip, it was to his benefit if he didn't make them wait. He had to tell them her side of the Fenris story, and he had to make sure they knew he had his territory in hand.

To expedite things, he'd used the Booker Brothers' plane—one of the perks he liked best—to fly to the Council's private airstrip just outside the city. A car and driver were waiting for him there to ferry him to the Council Building on the north side of Chicago.

He grimaced when he felt the cold wind off the lake do its best to tear the skin from his face on the walk into the building. Gods, he fucking hated this city.

Once inside, he checked in at the desk, nodded to the security detail, and took the elevator. *Going down.* The Council members had offices in the building, libraries, labs, and various other useful resources, but the meeting area that he called the Arena was belowdecks. Meeting underground was an ancient tradition, a holdover from when the Fae ruled the Council, but it still made for an impressive sight.

The meeting area was a circular room with auditorium seating all the way around and a large, round table in the middle. The acoustics had been magically enhanced to ensure that anyone who spoke could be heard anywhere in the room, if they willed it so. Booker had only ever seen Council members there, never an audience, but he knew that when large decisions were being considered that would have ramifications for many species and their various factions, the auditorium seats would be packed with representatives and delegates. It was rather like a typical human city council meeting, except the "city" was the worldwide supernatural community.

Booker had never seen one of those meetings, but his father had.

Today, he expected it would be simply him and the seven Council members—all of whom he already knew. When he arrived at the Arena, he was shown to a waiting room and told that he would be called when the entire Council had gathered.

Booker settled in to wait.

The Council expanded or shrank in size, over time, depending upon population and power distribution among the various different supernatural groups. At present, two members of the Council were Fae, one elder and one younger, and there was one hag, whom he thought was a dream hag—the most cooperative of that particular faction.

There were two shifters, one Native American man and one African woman.

Then there was Aisling, or at least that was the name she was going by these days. She was a particularly long-lived witch who had been on the Council for centuries. Most witches lived longer than regular humans, as magic use tended to slow down the aging process, but never so long as Ais. She looked no older than 25, and she was quite active. She was the Council's resident cat—she showed up when she wanted, stayed until it no longer suited her, and had no compunctions about using the Council to her own ends.

Art hated her, of course. Booker simply didn't trust her. The Council had its own reasons for keeping her there. She was clearly powerful, but it was possible that her own brand of wisdom was of use too. Either way, the Council sought her out when she was useful but otherwise gave her a wide berth. The Fae members of the Council had been there longer than Aisling, so at least she didn't have seniority. The rest, including Art Booker, were newcomers, comparatively speaking—and Art was the first wolf sworn in on the Council over a century ago.

His seat had been empty for years before then, as the Council took its sweet time debating whether wolves should be allowed a voice. Their minds were very old, especially the Fae minds, and they didn't adapt as easily as the werewolves did. While they weren't paying attention, the wolves had grown in power and in numbers. Art had been a major power long before he joined the Council, as the werewolves had gained a massive amount of territory in North America during the 1800s. He had been elected as the werewolf Council representative over the Odin's Wolves alpha candidate by a wide margin.

Booker had taken to pacing by the time a smiling young Fae—well, "young" was a relative term with Fae; this boy was probably at least 50 years old—bid him to come to the Council table.

As he emerged onto the central floor of the Arena, Booker first sought out Art, and when he saw the slight frown on his father's weathered but still handsome face, Booker's shoulders tensed. *Probably not going to enjoy this meeting.*

Telling himself to keep an open mind, Booker sat down at the table directly across from his father and formally greeted the Council members, thanking them for meeting with him.

"I have learned the details of Josephine Murphy's role in the Fenris' disappearance," he said, then provided them with the story, up to and including the money she had taken. The supernatural community's rule about wealth in the event of defeat was that the victor had the right to anything they wished that belonged to the vanquished, so long as what was taken didn't violate any important species law or tradition. Money wasn't one of those things.

However, he hadn't anticipated that there was more where that was concerned.

The elder Fae said ponderously, "The witch is due more of the Fenris' holdings than simply that. The Council has taken pains to see that ample sums and holdings have long since been transferred to the families of the vanished Fenris. However, much remains unclaimed."

Booker frowned. "Does Ms. Murphy have to claim it?"

"It is hers in perpetuity until she either claims it or denies it. If she denies, then it will revert to the Council to use as we see fit."

Booker thought rapidly. If Jo accepted the Fenris' holdings, he knew that some members of the Council would see it as her making a move to be considered a "power" in the community. It would open her up to more scrutiny, make her a target.

He projected as much confidence and certainty as he could muster. "The witch does not want the Fenris' holdings," he said. "She took the money from the den under duress, under the influence of her goddess."

Unfortunately, that roused Aisling from her lazy disregard. "You speak with authority for someone who is not present. Do you have a telepathic connection with the witch? Does she know about this already?"

Booker realized he was clenching his jaw and commanded it to loosen. "She does not," he allowed. "More importantly, she's too young to know anything about that particular ancient custom." He paused, debating how much to say. "Other than having natural talent, an ability to research answers, and a strong connection to Hecate, she really knows very little about our world."

Ais tilted her head, allowing her sleek, blonde high ponytail to bounce with the movement, and regarded him with expertly made-up emerald eyes.

"Then perhaps you should supply her with all the pertinent information and not simply assume."

"I will, my lady."

"Perhaps she should notify us herself." Aisling smiled. "I find myself intrigued by your mirror witch, although my own dealings with the Lady of the Crossroads have been modest."

Booker smiled back and made certain that it wasn't just a baring of teeth. Over his dead fucking body would he bring Jo here—he wanted to keep her as far from Aisling and her ilk as possible. Keep her as far from Council politics as he could for as long as he could. "I'll consult with her. Once her decision is made, the Council will be informed, and the appropriate contracts can be prepared."

Aisling simply nodded.

"There's still the matter of Josephine Murphy's power." The hag, her lined face and pure-white hair at odds with her bright, ageless eyes, looked to the other members of the Council, who nodded in agreement. "Many of our factions are uneasy about the scope of her magical abilities."

"She made an entire population within the supernatural community disappear," the elder Fae added.

Booker looked to Art. His father wanted him to be careful. Diplomatic. Booker could do that.

"She's sworn to Hecate," Booker said. "As she related it to me, it seemed clear that Hecate Herself took a direct role in pulling the Fenris from the world."

Art stepped in. "Josephine Murphy has avoided other interactions with the rest of the community in the years since. The only reason she's surfaced now is because she's established herself."

"If she simply wishes to run a shop and be ignored, the shifter community supports that decision," put in the Native American shifter. "She did the world a favor by ridding us of the Fenris. Let's not forget it."

There were nods around the table, but not all of them happy ones.

Booker narrowed his eyes. "She saved you from an inevitable war by praying for her own death." Art gave him a warning look, but Booker was done with diplomacy on that particular front. "Be grateful."

"Agreed," said the African shifter, and Booker gave her a respectful nod.

The younger Fae, frowning, broke in. "I believe we've covered the pertinent issues when it comes to the mirror witch and her role in the Fenris' disappearance. In deference to Hecate's involvement, the Council will leave you, young Booker, as her liaison. She's your responsibility."

The dream hag looked at Booker. "See to it that she's properly educated about our community and where she fits. Ignorance will win her no allies or friends."

Booker nodded. "I agree, and I have plans to gather materials for her education while I'm here, by the Council's leave."

Art held up a hand. "I will add myself as a co-liaison to and an official voucher for Josephine Murphy." Booker wondered for a split second what Art had up his sleeve, but then Art added, "Since she has allied herself with my son, she has become an ally to all Diana's Wolves, and since she has no clan or people of her own, I would have her recognized as an honorary part of our clan."

At this announcement, a warm wave of relief and gratitude swept through Booker. He'd planned to talk with Art after the meeting about giving Jo the official protection of the St. Louis faction of Diana's Wolves, but he should have known his canny father would have already thought of that and taken it a step further. Jo was a boon to all werewolves, but Booker knew that Art made the decision at least in part because of Booker. Art could and did play the games of politics well, but when it came down to it, his decisions always seemed to make Booker's life easier.

The Council absorbed this and put it to a vote. All but Aisling were in favor. "Accepted," the elder Fae said. "The witch Josephine Murphy is now subject to the rules and protection of the Diana's Wolves clan first and the Council second."

Booker sent his father and alpha a wave of gratitude, which Art only briefly acknowledged. In one fell swoop, Art had ensured that Jo was already removed from the worst of the Council's scrutiny and protected from the likes of Aisling.

"Now that the witch has been claimed by the wolves," Aisling said, with only a slight roll of her eyes in Art's direction, "what is your progress with the necromancer?"

Booker filled them in on the Hel's Belles situation, enjoying the way their collective noses wrinkled in distaste at the description of the band's music and members. He also identified Heloise as the primary antagonist, so far as they could tell, and the Council was seriously displeased at the wanton use of runes and mass energy drains from their human victims. Not because it was inhumane or wrong, but because it was messy and indiscreet.

"Our witches are working on tracing the magic, but much seems to be hidden from their sight," the elder Fae said. "We'll keep open communication, but in the meantime, have your wolves ready for engagement."

"We're ready," Booker said, baring his teeth at the thought.

With his part in the proceedings done, he retreated to the waiting room again. He doubted that the Council was going to do anything to harm Jo, especially now that his father had claimed her as pack. He knew that if anything bad was going to come his way, Art would warn him. Art, better than anyone, knew how to balance the needs of his wolves with the needs of the community as a whole.

Art also knew most of the ins and outs of Jo's creative use of the geas and its effect on the wolves, but Booker saw no point in sharing the details with the Council. They hadn't asked him, specifically, what she had done at the Sanctum, so he hadn't supplied that information.

Jo certainly had a lot of natural power, but she was still playing with her magic, still learning. She'd effortlessly made something of a magical fortress out of her building. She enjoyed running her Sanctum and walking through mirrors, but if the Council, or Aisling, sucked her in at this point, that wouldn't last much longer. Everything would have an ulterior motive, a price, or both.

He knew that Jo never really had much of a childhood once her grandparents had died, but she loved that building of hers. It had allowed her to recapture some of the stability she'd been missing during that lost childhood and the years on the run, and her joy in it showed in ways both little and big. He was certain she was unaware of it, but she always smiled when she walked through a mirror, regardless of her emotional state—and half the time, she'd giggle.

No, the Council would certainly educate her about the supernatural world and her place in it, but he doubted she'd laugh as she walked through mirrors when they were finished.

As Booker waited for his father to emerge from the meeting, he replayed his morning interactions with Jo. He'd brought the cat around with the raw meat the day before, so he sealed the deal with the Fancy Feast. It hadn't occurred to him until it was too late that he wouldn't be able to kiss Jo after eating the raw hamburger—her disgust at seeing him eat it had been palpable—so he wasn't going to make that mistake again. Cole no longer considered him a threat, so everything worked out.

Booker didn't want to jinx himself, but he was pretty certain he was figuring Jo out. He gathered a lot of information from that mind-blowing kiss. He'd never experienced that particular kind of sharing with someone who wasn't a wolf before. In the midst of being amazed that it happened at all, he found her emotions were still laced with fear, just a different kind. Jo wasn't afraid of him anymore, but she did seem afraid of liking him. He thought of the moment again to try to pinpoint exactly what her feeling was trying to convey.

People aren't permanent was the thought that coalesced in his mind from hers.

That was easy enough to fix. He wasn't "people."

Mostly what he got from the first initial emotions coming from her was anxiety, but a lot of it seemed to be directed at him with no real thought behind it other than *Run!* For most of the past decade, her instinctive answer to any problem was to literally run. She'd never stayed in one place longer than six months, often less than that, at least from what they could piece together. There were still years of her life that he hadn't been able to recreate. Years of her life where no one had any idea where she was.

The mere thought of not knowing her location was enough to make him break out in a cold sweat. Thank Diana she'd asked him for help. From now on, someone would always know how to reach her if she was in trouble. She was part of Diana's Wolves now, and her status with the pack wouldn't change even if something happened to Booker.

It would probably take a few years for Jo to stop thinking of running away from things that scared her. Things like him and his feelings for her. He was prepared for that. While she probably wouldn't leave the Sanctum, there were all kinds of ways that she might try to run from him.

He was impatient to have the investigation over. He wanted to get settled into the city and begin his plans for developing the area around the Sanctum, and he wanted to spend more time with Jo—in every way, any way, he could have her. However, until they found a breakthrough for an attack or Hel's acolytes and their shitty band made a move or made a mistake, they were stuck in this damned holding pattern. Waiting.

He was looking forward to the day when his priorities could be a little bit more pleasant.

Booker checked his phone. Nothing from Nick or Max. A general all clear from Ethan and his post near Purgatory. Nothing from Jo, but he'd told her he might not be able to text.

There was a quiet knock on the waiting room door, and then Art stepped in. "No worries on this end, son. They're willing to wait and see what happens."

"Thanks, Dad. For everything you did in there." Art's actions weren't just for his son, Booker knew. Art knew a lot more pregnant werewolves and was just as worried about the future of the clans, so he was inclined to make sure that the Council gave Jo breathing room too, but there was no denying that his declaration made life easier for Jo.

"Please convey my welcome and my gratitude to your witch," Art said. "I look forward to meeting her when the necromancer situation is resolved."

Booker grinned. "You'll like her."

"One more thing," Art said. "The Council really does want her educated in our ways, so they're going to be checking in."

"I figured as much," Booker said wryly.

"If she breaks any major laws, it'll bite us all in the ass."

"I know. Ignorance will get her killed." His wolf growled at the thought, but Booker reminded him that she was safe. For now. "I have no intention of letting anything happen to her."

"I've gotten you permission to go up to the library," Art said. "They're sending you home with some books, and you'll receive copies of more later." He cocked his head. "I hope your witch likes to read."

Booker laughed, thinking of how excited his witch would be. Hoping he would be able to claim her as "his" sooner rather than later. "She lives to learn."

CHAPTER 26

WOLVES ARE FROM MARS, WITCHES ARE FROM VENUS

JO

GRACE AND I TALKED MUCH OF THE MORNING, AND IN ADDITION to helping me with inventory, she suggested that I train one of Booker's younger wolves to help around the shop. "That's just a smart use of resources, especially since so much of the renovations are done," Grace said. "I'm sure Booker won't mind."

I ignored the part of me that wanted to insist, *No more wolves, dammit!* and instead gave in to the logic. "Anyone in particular who has experience in retail?"

She smiled, and her eyes danced. "My cousin Rochelle would be perfect," she said. "She's new to the pack, so this would help me and my family. They'd worry less."

It sounded right, but I couldn't resist the urge to pull a card, so I excused myself to go back to my office. A quick shuffle of my favorite decks, then I closed my eyes and drew. *10 of Cups.* My favorite card, full of nothing but win. I frowned, but there was no denying it. Hiring Grace's cousin would be a good move, and I'd be a fool not to take advantage of it.

When I came back out, I told Grace that I'd love to set up an interview, so she immediately texted Rochelle. After a bit of text-tag, I was on the phone with Rochelle myself, asking her a few basic questions. I liked her immediately just from her vibe and her voice, so we set up an interview for the following week.

I hadn't even had to do a summoning spell.

I had two tarot clients come in for readings back-to-back, and luckily Grace didn't mind watching the store with help from Max. The first client ended her session with an emotional breakthrough that brought me to tears, which was odd. I didn't usually cry during readings, although my clients often did. When the second client burst into tears halfway through the reading and I did too, I realized that it was just going to be one of those days. I didn't know if it was the energy in the Sanctum, the stress over Hel's Belles, or my own emotional turmoil over Booker, but it was going to be a Day of Tears. Normally, it would be cathartic to release those emotions, but I was tired and moody and didn't want to cry. I just wasn't going to be able to do readings today.

When the second customer left, thankfully more composed by then, John was in the shop, and he and Grace were chatting.

"Someone else came in for a reading, but you were busy," Grace said apologetically. "I told them they could wait, but they said they'd come back another time."

"Crap," I muttered. "It's one of those days, apparently."

I called two of the tarot readers who worked at the Sanctum on weekends to see if they could come in or at least be on call for phone readings if necessary. Neither of them answered, so I just left voicemails. John came in while I was calling them.

"Why don't *you* want to read today?" he asked.

I sighed. "Something's up."

Because it was the Day of Tears, neither tarot reader called me back, so I ended up crying along with a few more weeping customers before the day was over. I always felt bad for the ones going through a difficult time. I wanted to make things better, but most of their problems did not come with easy-fix solutions. The only thing to do was to listen and give them my attention and whatever hope I could bring them. One of the things about life I'd realized through reading tarot is that most adversity is temporary. Pain stays, but with patience, the cause of the pain often blows over within a period of time.

Once the afternoon crowd started to dissipate, Grace headed up to her apartment for a nap, leaving me and John in the store. It was easier to give Booker a promise I would stay indoors than it was to keep that promise after yesterday's outing. All afternoon, I thought of a million other things I'd seen out in the neighborhood, places I'd earmarked to go to later, but none of them would have constituted necessary trips and I knew it. I just wanted to go outside because my Guardian Wolf had made me promise not to.

Between the weird day of sad readings, emotional outbursts, and that irrational cooped-up feeling, I was elated when the shop closed and I was free to go up on the roof with some delivered food and sit with Stanley. When I stepped out of the mirror into the fresh air, Cole was curled up on the ledge next to Stanley. In my spot.

Great. Cole's still popping up everywhere he shouldn't be. Good to know.

"Dude, really?" I said to him, without heat. He meowed a greeting.

I walked over to Cole and Stanley with my dinner, pushed Cole to the side, and sat down in my usual spot. For a moment, I rested my head on the cool stone of Stanley's side. As I did, I tried to let the residual sadness of the day seep out of me and back into the earth. Filtered through the earth, I visualized the energy being cleansed, then added the energy into the protective shield I had around the building.

It took a little longer than simply powering the shields with the emotion, but the exercise in visualization was soothing. When I felt cleansed of that last part of my day, I opened my eyes and grabbed the bag of food.

Cole had positioned himself within optimal begging distance. I ate the chicken gyro I'd ordered and pulled off pieces of meat for Cole. After it was gone, Cole curled up on my lap. I angled myself so that the worst fall he'd take was from my lap to the roof. I leaned into the cool, stony solidness that was Stanley and told him about my day as we watched the Mississippi River reflect the last light from the sun.

It felt like I'd only been on the roof for ten minutes, but when I came through the mirror into my apartment, the clock showed me that it had been two hours since I left work. I texted Nick to let him know that I was in my apartment for the night. He responded with a thumbs-up emoji.

When I was on the road, a day like today would end in the inevitable crash of eating dinner, crying, and going to bed. There seemed to be a much heavier crash when I was younger. Thankfully, I'd improved over the years.

It helped to learn how to ground my own energy, but having something permanent to feed the energy into worked wonders. Even though I hadn't been here long, my little ritual of being on the roof with Stanley and flowing energy into this building and its shields provided more happiness than I was used to on a regular basis.

Since I was tired but still feeling cooped up, I made up for the morning yoga I'd missed earlier while talking with Booker. I was finishing up when I could tell he was there. Not just that someone was watching me—I knew it was him. That emotional connection sparked in me.

I stood up and shook out my limbs, taking my time, before I looked over to him where he was leaning against the wall, barefoot in jeans and a T-shirt. *How in the world does he make bare feet look so good?* "You know," I said, casting him an amused glance, "I've been meaning to ask you if you've been picking the lock to get in here."

"You still haven't," he pointed out. "Besides, a sharp look would unlock that door."

I stretched my arms over my head and brought them back down. "How was your trip?"

"Productive." He began to walk in my direction, not really stalking me, but all laser focus and molten-honey eyes. "I'll tell you about it. Later."

My body was already humming with delicious tension, so when I felt his intent, his heat and desire, I couldn't help but shiver a little. *Finally, I get to have him.* "Fair enough." Just because I wanted to, I stayed where I was, making him come to me.

"I probably should have made some noise to let you know I was here," he admitted. "But you have a clever face and expressive eyes. I like to watch you." The words should have come off as creepy, but I couldn't think of him that way. It was Booker, and knowing that he liked to look at me, that he thought of me that way, sent a thrill and a healthy zing of lust through me.

Instead of trusting my voice, I smiled a welcome at him, and that seemed to break some sort of inner tension that had kept him at bay. In three quick strides, his hands were on me and his mouth was hungry on mine. I sighed and leaned into him, his warmth and his scent. The movement brought my stomach up against his hardness, and he growled into my mouth with approval.

He wrapped one arm around my back and slid his hand down to cup my bottom, pulling me in and dragging my body up the length of him, urging my legs to wrap around his waist. The effort of holding me didn't seem to faze him—*gotta love that werewolf strength*. My hands were busy, pulling his shirt out of the way and sliding it up his naked back, stroking his smooth, warm muscles, as he walked us into my bedroom. I needed to feel his skin against mine. I wanted to be closer, even though only the fabric of our clothes separated us. Once my hands found flesh, the sense of relief and contentment was dulled only by the lust pounding in my veins and pulsing in my core.

Booker sat me gently on the edge of my bed, then took off his shirt. I gazed on those muscles I'd wanted to see for days and grinned. "You've been holding out on me." Where I was naturally pale, he was tanned, the type of coloring where after one day in the sun, he would stay golden brown. From the looks of it, I would bet that he did more than just wolfing out to keep his physique. If not, then werewolves had a seriously unfair advantage.

Rather than waiting for him to move, I reached forward and unbuttoned his jeans, letting my fingers linger on the prominent bulge there. The zipper slid down almost by itself. Apparently, Booker wasn't a big believer in underwear—beneath the jeans was nothing but him. His cock was fully erect and gorgeous, and I took him in my hand, slowly stroking up and down a few times before lowering my mouth over him. His hands fisted in my hair, but he took care not to put pressure on me. I moved my mouth, used my tongue, and he moaned, sending another shaft of heat between my legs.

His sandalwood and cedar scent was darker, more sensual now, and the taste of him, all salt and warm skin, was almost as intoxicating as the sounds he was making. I could have stayed there for a while, driving him crazy the way he'd been teasing me for days, but he pulled away from me with a final, desperate groan.

"If you keep doing that, this will be over before it starts," he warned, his voice gruff, his eyes hot and heavy-lidded as he stepped out of his jeans.

Then I was on my back and he was above me on the bed, kissing me, urging my shirt up and off, unhooking my bra with startling speed, only to heave a growling sigh when he saw my breasts. His eyes were glowing now, his mouth quirking up in a hungry smile, as he traced those long, clever fingers over my nipples, then bent his head to lick at them, then to suck.

The pleasure held me in its grip, my breath coming in short, frantic bursts. I ran my hands over his back muscles, loving the feel of him moving over me, and then he nipped at one nipple with his teeth and I gasped, my fingernails digging into his skin. That met with a muted grunt of approval before he slid down my body, unbuttoning my jeans and taking down the zipper with a remarkable haste that ended with my jeans flung somewhere in the room.

I was bare now, my whole body too aroused to be cold or to be shy, and he paused above me, our bodies separate for the moment, his aura tense and throbbing with his need. For me.

"You're okay?" His voice was so low that the words almost didn't register, but he wasn't moving until I gave him an answer. I knew that as sure as I knew my own name.

"Yes." I breathed it, a half-groan of fiery want, and reached for him—my arms, my heart, my aura. "Please." Everything in me needed Booker there too.

Without another word, he came back, his skin finally against mine, and when we kissed, that channel opened up again—I could feel his lust and his affection for me just as surely as I could feel his clever fingers sliding down my stomach, delving into the wet heat of my core. I gasped, and I felt him smile against my neck as he touched me—everywhere but where I needed him most. I'd wanted him for days, weeks, and he wanted to tease me.

Two can play at that game. I reached for him, then his smooth, hard length hot in my hand, then played my fingertips around the sensitive tip. He moved against me, groaning, his hips almost desperate, and then his fingers were gone, and I nearly screamed in frustration before he spread my legs and then his tongue was there. Right where I wanted it. Where I needed all that hot, stroking rhythm.

I did scream then, on a cresting wave of pleasure that made my body convulse. I saw stars behind my eyes, clenched tightly closed. He said, "Look at me, Jo," and I opened my eyes to stare down into his while the waves of bliss rolled through me again and again. All my pleasure was the color of amber, and I felt like he was drinking me in. Bottomless. Unblinking. Worshipful.

"Now," I told him, voice shaking. My hands were on his shoulders, and he slid up to kiss me again, his tongue tasting of my pleasure—and if he'd been hungry before, he was starving now. I ended the kiss with a nip of his tongue that had him growling again.

His deep voice vibrated against the skin of my neck. "Are you sure? You're ready?"

I knew what he meant. The bond between us had already grown beyond my control. So be it. I wanted this. Needed it. "Inside." I opened my legs to him, pulling him to me, raising myself up—offering him the fire.

His aura darkened again, and I shuddered to feel the way it hungered, his warm body finding its way along me until he rolled on a condom and finally, *finally* slid into my body. For a moment, we both stared at each other, the connection between us weaving threads of emotion through the excruciating pleasure. The glow in his eyes was white-hot now, and he shifted his weight to cradle my hips in his hands. I couldn't hold back a sigh of relief when his hardness moved inside me, and I slid my hands up to his neck and gave him a bright smile.

That seemed to snap his control entirely, and his hips took over the rhythm as I gave myself up to it, riding the pulsing waves of another orgasm, rocking up to meet him while he gave to me and took from me with every thrust. I wanted his skin though—all of that delicious heat was too far away. I wanted it against my belly, against my aching breasts. I wanted to taste it with my tongue like he'd tasted me.

No sooner had that thought crystallized in my hazed brain than Booker rolled us, disconnecting only long enough to reposition himself on the edge of the bed, before sitting and then urging me back to straddle him.

This, yes. I sighed in satisfaction when we were chest to chest, and despite the lust that charged all his energy, he grinned at me—*those dimples* —so I slid my tongue into his mouth again as he slid his hardness back into my wet core, his arms solid, his hips wild now, thrusting up into me, the friction so exquisite that I couldn't hold back mindless sounds of pleasure, encouragement, my hands digging into his back, clutching his hair. With a muffled curse, his hands went tense around me and then pulled me down on him, holding me there by my hips, filling me so completely that my head fell to his shoulder and I sank my teeth into his neck. He came, shuddering, groaning my name, his hardness pulsing inside of me, tipping me over the edge into another quaking orgasm.

It was molten honey. His pleasure and mine, flowing open between us. Pure, undiluted rapture. I'd never felt anything like it. Ever.

There's nothing like this in the wide world.

"Nothing," Booker echoed, burying his face in my hair, his heart still pounding against mine. I rested there, my body still locked to his, sated and exhausted and thrilled to the marrow, as our heartbeats slowed and our breaths evened out. One of his hands stroked up and down my back while the other rested on my thigh, his thumb lightly whisking back and forth across the soft, pale skin there.

As the connection between us eased, reality began to creep in. The sweat, the mess, the intensity. I eased myself back from him and began the awkward process of dismounting, but Booker held onto me. He brushed the stray hair back from my face, his amber gaze now glowing warm, no longer white-hot. When my breath caught, he kissed me, slow and sweet, like dessert after a good meal.

I'd had lovers over the years, despite my trauma—or at first, because of it. I was so determined not to let the Fenris steal a healthy sex life from me too. I chose them carefully, so they were nearly all good experiences, with one or two great ones. Physical intimacy was easy enough, but the way Booker had sex wasn't just mere physical. He brought an intensity, a presence with him, that demanded attention. When that combined with our newfound psychic connection—whatever it was—it was even more. I wasn't just naked with him. I was completely exposed.

Goddess help me, I stopped caring, stopped worrying, when Booker's hand came up to cradle my jaw as his lips lingered over mine. He melted all the defenses I'd begun to half-heartedly throw up between us.

After endless minutes of this, he paused, giving my bottom lip a last, quick swipe of his tongue that made the sore place between my legs tingle all over again. "Where were you going to run off to?" he murmured, arching a brow.

I took a breath, then let it out. Having a lover who knew when you were lying was inconvenient as hell. I chose my words carefully. "I want to take a shower," I said, with complete truth. "Sex is messy."

He grinned and picked me up. "That it is," he said, looking immensely pleased that sex was messy. He set me down only long enough to pull another condom from his jeans pocket, and then he walked into the bathroom, me holding on for dear life, and turned on my shower. Holy Hecate, he was strong enough to hold me with one hand while getting the shower temp right with the other. Since I had no other options, I just waited, clinging to him, half-irritated and half-aroused.

He tested the water a few times with his fingers, and when it reached what I assumed was optimum temp, he stepped us both into the shower and made a noise of contentment, closing his eyes as the warm water ran over us both. I stopped being irritated. How could anyone stay mad at Happy Booker?

I couldn't help it. I leaned forward and brushed a gentle kiss against his lips. I'm not sure what I meant it to be. A thank you. An invitation. A benediction. A confession.

Slowly his amber eyes drifted open, and a lazy smile spread across his handsome face. For a moment, I stared at him. *Who is this man? This wolf?* I reached up to his chin, framed my hands around his face, and just looked into him. All I saw was love and want, and it should have scared me. Should have made me want to run.

Instead, I kissed him again, and he turned me, pressing my back against the shower wall and nudging himself inside me in one fluid motion. I let my eyes close—*so good*—and when I moved my hips into his, joining his rhythm, he murmured his approval in my ear. This time, it was all long slow strokes that built gradually. He wanted to take his time, even when it drove me insane. Every effort I made to speed things up, he slowed back down. I could feel our psychic connection again, a burst of agonizing double pleasure with every movement, a haze of happiness and affection and need blanketing us both.

When I finally came from those long, slow strokes, he kissed me, taking my cries into his mouth while he drove into me, stroking me from the inside while my release went on and on. When the aftershocks of my orgasm receded, only then did he speed up the pace, and I sucked on his tongue when he growled into my mouth and then pulled his head back with a loud shout of release.

Watching him come was almost as satisfying as experiencing it myself. I smiled and leaned into him, bringing his mouth back down to mine while he rode out his ecstasy and my body milked his.

While we caught our breath, I let my unsteady legs fall from around his hips, and he set me down on the shower floor, making sure I was standing firmly before he let me go. Our connection receded again, leaving me with that exposed feeling—although I felt less self-conscious about it this time.

Since the shower was still running, I escaped the intensity of Booker's gaze by busying myself with washing up, shampooing my hair, then rinsing it. I met his gaze again when I put conditioner in my hair. His bright amber eyes were taking in every moment.

When I started to soap myself up, he blinked. In silence, he took the lavender soap and the loofah and began to wash me himself. My heart flip-flopped in my chest as he meticulously and thoroughly cleaned my body, the warm smell of lavender all around us—his attention focused on every part of my body, one by one. I simply let him do it, standing there, trying not to tremble.

Then he set the loofah aside and just used his still soapy hands to stroke up and down my body, sliding over every curve, dancing on my breasts and nipples, lingering on my buttocks and between my legs. It was like he needed to touch me everywhere, discover all my secrets, and the slickness of the soap on his rough hands made it all possible. All I could hear was the water and my own breathing, all I could smell was the lavender. All I could see was him.

When his hands began to slow and his eyes returned to mine, now glowing again, his mouth soft with arousal, I took the soap from him and gave him the same torture, letting my hands possess him as I cleaned his body. He stood passive, only the occasional twitch of a muscle and his fisted hands betraying his inner tension. He was tan all over—my pale hands on his darker skin made an interesting contrast—and I found all the places on him I'd wondered about before. I traced the light dustings of brown hair over his arms, down his legs, and on his chest, as it moved with his breath. That breath quickened when my soapy fingers followed the trail down his stomach and found his erect cock waiting for me.

Is this thing always ready to go? Is that what the legends mean by werewolves being cursed?

I almost laughed out loud, but Booker was pushing himself into my hands, so I leaned my body into his, letting my slick fingers play over the length of him, loving the rumbling in his chest against my ear. He moved then, as if he couldn't stop himself, and I gripped him gently, stroking him like he'd stroked me—*slowly, slowly*—even when he groaned and cursed and flexed his hands on my body.

What they say about absolute power is true. It does corrupt absolutely. I kept him in a near-agony for as long as I could, scattering nips and kisses over his chest, letting my free hand roam his body, until he rasped out a "Jo, please," and I leaned my head back to look into those glowing eyes, heavy-lidded and desperate. I gave him what he needed then, squeezing him gently, letting him pump wildly into my fist, rising up on my tiptoes to kiss him, sweeping my tongue between his open lips—and he came then, and I swallowed his hoarse bark of release, loving how it vibrated on my tongue.

He sank to his knees as if in a dream, parting my legs, pulling my left up and hooking it over his shoulder. I held on to the shower rod, my body relaxing there against the shower wall—I already knew Booker wouldn't let me fall—and watched him lick into me, let the luscious pleasure roll through my body as he tasted me.

This time when I came, it was an endless, rising tidal wave, my hips and legs quivering as he drank from me, wanting me to give him more. Give him everything. I did, rolling my hips into his questing tongue, my mouth open in a blissful sigh that went on and on.

There was nothing like this. Never had been. Never could be.

Because it was *him*.

I barely remember the rest, just Booker's fingers moving in my hair as he rinsed out the conditioner I'd forgotten, the spray of the water growing lukewarm as it chased soap suds from our bodies. A towel gently abraded my skin. Arms curled around me, lifting me, settling my naked body in all its bone-deep exhaustion into bed.

"We're going to get the pillows damp," I mumbled, and Booker chuckled. He was right behind me, crawling in next to me, and I wrapped my arms around him, resting my head on his chest. Now he smelled like sandalwood, cedar, and lavender, and the last thing I remember before I fell asleep was that we both smelled perfect now.

Chapter 27

Hecate's Dream Theater

JO

Tonight, the dream was different. Instead of being an active participant, I watched it as if it were a movie. Most of it seemed to flow by quickly—the capture, being hunted, being beaten, being violated—but a few different points slowed down. The first was during the second day. A Fenris wolf I'd never seen before—one with long, greasy, black hair and a sleeve of tattoos—came into the room to hit me, and I saw myself glaring at him through bruised, blue eyes that blazed with loathing.

What I'd never noticed before was that this Fenris seemed unnerved by me. The hatred in my eyes gave the illusion that they glowed, almost like Booker's, and it seemed to make the wolf pause for a moment. He approached me warily, circling me, sniffing the air, before he leapt toward me and landed an uppercut, and my eyes dulled again with pain.

It went on. I saw the female Fenris and her phone camera. I saw the unlucky bastard who'd forced me to give him a blow job he'd never forget. When I watched myself spit out the remains of that Fenris wolf's penis, I saw her grin with bloody teeth before he scrambled to his feet and plowed his fist into her face.

When I relived the experience in my dreams before, the suffering and despair of the moment always made my mental image—as it was then, I suppose—that of a beaten and cowed woman. That was how I felt at the time. However, in this external view, my face didn't look like someone who was beaten down.

The woman those Fenris were trying to hurt did cry and scream when they injured her, but she wore her hatred and disgust for them on her battered face. Watching it from a distance, this time around, I could see that my expression unsettled several of the more observant wolves. Not enough to stop, of course, and for some of them, I think my defiant hate coupled with my lack of begging spurred them on to be even more sadistic.

I could see, though, that defiant hate was all we had left.

The events sped up again until the tail end of the dream. My broken body, belly-down on the floor, trying to crawl away, swollen lips moving as I prayed for my own death. In my other dreams, my memory had always shown that I'd crawled away while they were distracted, but this time, from the perspective of a watcher, I saw the truth—they weren't distracted. They knew what I was doing, but they couldn't stop me. They clawed at the air around me, stabbed it with knives, but they couldn't penetrate the protective shield of energy. Still I crawled away, and still my lips moved.

Then I got to the point when I spoke with Hecate. From this perspective, it was much more literal. We were still in that filthy room, the Fenris all there around us, as Hecate and I sat talking on the log in the clearing. The green, leafy edges of the clearing bled into the dark edges of the Fenris' den, and the wolves were there, just beyond, immobilized or simply outside the time frame of Hecate's visitation.

The woman I saw there on the log with Hecate looked different too, free from the physical injuries. Attentive to the goddess as if to a particularly fascinating teacher. Then I watched myself stand up and move my hands—I could see the golden thread, but only barely—and then I disappeared, along with all the Fenris.

What I didn't see was me walking through the mirror, although I know I did. Maybe the mirror was something only I could see in the moment. Or maybe it was only in my head.

A few seconds later, I reappeared in the same spot, looking like myself but also very different. It wasn't just my hair, now raven-black—it was the body language. The way I carried myself. Walking through that mirror, leaving the Fenris behind with Hecate, was like being darkly reborn into a scarier world that promised no safety.

The expression on my face was one of exhausted, bleak determination.

I watched my younger self as she searched for and found ill-fitting but clean clothes, just to have something to cover herself, before she found the bathroom and shower. I'd never seen this part of the dream before, had never filled this gap in the memories of that horrible day. I watched and marveled at her—at myself. The fact that I actually showered there before leaving was the part I couldn't get past.

"What was I thinking?" I asked myself in the dream.

"You weren't. You were in shock," Hecate said from beside me, Her voice clear and musical but with a slight echo. It should have startled me, but somehow I'd known She was there, watching the same memory. "You needed to cleanse yourself. You needed to cover yourself. A tiny bit of mental fugue sometimes helps the immediate needs get met."

My younger self had found the shower, and now I could remember that shower all too well—such a far cry from the one I'd taken with Booker. She shampooed her hair three times, scrubbed herself all over three times, holding on to the overwhelming relief of being able to wash off the dried blood and all the other things I didn't want to think about. Washing off the old life and getting ready for the new one.

Once dream me had showered and dressed, I watched myself wander through the huge den, searching for money in the nooks and crannies, any clothing, any dresser, any cabinet. *Enough cash for a hotel*—that's what she was thinking about then. She hadn't even begun to think about how she was leaving the house or where to look for her own car, which had all of her worldly possessions in it. She just knew she needed money if she wanted to have a room for the night with a lock on the door. Eventually, in a corridor off the main part of the building, she found what could only be called a counting room.

The room had one long table piled with bags containing bills of different denominations, envelopes of cash, and a counting machine. They'd made quite a dent in counting their tribute but hadn't finished. So dream me took over.

I watched as she sat down in the house of her rapists to count their money. I knew I'd walked out of there with a fortune, but I didn't remember how. I'd simply imagined that I'd tried desperately to leave as quickly as possible, to run as far away as I could. However, dream me was methodical about counting the money, although she would occasionally pause to shake herself, wrap her arms around herself, rock herself, before getting back to work. I guess my autopilot was more efficient than I had been at that point.

In the end, dream me packed all the money neatly into two bags and went to the door before she turned to face the interior again, her eyes glowing nearly white as she extended her power. Then she walked away as the building burned to the ground. The conflagration started big, and not much would be left—but somewhere in the rubble that remained, Booker and the Council would find the phone that contained the video of so many key points. Including the part where the Fenris bitch holding the phone was pulled out of this dimension, leaving the phone to drop to the ground and bounce underneath something that sheltered it, so the recording would survive.

"It's about time you let the dream show you this through different eyes," Hecate told me. "You weren't the victim here. You were the victor."

I didn't feel particularly victorious, even watching my younger self walk away at the peak of her vengeance. It was lonely and hollow, watching myself, knowing that the next years of my life would be that of the constant nomad, with only a few small moments of connection surrounded by an ocean of fear, loneliness, and isolation.

"You bore it well and used the time wisely," Hecate said. Because, of course, She could read my mind. She put a hand lightly on my shoulder, turning me to face Her. "The Fenris didn't know what they did when they captured you. They changed the world. They opened the way. Now..." She paused. "Now is the time for witches, my daughter. Witches as they were meant to be."

The dream faded, leaving me bereft. I tucked away Hecate's comment about "the time for witches," knowing I would remember it when I was supposed to, and let the feeling of loss chase through my dreams for the rest of the night.

When I woke, my cheeks were cold with tears, so it was a relief to immediately register the warm, naked man wrapped around me. I nuzzled my damp face into his chest, happy to have Booker there with me, solid and real. *Mine.*

The small movement on my part woke him, and he tucked his head down to put his nose on my neck, inhaling with a contented sigh. I sighed too, wiping at my cheeks and eyes.

Booker lay his head back on his pillow, raising his hand to rub at the salt tracks on my face with a thumb, his eyebrows creasing in silent concern.

"Oh, sad dream," I said, tightening my arm around his waist. "Sometimes the sadness seeps out of the dreams and stays with me."

He shifted his arms to bring me in closer. "Tell me," he said, his deep voice a soothing rumble. In gratitude, I dropped a kiss on his chest and began to speak.

While I recounted the dream, his warm hands moved up and down the length of my torso slowly, gentling me, chasing away that sense of loss. As I spoke, it occurred to me that because the sadness and loss had been so overwhelming at the time, I missed the overall point of the dream—which I think was what Hecate was trying to show me.

This version of the dream wasn't about reliving the past—it was about learning from the past to make a better future. She showed me that, during the time I felt the weakest and most vulnerable, I still had strength. Before praying to Hecate, I had manifested protection, even if I hadn't been aware of it. I'd kept the Fenris off me simply through my all-consuming focus on my need to pray for death.

I'd always thought that the power that manifested inside me after that—the mirror-walking, the psychic abilities, and all of it—came from Hecate. A gift of protection or something. But no. It existed before I'd called on Her, buried inside me. Dormant. Waiting. A crucial truth that I needed to know.

Thankfully, Booker was a patient listener, and he let me babble, backtrack, correct myself throughout without comment.

"Hecate wanted me to see my own power," I said when I'd reached the end of the dream. "She wouldn't have shown me this perspective, given me this version of the dream, if She hadn't wanted me to know."

When I lapsed into silence, throat dry, he nodded and finally spoke. "I think it's confirmation of what we've all known for a while." When I raised my head to look inquiringly into his eyes, he smiled, dimples peeking. "You price yourself too low."

I laughed. Trust a wolf to be so cavalier about all this. Talking to gods. Manifestations of power. Just another Sunday for Diana's favorite cannon-fodder wolf.

I sighed and laid my cheek back on his chest, hearing his strong, steady heartbeat. "Maybe so. Maybe She really had to come into my dreams to show me something I should have realized before. I mean, I'm constantly looking into mirrors without really seeing myself. You'd think I'd be better at personal reflection," I said, meaning for it to be a light and funny comment.

Booker didn't laugh though. He just looked thoughtful for a moment, then smiled as if he'd had a tremendously clever idea. "We can take pictures and video of you. Then you can see yourself without the mirror in the way," he said, sounding pleased with himself.

I found the idea horrifying. "Booker. The world has basically no pictures of me in it, and I'm fine with that. Please, I was just trying to joke around."

"No, you weren't," he said, with the assuredness of a lie-detecting wolf. "Besides, it will be fun."

He was as good as his word. By the time we were finished with breakfast, Booker had taken pictures of me in bed, eating breakfast, feeding the cat, and more—I forbade him from bringing his phone into the bathroom, or no doubt I'd have had pictures of myself on the toilet.

I was learning that once you let them in, wolves don't really do "personal space." Booker seemed only too happy to be in whatever space I happened to be occupying, and he enjoyed taking those pictures so much that it was impossible not to laugh at him, even when I was insisting that he put his damned phone away.

"Just come look," said the half-naked werewolf sitting at my kitchen table, so I went to him. He pulled me into his lap and showed off his photography skills, making sure I saw every single one and swatting my hand away when I tried to delete any, kissing the side of my neck, rubbing his morning stubble into my skin to distract me while he took selfies of us together. I had to roll my eyes at the whole thing, but I secretly loved a few of the pictures, especially the ones that had captured me laughing at him.

I'd never seen myself look so happy. Ever.

I fully made his day when I gave in and asked him to text me a few of his favorites, which included one of his pictures of the two of us on the chair, with his head bent into my neck and the wide grin on his profile showing one dimple while I laughed helplessly, hair in my eyes, with one hand stretched out toward the phone. That one took my breath, which he noted when I saw it, and he texted it to me immediately with obvious pride before he bounced up and carried me back into the bedroom.

"No, Booker," I said, pounding lightly on his shoulders with my fists. "I know the shop's closed, but we have things to do."

His dimpled grin was positively sinful. "We definitely have things to do." He fell down onto the bed with me, rolling me beneath him. "I have one thing in particular that needs doing."

"Booker!" His head was beneath my Kiki's Delivery Service T-shirt now, his tongue busy on the soft skin of my stomach.

"Yes, Jo?" His teeth scraped over my ribs.

I shuddered and arched up into him. "You're lucky it's my day off," I mock-grumbled before he pulled back and stripped the shirt up and over my head. Then his mouth was on mine and his hands were full of my breasts and what else was there to do but slide my hands into his short hair and let him seduce me all over again?

It meant another shower, but I'd just make him pay the water bill this month.

When we finally made it downstairs, we met with Nick, Max, and Ethan in Booker's War Room—and as I'd assumed, all three of the wolves zeroed in on Booker and me with their unblinking eyes. Nick stopped mid-sentence when we walked in, and it wasn't because he'd been talking about me.

I could have sworn I could see their nostrils flaring.

There was really no way to hide that Booker and I had been all over each other for the past twelve hours, so I'd been determined not to worry about it.

All that careful planning went out the window the instant three pairs of werewolf eyes focused directly on me. My face flamed hot.

Booker just nodded a greeting to his pack members and put his arm around me, drawing me close to him. He kissed the top of my head and then smiled at them, ignoring my embarrassment. Max grinned at first Booker, then me, and Nick winked at me. Ethan's face was impassive, as if he was reserving judgment.

From what Booker had told me, and what I'd gleaned myself from watching them, I knew that body language was all-important to the wolves. It trumped verbal communication for them every time. Booker had just basically shouted out our shifting relationship with one move—letting the wolves know that everything their noses were telling them about our mingled scents was true.

I tried to smile at them, but I'm sure it looked more like a chagrined, apologetic baring of teeth. *Damn it, Booker, you had to make it weirder for all of us.*

"Status report?" Booker asked.

Nick was the first to recover, and some of the info he had was useful at least. They'd finally found that two key figures in the Hel's Belles situation, my new buddy Heloise and the as yet unseen Nigel Hades, were apparently a brother and sister from Florida who'd gone on the road as a folk rock duo five years before.

"Hilary and Keith Dunlap," I said, looking at the picture of Hilary, now Heloise. It was from her driver's license, but even so, it showed her with a fresh, pretty face and masses of chestnut hair. Yes, it was her. Her brother likewise sported the same hair, along with a pair of intense blue eyes in his own driver's license photo. They were both smiling and looked so...normal.

While I looked at the pictures, Booker and Nick talked over the situation. "This is a start, but it's not going to draw them out unless we can somehow use this," Booker was saying.

"We can send an email to 'Nigel' via the Purgatory website, threaten to leak this to the press, and plaster it all over social media if they don't agree to a meeting," Max suggested.

"That might work," Booker said. "Jo?"

"Yeah," I said, putting the photocopies down. "Their image is important to them. Let's see if it's more important than killing me."

Nick nodded. "I'm on it."

"We're going to go out for a walk," Booker said, then to me added, "I want to start doing some training with you."

My eyebrows raised. "Training?"

As it turned out, Booker wanted me to get some practice spotting hostiles in the field—which meant a werewolf version of hide-and-seek.

While we walked around the neighborhood that morning, Ethan found places to hide, or more accurately, blend in with the people and surroundings. My job was to practice scanning for him while walking. Ethan, like the other Sanctum wolves, was visible to me on a magical level because of the geas he'd signed, but Booker insisted that I work on training my eyes to find someone who was watching me. "You can't always rely on your magical sight—and our enemies may not be visible to you that way," he explained.

He chose Ethan for the task, I suspected, because I didn't know Ethan well. Aside from the day he'd signed his contract geas, we'd been in the same room together maybe one other time before today—he'd been leading the teams watching the Sanctum and Purgatory until Booker brought him in today. Grace was getting close to her due date, so Nick might be called away at any time. Kirsten was in charge of the surveillance teams now, and she seemed keen to do the job.

Of all of Booker's wolves, I found Ethan to be the most intimidating—Nick was friendly, and Max was a bit of a goofball, but Ethan's general demeanor was "menace." His aura was clean but murky enough that I could tell violence was part of his toolbox. It was hard not to be gun-shy around him. He wasn't as tall as the others, but he was solidly built, and he had a tattoo that curled up from the neck of his shirts. I couldn't tell what it was. I'd have had to look directly at him to be sure, and we weren't quite there yet.

As soon as I walked out the door, the air felt heavy, oppressive—very much at odds with the usual fall crispness. The smells and sounds were the same, pretty typical for a Sunday in this area of the city, but something wasn't quite right.

"Do you feel that?" I asked Booker.

He nodded, his handsome face grim, his aura on edge for the first time that day. He took my hand in his, and we set off down the street.

Since the whole point was to lure someone out, I walked as if I didn't sense anything, but all of the hairs on the back of my neck stood up and I couldn't quite relax. Playing hide-and-seek with Ethan kept my mind busy at least.

The street traffic in the developed areas was thinner than the Saturday crowd, but there were still enough people out and about to confuse and distract the eye. Ethan used every trick he had, and given his werewolf speed and ability to blend in, it took me a bit to find him the first time. I had to make direct eye contact to "win," and when I did, catching him right behind a group of people dressed for paintball, I grinned.

He didn't smile, but he gave me a nod and then he was gone.

Despite the ominous weight of the air distracting me, I found him quicker and quicker each time. Booker was busy scanning the perimeter, but when I finally caught Ethan around one corner of a building, I muttered a triumphant "Yes," and Booker gave me a brief, pleased smile.

To my eternal surprise, Ethan winked at me before he disappeared into the crowd again. By the end of the hour-long walk, I'd practiced enough that even Booker was impressed. Still no sign of any zombies or necromancers, so we headed back to the Sanctum.

Despite my enjoyment of the game and the sunshine on my face, despite the delicious lingering soreness between my legs and Booker's hand in mine, there was still a quivering fear between my shoulder blades. Once we got close to my building, the feeling lessened, but it didn't go away.

We walked toward the entryway on the side of the building for the apartments, and I didn't have time to continue worrying about that bad feeling. Another of Booker's wolves, Shannon, came out and beckoned to us. "Booker, Grace has gone into labor. Nick's with her, but we need you."

"Why did no one call me?" Booker snarled. I side-eyed him—this was new. He was genuinely angry with one of his wolves, and his aura swelled with it. Shannon took a step back and looked down. If she'd been in wolf form, her ears would have flattened and her tail would have been between her legs.

"I'm so sorry. It just happened. We could see you from the window."

"I see." His voice gentled, but he nodded curtly. Poor Shannon finally raised her head. Booker turned to me. "Stay with Ethan, please."

"I will. Give Grace my love, and if you need me, call."

He gave me a quick hug and nodded to Ethan, who said, "Go, Booker. I've got this."

I didn't enjoy being a "this," but I allowed it under the circumstances. In a second, Booker was inside and leaping up the stairs, with the other two wolves who'd been out with us following behind.

CHAPTER 28

TWO WOLVES, A WITCH, AND AN ARGUMENT

JO

ETHAN USHERED ME INSIDE THE BUILDING AND MADE SURE THE door was locked behind us, and then we regarded each other.

"You're really good at hide-and-seek," I ventured.

That got him to quirk his lips at least. "You got pretty good by the end." His voice was deep and a little gravelly, in a pleasant way.

"Now what?" I thought about inviting him up to the roof, but he surprised me again.

"Do you want to see the rest of the renovations? It's your building, after all."

That definitely piqued my interest. I'd only seen a few rooms, and I knew that the construction crew had been working long hours the past few days. "Sure."

I'd seen the sixth floor already—it was Booker's open concept place, like my apartment but with more bedrooms. I found out that Ethan and Max lived there with Booker. So Ethan and I started on the fourth floor, where I got to peek into the apartments. Grace and Nick lived in one, so we didn't stay long on that floor—I could feel the energy emanating from their place and was relieved that it didn't feel negative. That probably boded well for the birth.

On the fifth floor, things were still in progress on one half, but the other half was the big open space that had been fashioned into the home theater. The other side was being prepared as a gym, Ethan told me, but the equipment had yet to arrive. "I'll bet you guys go through the treadmill belts," I said, imagining Booker running full-tilt on one. That got me another half-smile and a low exhalation of breath that might have been Ethan's version of a laugh.

I'd thought it was finished before, but they'd added more furniture and some freestanding storage closets since I'd looked in here a few days ago. Since the lights were on this time, I could see that the windows hadn't just been covered—they'd been drywalled over, and the walls were painted now, a dark brown that made me think of tree bark and forests at night. The ceiling was a deep green.

The nature tones continued to the furniture, various chairs and couches in shades of green and brown, with even more pillows in the same theme. No camo, though, thank Hecate. The carpeting was a mossy green and thick enough that my feet sank into it. Ethan went over to a cabinet. He pressed a button on one of the remotes and the huge movie screen blinked on, showing a lovely if generic screensaver. The entire effect of the big open space with the colors of a nighttime forest was as if we were outside watching a movie. Then Ethan turned off the lights.

"This is fantastic," I murmured, turning in a circle.

The way the light from the screen played around the room, it seemed like we were in the forest. In the dark, with the shadows created by the screen, the walls seemed alive and full of movement. The green ceiling also came to life, looking as if leaves moved around in a wind that wasn't there. I had no idea how they did this, whether it was magic or just cleverly textured painting.

It was wonderful. Suddenly, I hoped that maybe sometime they would invite me to a movie night. Sure, they'd watched the Hel's Belles performance videos with that eerie stillness, but maybe it would be different if it was just for entertainment.

I thought about the couches I'd gotten and never really used for company. The solitary life I'd led for so long. Before the Fenris had changed my life, I used to love watching movies with people, laughing and gasping along with them. Before I'd settled in St. Louis and established my Sanctum, I'd fed that hunger by going to theaters, sitting in the back row, and enjoying the energy of the crowd. I'd gotten so caught up in renovations and running the shop that I couldn't remember the last time I'd been out to a movie.

My chest began to ache. In that big, inviting room, I realized how very lonely I was. Before, I'd thought of it as simply being solitary. Solitary was different. Solitary was a choice—a smart one. Since Booker and his wolves had barged into my life, since I'd been witness to their pack dynamics—since I'd been all but dragged into them myself—I found that I craved their company. Talking with Grace in the shop, joking with Max about food and his freakish height. And Booker. *Always Booker.* I wondered if he would hold my hand, cuddle with me on one of those couches with his pack around us.

Hecate, help me. I had to be seriously lonely if I was getting all wistful thinking about watching movies with a pack of werewolves.

After a few seconds, Ethan said, "It's probably going to be a bit until we hear anything. You like horror movies?"

I took a breath and let it out. "I really do."

By the time the movie was over, I had kicked off my shoes and stretched out on one of the couches in front of the screen, while Ethan had taken the armchair nearest the door. I was delighted to find out that Ethan had picked a movie that was both scary and funny—and that Mr. Intimidation did know how to laugh.

I sat up while the credits rolled. "That was awesome," I told Ethan. "Thank you."

"No problem."

I sighed, stretched, and slipped my Chuck Taylors back on. "I should probably go upstairs."

Ethan didn't say anything, but his aura shifted. I could feel a new tension.

Maybe he hadn't understood my meaning. I suppressed a twinge of unease. "Ethan," I said. "I'd like to head up to the roof."

A beat of silence. Then, "Why don't we put on another movie?" he said. His voice was level and calm.

I looked around and realized for the first time that this room had no mirrors. Every floor had at least one full-length mirror. There had been one on the far wall before—I'd mounted it myself when I moved in. When Ethan brought me here, I'd been so enchanted by the play of light along the walls and ceiling that I hadn't even noticed.

I was alone in a room with a wolf who I didn't know well, and he was between me and the only way out. Fear stabbed through me, sharp and quick enough I barely stifled a gasp. The only thing that kept me from a full-on panic attack was the knowledge that he couldn't hurt me in the Sanctum. *He signed the geas, he signed the geas, he signed the geas, hesignedthegeas hesignedthegeas.*

I closed my eyes and took a breath, gathering energy from the Sanctum into myself. "I'd like to leave now." The oppressive weight of the outside, that menace, now seemed centered in Ethan, even though I knew it wasn't. It couldn't be.

When he stood up and turned on the light, I saw the expression on his face. It wasn't one of anger or malice—it was resolution. With a hint of regret.

Just like that, I knew what had happened, and I let the energy drain back into the Sanctum before my mounting rage got the better of me and I was tempted to try to blow a hole through the middle of this lovely room. I took a few slow, deep breaths, willing myself to regain my mental footing. Ethan had been instructed to look after me, and he'd done so by bringing me somewhere that I'd be guaranteed to stay.

Because it had been designed as a room that I, specifically, couldn't leave without using the door.

I marshalled my anger, prepared myself to say something to Ethan—I'm not sure what, but I had some idea that I should let him know that my quite palpable anger wasn't directed at him. Right then, however, Booker walked in with a bounce in his step and a big smile on his face. As soon as he stepped into the room, however, the bounce left and the smile vanished. He looked hard at Ethan, tilting his head ever so slightly.

Ethan shrugged and raised his eyebrows, frowning, with a quick headshake.

Booker's mouth went flat.

I really wished these damn wolves would use more words. I'd crack their code eventually, but right now I just wanted to smack them. Especially *him*.

"Hi. Standing right here. Care to share, using words?" I asked in an acid-sweet singsong voice. Since anger had helped me get past my fear, I leaned into it.

Werewolves, there's a new bitch in town.

Booker glanced at me, then inclined his head at Ethan. Ethan sent me a look that was definitely a wordless wolf apology, then he nodded at Booker and left the room.

Damn it. They all treated Booker like he was the werewolf equivalent of a king.

Well, he wasn't my king or my alpha. He was supposed to be my partner, not my keeper. Nausea rolled over in my stomach. "When did you take out the mirror?"

Booker sighed. I searched his face for any sign of remorse or guilt and saw none. "I needed to know that you'd be safe."

Do not cry right now. "You needed to basically lock me up with a werewolf who I don't know very well."

Booker took a step toward me, and I edged back. His jaw tensed. "All the wolves here are Diana's Wolves. All the wolves here signed the geas. You know that. You couldn't have been harmed. They all work with me. For me." He rubbed the back of his neck. "Even Grace. She's an accountant, but she's also part of Booker Brothers' management."

Grace was management at Booker Brothers? I'd offered her minimum wage to be my part-time accountant. My chuckle wasn't one of amusement, but it chased away the residual fear the anger hadn't driven off. "So you're managing me like you manage your wolves? Just putting me where you need me to be and expecting me to stay put?"

"You asked me to keep you alive. Ethan's about the best there is at that."

"I'm alive. I'm safe. In *my building*, I'm safe."

Booker started to speak, then stopped himself. I could feel his irritation growing. Well, that made two of us. This connection we had was one hell of a bumpy two-way street.

He ran his tongue over his teeth. "You felt the air out there," he said, keeping his voice lower than normal. His eyes had gone turbulent, glowing with a light I'd never seen. "Something is up. It's not Grace's delivery. Something's going to happen—something *bad*—and until it does, I need to know where you are at all times." He stopped again. "I can't take any chances with you."

I shook my head, once. "All you have to do is text me. And trust me."

"Jo." His aura grew stormy with concern and anger. "Can you please just do as I say for once?"

"*For once?* Are you fucking kidding me?" I stepped closer to him. "You took the mirror out of this room. *On purpose.* Then you told Ethan to bring me here, not even considering that you put a traumatized person into a windowless room with one fucking door and put a werewolf in front of that door."

Booker scowled. "Ethan wouldn't harm you."

"No." It came out on an angry exhale of breath. "He was just here, between me and the exit. Like you told him to be. My fucked-up brain did the rest." When Booker didn't speak, only watched me with those unblinking eyes, I threw up my hands. "I got scared, all right? It doesn't have to be logical. I wish you could get it."

Booker's jaw worked, and his hands lifted as if to reach for me before he folded his arms. *That was the right choice, buddy.*

I gestured at him. "You're the one who doesn't want me lying to you. If I'd said I was fine, you'd have gotten pissed. Well, here's the truth: I damn near had a panic attack because you didn't give me enough information about your plan."

Now hurt shaded his aura's growing anger. "I shouldn't have to tell you everything," he said, keeping his voice even. "You should know by now that you can trust me. Always." Despite the pain in his voice, he was still trying to manipulate me. Get me to back down, like I would if I were one of his wolves.

But I could feel his fear underneath it. Fear for me. Fear for us all.

"If you want me to trust you, you're going to have to remember that I'm not one of your pack. You're not my king. You're not my boss. There are going to be times when I'm going to get scared around wolves, especially if I feel trapped. I won't be able to control it." I stopped and I gave him my best approximation of his unblinking werewolf stare. "And you acting all threatening Big Bad Wolf with the scary aura isn't helping me feel better about my life choices right now."

The intimidation radiating from him was gone as if someone had flipped off a light. He heaved a huge sigh and flopped down into a chair. Taking himself out from between me and the door. Giving me the escape route I craved. Showing me that he wasn't a threat.

"I apologize," he said after a second, scrubbing his hands over his face. "In that moment...the stress. I wasn't thinking, but it's no excuse." He looked more tired, more human, than I'd ever seen him. It tugged at me, but I ignored that. "I've gotten used to being obeyed, I guess, since I've been in St. Louis. Being an alpha. Leading a pack. I forget, sometimes, with you."

I walked over to stand in the doorway. Threshold spaces like doorways are a lot like crossroads, mirrors, and bridges. Those in-between spaces were sources of power and magic for me, so even just being in that doorway made me feel more secure. It also drove home my point—that he'd taken something from me without permission. My freedom.

I thought about Shannon. About Ethan. The pack bonds that I knew existed between them all. Like the Fenris were bound together.

"Your wolves obey you. Even ones you treat like family. Like Grace. Nick." I took a breath. "Is it freely given? Their obedience?"

"Yes." He closed his eyes. "You said 'king' before." When those amber eyes opened again, they were resigned. Unhappy. "Alphas aren't werewolf kings, although they did have them back in the day. Once upon a time, if you will."

"Whoa. Stop for a minute." I leaned against the frame of the doorway. "When we're done being mad at each other, I'm going to want to hear that bit of werewolf history."

His smile was faint, but it looked more like the Booker I knew. "You live to learn."

"I do." I gave him the tiniest of smiles in return. "I need you to tell me about the pack bonds. I need to understand."

Booker sighed. "I told you before that I claimed this territory, and a pack formed around me. Many of them, the wolves who work with me, followed me here. The others heard about my pack and decided to join." He paused. "These wolves are used to giving and getting orders, so it works really well for me and for them. Obedience is a habit based on trust. It's part of the pack bond."

"Right, but is it *freely* given?" I could feel his aura searching mine like my eyes searched his face. I *needed* to know how his pack worked. I'd seen that in the Fenris—I knew that the stronger ones could boss around the others. Tell them to do things. Force them to do things.

"Most magical control doesn't really affect free will," he said. "It affects desires. When dealing with an alpha, pack members are still free to act however they want, but how they *want* to act is different." He paused. "It's a lot like love that way."

"No, that's not true." My throat began to close. *Do not panic-attack right now.* "You can make them do what you want them to do. The Fenris could do that. They made some of the wolves...the ones who hadn't wanted to..." I stopped, swallowed. "They made the weaker wolves do things against their will."

Those were the worst times, because of the laughter of the strong ones—double the pain for them to feed from.

Booker clenched his teeth, and I felt the swell of anger in him. I heard him in my memories, asking me not to paint him and his wolves with the same brush the Fenris had given me. But I needed to *know*. To understand.

"Those wolves," Booker began tightly. "They *chose* to be Fenris. To be abominations. The Fenris were worse than any of us thought, but everything you described, everything we've learned and seen since then, isn't surprising to anyone who heard Loki's call." His expression was tinged with sadness now. "Loki didn't leave anyone with illusions about what they were getting into. They may have been forced to do some things, but they chose that life when they chose to be Fenris. They weren't victims. Not like the people they tortured."

He got up and paced the length of the room, coming to a stop in front of me where I stood.

"There are times when obedience is necessary, but all of the wolves here have chosen to be here. They have chosen to follow." Booker bent his head down to me. "Their vow of obedience to me keeps some of them from getting hurt or hurting others. Some adult wolves don't have enough control to function well in the human world. They need a dominant wolf to keep them in check, help them find control."

I got his point, but not being raised a werewolf, I found the idea horrifying. He took my hand in his and grimaced. "I know it sounds awful to you. I get why." His amber eyes begged me to understand. "But being pack, having those bonds? Wolves crave it. We need it. It's how our culture works."

"So your word as alpha trumps everything? Even their own bonds, their own wants and needs?" When he shook his head, I clarified. "If Grace didn't want Nick to do something that you wanted Nick to do, would Nick obey you or Grace?"

His hand tensed on mine for just a second. "First of all, I would do my damnedest not to put Nick in that position," he said. "Any good alpha would."

"But if you had to?"

"Then Nick would have to make that choice, and he'd have to work it out with me and with Grace." He sighed. "Committed relationships are complicated even in the human world. You know that. Work-life balance."

"Otherwise known as 'Life sucks. Get a helmet.'"

He huffed out a soft laugh. "Something like that, I guess."

"Booker." I wet my lips, then met his eyes. "I don't know how I feel about all of this. How I'll be able to deal with it."

His thumb rubbed the back of my hand. His free hand came up to my face. "I'm still trying to figure it out. How it will work with us."

"If there can be an us." Something inside me bled when I said it, but I had to. I couldn't just dive in headfirst, even with my feelings for him, our bond, as a helmet of sorts.

There was a burst of anguish from him. Booker went very still, then forced himself to relax. I could feel it. "Jo. How I feel about you..."

"I know." I raised my face to his, not quite close enough to kiss, but close enough for us to be breathing the same air. "I...well, I think you know." His eyes were glowing again, but before he could touch his lips to mine, pull us both into that madness again, I moved my head back, just a bit. "I need a little time. Alone. I'm...kind of a mess." *Goddess, were truer words ever spoken?*

When he didn't speak, I tried to smile. "You know when I say that, I'm not just talking about right now. Although," I heaved a breath, "I'm currently feeling about five different things all at once. I don't know if I need to scream or cry or laugh." I looked down. "Look. Emotions are stupid. I know that. The fear I felt earlier wasn't rational. Even if it was valid. It overwhelmed me, and I need to process. I need to get some control back."

Another wave of sadness. Booker rested his forehead on mine. "You want to run."

We both knew he didn't mean physically. "Not far," I said, hoping I meant it. "Just the roof. Just for a while. I need to talk to Stanley."

"I suppose I shouldn't worry about you up there." It wasn't a question.

"It's my place," I said simply. "It's where I go. To feel safe."

He shuddered out a sigh. "I want you to feel safe."

"Then let me go." I pulled back a little, enough to bring my hand up to touch his cheek, tentatively. To linger there, petting him a little. The way he'd petted me after the dream. "Let me think. Give me time."

He nodded, and then he leaned into my hand. "Grace had three human-born babies. Two boys and a girl." He drew in a slow breath, swallowed. "They're beautiful."

"Booker, that's amazing," I said, closing my eyes, remembering how happy he'd been when he came into the room to tell us the news. "I'm so happy for Grace and Nick. For you." Happy Booker was impossible to resist, but it was Sad Booker who held me here now—and so much of me wanted to make that pain go away. To tell him I trusted him with my life. With everything. Still, I kept that part back. It was too much.

I was afraid *he* was too much.

People aren't permanent.

"I'm not 'people,'" he said, and he raised his head enough to press a soft kiss to my temple. "While you're thinking, while you're taking time. Please remember that."

Booker stepped back from me. Letting me go.

Before I could stop myself, I turned and walked away.

CHAPTER 29

CAN'T JUDGE A WOLF BY HIS COVER

JO

I'D NEVER BEEN MUCH FOR REGULAR MEDITATION, BUT SINCE getting this building, sitting with Stanley and talking through my thoughts with him seemed to have the same effect for me. It calmed me, helped me think. Meditation was supposed to be a quiet endeavor, but I found that watching the river, talking through my day, and feeding energy into the many magical constructs I had in the building worked better for my scattered mind. Kate called it "letting yourself be inside yourself."

I needed to be myself inside myself after everything with Booker. Last night, this morning, this afternoon. Holy Hecate, it felt like I'd experienced every emotion in the spectrum in less than twenty-four hours. Twice.

Once I was alone on the roof, sitting in my spot, I did my slow routine of letting the emotions of the day sink down into the ground. Today, the variation that I used was sending the energy down the support beams. There were several throughout the building, and they went into the ground. I visualized all my unruly, unresolved emotions traveling down the support structure and being grounded by the earth.

I played with the energy a bit, and instead of feeding it back into the shield around the building, I fed it into the ground instead. Visualizing the ground healthy and strong and green, I fed the building and the land my stirred-up emotions, as I told Stanley about them.

It felt weird to talk to a gargoyle about my sex life, so I skimmed over that part with the bare details before getting to the meat of what was really bothering me. Part of that was my connection to Booker, but the other part was Booker's power over his wolves. It went against so much of my life's experience.

"The wolves seem to be happy and fine with it, and they aren't Fenris," I told him, my head resting on his side. "But there's so much that could go wrong. Being held down and forced is beyond awful, but being forced to participate in it, to be a willing partner, that would have been much, much worse." I sighed. "That's what Booker has the power to do if he wanted."

"No, it's not," Ethan said from somewhere behind me.

I recognized his voice immediately. Even so, I stopped feeding energy into the building and used it to shield myself before I turned to look at him. "How did you get up here?" I was proud of my voice for not wobbling.

He shrugged. "I'm a good climber."

The matter-of-fact expression on his face made me want to roll my eyes. *Wolves.* I figured I'd been so focused on the magic I was feeding into the building that I just hadn't heard him open the roof-access door. Given what Booker had said about him earlier, plus this newest evidence, I might not have heard him if I had been paying attention. Even loaded down with a large backpack as he was now, the dude was silence on two feet. Probably on four as well.

I climbed down to stand on the roof, facing him. "Ninja wolf, huh?"

Ethan ignored that. "What you were describing? Booker doesn't have that kind of power over us. None of us could do something like that. You choose what vows you take." He paused. "When it comes to things like you're thinking of—rape, murder, and the like? That's not even an option."

"You're telling me you've never killed someone?"

"I'm telling you I've never killed an innocent. None of us have. If we did, as collateral damage or by accident? We'd have to deal with that. Wolves have laws. Justice. Both as a species and as separate clans." Ethan shook his head. "Not to mention the personal guilt."

I met his dark, unblinking eyes squarely, and after a second, I let the shield energy slip back down into the building at my feet.

"Rape is the same," Ethan continued. "None of us would think of raping someone, or of forcing someone else to do it for us. The very thought is disgusting and dishonorable. I've yet to meet a wolf of Diana's who wasn't completely revolted by that kind of violation even before they pledged fealty to Her."

Booker had said that, but I hadn't completely believed him. The shame of it flooded me while Ethan's impassive eyes watched.

He added, eyebrows up for emphasis, "It's why I pledged to Her. I didn't grow up in the Dianic clans. My parents were pledged to Odin, like Max's."

Odin? Ew. My face must have given away my thoughts, because Ethan gave me a fleeting, sardonic half-smile. "It's about what you think. Very 'macho warrior,' 'real wolves don't live in human cities' kind of thing. Nothing like the Fenris, but they're not very concerned about protecting anyone who isn't a wolf." He paused. "Odin's Wolves also aren't nearly as accepting of wolves from diverse cultures. Racism's everywhere, even in the clans."

"Is your family Chinese?" I hadn't thought much about his Asian heritage, although it was clearly stamped on his face.

"My ancestors came over and worked on the railroad. Most of my family lives in Northern California—the big old-growth forests and mountains, that's Odin's Wolves territory. Most of the Pacific Northwest, up into Canada."

"Wow." I shook my head. There was so much history to this world I'd stumbled into. How would I ever understand it all?

"I don't blame you for being worried, for not quite understanding our culture," Ethan said. "It's a lot. I don't know your full history with the Fenris, but I can guess. Any time Booker thinks about it, his smell goes dark. Rage-smell. I don't go poking into my alpha's emotions but..." Ethan shook his head. "He's not good at hiding certain things. He'll get there, once he's been alpha for a few more years."

I thought about Booker's reactions when I'd told him about the dreams. He'd always seemed so calm, comforting. He'd obviously been hiding his feelings, trying not to scare me.

"About earlier..." Ethan sighed, scowling, but not at me. "I was absolutely guarding you on Booker's orders, and he suggested the theater, but I also thought you'd like the room."

"I did," I said. "And the movie. You have good taste."

He gave me a nod. "Booker may have tipped me off."

Do not let that make you feel warm and cuddly.

"With everything happening all at once, he forgot to give you this." He shrugged out of the backpack and unzipped it to show me...books. Some that looked very old, and others that were more recently published. Like, as in less than fifty years ago. "Booker got them for you from the Council. They're to help with the necromancer, but also to help you learn more about the supernatural world."

Staggered, I could only stare. "For me?"

"To borrow." He cocked his head. "It goes without saying, I'm sure, but handle with care." Suddenly, Cole was there, nosing into the backpack and then winding himself around Ethan's ankles.

I laughed, but it was a soft, shaky sound. "Of course." Booker had gotten me books. He was trying to help me understand his world. Help me find my own way.

"This one, though, is from me." Ethan handed me a brown paper bag. When I opened it, I saw a black leather book.

Ethan bent to pet Cole, then picked him up, stroking his fur, while Cole settled his front paws on the werewolf's shoulder. "You're basically surrounded by wolves, getting all your information from wolves. How can you trust information from us? Booker's never told us to lie to you, but you have no way of knowing that." He looked at the book. "This is an old one, but it's a history book about the American clans and their cultures. It also details some of our interactions with other supernatural species." He paused. "Don't worry—it's been digitized. My grandfather was a scholar. He wrote it for Odin's Wolves, and the original came with me when I pledged to Diana."

I started to speak, but he waved his free hand, then brought it back to rub Cole behind the ears. I could hear the cat purring even five feet away. "It's not comprehensive, but I thought you might like to borrow it. It's as close to a manual on werewolf culture that exists, as far as I know."

I held the book in my hands as gently as I might have cradled a newborn kitten. "I don't know what to say."

"It's the least I can do," he said. When my mouth dropped open in confusion, he shook his head, scowling again. This one was definitely for me. "You really don't get what you mean to us, do you?"

"Booker says I price myself too low."

"That's because you can't put a price on this place. On a better future." He gave me a level wolf stare. "Thank you."

Somehow, his gruff abruptness made me like him even more. *Wolves*, I thought again, but this time on a wave of affection. "You're welcome." I lifted the book a little, my hands still clutching it as if it were made of glass. "I appreciate the help." I smiled. "I live to learn."

"Keep learning. Keep asking questions. Keep challenging Booker." His real smile was wide and a little shy, and it completely changed his harshly handsome face. "You're good for him, you know? He needs someone who won't back down. Keeps him on his toes."

When my jaw dropped, he resumed his normal stoicism, put Cole back down, then straightened, nodded at me, and turned, going back to the edge of the roof and swinging himself over. "Show-off," I muttered, but without heat. Then I glared at Cole. "What's with you? Are you a wolf fan now too?"

Cole sauntered over to me and allowed me to pet him, but when he discovered I didn't have food, he walked over to sit beside Stanley and washed his face with a paw.

"Oh, Stanley," I murmured, looking at the treasure trove of books I'd been given. Remembering the pain on Booker's face. In his heart. "It's another fine mess I've gotten us into."

At some point later, Max called me. I'd already stashed the books in my apartment, had already made stacks of what to read and in what order. However, the one I'd kept coming back to was Ethan's grandfather's book, *A History of North American Wolf Clans to 1945*, so that's what I'd started reading first.

I'd started taking notes too. My first one? I knew Ethan's last name was Lang, from when he signed the geas, and his grandfather's name was Jian Lang. I wondered if "Ethan Lang" was an Americanized version of that, since the sounds seemed a little similar, and I scrawled it in my notes so I could ask him. If Ethan was going to do stuff like this and be all secretly soft on the inside while being gruff on the outside and make me want to be his friend, then I was going to ask him any damn question that I wanted.

Even though the reading was fascinating, I kept checking my phone every few minutes, wondering if Booker would text or call. When a notification finally sounded, my heart made an embarrassing leap, only to fall back in a heap when I saw it was a text from Max asking me to come down to my office.

After a few moments of deep breathing, I stepped through my mirror. "What's up?" I asked Max. "Is Booker here?"

Max shook his head. "He's out checking some of the properties he bought nearby," he said. "He wants to have something ready for the full moon."

Suddenly, every molecule of my body was on high alert. I pulled out my phone, checking to see if he'd texted or called. Nothing. Taking a deep breath and tamping down my growing sense of dread, I texted Booker: "Hey. Call me when you get this."

Max was still talking. "...got several pack members who want to visit Grace and the babies—some of her family, some of Nick's. Can you whip up, like, a temporary geas so they can visit? Like a visitor badge? We want them to get the peace vibe, let them know you're not the Wicked Witch of the Central East End."

"That's what you think," I said, my brain apparently on auto-snark. It made Max chuckle. "But yeah, I can do that."

I looked at my phone again, willing Booker to call or even text back. I'd already texted Nick my congratulations for him and Grace, told him to let me know if he needed anything. I also told him Grace and I had already talked about the wiccaning, which she now jokingly called "the Wolfening," and they just needed to let me know when they were ready. Loki couldn't reach anyone in the Sanctum, at least, so we'd probably do it right before they left.

The thought of Grace leaving penetrated my sudden bout of paranoia and gave me a pang of sadness. We'd become good friends in such a short time, although I knew she'd be busy with her triplets. Booker might think he'd found a loophole in "people aren't permanent," but the jury was still out.

Of course, there's a five-year lease in my drawer that at least implies a level of permanence, I couldn't help reminding myself. *If something hasn't happened to him already.*

Suddenly, everything in me wanted to see Booker. Even above and beyond this bad feeling I couldn't shake, I needed to talk to him—sort all this out. As much as I liked to pretend otherwise, I couldn't do that by talking to my gargoyle or my cat.

Max seemed to be waiting for more info from me, so I shook myself back into the conversation, with some effort. "I can work something up tonight so they can start visiting tomorrow," I said. "Will that work?"

"Sure," he said. "Grace's already worn out from just the pack members who are already here. Everybody wants to hold babies all of a sudden." He shook his head good-naturedly and typed out a quick text and sent it—I assumed to Nick, so he could notify their families—and then tilted his big, blond head at me. "What's up, witchy witch? You okay?"

I swallowed, wishing I didn't feel like I was about to jump out of my skin. Wishing Booker would call. "I just...I need to see Booker. Can you maybe take me to him?"

He nodded. "Say no more." He started to send a text, then looked at me, his blue eyes keen. *So many wolf eyes in my life now. So little blinking.* "Don't get mad at me, but I'm pretty sure the boss man isn't going to want you outside the building. If I text him, and he says no, I won't be able to take you. It's his call."

Gods damn it all. "I already tried texting, and he's not answering. I need to see him, Max." Something cold dropped into my spine from somewhere. "I need to make sure he's safe. This one's *my* call."

He watched me, frowning, and chewed his lip, then nodded. "Let's go." He put his phone in his jacket pocket. Unlike Booker, who tended on the upscale end of Midwest fashion, Max favored checkered shirts and fleece-lined denim, which made him look like a corn-fed Wisconsin farm boy. "But you've got to promise to stay close to me. Arm's reach, the whole time." Those blue eyes were harder now. "Ethan's got to come too."

I let out a breath I hadn't realized I'd been holding. "Absolutely."

After a quick call, Ethan met us at the shop entrance. He gave me a nod, then we set out. The air settled around me again, heavy as a blanket, and I shivered. Ethan and Max stayed on either side, Max on my right, a step

ahead, and Ethan on the left, a step to the back. A Mini-Wall o' Wolves this
time.

I should have found that funny, but it was hard to find anything
amusing when a sense of dread had me certain something was going to
happen.

I heard a call from across the street, and my heart leapt when I saw
Booker coming toward us with two wolves I couldn't recognize at this
distance. *Thank you, Hecate. He's okay.*

Then I heard a familiar meow and felt something brush against my leg.
"Cole, what the hell?" I looked over at Ethan. "Did he come out here
with us?"

Ethan shrugged.

Max was getting that flattened-ears feeling, and I knew why—Booker
was angry.

"Here, wait," I said, picking up my sneak-and-a-half of a cat. "Let me
take him back inside." Maybe that would give my irate wolf a second to calm
down.

If he was still *mine*.

I'd dropped Cole inside the door and closed it again, but the latch
hadn't even clicked yet when the first gunshot cracked out, muted but
vicious.

Several more shots followed in quick succession, followed by shouts
from various directions. Silencers really weren't silent, although I knew the
shots would have been so much louder without them.

I crouched low before I could register it all, but I craned my head back
and forth, heart pounding, trying to see where the shots came from.

Then I felt a pain that wasn't from my physical body.

"No," I said and turned, rising up, to see Booker, still outside of my
shield near the street, crumple to the ground. "*No!*"

I don't remember telling my legs to move, but I ran for him, reaching
out my mind to him. All I could feel was pain. Fear. I didn't make it far
before Ethan—*ninja wolf*—tackled me and threw me over his shoulder in a
fireman's carry, cursing under his breath.

More shots. Someone shouting.

"No!" I tried to scream, but my breath still hadn't come back properly after the impact of Ethan's body on mine. I heard the bells on my shop door ring out, and then I was dumped on the floor.

"Stay here!" Ethan shouted, slamming the door behind him.

No fucking way. I crawled to the counter, wincing a little from the bumps and bruises, and got my gun, rising up cautiously to look out the windows.

Two other wolves were down, but I couldn't see Booker. Couldn't feel him.

No.

Ethan and Max picked up one of the fallen wolves, and two others picked up the second—*why the fuck don't I remember all their names? I should know this by now*—and I went to the door and opened it.

I let them pass, and then I stepped over the threshold, but strong arms from behind pulled me away from the door. It was Nick.

"Easy, easy, stop. You can't go outside." When he turned me around, his face was grim. "By the time I got out there, the shooting was done, but the sniper might still be in position. I called in a team from the agency. I've got a healer on the way, but Booker's already gone."

Gone? As in dead?

I didn't think I said it out loud, but Nick shook his head and bared his teeth. I could feel his wolf's rage, but I knew it wasn't directed at me. "No. Disappeared. They took him."

CHAPTER 30

SILVER AND BLOOD, SILVER AND BLOOD

JO

THE INJURED WOLVES WERE IN MY OFFICE AND DOWNSTAIRS reading room when I went back to check on them. Inside, I was still reeling. Still unable to process.

They'd taken Booker. There was no question who "they" were.

Max was on his phone in the hallway, describing the injuries of one of the wolves. There was blood on his jacket and on his hands. He looked over at me and mouthed the words *First aid kit?*

I nodded and went to fetch the kit, grabbing some towels and filling my electric kettle for good measure.

Too bad I didn't know any spells that used werewolf blood. It seemed like I had plenty.

I came back with the first aid kit, towels, and anything remotely medical-looking I could find along the way. Max and Ethan went to work on the two injured wolves.

I recognized one of them as Shannon, and she looked like she was in pretty bad shape. The other one's name was something I couldn't remember —he looked better, but he was still hurt.

The pain-filled energy in the room ate at me. I could heal myself more quickly than normal, but Kate was the one who was better at it. *Potions.*

When I called Kate, she answered with, "What the hell is going on? We heard gunshots and the kids are *freaked.*"

I filled her in as quickly as possible and asked her for any healing potions she had already brewed. "I only have three, and they're not really for gunshots," she said.

"I'll take them," I said. "I'll be there in a minute."

When I appeared in her room, she was already there with the vials in hand. Her eyes scanned me quickly for injuries. "I can't come with you," she said. "I can't leave the kids unprotected."

"I understand," I said, giving her a quick hug. "Maybe if you could brew up something stronger." I set my teeth. "We may need it before this is done."

Kate held me close, and I breathed in the soothing sage-tinged scent of her. My friend. My sister. *Now is the time of the witches,* Hecate had said. I tried to hold onto that as I held onto Kate.

When I pulled back, she held my shoulders, her pale eyes keen. "Remember," she said. "Be smart. Be safe."

I nodded, swallowing the lump in my throat. "See you around the next bend."

When I popped back to the Sanctum, the wolves were in full triage mode. I took the potions to Nick and Ethan and explained their use. "Give them water too," I said. "That stuff's nasty." I grabbed water bottles from my fridge.

"Can you talk and work at the same time, Ethan?" I asked. I needed information, but I had no idea how much concentration he needed—it looked like he was removing the bullet.

He nodded without looking up at me, and he spoke low and quick. "Only one sniper, near as we could tell, but well-hidden and fast. Two zombies with guns in a car, but they weren't good shots. Otherwise, these two would be dead." The wolf groaned, and Ethan pulled the lump of metal free from his leg. "Silver."

That meant Booker had been shot with silver bullets too. "Goddess," I muttered, fighting back a wave of nausea. "What does it do to you?"

"We can heal from most things, but silver slows all that down," he said, putting down the pliers and grabbing a bottle of peroxide. "It's like a bad allergy. Only without the option of an EpiPen."

That explained the unresponsive Shannon, who was getting similar treatment from Max and another pack member—it looked like she'd been shot several times. Ethan's patient sighed and looked up at him with dulled eyes and sweat running down his face. "There's one more in there, Trey. I'm going to wrap this up, but I've got to get the other one next."

Trey—*damn it, I knew that*—nodded and laid his head back, closing his eyes. Ethan disinfected the wound. "They were clearly targeting Booker," he said to me. "The sniper waited until he was in the street and focused his fire on him, then the zombies drove by and snatched him."

While Ethan started wrapping Trey's wound, I looked hard at the bloody lump of metal he'd laid down beside him. That could be useful. "I want the bullets after you're done," I said to Ethan. "If the wolves would consent to leaving the blood on them, that would be helpful, but if they aren't comfortable doing that, the bullets will do."

"T?" Ethan asked.

Trey gave me a weak nod.

"As soon as the other bullet is out, make him drink that potion," I told Ethan. "Tell Max the same for Shannon."

Ethan nodded at me. "Go talk to Nick. Make a plan. I've got this."

Nick was out in the shop on his phone, pacing in one of those werewolf circles as he kept his eyes on the windows. When he saw me, he covered the mouthpiece of the phone with his free hand. "Jo, our healer's in a car right now headed this way. She's young but trustworthy—we've had her on the Booker Brothers' payroll for two years now. Will you allow her entry?"

Such a formal request when Booker had been throwing werewolves at me for days. *Curiouser and curiouser.* I lowered my voice. "What kind of supernatural creature are we talking about?"

He gave me a sardonic look. "She's a witch."

Ah. Well. Despite the territorial pangs this revelation brought on, I nodded. "Can I talk to her first?"

He handed me the phone. "Hello?" I said, feeling weirdly shy.

"Hi. I'm Claire. You must be Jo." The voice was female. Definitely young. Oddly cheerful. "I've heard good things."

Against my baser nature, I said, "Ditto."

Her friendly voice turned solemn. "I vow not to disturb any of your magic with my own. I will only use my power to heal in your territory, if I have your permission to enter."

I took a breath. It wasn't much—a verbal agreement wasn't fully binding. I could make it stick, in the magical sense, if I needed to, but I doubted that would be necessary. The sound of her voice was comforting, and my intuition was telling me that Claire the Witch could be trusted, that she was much like me.

The time of the witches.

"You have my permission to enter, and you will be welcome here, Claire." I paused, then added, "Thank you for asking. I'm giving you back to Nick now."

After another short exchange, Nick ended the call and looked at me. "Did you see anything earlier?"

I shook my head. "The air was ominous today—I had a feeling something was going to happen. I thought it was Grace at first. Werewolf going into labor in the Sanctum equals magical disturbance." I wrapped my arms around myself and did a little pacing of my own. "Otherwise, I was on the roof earlier with Ethan, but I didn't see anyone." Granted, I wasn't looking for a sniper, but I did tend to notice things around here.

"It's not your fault," Nick said. "None of us saw it coming."

I stopped pacing. "I mean, why a sniper *now,* when I'm not out there? You'd think someone making zombies would have just used a gun in the first place. Take me out during a bait-walk days ago."

Nick slid his phone into his pocket, shaking his head. "Supernatural creatures rarely use guns, especially ones with magic. We do because of our day job, but most supes want to kill you with their power." He spread his hands, his unblinking brown gaze on me. "In my experience? Power needs to be used. It *likes* to be used. Killing with a gun defeats the purpose."

"The purpose of feeling powerful and using your power?"

"That's the one." Nick paused, seeming to search for the right words. "If you were a nonmagical human with a human threat coming after you, we'd worry about snipers. A witch who's being attacked by a necromancer, who has zombies coming after her, being shot at? Definitely not the usual."

"But maybe it is for a necromancer who's a newbie and can't figure out how to get past the Sanctum's wards." Nick's eyebrows rose, and I shrugged.

"If I didn't know too much about 'the supernatural world and its rules,' I'd use a gun."

I still might, if I get the chance.

A low sound came from Nick's throat. "You've got a point."

Thoughts began clicking into place rapidly now. "Taking Booker—probably to Purgatory, right? Where else would Heloise take him?" I chewed on my lower lip. "They'd have to relax their werewolf wards to get him inside, or put a spell on him to make him an exception."

"According to our wolves at the perimeter, the wards are still up," Nick said, his voice flat. "They don't want us in there."

I swallowed. "Nope. They want *me* in there." The ember that was inside me had sparked to life with a newfound rage. "They want me to come after him. Alone."

"You can't do that," Nick said, his voice going hard. "It's a trap. Booker wouldn't want—"

"I don't care," I snapped. "I'm not letting him die." Not for some illusion of temporary safety. Not for some misguided sense of keeping me safe. Not for anything. I gave Nick my go-to-hell eyes, wishing they would glow like Booker's. "Don't try to stop me."

Nick grimaced. "Just wait until we can get a plan together." I could feel his aura butting up against mine. His fear and worry tangling with my rage and worry. Booker was his alpha, and I'd faced down Booker twice. Nick never stood a chance.

Still, to some extent, Nick was right. "We'll come up with a plan," I said. I wasn't going to walk into Purgatory without arming myself in every way possible. *No cannon fodder here, thank you very much.* But that didn't mean the wolves were going to be running the show.

While Nick checked on Trey and Shannon, I made my own plan and busied myself gathering what I thought I might need.

Within ten minutes, Claire the healer arrived—and if it was possible, she looked less like a witch than I did, at least from the neck down. Her dark hair was shaved around the bottom and halfway up one side, and the rest was waved up into a blue-dyed tumble that came down to her chin on the other. The best part, though, was the red cats-eye glasses. She was dressed in what looked more like workout clothes than anything else—sneakers, soft-looking black sweatpants, and a red hoodie—and she wore a backpack, which I assumed held whatever she would need to perform the healing.

Claire wore an intrigued, bemused smile as she walked into the Sanctum. I ignored the territorial pang I felt when she stepped into the shop, tamping down the emotions and pulling my aura in close around myself—I didn't want to get her hackles up or offend her. She was doing us a favor, and there was every chance she'd be the only one who could save Booker if we got him back.

When I get him back.

I wondered if she was one of those "Hail and well-met" witches, but all that vanished when she came right up to me, the smile still on her face and in her large gray eyes behind the lenses of her glasses. "Hey," she said, holding out a hand. "Claire Sanderson."

I didn't hesitate to take her hand. "Jo Murphy," I said, glad I was able to give her a real, if brief, smile. The connection, like the handshake, was quick, but the bulk of my buried anxieties and that urge to chase her out of my territory ebbed away. As I'd felt when I'd heard her voice on the phone, there was something about her that I recognized.

I couldn't think much about that now. Not until I found Booker.

"Gotta say, I love what you've done with this place," she said. "Feels like walking into a fortress." She paused, then cocked her head as if she was listening to something. "But, like, a cool, friendly one? Does that make sense?"

I couldn't laugh, but I nodded. "Thank you for coming."

Nick was hovering behind me, obviously willing to wait for us to do our metaphorical butt-sniffing and decide to be friendly—wolves understood the need for that kind of thing—but just as obviously keen to get Claire to work. I motioned for her to follow us, and we went into the back room.

Once she was in the room, Claire wasted no time. She shed her hoodie, revealing an old black T-shirt, one that she'd obviously worn and washed many times, and went to Shannon, who was still breathing, thankfully, but it was shallow. Irregular.

"We haven't been able to get all the bullets out," Max said, his face drawn and grim. "At least one is still in there."

Claire nodded, leaning down to lay a hand lightly on Shannon's forehead, frowning a little in concentration. "She has traces of silver in the other wounds." Then she ran her eyes down the rest of Shannon's body before she looked up at Ethan. "She's had a healing potion?"

"Yes." Ethan's deep voice was even more gruff than usual. "About ten minutes ago."

"It's trying to help, but it can't do much with all the silver in there." She lifted her hand from Shannon and motioned for Max and Ethan to move aside.

Max came over to stand by me, but Ethan stayed close, only stepping back a foot or two. His dark eyes stayed fixed on Claire, and he folded his arms and stood like a statue behind her. She sat beside Shannon and rummaged through her backpack until she came out with a little pouch and removed a small silver pendulum. Having found what she wanted, she put the pack on the chair and stood over Shannon, pendulum in hand.

"Let's find the silver first," she murmured.

She was talking to the pendulum, not herself, which was interesting. I wouldn't have known it if every single nerve I had—physical and metaphysical—wasn't wide open, trying to help me gather information. The pendulum set itself in motion as she moved it, seeming happy and eager to help as it tracked over Shannon's body, swinging wildly. While I couldn't tell the silver's location from the swinging of the pendulum, Claire nodded a few times as if the pendulum was speaking to her.

With a quick motion, Claire cupped the pendulum and wrapped it around her hand. She rested her hands on Shannon's leg, near one of the wounds, and hummed a little. "Come on...you don't belong here," she crooned, a musical entreaty not unlike the way I might try to get Cole to come out from under the bed after a thunderstorm. "Come join us out here. It will be more fun. Yes, that's it...come to me..." She coaxed the silver out of the body, calling it to her hands, something I'd never seen done with metal. I never actually saw the silver leave Shannon's body, but I did see the pendulum grow in size, ever so slightly.

Over the next few minutes, Claire placed her hands on a few other parts of Shannon, drawing silver from her steadily. Each time, her pendulum grew in size, and Shannon began to breathe more easily. A million questions flooded my brain, and it was all I could do to keep myself from blurting them out.

When Claire was done, she looked at me as if she could tell I was bursting with curiosity—and given her power, she may well have read my aura that accurately. She shrugged and put the pendulum in her pocket. "Silver prefers to be seen, not to be inside a body or a gun." I nodded and gave her a smile. That made sense. Silver had always felt like a good-time precious metal to me.

"We're not done yet, are we?" Claire walked up and down the length of Shannon where she lay on the desk, her hands hovering over the werewolf's body as she did so. As she reached Shannon's feet, she stopped and closed her hands over the soles of Shannon's bare feet as if she were about to begin a massage. I could see the energy she flowed into Shannon as she replaced the wolf's broken and hurt energy with her own healthy and vital energy. Her eyes took on a pale glow, the effect more eerie as the white light filled the lenses of her glasses.

Some of the damage she managed to ground, if a little clumsily—*I could help her learn to do that better*—but most of it ended up transferring out of Shannon and into her.

I really hoped the wolves paid Claire well. She looked like she was having fun with the silver and the pendulum, but for this energy healing, her face was carefully neutral, eyes glowing. I've seen that kind of look before, and it usually conceals a huge amount of emotion, mostly pain. If I'd known her any better, I'd have given her a hug.

Throughout it all, Ethan remained just less than an arm's length behind her. It was clear he was trying to hover casually, but if she collapsed suddenly, he would be able to catch her.

Once Shannon was healed to Claire's satisfaction, she released the wolf's feet and winced a little. She swayed on her feet, and Ethan immediately stepped to her, his hands supporting her for a long moment, his dark head bent to hers.

Then she pulled away and stood strong, assuming a mountain pose as she gathered energy into herself. I wanted to help her, but I didn't want to break her concentration. While I was considering opening a channel of energy from the Sanctum and sending it her way, the energy in the room pulsed blue-gray. This was Big Magic, and it looked less like she was healing Shannon and more like she was transferring Shannon's injuries into herself. I could see the blood beginning to form a wet patch on Claire's side. No wonder she'd worn old clothes. She'd known what would happen to what she wore if she was treating bullet wounds.

Once Shannon's color returned to normal and her breathing was deep and even, her wounds apparently cleansed of silver and infection, Claire let out a long breath. "She'll sleep now," she said, voice thready but clear. "She'll be able to heal on her own."

Claire pressed one hand to her side, blood now making dark patches on her legs, and Ethan came up to stand beside her, scowling. I couldn't hear what he murmured to her, but she shook her head and began to move toward Trey.

"He's already healing," Ethan said, loud enough for us all to hear, as he followed Claire—staying at least a foot away from her, I couldn't help but notice. Arms out. Ready. Like he didn't want to touch her unless he had to, but also like he was waiting to scoop her up. "That's not necessary."

Claire didn't even look back. "I'm already here, and he's in pain." She looked at Trey with sympathetic eyes. He stirred and looked up at her, and she smiled a little. "Haven't learned how to dodge bullets yet, T? You promised me last time."

"Claire," he said and winced. "Not much silver left in me, I don't think. Ethan got all of it." Behind her, Ethan nodded, brows low.

"Ethan did an excellent job, but you're not clean yet." She pulled out her pendulum. "You should be healing on your own, but the silver is fighting you." She did her pendulum trick again, humming and singing to the silver while the pendulum grew, this time only an infinitesimal amount—but it was enough. Trey's sigh of relief was proof enough.

"There we go." Claire sat beside him where Ethan had sat earlier, and instead of scanning him, she simply took his hand, holding it gently in both of hers. "Now, where is it...where is it hiding?" She sought the wolf's pain this time, not the silver, and her eyes unfocused as she searched.

When she found it, she smiled a little in triumph. This time the blue-gray pulse of energy was weaker, and it looked as if she was taking on a lot more damage than before, but she was determined not to stop, her eyes glowing again. I heard Ethan growl a little behind her, his aura darkening with...fear?

I couldn't help myself from trying to add my energy flow to hers, reaching into my grounded energy from the Sanctum and trying to direct it so that it would flow through her. Claire was getting low, and the blood was running more freely from her absorbed wounds now—it was a damned good thing she was sitting down this time. When she felt my energy, she cast me a grateful look and a nod, then directed it through herself into Trey. I was relieved to see that it seemed to stymie her injuries, or at least perk her up.

Still, when she was done and brought her hands to the surface of the desk, her head drooped and she made a low sound of pain. This was apparently all the excuse Ethan needed to curse under his breath and simply pick her up, despite her annoyed-if-exhausted expression.

"I'll be fine in a minute," she muttered.

"Shut it," he advised tightly, his expression dark, turning to take her out of the room.

"Hey," I said, snagging him by the shoulder as he strode past me. "Give her this." I tucked the last of Kate's potions into the hand he was using to hold up her legs. "Plus lots of water. Tell her to tap into the Sanctum energy to heal herself."

Claire had given up and rested her head on his shoulder, closing her eyes behind her slightly askew glasses. She looked even younger now than she had when she got here, and her face was on the gray side of pale. His thunderous expression softened when he looked at her, then he gave me a brief nod and stepped out of the room.

The whole thing had taken less than ten minutes, and both wolves were now healing comfortably, despite the likelihood that one of them had been on the brink of death. Claire Sanderson had mojo like nothing I'd ever seen, and I was very, very glad she was on our side.

CHAPTER 31

FIND THE WOLF

JO

ONCE THE WOUNDED WOLVES HAD BEEN TAKEN UPSTAIRS TO their beds to sleep and finish healing, Nick, Max, and I gathered around a crude drawing of the interior layout of Purgatory. "I can get into the building," I said. "There are plenty of mirrors in that place, but I need to get an idea of where they're keeping Booker so I don't have to waste time looking for him."

"Don't you have a link with him through the geas?" Max asked.

"I can't get my magic in there." I'd already tried while we'd been waiting for Claire. Any of my attempts got cut off when I tried to extend them inside the building. It was galling to admit that Heloise had effectively forced my hand. It was indeed a trap.

But there was something I was betting she didn't know about: the wolves' pack bonds. Heloise might know about the werewolves and their existence, but I hoped she didn't know the extent of their magical links to each other. "Can you sense him in there?"

Nick and Max flicked glances at each other, then Nick looked back at me. "There's a simpler way." His unblinking brown gaze bored into mine. "The bond between you and Booker will be the strongest right now." I started to shake my head, but he cut me off. "Jo. You asked for his protection —that's part of it. Plus the emotional connection. You also slept with him?"

I could feel my entire face turning red from that bald question that wasn't a question. "Yes."

"Then you can find Booker," Nick said. "Just close your eyes and think about him. From there, you should be able to follow some kind of path to him."

I closed my eyes and thought of Booker the last time I'd seen him: lying on the sidewalk, bleeding, unconscious.

It tore at me, made me want to scream. *Not helpful.* I chased the thought from my mind, using my breathing to calm my racing heart. Then I saw the memory I wanted: Booker's eyes, his dimples, his arms. I felt the memory of him pulling me close, kissing me, the two of us entwined.

The smell of his cedar and sandalwood scent wafted to me, and I closed my eyes, let it clear my mind of everything else.

Then I followed it.

The scent became a forest green cord, soft but strong as a steel cable. I trailed my fingers on it, traveling down its length—everything that I was flowing down the path to him.

Into Purgatory.

Down to its basement.

He lay there in wolf form, and he was getting weaker with every passing minute. The blood smell was strong, and the silver was like a black mold on his aura as it poisoned him.

I opened my eyes. "I've got him." I took a breath, let it out. *Save that rage. Save it for the bastards who did this to him.* "Can we do anything about the silver?"

Max shook his head. "We have to get it out. Cleanse the wounds. Otherwise, it'll just keep getting worse."

"Fuck." I ground my teeth. "Any kind of timeframe on that?"

"Depends on the wolf. Depends on the silver. Depends on luck." He raised his hands in a frustrated shrug.

Ethan came in then. "How's Claire?" I asked.

"Resting. Healing. The potion was a good idea. Thank you." He took something from his pocket. "Your bullets." He handed me a baggie that held the blood-speckled chunks of silver.

Finally, something I can do.

I went to the mirror in the room, then took the bullets out and held them in my hand. They were warm, and I concentrated on that. *The blood of my allies. My pack.* I sat down in front of the mirror, held the bullets in my left hand, and put two fingers on the mirror. I focused on the malice and intent behind the bullets and blood.

I knew where Booker was, but now I needed to know if Heloise was our Big Bad, our real problem. I wanted all of this to end, but more than that I wanted to hurt the person who'd orchestrated Booker's shooting. Who'd killed Emma.

Something had been nagging me about this whole situation, about Hel's Belles. Something wasn't quite the way it seemed. That ancient rune on Emma, that sense of *wrong* I'd felt from Heloise in the club.

Mirrors were no longer made using silver, but just because their ingredients changed didn't mean their magical nature was that different. Even if they were cheaply made, mirrors still resonated with silver. I would find everyone involved in this through the silver they'd used and the mirrors that reflected them.

The mirror turned into a screen not unlike the one in the theater, only now I was looking into the basement of Purgatory. Booker lay in wolf form near a wall, not moving. He was neither caged nor chained—they clearly thought he was no threat. I swallowed, my throat suddenly dry.

Behind him, looking like life-size Victorian Dead dolls, were the members of Hel's Belles. They looked exactly the same as they did the night of the concert, only this time completely inert, too still. The driving charisma of the group was gone.

Next to them and in front of Booker-wolf paced a man who didn't resemble a monster so much as an irritated accountant. He was tall and peroxide blond, with a darker goatee and intense blue eyes. The face had lost the softness, the smile, from the driver's license photo.

This was Keith Dunlap, who'd assumed the asshole-ish name Nigel Hades. The manager of Hel's Belles. His sister's band.

The reflection was only visual. I couldn't hear what he was saying. I could only watch him saying it. However, I could clearly tell that Keith was a magic-user. The tendrils of power coming off of his aura and circling the Hel's Belles were pale but familiar.

It was the magic I'd seen being gathered from the crowd at the concert.

I'd thought Heloise was mesmerizing the crowd, drawing energy from them into herself, but it was her brother—the Heloise doll I saw now wasn't the puppet master but just another puppet. Keith had used her and used much of the crowd's adoration to fuel his spells, his magic.

I watched him pacing in front of Booker and analyzed what I could see of his magic, what I could feel of it.

All the while, the ember in me glowed brighter. Hotter.

This man had sent zombies after me. Had shot Trey and Shannon. Had shot and taken Booker. Was letting him die slowly, painfully, while silver ate at his insides.

This was the guy Emma had been alluding to, the hook-up she couldn't discuss—the one who'd made her eyes sparkle with mischief that night before she left the shop for the last time and went to the Hel's Belles show. I knew it without a doubt. Keith had played Emma, had strung her along, because she would be useful in getting to me.

This man had violated Emma. Killed her. Made her into his zombie puppet.

My hand fisted hard around the lumps of silver. I thought I'd never hate anyone or anything more than the Fenris wolves.

I was wrong.

CHAPTER 32

A WOLF IN PURGATORY

BOOKER

PAIN.

Booker was too weak to fight off the agony. Too drained of blood and energy to do much more than lie there, his wolf form limp. The two bullets in his guts burned him from the inside, the wolf frantic to escape from the pain, to try and run away from it, but the man knowing that moving would only make it worse.

Still, Booker could feel his human side fading into the wolf as his body weakened.

Pain. Fire. Enemy.

The last part made Booker emit a soft growl and try to raise his head from the floor, to look over to where the man who called himself Nigel Hades was pacing. Keith Dunlap from Florida had certainly been busy in the last five years—he'd helped his sister put together a band, managed them, and become a necromancer with access to magic far beyond his own abilities.

Dunlap had hidden himself behind the band, literally and figuratively, in order to conduct his magic without being detected. Meanwhile, they'd all thought it was Heloise orchestrating the attacks, even Jo.

Jo.

The thought of her roused him again. He tried to trace their bond—the one that had been cemented when they'd shared each other's bodies, felt each other's emotions, loved each other—but couldn't find the thread he needed. The Jo thread, the one that was violet and blue, the one that smelled of lavender. He knew it was there, but his thoughts weren't steady, weaving in and out of consciousness.

But he needed to warn her. It was all a trap. Keith had made his move with the sniper and the zombies out of desperation. They'd taken him as a lure. Jo's Sanctum was too strong, their bait-walks too heavily monitored. Keith could have taken her out with a bullet, but that wasn't what he'd been ordered to do.

Because there was something else at play here. Someone else, far more powerful, who wanted Jo dead—and not bullet-in-the-head dead. Magically killed. Punished. Eradicated.

The Hel's Belles themselves were not in control of their own will. At least one of them was dead. Booker's nose told him this. Was it possible that they'd been controlled during the concert he'd seen?

He didn't know how much it even mattered anymore.

All that mattered now was the pack. Booker could feel the pressure of the wolf warding on the place. They couldn't cross the barrier, much as he hadn't been able to come to the Sanctum until Jo allowed it. The warding was different from Jo's—hers felt like a tangible thing. Herbs, charms, infused with her magic.

This warding felt like it was centered in the man himself. Keith Dunlap may have borrowed the bulk of his mojo, but he was using it to the hilt.

That power meant that every time he got near Booker, he got weaker, more disoriented.

Like now. He could hear words from Dunlap, but he couldn't focus.

"...be here. I've got her..."

"...more power...she'll come..."

She'll come.

Booker knew that meant Jo.

No.

This was a place of death. Perversions of magic. Hatred and decay.

Jo. Don't come. Don't come here.

He tried again to mentally grasp his connection to Jo, to reach her somehow. *Stay safe. Stay away.*

His head lowered again, exhausted. He listened to Keith's ranting. "...thought she could...*suffer* for what she..."

What had Jo done to Keith Dunlap?

The question roused him again, brought Booker the Man back to the forefront. *Need to think.* Was this someone she'd come across during her years on the run? She hadn't recognized him or his sister from the ID pictures they'd found.

Had she offended him by coming to St. Louis? This seemed more likely. Witches tended not to like to work together—they could be competitive, territorial.

But this was more. This felt somehow...personal.

Booker was trying to think, trying to put it together, when he sensed another power. A feeling of something, someone, seeking him.

His connection to Jo, the one he'd kept failing to follow before, began to vibrate minutely. He felt it like a spider might feel an insect touching one of her threads.

Unfortunately, the spider in this scenario was Keith, and if Jo came here, she'd be snared, trapped in his web—and he wouldn't be able to help her. *Too weak. Infected. Dying.*

The warmth of Jo's approach through their connection made him want to lean in and pull away at the same time, but it gave him the burst of energy he needed to finally grasp their bond.

The heat of the connection warmed him, reminded him of those hours they'd had together. The best hours of his long life. It was appropriate that they'd happened just before the end. Flashes of memory. Her reaction to his smile. Her silly T-shirts. Her eyes when he'd made her laugh. The good-feeling smell of her hair, her skin. The taste of her smiling mouth. The feel of her warm, naked body on his.

He began to fade away from the pain into a dream, a fantasy haze of Jo smiling at him, touching him, laughing with him. But then the dream turned red around the edges. Jo frowning at him, her fear-smell, her anger at his deception, her lack of trust. Her urge to run from him, from their bond.

Stay awake, damn it.

Deliberately, with what little strength he had, he moved his body on the hard concrete, and the arrowing burst of pain brought him out of his stupor. He was going to die here on this damp, unforgiving floor that stank of suffering and hate. He'd never see his pack again, although he knew Nick would lead them well. His father. His family. Jo. He'd never smell Jo again, never taste her again. He would never be able to make it right with her.

The thought made him want to howl.

When Grace had gone into labor in the middle of a day that had smelled like a disaster waiting to happen, he'd maneuvered Jo into a room that, to her mind, had been a trap not unlike Keith Dunlap's. His alpha brain had thought he needed to keep her safe, even if it meant taking away her choices. It was all he could think to do, but he'd done it wrong. He'd hurt her. He'd scared her. He'd broken her trust.

He couldn't make that up to her. He wouldn't get the chance, but he could save her, if he could concentrate.

He pushed the pain down away from himself, and he grasped the Jo-cord. As if he'd conjured her, she was there—he even smelled a hint of lavender, and a rush of pathetic gratitude swamped him. A tear trickled free. *One last good-feeling smell. Thank you, Diana.*

He could feel Jo's fear for him, her anguish at his injuries. The connection was hurting her, and Booker never wanted to hurt Jo. So he focused, tried to send the necessary words to her.

Keith. Trap.

Stay away.

The rest he could only feel—*stupid wolf,* she'd tell him, *use words,* but he couldn't find coherent words in the growing dark of his psyche. Only his emotions were there. They always swamped him when he thought of her, so he sent them instead. His love of everything she was. His regret for what he'd done, and for leaving her.

Finally, to break the connection, Booker gave in to the pain and let himself drift down, away from the light.

His last thought before he left consciousness behind was that he hoped he would dream of her. That he could take his memories into the dark.

CHAPTER 33

HEL'S BELLES

JO

ALL WAS HORRIBLY CLEAR NOW. BOOKER HAD BEEN TRYING TO tell me that Keith Dunlap was the one behind everything, that he was the real enemy. From what I'd been able to see, Booker was right, but that didn't change anything. I still planned to walk through a mirror into Purgatory and bring Booker home. I still meant to kill someone for what they'd done.

It just meant that Keith would be the focus of my rage.

What about Heloise, née Hilary Dunlap? Was she a victim or was she a partner in crime who'd been betrayed by her twin? As I watched them through the mirror, Keith walked over to his sister's doll-like body and leaned forward—and then he was kissing her passionately, fondling her passive body. Bile rose up in my throat when he pulled up her skirt and put his hand between her legs.

Since I was pretty certain she was dead, the whole scene reached new levels of gruesome ick. I wanted to look away, but her vacant eyes stared straight ahead like an automaton. Unnerving. Haunting.

When they moved just a fraction, I felt a shriek rising in my throat. *She can see me!* She was looking back at me from somewhere inside herself, like a mirror-perversion of the bond communication I'd shared with Booker.

Her eyes locked with mine as her brother continued to defile her, and I clamped down on my horror and disgust at the touch of her mind. Heloise needed me to know something, and when I allowed her in, a flood of information screamed through my brain.

This was unlike the simple *knowing* I'd normally get from a client or a friend. This was a frantic download, Heloise's desperate attempt for someone to help her. She'd been dead a week, and that was because she'd killed herself. She and Keith had both been witches, had been born with it, but Keith had been the one to study and really take it seriously. Heloise had used her magic for fun occasionally, but she was more interested in music. She'd taken Keith with her, and they'd ended up traveling to Nashville, desperately trying to get gigs. The only thing that had gone well for them was making connections with other musicians. That was when she'd met Donna, Lori, and Maggie.

Keith hadn't wanted to play guitar and sing, not when he could practice using their magic to benefit them. He'd taken himself out of the music side of things, he'd said, so he could make her successful—his way of attempting to get around the magical loopholes of self-gain. They'd come up with the Hel's Belles concept at Keith's urging, and they'd all changed their names to create their stage personas. Including Keith, who'd insisted on being called "Nigel" when he was around—which was rarely.

But he was only ever Keith to her.

Their goth trance-dance music transformation had gone over well, thanks to Keith's management. During their concerts, Keith had given them what he'd called "good luck charms." The runic necklaces fit with their stage costumes, so they'd been happy to wear his necklace for the concert. They trusted him.

While Heloise had been spending her time with her bandmates, writing music and practicing, Keith had been digging himself deeper and deeper into the pursuit of more powerful magics. He'd locked onto the goddess Hel, who'd whispered to him much the way Loki whispered to the wolves. Telling him how he could fulfill his darkest desires and help Her avenge a wrong.

Nine months ago, Hel had told Keith to go to St. Louis. She'd told him to find a place near a certain building, a place of power. Hel would show him the magic he needed to kill the witch who lived in that building, then She would reward him with powers beyond his wildest dreams.

Heloise hadn't understood this. "Why can't Hel do it?" she'd asked her brother, whose eyes were becoming increasingly unhinged after every meeting with the goddess.

Keith had only said, "She told me this witch is a daughter of the underworld."

As I renovated my building, Keith's power base grew. The necklaces gave him access to the will of others, and he was able to wield this will as if it were his own. Once they were established at Purgatory, Hel's Belles drew in the crowds, then Keith enhanced the music and drew on the power. At first, Heloise loved it. Performing was always a rush, but every night was a wild high. The larger the audience, the wilder the night. Heloise began blacking out during shows, and for a time after. She never drank alcohol or did drugs, but she would feel hungover the next day.

The more often they performed, the worse it became. Sometimes there would be whole days missing from her memory. Heloise wasn't as knowledgeable a witch as Keith, but she was intuitive. During their next concert, instead of letting the music overtake her, she held herself back and watched the crowd and the band. What she saw horrified her. They drew in the will of the crowd and were able to control them, but that wasn't all. The energy of the audience was being drawn into magical chains around the throats of her and the rest of Hel's Belles. The chain around her own throat glowed the brightest.

Heloise kept herself aware during the entire concert and the aftermath. Afterward, before Keith could compel her to wait docilely for him, she found a doll in his office, one with her blonde hair and white dress. It was wrapped in a black cloth. Her twin had bound her, kept her from seeing the truth.

That truth, the extent of what he'd been doing, nearly knocked her unconscious when he freed the doll from the cloth. She was strong enough to keep herself from blacking out, but not strong enough to keep Keith from compelling her to go to the band's dressing room to wait patiently for Keith to arrive. She couldn't move or do anything other than wait, because Keith didn't want her to. Belladonna and the others sat with a glazed expression on their painted faces.

Keith came in, beaming like a proud father. He went to Heloise and kissed her, and she had to kiss him back, because he wanted it. She could feel his hands on her, all over her. Her brother. Her twin.

He'd done it before. So many times.

She knew that now. She knew all of it.

"I'm so proud of you. You know what's going on," he panted as he took her clothes off. "That's going to make this so much more fun."

After that, she was always aware. She remembered everything. Eventually, so did Belladonna. Keith delighted in that. Heloise couldn't believe he'd become so dark and full of malice. He enjoyed forcing them into acts of depravity. It made him laugh.

When Keith came to them after a show, flushed and aroused with power, he always started with her for some reason. The first few times she spent the duration in shock and wondering what she had ever done to him to make him so cruel, so sick. He forced her to act like a whore, then he'd told her she was a whore. Eventually, she stopped caring. She just wanted him to die, so she'd made a plan.

It had happened a few days before that last concert. Heloise had studied the eddies and currents of the magic and learned how to siphon off some of the crowd's energy. Keith's energy was similar to her own, so it worked well. He enjoyed the rush so much and was so confident in his abilities that he didn't even notice when she was skimming. Finally, one night, as she sat and waited for him to join them after the concert, she wasn't under his will—she was under her own.

When he came over to her, wild with anticipation, she stabbed him in the chest with a knife. Keith looked at her, his eyes blank with shock, then anger clouded them over. That was when Heloise knew he was too powerful. She wouldn't be able to kill him. So she pulled the knife out of him and stabbed it into her own chest.

Keith didn't say a word to Heloise as he watched her die on the floor of the dressing room, the other three band members assembled like dolls nearby on the couch. Instead, he performed some kind of magic while it happened.

Whatever Keith had done, it ended up a curse. Death didn't free Heloise. It didn't take her away from her body. Instead, Keith had trapped her in it—only now, she couldn't move it at all. She was one of his zombies, completely under his control.

The only good news was that she could no longer feel any of the pain and degradation he inflicted upon her. But she still wanted—needed—him to die.

Kill him, kill him, KILL HIM!!!

She screamed it into my overwhelmed mind.

My fingers fell limply from the mirror, and it once again became a reflection of me and the werewolves behind me. My ears rang with the psychic scream, an icy spike of pain in my head, and when I tried to take a step away, I fell to my knees, blood dripping from my nose onto the ground. Tears soon followed. I cried when I was sad, but I also cried when I was furious—and this was a mixture of the two.

Nick and Max were beside me in an instant. "What happened?" Nick asked.

I tried to speak, but the information overload, the sheer power of the thought blast, was too much. I tried to rise and couldn't. I didn't think Heloise was trying to harm me, but her desperation and strength had done some damage. Unfortunately, we didn't have time for that.

I was standing now, being held up by two increasingly frantic werewolves. Blood stained the front of my Must Be the Season of the Witch T-shirt. *Of course. That's what happens when you wear pale blue, Murphy.*

"Jo," Nick said, his voice controlled, as he held a tissue to my nose. "What happened?"

Breathe in and out. In and out. "I know more," I managed. "It's Keith."

"What happened?" Max demanded. "We were all seeing through the mirror for just a few seconds, and then you collapsed."

A few seconds? It had felt like years.

Also, it was news to me that the wolves had been able to see through the mirror as I could. I'd never done that before.

When I could stand on my own, Max let me go. "We have to get in there," he said.

"You can't." I tried to stem the blood flow by shoving the tissue up into my nostrils. "Not until Keith goes down. The warding is tied to him." It sounded ridiculous with the tissue blocking my nose: *Duh war-dine-guh is died do him.*

"You can't go alone," Nick said.

I took the tissue from my nose, wiped it again. The flow of blood had ceased, thankfully. "Kate can't come with me—she's got her kids to think about."

"What about John?"

"John?" My bewilderment was real. "I'm not involving him in this."

They gave each other a look, but let it drop. I filed that away for later.

"The best bet is for me to go in and rush him." I lifted my chin at their mutinous expressions. "I'll take my gun. He won't be expecting it."

"We have more wolves outside, waiting." Max looked at Nick. "She's got a point. If she can ambush him by going through the mirror, we can get in the building as soon as she takes the necromancer down."

"He only has the four Hel's Belles in there with him that I could see," I said, with a bravado I didn't feel. "He knows the wolves can't get in, so he didn't think he needed more zombies. I'll be prepared—we'll all take anti-zombie charm bags." Nick shook his head, but I could tell that he was coming around. I had to press my advantage. "Nick. He's dying."

Nick still hesitated, so I stopped being gentle. "Look. I'm going whether you approve or not. So you can either help me or not. It doesn't matter." He and Max looked at the mirror. "I swear unto my goddess that if you break that mirror or any mirror in my building, the seven years of bad luck will be *me*. I will make your wolfy lives so much fucking hell that you'll wish your whole litter had never been birthed."

They looked at each other, then back at me. I got that ears-flattened, tail-tucked feeling from their auras. *Good puppies.* "Let's take another look inside, so we can utilize all entrances."

I went back to the mirror and placed two fingers on it and thought about Purgatory, the bullets in my hand, and seeing things from multiple perspectives. There were four more mirrors. One was in a dingy bathroom in the basement, two in the bathrooms on the main floor, and another one in the dressing room backstage on the main floor. I suppressed a shudder at that one, remembering what had happened to Heloise and her friends there.

Nick gave me a quick nod when they were done mentally mapping out what the mirrors told us. Since they knew the layout of the club, the mirror information helped them a little, memory did the rest. Nick and Max made plans quickly and with little conversation. By the time they were ready to gather the wolves, we had all our parts in place.

"Take care of yourself," was Nick's only instruction before they walked out the door.

I gave him a grim, tight smile. "You too."

As soon as they were out the door, I went back to the mirror. This mess was of my making. I'd asked Booker for help, and he'd been shot and kidnapped doing the job. I hadn't been able to find Keith, to stop him in time. I'd failed to realize that Purgatory had housed such a dangerous abomination of power, growing all those months just a few blocks away.

Not realizing that—focusing too much on myself and my Sanctum— had led to Emma's death.

Now these wolves were in danger—these wolves I'd bonded with, had come to respect and like. These wolves who acted like my Sanctum, my powers, were a gift. The peace they'd found here and the small miracle that was Grace and her children upstairs were proof.

All that was on the line now.

Booker was on the line now. I didn't know what the rest of my life would look like without him, and I'd be damned if I was going to let a disgusting shit-weasel like Keith Dunlap or even Hel Herself take him away from me and his pack. We all needed him.

And right now, he needed me.

I took a deep breath and sent a quick prayer to Hecate, then checked my jacket pockets to make sure that I had everything I needed.

Then I stepped through the mirror into Purgatory.

CHAPTER 34

LIFE'S A WITCH, THEN YOU DIE

JO

When I passed through, the aura of depraved sexual excitement was almost as overwhelming as the smell, rot and sewer combined—not the dankness of a wet basement, but the stench of darkness, death, and a touch of madness. I realized it was the smell, the feel, of Keith's power, and it staggered me for just a moment before I recovered myself.

Heloise saw me, her eyes wide and blank, as I crept over to Booker-wolf, who was breathing evenly but seemed to be passed out. Keith was busy having her hand-rub him through his suit pants, panting into her mouth, murmuring things to her. I kept myself shielded, hoping it would keep my aura and my power from warning Keith I was in the building. He was apparently counting on Heloise to warn him, but he didn't know how badly she wanted him dead.

KILL HIM.

It was another full-on mental blast from her, and I winced, trying to keep myself on my feet. *I will. WAIT.*

Finally, my hand was on Booker-wolf, in his fur, and I tried to find him again, using our connection to reach his unconscious mind. I'd forgotten how huge the wolf forms could be. On my knees beside him while he was laying down, the wolf's shoulders were almost as tall as mine. If we were both standing, he'd be close to my height.

I could feel the agony inside him, although he couldn't, not right now. He was insensible, drifting away.

There was no way I was going to be able to drag him through the mirror, so he had to help me. I tucked one of the anti-zombie charm bags I'd brought beneath him, keeping the other in my pocket, and envisioned a shield around Booker. Keith's magic had felt like electricity, so I constructed a shield around Booker that was the essence of earth and trees. Earth and trees would comfort his wolf-form and the energy would hopefully negate any magic Keith sent his way. In some situations, very specific shielding worked better.

I hurried through the process, although good old Keith was not paying Booker or me any attention. His attention was entirely for Heloise.

Once it was set, I drew my gun and aimed for Keith, but Heloise saw.

YES. YES! KILL!!!

The blast was so brutal, so full of violent anticipation, that it nearly put me on my knees, driving that spike back into my brain. I felt blood oozing out of my nose again.

Unfortunately, two things happened then. Booker-wolf woke up, apparently roused by my pain, and Keith finally realized I was here.

"Welcome," he announced, turning to me with arms theatrically wide. "It's about time."

He snapped his fingers, animating the rest of the Hel's Belles. Belladonna lunged at me, with Leonora and Magdalena hot on her heels. Heloise didn't move, standing still behind Keith.

I got a shot off at Keith before I had to dodge their grasping hands, but it went wide. Then I was holding off three mind-controlled women—not dead like Heloise, but close to it by now.

I didn't want to kill any of them. All I could think when I looked at their blank faces was that they were being used, that they were victims. Maybe not totally innocent, but who was?

The problem was that they were fast and viciously strong, clawing away at my protections, while my pain and shock were weakening my force field.

Booker wanted me to escape, to run, to leave him and get back to the

Sanctum. I could feel his fear for me, his bloodthirsty rage at Keith, as he tried to get to his feet.

I'm not leaving without you. Stay in your shield, you stupid wolf.

I'd have a chance if I could remove the women's necklaces—the ones that tied them to Keith's power. So I tucked my gun into its holster and transferred all my shields to Booker. I rushed at Belladonna, who hit me in the gut—which I was kind of prepared for, but not really. My forward momentum got me to her, though, and I grabbed the necklace and yanked it free, only to be confronted with a raw-looking wound in the center of her chest, in the same pattern of the ancient Hel rune.

Great Goddess Hecate, he'd *branded* them. It looked like it had happened recently, as the skin wasn't even remotely healed.

Belladonna flicked her wrist and pulled out some kind of blade. *That's bad, that's bad, that's bad.* I leapt back from her.

I could win the fight if I simply killed them, but even as bad as things were getting, I couldn't make myself do it. However, I couldn't leave them like this. I couldn't let Keith continue to torture and abuse them.

Unfortunately, avoiding their attacks proved impossible. There were three of them and one of me. It would have been more efficient for two of them to hold me while one cut me, but apparently Keith wasn't interested in going for the quick, efficient kill. He was more interested in being entertained.

Leonora liked to kick, and she had knocked my leg out from under me a couple of times. I dodged a few, but it was getting difficult to stand and move. Belladonna didn't stab me, but her slashes were deep. One slice came down my chest and off to the side. I cheered silently for the protective nature of rib bones. I had a slice on my cheek, another along my upper right arm, and another one along my hip that bled like crazy.

Meanwhile, Magdalena enjoyed punching. Her aim wasn't great, but she had power behind it. My back got most of her attention, but a few of her blows landed on my arm, and the pain was causing it to go numb. Both legs were unsteady and one was numb.

Sure, just remove their necklaces. That'll free them. My genius plan was going splendidly, and Booker-wolf's aura was going crazy. Thank the Goddess he couldn't move, or he'd have been up and out of my shield.

It didn't take more than a few seconds before I inevitably went down. I knew it was going to happen, so I'd tried to angle myself toward the shield I'd constructed for Booker. I fell with one hand within the shield. I could work with that. Just as I was getting ready to expand the shield over my body, teeth clamped firmly over my wrist. Booker-wolf could barely stand on all fours, but he was trying to drag me into the shield with him. Before I could even tell him to stop or try to expand the shield, I was inside.

I was bleeding everywhere, but at least I had temporary shelter—although pride forced me to stand back up. I refused to cower before them. My hip had a pretty deep cut in it, but at least I could feel that leg. The other one was numb, but I knew it was there. I remained upright, and through sheer force of will, I didn't wobble. Booker-wolf collapsed again, but he didn't lose consciousness. Of course. It would have been easier if he had, if I didn't have him in my head urging me to *run, run, run*.

Keith motioned his hand, and the three Hel's Belles stood back. He looked at me and smiled. The stench that I first noticed in this place grew. The air became heavier. It was him, gathering his power.

"Kneel," he said, the power in his aura working in collaboration with my injuries to finally bring me to my knees.

The ember in me flared. I was so pissed off now that the shield around us solidified and glowed a furious, fiery red, matching the building glow of the ember in my chest.

Booker-wolf's aura seeped into the foreground of my consciousness, still begging me to leave, to run. On a burst of raw energy, his emotions slammed into me all at once—no longer a voice but a tidal wave. Booker was wild with pain, with fear, with rage, with despair. The energy felt less like the man and almost entirely like the wolf. I remembered what he'd told me: *When we're in wolf form, when we're in pain, it's harder to remember how to be a human.*

Well, whichever of them was running the show in there needed to stop or it was going to get us both killed. Holding the shield while bleeding and in pain was hard enough, but fighting Booker's will on top of it was too much.

"Booker, please *stop*," I said, firmly, willing my voice not to tremble, panting with the effort of holding them off. "I can't hold our shield with you in my head. Shut the fuck up!" I had no idea if the words were even making sense to him at this point, but if he didn't stop fighting me, we were going to die.

Thank Hecate, or Diana, or Whoever was listening, because he emitted a low howl and finally quieted, breathing in heavy shudders, his head near my legs. I curled one hand in his fur, stroking him. Thanking him.

I stayed on my knees for convenience—easier to concentrate on magic when I wasn't expending energy staying upright. Let Keith think that I was on the floor because of his will. Now that I was no longer being attacked, I was able to shield against it. Belladonna, Leonora, and Magdalena had resumed kicking, punching, and hitting the shield. It stung me, occasionally distracted me, but I could manage it.

While Keith shouted at them to kill me, I threw my rage and Booker's rage into the shield and felt it power up against Keith's dark aura and his stench. I could feel all the things he'd done to his sister all over again. I could feel how much he wanted to make me suffer. It hit me, there in that awful basement, that after all of these years of running, I was once again dealing with a mind-controlling rapist. I'd come full circle.

Fuck, there were even werewolves involved. Well, werewolf. But this one was *my* werewolf. I wasn't going to let him die.

Keith took a few slow steps away from Heloise, moving toward me. That was good. Heloise was already dead, but still, I didn't want her in the line of fire. His blue eyes were narrow and glowing with power. "Hel hates you, you know," he said, enhancing his voice magically, which I think was supposed to be intimidating, but all it did was irritate. *What a fucking waste of energy. You're like ten feet from me, dickhead.*

Still, he was right, damn it. I should have seen it before. Hel and the Fenris wolf were brother and sister, both children of Loki. I'd gotten rid of her brother's minions and thwarted her father's attempts to get more werewolves under his control. Not the best family to piss off.

However, Hel wasn't here right now. Keith was the immediate problem, and the only plan I had hinged on getting him to come closer to me while I was still shielded. The gun was in my hand, half-hidden behind me. I could drop the shield and get off a shot before the three Hel's Belles got to me. It was possible, but he needed to be close—I couldn't afford to miss again. *What would get him over here? Fucking* think, *Murphy.* Booker-wolf stirred under my hand, a low noise in his throat. The cut on my hip ached.

"It was fun, coming here." Keith stopped, a foot or two farther back than I wanted him. He snapped his fingers, and the three Hel's Belles stopped attacking the shield, but they were still crouched to spring. "We're going to stay. She's promised us this city."

The arrogant bastard seemed to delight in everyone's pain almost as much as the sound of his own voice. Through Heloise's memories, I'd seen him talk to her for hours, going over and over the same information multiple times. I was a new audience, I was on my knees, and he wanted my attention. I gave him that attention, doing my best to look scared. Cowed. Beaten. *Come on, asshole. Come get me.*

I almost couldn't feel Booker's energy. I tugged his gray fur. It was soft —so much softer than I'd thought it could be. He didn't respond. *Booker. Stay with me.*

I was running out of time.

"Don't kill me," I whined, trying to keep the disgust out of my voice, to convince him that I was beaten. "Please. Please, Keith."

His face changed. Fuck, I'd used his real name and made him angrier. "My name is *Nigel Hades*, bitch." Then he grinned. "Still, I like hearing you beg. I'll make you do it again before I'm done. Your little friend begged me. Sweet, tender Emma."

In the rising tide of my anger, I could feel Heloise's crazed rage simmering behind him. I thought fast. *Can you push him?* I asked her. *Mind-blast him—use your twin connection. Do something. Help me avenge you. Help me end this.*

He was so confident in his own magic and his control of people's minds that he'd gotten cocky. He hadn't bargained on Heloise having any autonomy. In the next moment, I felt her gather what power she had in her dead, broken body and push it into her brother's mind—her hate and her agony and her rage.

It stunned him, like it had me. That was all I needed. When Keith dropped to his knees, his face blank with shock and pain, I raised my .38, dropped my shield, and shot him in the chest. Once. Twice.

He went down the rest of the way. Still alive, gods damn it, but it was a start.

The women lunged at me, but I was up and moving, ignoring protests of a dozen injuries, and as I ran toward Keith, I kept shooting. I emptied my gun into his body, making sure to get him at least once in the head. Heloise dropped to the floor like a marionette whose strings had been cut. The other three women simply stopped moving and stood still, doll-like, again.

"Thank you, Goddess," I whispered, sagging a little with relief. Not all magical problems required a magical solution.

I looked down at his body. It felt right to kill a power-hungry bastard like Keith with something so mundane as a gun.

"Fuck you, *Keith*," I muttered, and suddenly, wolves flooded the room. *Hello, cavalry,* I thought, light-headed with relief, and my cut leg buckled beneath me, almost sending me to the floor. Strong hands caught me on the way down.

It was Ethan. "Damn it, you're a mess."

He tried to look at my wounds, but I shook him off, still feeling the adrenaline of the confrontation. "Booker," I said, my voice gaining strength. "Get him out of here."

Nick and Max were beside Booker, but they couldn't get to him. "Jo!" Nick barked. "Your shield!"

I pulled the energy around Booker back into myself, and they began working on him. *Please, Hecate, Diana. Help Booker.*

Ethan reached for me again. "You're coming with us."

I shook my head, looking over at the ruined mess of the four women who'd been unlucky enough to become the playthings of Hel and Keith Dunlap. Heloise lay crumpled behind Keith's body, while the other three stood motionless amid the flurry of activity around them—how much awareness did they even have at this point? "I have to clean up this mess."

At my request, Ethan brought Heloise's limp body over to the other three, and I motioned for him to step back as I walked over to the women, trying to figure out the magic that bound them. Only Heloise was dead, but the rest had no will of their own. I had no idea how to return their will to them or release Heloise from her body.

I tried to reach into them with my energy, tried to figure out what residual magic was keeping them from exercising free will, but could only see the chains around their necks.

As I stood there trying to figure out what to do with them next, the world started graying out around me, much as it had when I'd last been in a place that stank of death and pain.

Then I heard a familiar voice speaking to me in the gray in-between world of unconsciousness. "You did well, my daughter, but your job is not yet finished," Hecate said. Then She told me what needed to be done.

"*No*," I said. It was torn from me, a struggle, to deny to my goddess. "It's not right." *Not fair.*

"You must. There is no other way for them."

I looked at the women again. Tried to reach them again. But there was nothing to reach. Hecate was right. Any other solutions wouldn't be permanent.

"A woman without a will of her own cannot last long in this world." Hecate's words were gentle but firm.

I came back into my body again—and all of its aches and pains—still standing upright, most of my weight on my uninjured leg. Max and Nick had picked up Booker-wolf and were carrying him away while Nick yelled to Ethan to bring me.

I enclosed myself in a shield, and Ethan couldn't get to me.

I nearly smiled at his disgruntled, worried expression, but everything was still too wrong. "Go, Ethan," I said. "I've got work to do here."

Hecate had shown me that Belladonna, Leonora, and Magdalena were all still bound by the chain that Keith had placed on them. Removing the brand on their bodies wouldn't work, as the magic had seeped too far into them from too much use. Killing them wouldn't work—they'd just end up trapped in a corpse-state, like Heloise.

Purgatory. They were in-between, existing in a liminal space.

Lucky for all of us, those were spaces I knew well. My goddess had given me all the knowledge I needed.

Much like I did with the golden thread of the Fenris, I picked up the chains binding all four women. I sent tendrils of my will through the chains so that they would follow me, almost gagging in revulsion at the act, and I limped over to the large mirror on the wall, the four women stumbling behind me.

Echoes of Heloise's memories bled into my mind when I looked back at them. I could see all of them, young, happy, and vibrant. So talented. So *alive* and full of potential. I couldn't stop the tears. They had been there since the fight, thanks to my own physical pain and rage. The ember within me grew hot again, but I tamped it back.

Hilary. Donna. Lori. Maggie. Come with me.

Their dead-doll gazes fixed on mine—there was nothing left behind those eyes, I knew, so it was just my imagination that made me feel like they trusted me—and they followed. Before I could take them through the mirror to Hecate, the stench of rot grew stronger in the basement, a heavy, awful pressure building in the dank air.

My blood went cold in my veins when I saw a blue and black figure, indistinct but fluidly corporeal, walk out of one of the shadows. It was large, female, and angry, and its very presence made the wolves left in the room— on two legs or four—flatten their ears and growl.

It seemed Hel had decided to make an appearance.

CHAPTER 35

THE TORCHBEARER

JO

THE MORE I TRIED TO FOCUS ON HEL'S FEATURES, THE LESS defined She became. It was almost as if She blurred the more She was noticed. There was decay and rot throughout Her form, Her body a corpse that moved of its own volition.

I was suddenly very glad that I couldn't see Her clearly.

"Leave. Go," I hissed to the wolves, but they seemed to be frozen in place, unable to stop growling. Even Booker-wolf, as weak as he was, made a low, rough sound—and as much as I hated knowing he was afraid, the sound cheered me. He was still alive.

For now.

Hel stalked-oozed over to Keith's body and reached down, pulling his spirit free. It was a wisp of nothing with a vague shape, but it had a Keith feel to it as it hovered above his dead body.

In true Keith fashion, it began to rant and rave at his erstwhile benefactress. "Bring me back!" His voice sounded tinny and far away. "How could you let me die before I killed her? We had a deal!"

My jaw dropped, and if I hadn't been so terrified, I might have laughed. *Dumb shit, you don't make demands of a goddess.*

The air thickened around the two of them—I could see it as well as feel it—and Hel simply passed a gray-fleshed hand through his spirit, dispersing him like a puff of steam. In the next instant, his body ignited and burned below it.

Then She turned to the wolves.

I maneuvered myself so that I was between Hel and Booker-wolf while still holding the chains of the enslaved women. Then I lowered my eyes and kept quiet—unlike Keith, I knew not to speak to a goddess until spoken to.

When Hel spoke, Her voice came from all around me, and the stench of Her threatened to choke me into vomiting. *Am I to believe that now you protect wolves, Murderer of the Fenris?*

I think the question was meant to be rhetorical, but I answered anyway. "Yes, I protect these wolves. They are my allies," I said, trying to keep my voice strong. "I didn't murder the Fenris. They still exist, but they are no longer wolves." She didn't speak, but I could feel Her disbelief, so I added, "They no longer live on this plane of existence." Might as well make it all clear. If Hel was going to kill me, She should at least do so for accurate reasons.

The Fenris still live? Her voice was less angry now. It sounded sullen but thoughtful.

"Yes, as neutered dogs." I couldn't stop myself from adding, "They deserved worse." Fear and injury had rendered my mouth too dry, so I was able to refrain from spitting on the ground.

There was a beat of fulminating silence, and then Her smell began to recede. *If the Fenris still live, witch, then our conflict is over.*

I didn't answer this. I didn't want to thank Hel for anything, and I didn't know how to tell Her to get lost without antagonizing Her.

But...I will not leave without my due. After this pronouncement, Hel's desiccated body moved faster than I could see. One second I was holding the horrible chains that bound the Hel's Belles, and the next the chains were in Her hand and I was knocked to the ground.

Hel was taking the women with Her to the land of the dead.

"No!" I screamed, reaching out to catch them with my power, but Hel deflected it easily. I got to my feet and scrambled out of my force field, trying to run after them, to find them in the shadows—*I could move there too,* I thought, maybe crazily—only to be caught by Ethan's restraining hand.

"Stop, Jo," he said. "They're gone."

Tears burned hot in my eyes. Hel was indeed gone, but the stench of Her remained. Every part of the room was infused with it, every corner of this building tainted by Keith and his perversions of magic.

This place was cursed. It deserved to die.

"Leave me," I said in a voice I didn't recognize. Ethan scowled, not wanting to obey, but the rest of the wolves were leaving. "I'll return through the mirror. Go with the pack. Help Claire heal Booker."

I'd used the magic word: Claire. Ethan ground out a low curse, but then he nodded once, turning and following them out.

I looked over at the mirror, seeing myself. The wounds, the blood, the anger and sadness twisting my face. I wished I hadn't given Hel the chance to take the Hel's Belles. That I'd been fast enough to save them.

No. Not "Hel's Belles." She took four people. Four women. Hilary. Donna. Lori. Maggie. There was no telling what Hel would do to them once they were in Her realm, but they didn't deserve more suffering.

Just like Emma. She hadn't deserved her fate either.

I didn't include myself in this. What the Fenris had done to me. I hadn't deserved it, but it had been part of my journey to become who I needed to be. At least I had survived. I'd been reborn onto a new path—for better or for worse.

Suddenly the mirror changed. I no longer saw myself or the Purgatory basement—I saw Hecate, no longer young as She'd been in the forest so many years ago, but a confident older woman, simply dressed, surrounded by the dogs that were once the Fenris.

She nodded at me and said, "All will be well." I wanted to have faith in that, but a goddess's view of what was "well" was vastly different than mine.

I have no idea how long I stood in front of the mirror, but when I became aware of the room again, it was because of the silence that surrounded me. I was alone in this building that had been ruined by Keith's human evil, by Hel's presence. My body sagged with injury and pain, but the ember inside had caught fire with my fury. I could feel the flames licking at my insides.

Injustice. Those four women were young and bright, with their whole lives ahead of them. They'd had talent and charisma. Emma's kind spirit had brightened the world, had helped me feel like a real person again. Then one man had decided that he had to own them, that he had the right to use them, and he'd killed them all. What should have been the happiest time of their lives had turned out to be a nightmare. A tragedy.

Their loved ones, their families wouldn't even know what had really happened to them. They would all be burying empty caskets. I thought back to the zombies Keith had used to attack me at the Hecate's Home carnival. They, too, would never be found by the people who loved them.

So many lives lost, so many other lives bruised—and those were only the ones I knew about.

Tears again, running unimpeded down my cheeks. I closed my eyes and let my despair feed the flames inside me, slumping to my knees and falling to the floor.

Keith Dunlap had a lot to answer for. I supposed I should be glad that Hel had taken *him* at least. He'd reaped what he'd sown.

Still, I wanted to kill Keith again, this time slower. I wanted to kill the Fenris, instead of merely taking them to a different plane of existence. I wanted to no longer have the memory of watching four helpless girls be taken by a rotted corpse of a goddess.

I didn't save Emma.

I couldn't save any of them.

It all built inside me, despair and guilt turning to pure fury, the fiery rage fueled by every breath of stinking, defiled air.

This place needed to die.

The scream ripped from my throat without warning and shattered the mirror behind me, the windows above me. Still, I screamed. The power of my rage broke Purgatory, and something inside me shifted. That flaming ember poured power out of me and into the world, and I gloried in the rush.

The shield that had once surrounded Booker flamed back into life, a fiery circle surrounding me. This was the magical fire that I'd summoned before, that I'd manifested. Only this time, I was the one who commanded it, and my fire whirled and danced around me, greedy. *Hungry.*

I was no longer screaming. My throat was raw, but I hardly noticed. This all-consuming focus was like meditation, only I was no longer being my self inside myself—I was being my self in bright, vengeful flames, the circle of them no longer feeding from me, but begging for more.

I lifted my arm to trace my eyes over the Hecate's wheel tattoo there. My goddess had many symbols. One of them was the torch, the light in dark places.

She'd said I was the torchbearer.

Fire-bringer.

Oh, yes.

I asked my hungry fire if it would enjoy something like the curtains on the stage upstairs. Or the liquor stored on the second and third floors. Perhaps the wood of the frames inside the walls.

When it eagerly agreed, I took the flames of my fire shield, bit by bit, and placed the fire where it could really have fun, leaving the shield around me. The sound of my fire devouring Purgatory delighted me. I thought of the brick on the outside of the building. *The hotter you are, the better it'll taste,* I told the fire, and the fire complied.

I kept my attention on the fire, making sure it went everywhere. I couldn't control it, not really—fire, like all the elements, has a will of its own ultimately—but the fire liked me because I'd created it. I'd fed it. Its needs meshed with mine in ways that pleased us both.

I showed the fire where it could be happy. Happy fire spreads.

My fire was deliriously happy. Furiously happy.

Smoke filled the room. My shield kept the worst of it from getting in, but I loved the smell of it. *So much better than suffering and death.*

I was still on the floor in front of the broken mirror, too tired to move, too tired for anything other than fueling the fire. Somewhere inside me, I noted dimly that the mirrors were broken. I couldn't travel through the shards—I could only travel through a mirror large enough for my body.

Since I had nowhere else to go, since it was the only thing I could do, I fed my energy into the fire. Let it clean up the mess.

Let it take me with it.

NO. COME BACK.

The voice—low, graveled, inhuman—echoed in my head, startling me out of my joy in the destruction around me. It felt familiar, but it was not Hecate. It wasn't one of the wolves.

YOU MUST RETURN.

I watched the fire, felt the burn of the smoke in my lungs. "I must finish," I whispered, my voice so hoarse and harsh that I hardly recognized it.

YOU HAVE FINISHED. IT WILL ALL BECOME ASH. RETURN.

With some effort, I swallowed, my throat so raw that it reminded me of the day Zombie Emma choked me. When Booker had come to help me.

I tried to wet my lips with a dry-sandpaper tongue. *Booker.*

YES. YOUR WOLF NEEDS YOU. YOUR SISTERS NEED YOU. RETURN.

Sisters?

"I can't." It croaked out of my mouth. "Too late." First one, then another hot tear slipped down my cheeks. *Booker.* I'd only just found him. I'd only just figured out that I wasn't afraid anymore.

YOU CAN. YOU MUST, DAUGHTER OF THE UNDERWORLD.

The noise behind me was slight, but when I turned, the shards of the mirror had assembled themselves. I could still see the cracks between the shards. Had I done that? Would it even work? I rose, shaking, stumbling, to my feet.

There was a shadow behind the mirror, too large to be mine. It dwarfed even the wolves. It had...wings? *COME HOME, JO MURPHY.*

I turned to the shadow, moving as if in a dream, and I thought about home. The Sanctum. The wolves. My pack. Suddenly, through the reassembled mirror, I could see the shop. I could see Nick. I could see Max. They were shouting at me, gesturing.

I took a last look at my flames, felt a last burst of yearning to stay and be consumed by my joyously raging fire. *No.* I wished my fire well and turned away. *Time to go home.* Then I limped away, through the reassembled mirror, out of that place of suffering and ruination.

It would not ruin me.

The air in my shop, my home, was clean in my lungs, searing them with fresh oxygen. I breathed it deep between bouts of coughing, and ignoring Nick and Max's muttering about crazy witches and blood loss, I left my finger on the mirror and watched as my rage ate that cursed building. Even with me gone, the fire still burned brightly.

My last thought before I collapsed into unconsciousness, my wolves cursing and shouting as I slipped to the ground, was that it was amazing how fast some of these old buildings would burn.

CHAPTER 36

SOME OTHER BEGINNING'S END

JO

I WOKE UP IN MY OWN BED, FEELING LIKE I'D BEEN SET ON FIRE and thrown through a building. Everything hurt. I looked down to see bandages in various places and raised my hand to my cheek to feel a bandage there.

When I turned my head, I saw Booker sitting in a chair beside the bed, asleep. He looked almost normal—except for the pale cast to his tanned skin and the worry that flavored his aura.

He was alive. We both were.

And...we were also both awake.

I frowned. Goddess, even my forehead hurt. "I know you're not asleep," I rasped. "You can stop pretending."

He sighed and sat up, wincing a little as he opened those glorious amber eyes. "I thought it might make you more comfortable to not have me watching you when you woke up." When I rolled my head toward him and raised my eyebrows, he shrugged. "I hear we don't blink much. It can be unnerving."

The rush of happiness that he was here, alive, once again invading my space and trying to make me comfortable with it, made me smile. I felt his relief before he grinned back at me, his dimples peeking out.

Only hours before, I'd thought I'd never see them again.

Suddenly my vision blurred, and tears began to soak my hair and my pillow. Booker knelt beside me, his hands warm on my arms, trying to touch me where I wasn't wounded, gathering me up as gently as he could. "It's okay," he crooned. "It's okay."

It wasn't, not really—but this part was, so I let myself cry in his arms until I fell asleep again.

The next time I woke up I was alone, and the shadows fell across the room. It must have been late afternoon. Moving seemed like a bad idea, but my bladder insisted on immediate action. There were crutches beside the bed, no doubt a gift from Booker or possibly Kate—I could smell her rose perfume in the air—so I used them to help myself get to the bathroom.

When I looked in the mirror, I saw only myself: pale, eyes red-rimmed and smudged beneath with black shadows, rumpled black hair. When I checked my cheek bandage—*Belladonna's knife, flashing red and silver toward my face*—I saw only a healing pink wound.

Kate must have brewed up the strong stuff.

I threw away the bandage and splashed water on my face, then drank some from my hands, feeling a little more clearheaded.

My stomach was empty, so I hobbled into my kitchen on the crutches and managed to brew some tea and make some toast. By the time I'd finished, I was worn out again but could no longer stand being alone in the apartment. Cole was missing—Booker had probably taken him down to his place to keep him from disturbing me.

I needed to get up to the roof. Feel the fresh air. Talk to Stanley.

I pulled a hoodie over my pajamas, briefly wondering who had dressed me, and crutched myself through the mirror.

The rooftop was exactly as I'd left it yesterday when I'd taken the books into my apartment. After I'd talked to Ethan. That made me think of Claire, and I hoped she was better. If she'd taken on the brunt of Booker's injuries when she healed him—and she must have or he wouldn't have been sitting with me earlier—she would be in rough shape. Three werewolf healings in one day were a hell of a lot to take on.

However, I got the feeling Claire was tough.

She was going to have to be.

I raised my face to the early evening breeze, smelled the river there. *Home.* Then I turned and limped over to Stanley, but I couldn't hop up to the ledge to sit in my spot—there was just no way to manage it. However, Stanley wasn't alone. Cole uncurled himself from his own spot on the ledge and yawned, stretching, before he regarded me with bright green eyes, meowing a welcome.

"I suppose I shouldn't be surprised," I said, reaching out to stroke him when he padded over to me. My voice still sounded rusty, but my throat no longer hurt, thankfully.

Then I turned back to my gargoyle, perched on the roof, facing the city. "Well, boys, I hope you're ready for one hell of a story." I paused. "So to speak."

I stood behind Stanley, bracketed by his wings, and rested my hand on his back. I could still see the river from here, and I kept my eyes on its steady, churning current as I told Stanley all about yesterday. Because it was just Stanley and Cole, and no one else was around to judge me for it, I told them all about Heloise and her friends, about saving Booker, about killing Keith, and I let myself weep when I needed to.

They listened. They always did.

By the time I told them about Hel's interference, I felt a little better. Even a little stronger. However, when I got to the end, when I told them about the fire, that was the only place that I faltered. I'd lost control pretty badly when I set Purgatory on fire, and I had no excuse for it, but I wasn't sorry. The only thing that I regretted was being willing to lose myself to the fire in the process.

"Something called me back," I said, the memory rushing back to me. The mirror. The voice. The shadow. The wings. *COME HOME*, it had said.

Much like when I'd reached out to the Sanctum when I was being attacked and it had helped me see the amulet. *FOCUS*, it had said.

I leaned into Stanley's back then, and I whispered, just for him, almost soundlessly, "If that was you, my friend...thank you." A tear dripped onto his stony back, and I pulled back and shook my head in disgust, sniffling. Fucking hell, you'd think I'd be dry by now.

"Anyway," I said, pulling one arm free to wipe my eyes. "I lived. Now I have no idea if I've just completely freaked out the wolves or what." I sighed, reaching over to run my hand over the surface of one of Stanley's wings. I loved the texture of his stone—smooth and cool. "I guess I should tell them that I wouldn't have burned the place down around them."

"You borrow problems, and when you can't, you create them out of nothing," Booker said from the roof-access door.

I hadn't heard him coming up behind me, but I should have felt his aura. I suppose I was too focused on Stanley and Cole. However, nothing about his sudden appearance scared me. It was Booker. *Always Booker.* "You forgot to tell me that I price myself too low," I said with a sigh.

An impatient huff was his only acknowledgement of what I'd thought was a lovely joke. Then he was moving, prowling around the roof with nary a misstep. *He must be fully healed.*

While one part of me celebrated that, the other part seethed with envy. I wished I could pace just then. Burn off some of the nervous energy that had begun zinging through me.

Since I couldn't pace, I stroked my fingers along the bottom of one of Stanley's wings. Seriously, what was that stone? It wasn't marble, but it had the same smooth texture. Petting Stanley soothed me. Somewhat.

"Is everyone okay?" I ventured.

He didn't break stride. "Trey's back to normal, feeling good. Shannon's still resting but should be up and around tomorrow."

"Claire?"

"She's recovering quicker than usual." He stuffed his hand in his pockets. "Kate's potions helped her a great deal."

"And Ethan?"

"Worried. Hovering. As usual." He snorted, still moving. "You picked up on that, huh?"

I smiled at Stanley's wing. "I think the only one who hasn't picked up on it yet is Claire."

This time, he grunted.

"I'm glad you're alive," I said, still not looking at him. "You had me worried there for a minute."

That brought him to a screeching halt. If he'd been a cartoon, he'd have skidded on his heels for a foot or two. "*I* had *you* worried?"

When I finally met his gaze, his eyes were nearly glowing with suppressed emotion—although his aura was so tangled up, I couldn't quite get a lock on it. Probably because he didn't know himself.

"You nearly died," he said, like an accusation.

"So did you."

"Yeah, but I got shot. You nearly burned yourself alive."

I closed my eyes briefly. He had me there.

He took a step closer to me, his hands out of his pockets now. "You know, you didn't freak the wolves out. You impressed them, although I'm still wondering how in the fucking hell you got Nick to let you go there alone—walking into a goddamned *trap*—when it was against everything I've ever told him."

"It was the only way." I met his frustration with calm certainty. "Nick knew that."

"Apparently, you also threatened him."

I shrugged. "It worked."

"Yeah." He paused, then burst out, "You asked me to keep you alive, and then you walk into a trap." He gestured at nothing. "You're worse than Cole. You never stay where you're supposed to be."

He stopped there, his expression stricken.

"Jo. I didn't mean it like—I swear on my pack that I will never try to take away your choices again." He swallowed, his throat working. "I was wrong to do that before. Having Ethan keep you in the theater."

He was apologizing. I couldn't help but be warmed by it.

However, he wasn't finished. His voice deepened. "You aren't supposed to kill yourself to try to help me."

"Like I was going to let you die, when it was my fault?" He opened his mouth to retort, but I lifted my hand. "No. Listen. What I did was the only way to keep us both alive." I turned to fully face him now, shifting myself carefully. "I don't know how much of it you got when you were there, but it wasn't just Keith who was after me. It was Hel Herself. The goddess. The only reason She's backed off now is because I finally got a chance to talk to Her, tell Her what really happened to the Fenris."

He didn't speak, so I did. "You've told me a lot about what it means to be a wolf. Some of it I still don't quite get, but I'm learning." I gave him a half-smile. "I've been reading quite a bit, thanks to you."

He nearly smiled. "I'm glad."

"So am I. But something *you* need to know about being a witch..." I paused, tried to sort out what I wanted to say and how to say it. He waited, more or less patiently. "For me, part of how I work is acting on intuition. The knowing of the moment. It's part of the gift—it's why tarot cards work for me. Why I know when I can trust certain people but not others before they even talk to me. The way they walk, the feel of their auras. What I know about any given situation." I paused again. "Part of that was life on the road. It's one of the reasons I stayed alive. Why the Council couldn't find me. I followed my intuition." I looked at him, silently begging him to understand. "Does this make sense?"

He nodded. His aura was still turbulent with emotion, but he was listening.

I took a breath. "Last night? I knew I needed to be there. To save you, yes, but also to end this for good—I didn't know how, but I knew it would be settled." I shook my head. "That was hard to explain to the wolves. They're so used to moving as a unit, to that wolfy shorthand you have. My words weren't cutting it."

"So you promised to make Nick and Max's lives so much fucking hell that they'd wish their litter had never been birthed."

Despite myself, I chuckled. It was a good line.

His lips quirked. "It got to them," he admitted. "Not just the words, but *you*. That's impressive." He paused. "I guess I can understand that part. Following the intuition. Instinct is also part of our nature."

"That feeling I had, Booker." I raised one hand in a vague gesture. "It was more than instinct. I *knew* I was supposed to be there. That's why I can't apologize for it. I won't. Because it was the right way." I stopped and bit my lip. "The only thing I'm sorry for is scaring you. Hurting you. But I'm not sorry for trying to save those women. They didn't deserve what happened to them. They still don't. I'm not sorry for burning that fucking building to the ground." I met his gaze squarely. "I'm *not* sorry for making sure you survived."

He looked away, his jaw flexing, but he nodded, once. I could feel him trying to get himself back under control, so I waited, let him work it out.

Eventually, he looked back to me, amber eyes molten. "Your heart stopped. Did you know that?"

Whoa. "No," I said. It came out shaky.

"It did. Just stopped beating." He folded his arms and took a deep breath. "For almost a full fucking minute, before you came back." When I didn't speak, he nodded. "When they brought me back here, I could hear your scream from outside. It woke me. I begged them to go back and get you." His mouth was flat. "I was awake when Claire began healing me, and they had to hold me down, until the mirror showed you there, in the middle of the burning."

He walked over to me. "Your eyes were glowing red. So was your hair." His hand was gentle as he reached out to touch the ends of my hair where it touched my shoulder. My breath caught. "It's black, usually, but black like a living thing. Like a crow or a grackle. When we're outside, in the sun, it picks up a sheen. Blue or purple, like a crow's wing."

He let it slip through his fingers. "When you came back through the mirror, it was red. You started to look like fire. It was as if you were melting away and being replaced with flames. I couldn't—" He swallowed, his hands fisting at his sides. "I tried to get to you, but they held me down. We could feel the heat when you walked back into the shop. It was pouring off you."

"That's...scary." I'd never connected with fire before on that level, felt that ember and what it could do—not consciously anyway. In that basement, the fire and I had understood each other. Maybe I'd over-sympathized a bit, given my own emotional state at the time.

I'd need to practice controlling it, and myself, in the future. *Better invest in more fire extinguishers first.* Looking at the solemnity on Booker's face, I decided not to share that thought.

"Scary. Yes." He rubbed a hand over his mouth. "Then you collapsed and your heart just stopped. No one could get close enough to do CPR because of the heat."

I took a breath. "Booker—"

"For a *full minute*. I thought you were dead." He shook his head as if to rid it of the memory. "Then your heart started beating again. The heat just... leached away. Your hair went back to normal, and you were *you* again. Alive again."

He was drowning in emotion again, and I didn't know what to say—*I'm sorry I wanted to be fire for a while and it made my heart stop beating?* I wasn't sorry, and he didn't want me to lie, so I simply said, "I didn't know."

He nodded again. "You really can burn a place down though. I'll give you that."

"Well. I was properly motivated."

Booker barked out one of those surprised laughs. He didn't need obedience from people—he could get anyone to do what he wanted with just those dimples alone. I smiled at him, willing him to understand. I hated what he'd gone through, seeing me like that, but it wasn't something I could change.

He finally lifted his hand to my cheek, looking at my wound with his amber wolf's eyes, now calmer. Then he checked the rest of me. His fingers and eyes wandered over me gently, methodically examining the various cuts and bruises. He stopped at the cut on my hip, which was covered by my pajamas. I waited, wondering what he would do—wondering if he was going to pull my pants down right then and there to make sure he'd checked all my wounds thoroughly.

He looked around, a humming noise in his throat, but in the end he apparently decided not to partially disrobe me on the rooftop, though he didn't like it. "How's your leg?" he asked instead, his voice low, gruff.

"Stiff, but functional. Not healed enough for me to sit next to Stanley," I said, casting a rueful glance at my normal perch. "The crutches helped."

"You should be in bed," he rumbled, touching my cheek again, looking into my eyes.

"I needed to be up here."

Then, to my great surprise, Booker picked me up and put me down where I normally sat on the wide ledge next to Stanley. Only instead of facing the river, I was facing him. We'd talked before like this, I remembered, back when I'd first brought him up here.

I looked at him expectantly, but instead of talking, Booker took a shuddering breath and put his arms around me, tucking his nose down into my neck. He breathed in my scent and gently rocked back and forth with me —and this close, our bodies touching skin to skin, I could feel all those emotions he'd been holding back. I knew the rocking was more for his benefit than mine.

Oh, Booker.

I stroked my hands down his back, like I had when he was in wolf form. When I'd been so afraid that I would lose him. I let him feel those feelings, let our auras mingle, and I breathed deep too. There was no way I'd ever get enough of his smell, that warm cedar and sandalwood that was becoming categorized simply as "Booker" in my head. In my heart.

Some knot in my stomach that I hadn't realized was there loosened as he held me, and I leaned my head onto his.

BOOKER

Booker breathed deeply of the lavender smell that was Jo and let the rocking soothe him. When she opened herself to him, he absorbed her emotions and was grateful for it—her memories of rage over his capture, pain at seeing him hurt, anguish at the thought that he might die. It was selfish as hell, he knew, but he was glad to see that it hadn't all just been about justice for her.

He could see the rage in her over the fates of those women. Over Emma. He understood that, and he understood why she had to burn Purgatory. It was the Fenris for her all over again—but worse, because she'd failed to save them.

Jo thought he was healed, but he wasn't fully back to normal. Ethan and Max wanted him to be resting, like Shannon, but he couldn't stay away from Jo. He'd at least been allowed to stay with her until she woke up the first time, on the condition that he stay sitting and keep drinking water to flush out his system. Claire was a wonder with silver, but even she hadn't been able to fully scrub his body—the silver bullets had been in him too long. Only time would clear it all away.

Claire had been in bad shape again when she was done healing him, and Ethan had all but tore out his own hair by the time Booker was well enough to walk out of the wolfirmary, as Claire had called it. He sympathized with Ethan—really, no one understood better than him the stoic warrior's poorly hidden feelings for the blue-haired healer—but not enough to keep from getting as healed as possible, as quickly as possible.

His wolf was pacing inside him, and it wouldn't settle until he could see that Jo was still alive. Was still *her*.

It had terrified him, seeing her become one with the fire. It had also fascinated him. Just another thing that was driving him crazy, inside and out. He'd known he was babbling when he talked with her on the roof, but the wolf was urging him to run over to her immediately to smell her and check her injuries. Trying to have a conversation at the same time had been difficult.

Still, he'd needed to rehash what had happened. Hear the story from her perspective, tell her the story from his. He hadn't expected to have to fight not only his wolf but his own emotions the whole damned time though.

Ain't love grand?

When she'd woken up that first time, he'd faked being asleep, forgetting that she'd probably see through that because of their connection—the same one that had told him she was waking up. Then she'd smiled at him, that heartbreakingly lovely smile of hers, and he'd felt like his heart was going to burst.

Then she'd wept while he held her, her emotions too jumbled and chaotic for him to sort, so he hadn't tried. He'd just held her, murmured comforting words to her, until she slipped back into a healing sleep.

He'd left her then, knowing she'd need time to herself. Then he'd reported to Kate, who'd demanded to be let into her room to do some healing while she slept. She hadn't liked having to make the request and go through a bunch of wolves to get to her friend either. "I won't wake her," she'd snapped, her aristocratic nostrils quivering with indignation. "She'll need help to heal faster."

He'd let it happen. Had been debriefed by Nick and Max. Had visited Grace and the babies. She'd named the girl Josephine, and it had made him laugh too hard, nearly making tears come to his eyes. His emotions were all too close to the surface, and Grace had hugged him hard before he left them. "Go see her," she'd murmured in his ear. "Talk to her."

He'd known the instant Jo was up and moving around, had waited until she'd settled again. She was on the roof, and he kept himself away for as long as he could—then, when he got to the top of the stairs, he'd heard much of her conversation with Stanley and Cole. After hearing what Heloise had shared with Jo, he understood her reaction better. His wolves had only seen her take the women to the mirror, then they and Hel were gone, leaving Jo broken, both body and heart.

Purgatory was the site of Heloise's hell, much like the Fenris' den had been for Jo, so Jo had destroyed it. She just came very close to destroying herself in the process.

He hadn't been able to keep himself from the anger that had leapt to the fore when she'd mentioned freaking out his wolves. Was she fucking kidding? Wolves understood going mad with rage, respected it as a battle tactic. Her power impressed the hell out of his pack, so long as she was fire-mad on their side.

More importantly, he knew that the pack mattered to her. The problem was that she kept forgetting, somehow, how much *she* mattered to the pack. To him.

Booker held her there on the roof, beside her gargoyle and her cat, rocking them both, inhaling her Jo-smell until his wolf was able to rest. A noseful of Jo, safe and healing, would do that eventually. There were tears as well, but they came and went without comment for both of them.

Then he stepped back and wiped his hand across his eyes, taking a moment to look out over the river. He could see why she loved it so much—the power, the steadiness. Always flowing. Moving forward, but on a mostly set path.

He needed Jo to know the path that he was on now, and that his path was her path. If she wanted it.

When he looked back at her, he smiled. Jo was going to have a scar on her cheek, but it did nothing to diminish her beauty. Not to him. Her big blue eyes were tired but calm, no longer as sad as they had been when they'd first begun talking. In the setting sun, her rumpled black hair shone with that blue iridescence that oddly matched her eyes. She was wearing pajamas with sugar skulls on them and a gray hoodie with frayed hems. She looked more like a lost kid than a witch, but he knew that was only on the surface.

She was strong, his mirror witch. His fire witch. She had spirit like he'd never seen before—it had pulled at him, had drawn him to her, from the first moment he'd laid eyes on her all those months ago. He'd wanted her then, in that awful occult shop in Ste. Genevieve, and he wanted her still.

Was it any wonder he'd fallen so completely for her? That she would be his match? His mate?

He took a deep breath. "When we were in Purgatory, I could barely move, couldn't protect you. The silver was still poisoning my system, on top of the blood loss. You protected me then, when I was at my weakest."

Her eyes were steady on his, so he kept going. "Then you came back, bleeding, blazing with heat. Fire. Your heart stopped, and I thought you were dead." He paused. "It turned me inside out, Jo. For those fucking endless seconds, I was destroyed."

Her lips parted. "I'm sorry," she murmured, and he knew she meant it—when it came to how he'd suffered at least. He held up a hand, and she nodded. He needed to get this out. He'd wrestled over it, whether to tell her about their bond and what it meant. But he couldn't help it. He needed her to know.

Apparently, he was going to have to pace again, not look directly at her, in order to get it out. So he began moving. "Werewolves mate for life," he said finally. "It doesn't happen for all of us. It did for Grace and Nick, but they're one of only a few in my pack here in the city. There are relationships that aren't mated pairings and just about every other flavor you can imagine, but when wolves truly find a mate, it's for life."

Jo was still now, her eyes huge, following him as he moved.

"Nick told me that you were able to find my location using our connection." He wished he could get his legs to stop moving. "It's not just because we had sex." *Mind-blowing, unbelievably soul-satisfying sex.* "It's because I love you."

She drew in a breath. Suddenly, he was back in front of her, his mouth seeking hers. Tasting that breath. Rediscovering her lips, her mouth. Her response was immediate, gratifying. Soothing. She felt it. She had to.

When he pulled back, he looked down into her eyes. "It's not unheard of for someone to find a mate who isn't a werewolf, but it is rare." Her mouth rounded on an unspoken *Oh.* "I wasn't sure at first, because I'd never heard of a mated wolf-witch combination. But my responses to you, your responses to me..." He traced her jaw with his thumb, slid his hand into her hair. "The way my wolves listen to you. The way you feel about them."

Her eyes went blank for a moment, but before she could shake her head, he bent down and kissed her again, gently. "Don't lie, remember."

As he'd hoped, that got a response other than shock and fear. She glared at him. "So now you're convinced we're mated for life?"

"The timing isn't ideal," he admitted. It was the understatement of the century. *Hey, you have a mate! Nope, you're going to die! Just kidding! But she's dead! Ha! Nope! Just kidding again!* "You have to feel it, Jo. You're my match. My mate. We belong to each other." He paused. "If you want to accept it. Accept me. That's your choice. It's always going to be your choice. I'm sorry I haven't made that more clear to you."

He took a deep breath and waited for her reaction. He'd wait for her however long she needed.

She didn't say he was wrong, didn't deny what he'd said. Her eyes were big, thoughtful, but she didn't look away. She didn't blink either. After a few moments, she raised one hand to his cheek, smoothing it over his jaw. "You're awfully pretty, you know. I've been meaning to tell you."

He exhaled a shaky chuckle, leaning into her hand as she stroked him. "That's not an answer."

"Oh," she said, full of mock-sweetness. "Did you ask me a question?"

He couldn't help it. He grinned, and he hoped those dimples she seemed to love so much would work their magic.

They did—she grinned back, holding him still and going on her tiptoes to kiss one of them. Then she dropped back down and sighed. "I'm not sure I believe in fated mates. Or that any match is for life," she said, meeting his eyes again. Then she gave him a lopsided smile, one that made his heart lurch with hope. "But Hecate help me," she sighed, "I do love you." She raised one hand to his cheek. "You did sign a five-year lease, so that's a start."

Booker kissed her again, gently, drinking in the joy of hearing her acknowledge her love. Out loud. He tried to get a lock on her state of mind, but the only thing he knew for certain was that she wanted him to stay. She wanted to believe in permanence. "I'll take it," he said, resting his forehead against hers, awash in relief and gratitude. Letting her feel how much he loved her. How much he needed her—body, heart, spirit, and all.

"Nothing like this in the wide world," she murmured, and when she lifted her mouth to his, he could feel her love there.

Epilogue

Lady of the Crossroads

JO

As I fell asleep that night in Booker's arms, I sought Hecate. With his warm body as an anchor, I tried to keep my focus on the goddess, hoping for a dream of my own making.

I found Her at the edges of a small clearing in the place between places, somewhere that can be accessed through dreams, if one can cross the threshold.

The goddess sat in a chair underneath an ancient-looking oak tree, and She smiled as I approached. "I was beginning to wonder if you were only ever going to come to me with blood in your teeth and fire in your veins," She said by way of greeting.

While the goddess often appeared to me in a modern guise, this time She was old-school Hecate with saffron robes, golden sandals, and snakes slithering around Her as decoration the way other people would wear jewelry.

That's a good way to scare the mundanes.

Hecate laughed. "The snakes have always been mine. Although I will admit," She mused, looking down to one arm to admire the snake curled there, "I don't mind them putting off the weak-hearted."

I nodded. Then I said what I came to say. "I failed to save those women. I tried, but I didn't move fast enough." Even in the dream, I felt the tug of grief and shame.

Hecate raised one hand in a gesture of acknowledgement, a small green snake twining itself around Her wrist. "You were broken at the time," She said, all magnanimity.

When silence fell between us, I ventured a question. "Can we put a chain around all the mind-controlling rapists in the world and pull them out like we did the Fenris?"

"You don't lack ambition, do you?" Her smile was sardonic. "Alas, the Fenris were a unit of sorts, so that was easy. It's simply not possible to do the same with disparate parts of humanity."

I figured as much, but it couldn't hurt to ask, even if the answer did sting.

There was another thing I had to say—and I had to be careful with my phrasing. "I don't want to whine like a child and scream that it isn't fair that Hilary, Donna, Lori, and Maggie were turned into unwilling sex dolls and then stolen away by Hel, but the lack of any kind of justice for them makes me want to burn down the entire world, not just Purgatory. You know, when I'm in my feels."

Hecate regarded me for a moment that seemed to go on and on. Being stared down by a goddess, even in a dream? About as uncomfortable as it gets. *Please let that not have sounded like an accusation.*

However, I wasn't wrong, so I managed to hold Her glowing gaze.

Finally, Her impassive face softened, and She held up Her other hand—a gold snake curling there, its head nestled in Her palm—to gesture with Her fingers.

At first it seemed like fog was simply gathering around Hecate, but then that fog swirled and solidified into the four women who had once been Hel's Belles. That Victorian Dead goth look was gone, however, and they looked like the young women they'd been before Keith Dunlap began using them for his own gain. They were Hilary, Donna, Lori, and Maggie once again, and while they didn't exactly look happy, they looked *free.*

None of them spoke to me, but Hilary smiled slightly when our eyes met, inclining her head.

When I could gather my wits again, all I could say was, "How?"

Hecate looked at the women. "I took Fenris wolves. Hel took witches. She wanted the Fenris, and witches by rights belong to me. It was a logical trade."

I nodded. At least with Hecate, they could have some sort of choice. *I hope.*

Hecate smiled. "I assure you, daughter, they have autonomy now, although their choices are limited. I was happy to accept them into my company when they chose not to move on." Then the women looked to Her, fierceness etched into their features and in their stance.

Whoa. Hecate traditionally rode with a horde, and that horde had gotten bigger by four.

The pressure on my heart and soul eased. It wasn't a perfect solution. I wanted them to be alive, unmolested and vibrant, but Keith had removed that option. At least now they could be themselves, and Hecate had given them a community within Her horde. A purpose.

I bowed, although it was awkward, because it felt like the right thing to do. "Thank you for this." I looked in Her glowing eyes again. "Thank you for doing what I failed to do."

Hecate raised Her shoulders in a movement too elegant to be termed a shrug. "You are a human. Hel is a goddess." She smiled slyly. "Luckily, I'm a Titan."

And to my utter shock, Hecate winked.

Thank you for reading! Did you enjoy? Please add your review because nothing helps an author more and encourages readers to take a chance on a book than a review.

And don't miss the next book of the Daughters of Hecate series coming soon!

Until then read <u>MARKED FOR GRACE</u>, by City Owl Author, K.C. Harper. Turn the page for a sneak peek!

Also be sure to sign up for the City Owl Press newsletter to receive notice of all book releases!

Sneak Peek of Marked for Grace

By K.C. Harper

It was one thing to stare at the dead, another entirely when they stared back.

Grace was seated in the cold, red pleather booth of a small cafe adjacent to the hospital where she worked. She twisted her long umber-colored hair around her finger as the thump of her heart rivaled the wailing sirens from an ambulance parked nearby.

Canting her head, she peered through her reflection in the window to her right. Blood coated the sun-lit sidewalk across the street, dripping from a man's hand where it hung from the gurney. His translucent soul hovered near the emergency entrance, its unblinking stare fixed on her. It didn't speak, didn't move. Nothing. Just existed.

Someone dropped into the seat across from her and she jumped. "You scared me to death, Noah," she said to her best friend and roommate.

He frowned. "Not sure why since you invited me here."

She waved a flippant hand. The vanilla and burnt coffee aroma dominated her senses while steam from an espresso machine behind the counter shot into the air.

Removing his gray parka, Noah hung it from a hook beside the table. "When did you get here?"

"A few minutes ago, so I can't stay long. My break is almost over." Her gaze drifted to the familiar, rippling glow of the two gold cuffs embedded along the soul's right arm, but whether they were a gift or a sanction, she didn't know.

She wanted to look away, but the dead commanded her attention like lightning striking down beside her. Even four years after her Sight appeared, their presence still affected her. No, they affected her *more*. It wasn't that she feared them, but she feared what they meant.

Lights from the ambulance painted the snow, the building, and everything else in the vicinity with a chaotic, staccato spray of red and white. The paramedics performed CPR on the too pale man while they wheeled him inside, but their efforts were for naught. He was well beyond saving.

Noah was midway through placing the lunch Grace had forgotten—and would desperately need before her shift was done—on the table when her hand shot out, snapping it from his grasp. She clutched it to her chest like a desperate lover. "You're a lifesaver."

The lines of his olive-toned skin creased when he laughed. "Easy, Gracie. I'd like to keep my arm."

"You assumed the risks when you agreed to bring my food, delivery boy. You know my hunger's an emotion."

"A dangerous one."

She offered a sharp nod before her attention returned to the soul. Its expression flat, unsmiling. It didn't look happy. Didn't look sad or scared. Didn't look anything. Like all the others she'd seen, it bore no signs of emotion, and she wondered if it had any awareness at all.

Noah followed her line of sight. "What is it?"

Her mouth ran dry. "One of them."

He looked away and shuddered.

"Pfft," she scoffed. "I don't know why they bother you. It's not like you can see them."

His honey-brown eyes settled on her. "That almost makes it worse. I hate knowing they're there."

She ran her palm over her baby blue scrub pants, smoothing the material again and again, thankful she had at least one person who knew her truth and believed her. "And yet you always ask about them."

"Because that," he flourished his hand toward her face, "is impossible to ignore."

She snickered.

He peered in the soul's general direction again. "Does it have any of the markings?"

"Just two."

His lips pursed. "I wish we knew what they meant."

"You're telling me." She curled the sleeve of her wool coat in her grasp, exposing the fair skin of her wrist. On some messed-up level, she figured becoming a nurse would make it easier. Like being around the dead would either give her answers or force her skin to thicken. Neither had happened. If anything, the oppressive questions had only grown deeper, more unnerving —worse. Her leg bounced under the table. "They *have* to mean something."

He flicked the side of his menu with a finger. "If that's true, logic dictates someone was meant to see them."

Her stomach torqued into a knot she wasn't sure could ever be undone because if he was right, then she had a purpose. But if he was wrong... "What if I'm losing my mind, Noah? What if this has all been in my head?"

"Don't go there."

She threw her hands up. "How can I not? If anyone at work finds out, I'll be deemed unfit to practice. I'll lose everything, my nursing license, my career," her voice hitched, "the house."

"You're not losing your mind, you're just upset because you're hungry, now take a breath, Gracie."

She did, sucking in deep and slow, then followed that one by another and another. "I can't tell anyone without risking everything, but then if I don't, I'll never find answers." And the idea of going through life without those explanations, knowing she was alone in this was more painful than she cared to admit.

Noah's gaze pinched at the corners as he reached across the table and gently squeezed her forearm. "It's too bad they don't share it with you."

"That might be difficult when they don't speak."

His brow furrowed. "You know what I mean, smartass."

She released an explosive exhale as a small smile tugged her lip. He always knew what to say to smother her wildfires. Withdrawing her arm, she gave him a spirited pat on the head. "You'd think I'd be used to them by now."

"I think there are some things we can never get used to," he replied, fixing the hair she'd mussed. "We could scour the internet again. There might be something new."

Sweet lord, anything but that! Her eyes rolled so aggressively it hurt. "And maybe while we're at it, we could join one of those ghost hunter's clubs."

"I'm fairly confident you're mocking me."

She offered him a tooth-baring grin while a raucous group of teenagers guffawed at one another across the café.

"Why are we friends again?"

Grace smacked his elbow. "Because I'm so lovable."

"Clearly," he grumbled as he rubbed his wound, then straightened. "Oh! Did you get my email?"

She fidgeted while the sharp scent of burnt toast filled her senses. "I haven't had a chance to check it yet. Why?"

"Some real estate lawyer named Gerald Martin came by. He's representing this company, G.R. Incorporated. They're considering building a business development in the area and are inquiring with homeowners about selling their properties. He left me his card and a bunch of documents. I sent pictures of both for you."

She pulled her phone from her coat pocket then brought up the file and scrolled down, eyes flying wide when they landed on the offer amount. "Holy crap!" Her brows climbed so high on her forehead it was a wonder they didn't slip free because the proposal was *well* above market value.

"That's what I thought. It'd more than cover the remaining mortgage debt."

Grace chewed the inside of her cheek as a waitress shimmied by, a tray of steaming drinks in hand. She shook her head and closed the message. "It doesn't matter how good the offer is, some things are more important than money. That house was Mom's." Her vision blurred when she fought back the tears stinging her eyes, the conversation an excruciating reminder of the night her mother died—a blood and agony-filled night she refused to think about.

Noah cleared his throat and looked away. "You're still good for your graduation lunch tomorrow?"

Heat flooded her body as she blinked her sight clean. "Everyone knows I graduated two months ago, right?"

"They sure do, but that's what you get when you have friends who do shift-work."

"Disorganized planning?"

He snickered. "Exactly!"

A series of piercing sirens drew closer, reverberating off the buildings and amplifying the sound. Her head snapped toward them. Several ambulances whipped into the hospital's lot accompanied by a slew of Arillia City Police vehicles. The hospital's P.A. system crackled, the announcement muffled from inside the restaurant.

She scrambled out of the booth, snapping to her feet. "I've gotta go."

Noah's voice was lost in the cacophony as she bolted from the café, aiming for the entrance of the E.R. A car whipped across her path, and she jolted to a stop. It passed so close its wind snapped her clothes. Her heart lurched when the distinct cry of metal-on-metal filled the world as the vehicle side-swiped one of the ambulances. Its tires screeched before it crashed to a halt and smashed into a concrete garbage can. Glass exploded from the windshield, tinkling across the ice-covered ground like freshly fallen snow.

A bloodied man exited and took three steps before dropping to his knees. His hands were clasped over his stomach like they could hold back the torrent of blood that leaked between his fingers. His shoulders heaved from his labored breathing. He was pale. Too pale.

Help, he mouthed.

Grace made for him and threw his arm over her shoulder, taking as much of his weight as she could. Her teeth clenched from her effort while she guided him toward the doors. The first wave of paramedics burst from their vehicles, rushing past with their bloodied patients, each of which was escorted by an officer and cuffed to their gurneys.

The distinct scent of copper saturated the air, heavy and clawing. It burned her throat like a sharp mineral acid and made her voice thick when she called, "What happened?"

"Gunshot wounds," one of the paramedics said.

"Bar brawl," an officer added, hand on her gun, eyes trained on the patient she followed.

Grace swallowed hard as Angie the Charge Nurse pushed outside, barking orders when she pointed to one of the lesser wounded men. "Get him to E.R. room four. Move that car out of the way and for the love of all that's holy, turn those damn sirens off!"

One of the prisoner-patients with a jagged gash across his cheek offered Grace an air kiss. "Hey there, blue eyes. You can take care of me if you want."

A poisonous shiver prowled across her skin. "That's Nurse Crawford to you. And you'll be dealt with when your friends stop bleeding."

The man she helped stumbled. She held tight but his momentum was too much. "He's going down," she warned. Several people lunged to catch him, too late. He collapsed, grunting when he landed hard. His hands dropped limp by his sides and his eyes rolled back in his head before they fell shut. Blood slithered from his slack mouth, crawling across his jaw like a life-stealing snake.

Grace cursed when she knelt by his side, searching for a pulse, and finding none. Setting her palms on his chest, she started compressions. "I need help over here!"

Dr. Rodan Brookes, a man in his late twenties, crouched across from her. His long-sleeved white lab coat skirted the ground while his keen, hazel stare took in the scene. He pressed his blue latex-gloved hands over the man's wound.

"He's lost a lot of blood," Grace told him. Her shoulders and back ached from her efforts while the chill from the wintery ground seeped into her skin, taking root in her bones. *Come on. Don't die on me. Come. On!*

"We need another gurney here," Dr. Brookes called over his shoulder before coming back to her. "Do you need to swap out?"

Grace heaved a breath and nodded. She pulled her hands from the patient's chest and pivoted to put them on his stomach but jerked back when his soul materialized. A diaphanous mist rolled from the body. It torqued and roiled as it took shape until it stood fully formed before her.

Her hands trembled as she stared, because its forearms were *covered* in markings. On the right were three golden bands, while on the left were seven blacker than coal, thickly scaled serpents. Each coiled around the arm, climbing higher and higher, binding.

She'd seen them before, but never that many on one soul and something about it felt wrong, so damn wrong. She couldn't say why, but it was a pervasive, indisputable sensation that's shadowed limbs spiralled around her and tightened like a vice, whispering of darkness.

"Here!" Angie called as she wheeled an empty gurney their way, snapping Grace back to her surroundings.

Dr. Brookes' stare was locked on her, narrowing when it flicked to the space above their very dead patient and back again. There was something strange in his expression but what it meant, she had no clue.

Biting her lip, Grace squirmed under his scrutiny. Or suspicion? God only knew. Regardless, she couldn't let him see something was...off about her. Needing his attention anywhere else, she threw herself forward and pressed her hands to the patient's stomach. *Please don't notice. Please don't notice.*

"I'm calling it." He leaned back and snapped his gloves off before shoving them into his pocket.

One of the injured men launched a brutal string of epithets his way.

The doctor checked his watch. "Time of death: Seventeen hundred hours and fifty-eight minutes."

Against every instinct, Grace lifted her eyes to his, but if she'd hoped for reassurance, she found none.

His jaw was clenched, movements rigid when he pushed to his feet. "We're needed inside." He pivoted on his heel and pulled his phone from his pocket as he stalked away.

He couldn't know anything. It wasn't possible. She was just reading into things that weren't really there. Fitting under the circumstances. She swallowed hard and removed her blood-soaked hands from the body. Releasing a shuddering breath, she took one last fleeting glance at the soul, then moved on.

* * *

At the end of her shift, Grace shuffled her way to the change room, barely able to lift her feet from exhaustion. She struggled to strip off her blood-stained scrubs then hopped in the shower trying not to, but unable to stop replaying the haunting moment with Dr. Brookes earlier.

Rolling her shoulders, she tried to release her taut muscles and failed miserably. She turned off the water, dried and dressed before rubbing her hands along the back of her arms to warm them–a useless effort since the cold had burrowed soul deep. Giving up, she grabbed her belongings and left, turning down the hall toward the staff exit.

She bit the inside of her cheek when she spotted Dr. Brookes speaking with two imposing men by the door. Both were tall, well above six feet. Their backs were to her, but their broad, solid frames and clenched fists made the tension that pulsed from them nothing short of menacing.

They turned at her approach and the weight of their scrutinizing stares almost crushed her. The first had a shaved head, chest-length dark beard, and offered her a glare that made her think it was personal; the second's chestnut brown stare pierced her, hunting her every move. The intensity he put off was a bizarre mix of threat and intrigue. To say he was gorgeous would have been an understatement, and the weight of his attention sent the heat of a blush crawling up her cheeks. He lifted his hand and raked it through chin-length blond hair, exposing the inside of his wrist.

Her heart shuddered in her chest. A mark, one she'd never seen before. It was similar to, yet wholly different from the ones on the dead, though this guy was very much alive. Did he see things too? Did he have the answers she wanted? The answers she craved?

The questions danced at the tip of her tongue, threatening to burst free, but a nagging caution told her to keep moving, fast. She couldn't override it and it set her teeth on edge. She nodded to acknowledge them, praying it covered any reaction she might've had before she slipped past the three and out into the night.

The wintery air hit her like a wall, and she drew her coat tighter to block the chill as she advanced, her legs pumping hard. Pulling out her keys, she unlocked her car, shoulders sagging while the familiar icy bite of the driver-side handle stung her skin. She was halfway through opening the door when someone reached past her and slammed it shut. Her body went rigid, and she sucked in a sharp breath before she whipped around.

The blond man loomed less than a foot away, eyes narrowed as he edged closer. His heat brushed her flesh when he penned her in. "Good evening, Grace Crawford. I believe we need to talk."

* * *

Don't stop now. Keep reading with your copy of <u>MARKED FOR GRACE</u>

Don't miss the next book in the Daughters of Hecate series coming soon, and find more from Phoebe Walker at www.phoebewalkerwrites.com

Until then, discover MARKED FOR GRACE, by City Owl Author, K.C. Harper!

What if the dead hunted you?

As an untrained soul seer, Grace Crawford has not a damn clue what they want. But she's about to find out.

After she finds a mark on the dead that kills the living, her quest to discover who unleashed it pivots to the half demon Gideon. She's got her eye on him, and he's got his on her too—every inch of her.

As the mark haunts humanity's steps and the death tolls climb, Grace realizes she's in way over her head. But the lines between good and evil are blurred and choosing who to trust is hard as hell, seeing as God is capable of wrath and Satan was once an angel.

Please sign up for the City Owl Press newsletter for chances to win special subscriber-only contests and giveaways as well as receiving information on upcoming releases and special excerpts.

All reviews are **welcome** and **appreciated**. Please consider leaving one on your favorite social media and book buying sites.

For books in the world of romance and speculative fiction that embody

Innovation, Creativity, and Affordability, check out City Owl Press at www.cityowlpress.com.

Acknowledgments

We set out on this adventure together during the pandemic, and it was one of the best things to come out of that scary time. We've been friends more than 20 years, but suddenly we couldn't visit each other and were too burned out on phone calls/video chats by our day jobs. However, we could *write* to each other. We started out by sending long letters and fun postcards back and forth to alleviate our frustration and need for communication, and we ended up writing a book together. We are both very, very grateful for each other.

We'd like to thank our spouses, Will and Ryan, for being endlessly supportive along the way and for being our favorite people in the world; we are also grateful to our families for caring about our author journeys even if they weren't always sure exactly what we were doing. *insert laughing emoji here*

Speaking of not always being sure what we were doing, we also want to thank our amazing beta readers Laura Jennings, Sarah T. Dubb, Karen Morris, and Tracy Gulovsen. Your feedback helped make MIRROR WITCH into the book it is today, and we are so grateful for your time and wisdom! Likewise, thanks to our longtime friend and devoted St. Louis resident Susan Kaman, whose insights into the city's history and unique neighborhoods were of immense value.

We both have endless amounts of gratitude for Lisa Green, editor supreme, and to the wonderful team at City Owl Press for making our dreams for this book and this series come true. And Lisa, thank you for giving us not just one chance but two to make you fall in love with Booker and Jo. We will never forget it!

Mary would like to thank the incomparable Laura Jennings (a.k.a. Laura Moher) and the amazing Jenn Roush and Christen Randall (Blush Puddles forever!) for being the best writing friends anyone could ever wish to have. I love you so much and am hugging you from afar as you read this! I am also grateful for the folks in the SmutFest 2.0 and Writing While Fat Discords for being supportive and welcoming environments for romance/WF/YA/etc. writers at all stages, and to the FridayKiss community and Romance Twitter in general for the support, the memes, and the fun.

Finally, we would both like to thank Hekate, for obvious reasons.

ABOUT THE AUTHORS

PHOEBE WALKER is the pen name of co-authors and longtime best friends Jennifer "Jay" Bull and Mary Morris. Jay lives with her husband and her cats in rural Illinois, where she works as a writer and a professional psychic. She began making up stories and characters in her mind at a very young age and always loved sharing them with others, so writing became a natural creative outlet. Jay collects tarot decks and cats, but her spouse has put a limit on cat collecting, so she only has the care of three tiny terror beasts. Mary grew up reading romance novels and SFF epics on a farm in southeastern Illinois. After earning an MFA in fiction, she has worked as a proofreader, copyeditor, reporter, English professor; today, she is a freelance writer and editor who has published short fiction and nonfiction in various lit mags. She lives near her childhood home with her husband, her children, and miscellaneous cats. Between family, friends, writing, reading, and watching TV, she can't remember the last time she was bored. (Probably the '90s.)

www.phoebewalkerwrites.com

About the Publisher

City Owl Press is a cutting edge indie publishing company, bringing the world of romance and speculative fiction to discerning readers.

Escape Your World. Get Lost in Ours!

www.cityowlpress.com

facebook.com/YourCityOwlPress

twitter.com/cityowlpress

instagram.com/cityowlbooks

pinterest.com/cityowlpress

www.ingramcontent.com/pod-product-compliance
Lightning Source LLC
Chambersburg PA
CBHW022208010726
47493CB00002B/473